Table of Contents

Prologue

Ranir opened his golden brown eyes. The wood on the ceiling mirrored the musky plank he was lying on. His entire body was throbbing with a dull pain. Sitting up, he could smell the daub and straw, mixed with the mountain rain. Shadows from the candles danced about the room.

"Where am I?" said Ranir, the dark, shaggy haired boy. He was near adult aged, a short scruffy beard covered his face.

"You are home. Well, my home, of course," replied a voice from a dark corner. Ranir couldn't make out who the deep voiced man was, in the shadows. He wasn't even sure that it was really a person at all.

"And just where would that be?" asked Ranir, sitting up and turning towards the shadowy corner of the room. Leaning forward from the creaking chair, the man shoved his face into the aura of the candlelight.

"That would be very near to your birthplace. Or... rebirth, is what I should say. We are in the Veörn Mountains," said the man.

Ranir could see through the shadows on the mans face. It was textured with scars and age. The golden light from the candle flame casted a foggy tone to his skin.

"What happened to me? And why am I back?" questioned Ranir.

The man stood up and moved closer to Ranir.

Something familiar about him struck Ranir. He knew that he had seen this man before. He simply couldn't be certain, though.

"You have been given yet another chance. The Old Gods aren't satisfied with the balance yet," he said, speaking with a voice that resonated from deep in his chest. He spoke through a long black beard, which seemingly muffled his voice ever so slightly.

Disbelief perplexed Ranir. He couldn't belief that his actions had drew a response from the four old gods. He had thought that maybe his work was done. What more could they want?

"Even if that is true, that doesn't explain why I am back here, of all places," Ranir said.

The man seemed annoyed with the repetitive question. He pursed his lips together as he took in a hearty breath. Pausing for moment before exhaling, he grasped his beard in his hand, letting the thick hair pass though his fingers.

"Just know that you are meant to do more in Gnariam. Your responsibilities are not fulfilled so easily and all your questions will be answered in time," answered the man. He was stern with his answers. Ranir thought it all seemed like riddles to him.

The Stranger was clad in a dark and dusty cloak. His boots were worn down, and a couple patches dotted his pants. Besides the way his character was so steadfast and the manner in which he carried himself and his conversations, Ranir would have thought he was a beggar.

"So for now, go home. Or what remains of your home. You will be called upon when the moment is right. There is much to discuss," said the man.

Ranir looked out the window as lightning dashed colorfully across the sky. A beautiful blue and yellow bolts dodged each other through the air. The thunder shook the entire shack. The arc of energy, spreading various hues of light, enveloped the room to a near blinding sense. Ranir could see all the details of grain in the old wood and the hole in the side of the far wall.

"Now, that is something I know," said Ranir, feeling the lightning in his core. It was as if that spark of energy was a part of him. He could feel the static raise his hair on his neck.

"How did this happen? Why did this happen?" he pondered to himself. Turning around to further question the man, Ranir was only left with silence, and an empty room. The man had gone. He began to recollect the events that transpired over this past year. He remembered that fateful night when he became The Lightning Rod.

Chapter 1:The Shifter and The Caster

The morning was warm. The moisture was evident everywhere, as it clung to every tree, and dampened every rock. The humid wind still remained from the passing storm. Spotted rays of sunlight moved, between the trees and the clouds above.

Ranir Trysfal was just waking from the loud crash of a branch nearby. The sound doubled his heart rate as he jumped up. Instinctively, he reached for his dagger.

"Always something," he thought, realizing it was just another casualty from the storm. He remembered the tempest rushing in through the late night. The skies a deep purple, lightning cracking across the sky. The thunder shook the ground. The downpour of rain washed out his fire, leaving Ranir with only his quick shelter.

Clambering to his feet, he put his dagger in the sheath on his belt. Pulling his tattered leather tunic on, Ranir could smell the moisture in the air, and on his clothes. He knew another storm was approaching. The storm from the previous night had shattered his makeshift shelter. Branches, leaves and vines littered about the small niche. Not wanting to experience another stormy night, Ranir picked up his deer hide sack and began gathering up his supplies. It was then he realized that he slept through the bulk of the storm. How was that even possible? He felt full of energy, though.

Scattered about was his water bag, torch, and rope. His bow was intact, but the quiver was broken at the seams. A few arrows lay broken on the ground. He gathered his blanket and what was left of the smoked rabbit he ironically stored in a rabbit pelt. Ranir knew that he had a half day journey back to the farm. He needed to get out from underneath the tree's canopy, to see the sun. Knowing the daylight hours was a crucial part of traveling so far, with minimal supplies, especially so close to the Veörn Mountains.

As he climbed out and saw the sun, Ranir knew that it was not yet midday. And yet, the humidity was already drawing sweat from his brow. He knew the risk of hunting close to the mountains. However, this is where the best vräel were. He could've stayed closer to home, and hunted deer with Marnos and Selendt His friends were always fearful of Veörn, the legendary story of the mountaintop temple.

Most of the villagers stayed within the forest, far from the mountains. Old stories of Gods, and monsters, had spread for millennia. Much like the villagers, the deer kept their distance as well. Not the vräel, though. These creatures were much bigger, and faster. They resembled a horse in size. They had horns protruding from the sides of their almost buffalo-like heads.

Vräel had broad shoulders like a lion. This, making it move faster than a horse, accumulated its weight almost seven-fold of a deer. Ranir knew if he could take one of these magnificent creatures down, he would be able to bargain for much more than normal at the market.

He hadn't planned to get so close to the Veörn Mountains. However, before the previous night's storm forced him into crafting a shelter, he was tracking a rather large vräel. Even with half of his arrows broken, Ranir still had confidence that he would secure a kill.

Sensing it was a small risk, to trek further to the mountains, he tightened his rucksack knots and continued his hunt. It was past midday by the time Ranir got to the base of the Veörn Mountains. He knew vräel traveled close to the mountains, but he didn't know exactly how close. The tracks that he was following led him straight into the mountains, becoming a dead end once they reached the jagged, black rock floor. He didn't realize just how much energy he had spent for a failed hunting track.

This was disheartening, for he had traveled much farther that he originally anticipated. He journeyed into potential danger. He was low on food and water. He would have to ration out the rest until he returned home, in Heramor. Looking up to the sky, Ranir knew that he wouldn't have enough daylight left to travel home. He knew he would have to make camp again tonight.

Ranir began unpacking his bag, worried of the minimal supplies that remained. He walked around for several minutes, collecting dead branches that were scattered at the edge of the forest.

He planned on fortifying his new shelter with stones and mud, as to mitigate the damage from the storm, that was cascading from the west, over the mountains. An hour had passed by the time Ranir had finished the shelter. Strangely, he thought it would have taken longer, but the material was all around him. He didn't have to travel far this time, to gather what he needed. It was time to collect more timber for a fire.

As he was nearing the forest edge, Ranir noticed the contrast of the mountain and the forest. The forest was teaming with life and color. The smell of evergreens flowed through the air. An ambient noise was constant from critters of all types. The mountain, however, seemed dead to him. It was very much devoid of color, and of life. All that existed here were sharp rocks, blackened.

As he was near the edge of the forest, he heard a cracking sound behind him, making him stop instantly in his tracks. Turning only his head to use his peripherals, Ranir could make out the figure of a creature, stagnant behind him. He didn't want to scare off a potential hunt, if he could make it to his bow. The animal behind him did not run. It did not move at all, after the rocks broke beneath its mass.

Ranir had, until this moment, hunted deer, vräel, wolves and mörcats. Whatever was behind him, and out of focus, sent a chill down his spine. This was altogether a new experience for him during a hunt. In that moment, he realized, something about this unknown creature was violent and infuriated. He could feel his hair raising at the base of his neck. His skin felt as if it were crawling with bumps, like the skin of chicken's foot.

Ranir knew he had to either run, which he had never ran away from a fight before, or face down the beast. Slowly and steadily, he drew his dagger out. His bow lay too far away, on his blanket. Looking down, he noticed his hand shaking. He began to turn around with his full body. Before he was fully turned around, he realized, that hunting and studying every creature in and around his village, had not prepared him for this. In a dark flash the beast slammed him in the side, taking his breath away, and knocked him 15 paces away. As he hit the ground, with a loud thud, he caught a better glimpse of this mysterious creature. He was dumbstruck and petrified. He dare not move just yet.

Looking up all the way, he saw something nefarious. The creature reminded him of a story he heard as a boy. This beast had scale-like, jet black fur. It's face was that of a wolf, but more like a wolf skull. It had razor sharp, bright white teeth. Ranir could almost hear the saliva dripping from the beast's jaw. It had a long arrow tipped tail. From the mountain, behind the creature, Ranir noticed movement among the rock. Ranir could almost make out the shadow of a man.

"*Azshul navok!*" came a bellow from the shadowy figure. Ranir hadn't had time to think. A bright orangish-white flame burst from seemingly nowhere and struck the creature.

Ranir couldn't believe it. As he watched the orb of fire strike the beast, the creature shifted into the form of a man in midair. The newly formed human landed perfectly on his feet, sliding a meter backwards in the gravel. He was stark naked, with long, jet black hair. His back was towards Ranir. He flashed a look over his shoulder, at Ranir. His eyes darkly matched his hair color. A smirk came across his face, baring razor sharp teeth. The man leaped into the air with inhuman strength. Ranir noticed the man shape shifting once more into a flying creature. Before he was in flight another sharp curse came from the man at the mountain base.

"*Sithak. Notith avol!*" cried out the caster of deep, red orange fire. An immense wall of flames horizontally fell atop the shifter, knocking him to the ground. Ranir could feel the presence of the caster, even standing back, the energy of the fire seemed to emanate all around and yet, seemed to pull the energy from him.

9

"Vile, pathetic beast! You don't belong here!" Yelled the caster, walking towards the man, once again in human form. Ranir could see muscles in the man's back that reminded him of thick ropes.

The shifter lay still on the ground, breathing heavily. The man in the shadows approached the shifter. He was wearing full black attire. His robe was pitch black with silver threading dancing around the sleeves and the bottom. His hair was dark brown, face covered in a black scarf. A long, hooded cloak was strewn across his back, and a dagger protruded from his belt. He moved about almost silently. Clearly, this man was highly skilled. That much was evident, immediately.

Ranir slowly rose to his feet, now closely watching the fire caster. He did not move from his landing spot, though. He studied the mystery hero, if that is what he was, if only for a moment.

"Who are you? And what, or who is that?" exclaimed Ranir. The man pulled his scarf from his face, revealing a scrubby, dark brown beard. The man seemed to be at least twice his age. Wrinkles littered his forehead.

"His name is Felg Eldìr. And he-" pointing at the shifter, " is my bounty. A shape-shifting murderer is what he is!" replied the man, now standing over the shifter. He was holding silver shackles in his hand.

Ranir had heard stories of bounty hunters in the past. He remembered that they were supposed to be some of the best in Sythestine at combat. Stories spread far and wide of a bounty hunter dressed in black. He wondered if this was the legend standing before him now.

"You? You are a bounty hunter? How were you doing that with the fire? What are you?" cried Ranir, still in disbelief of the events that had happened only moments ago.

"Yes I am a bounty hunter. I am a pyromage, as well. One of the Emphyres many, many mages. But only one of the few remaining bounty hunters, I'm afraid," answered the man.

"*Could he really be a mage?*" thought Ranir. So much had happened so quick that he had so many questions and no idea of what or how he should ask them.

He almost couldn't believe it. A mage, performing combat magic, or any magic, was too hard to believe. On top of that, he was fighting a shape-shifter. He had never heard of one before. He wasn't sure if this was a dream or real. Of course, Ranir had simply just witnessed it himself.

"My name is Detmés Ontaga," the man introduced himself, his voice of an unfamiliar accent to Ranir. His voice was deep, bold and brilliant all in one. The man spoke fast and with conviction.

"I am Ranir. And I have never seen anything like this-" pointing at the shifter. He was still disgusted seeing the shifter. His form was human and yet, seemed more reptilian or animal-like than human. His skin glistened like that of a slug.

"-or *you*! How is that possible? Is that actual Magic?" Ranir said, beginning to breath heavier now that reality seemed to be setting in. Could this actually be possible? Can magic like this exist? How had he never heard of it before? Of course, stories of old were thought to be fantasy."There has never been someone like you in Heramor. That's my village, 'bout a half day's travel from here," said Ranir. He just remembered that his friend, Marnos, was probably still looking for him to be coming through the forest.

His home village, Heramor, was small, mostly farmers and the poor. So much to get away from, and so much to miss. The thought of his village comforted him, compared to what had just transpired.

Detmés seemed intrigued, and almost amused. He turned more, to face Ranir."Son, do you know where you are?" asked Detmés.

"Of course, at the foot of the Veörn Mountains. I tracked my hunt all the way here!" boasted Ranir, confused.

The man let out a bellowing chuckle. It sounded like the had swallowed some glass and washed it down with some high end alcohol. It was almost like the sound of wood crackling in a fire.

"Oh whats so funny now, sir?" demanded Ranir.

"Boy, you must've hit your head harder than I thought. You are about a week's ride from Heramor." said Detmés.

"What are you talking about? I tracked a vräel all the way here through the forest!" exclaimed Ranir.

Suddenly, the smile vanished from Detmés's face. He now looked stricken with fear from unknown reason."Kid, vräel don't travel into the forest. Now, I don't know what you think you know about them, but they are vile creatures that stick to the mountains. Massive, and territorial. If you followed anything out of the forest, it was this thing!" he said, kicking the shifter laying silently on the ground.

"But. No wait. It was-" started Ranir.

"No! You wait! Listen now! If he lured you out of the forest, he most likely had help of another sorcerer, enticing you. Messing with your head!" said

Detmés.

The shifter laying in the gravel started shaking silently. Ranir realized he was trying to contain his maniacal laughing. He stopped chuckling as he looked up at Detmés.

"Gotcha this time, Bounty." said the shifter. His voice was smooth, like the hiss of a snake. Detmés glanced up at Ranir, a look of unsettledness struck across his face.

"Kid, don't move." he started to say. Detmés began to scan the area around them. His face grew hard, focused. His eyes were dark green, now that he was close enough for Ranir to see. They moved slowly around the background. He slowly turned towards the mountains, observing everything.

"*Shtak!*" came the sound behind Detmés.

"Aah!" exclaimed Detmés as he went down on one knee. Ranir noticed a deep red arrow, sticking out of Detmés's black cloak.

The arrow looked as if it were smoking, the red color pulsating like an ember in a fire.

"*Orshtu Alak!*" Detmés casted another spell. Ranir suddenly felt energy being pulled from himself. As he looked down, the shifter fainted on the jagged rock.

From the midst of the black rock, a fire circle formed underneath Ranir. Yet, he felt no heat from the flames. Ranir's vision seemed to weaken, as he tried to peer through the heatwaves.

"*Shunt!*" another arrow, of the same color, stuck Detmés in the back.

As he fell to the ground, on both knees now, he

13

muttered something under his breath. Ranir felt like something was pulling him down. Something was pulling him into the ground! The fire ring was swallowing him!

"Help! *Please!*" cried out Ranir.

"Hide, boy!" yelled Detmés.

Ranir didn't understand where he was supposed to hide. The circle of fire seemed like a cage, holding him in place. It was as if he was frozen.

The fire grew bright orange, almost white. It rose up, blocking Ranir's view of Detmés and everything else. Though he could see the waves of immense heat around him, he was unharmed by them.

Through the flames, he could hear the bounty hunter cry out another spell. Ranir wasn't sure what language the magic was being summoned with. He slammed his watering eyes shut. Suddenly, all fell silent.

Ranir opened his eyes. He was standing in the forest again. Looking around he noticed that he was barely outside Heramor. He could smell the wood burning in the fireplaces.

Then, he realized what the ring of fire was. The dauntless bounty hunter casted a teleportation spell. Could he have saved himself too? He saved Ranir's life. He wasn't sure whether Detmés survived or not. He didn't understand a lot in that moment.

He felt lightheaded. He stumbled as he walked toward the village. His whole body felt like he had rode for days without sleep. Ranir collapsed on the forest floor.

So many things swirled in his head. All he

could think about was the magic of what happened, and the mythical magic itself. He thought of the fire spellcasting bounty hunter, the shifter, and the unknown archer that attacked.

Why was he so depleted of energy? He could see the blurry sight of the tree canopy, light shining through. The haze seemed to coat his eyes, making it harder to focus Then he fainted, drifting into darkness.

Chapter 2: The Tracker

Images of the shifter, the bounty hunter, and the mysterious attacker swirled in Ranir's mind. He had so many questions and emotions about his savior, the pyromancer. How was any of that real? How was any of it possible?

Images floated around in his head, yet they were distorted. It felt like he was peering through stained glass windows. He can remember, perfectly, the shifter's face and his sharpened teeth. He was still unsure if they were that way by being a shifter, or if the man filed his teeth down to be more threatening, if not scarier.

From the side of the mountain, he could still imagine the two ember colored arrows, flying towards Detmés, from somewhere in the darkness. They appeared from seemingly nowhere. Ranir tried to get a glimpse of the shooter, but with no prevail. This re-imagining of the memory flashed forward in his mind as it happened, only it played out in a much slower pace, allowing Ranir to get a glimpse of more details. This made the memory much stronger.

From the depths of the deep shadows, by the mountains, he noticed something new. Rather, he noticed some one new in this nightmarish memory.

This person looked almost familiar to Ranir. He tried to call to the blurred figure, but no sound came out. His mouth was wide open, and not a single note emitted from within.

He could hear the faint cry, thrusting from the figure in the dark. The sound grew louder, and louder. Ranir realized the figure was calling his name. At first it was faint, then grew more clear with each iteration.

"Ranir! Wake *up!*" The voice sounded too familiar at this point. He knew this was only a memory and yet, the new stranger was not present during the events that occurred. This meant this was more than a memory, maybe. "Please! Wake up Ranir!" said the voice again. This time it was clear to Ranir. "*Ranir!*" This time the voice screaming to him. He jumped up from his slumber. He forced his eyes open to see his best friends, Marnos and Selendt. He was as shocked, to see them, as much as he was surprised by the mountain base occurrence.

"Marnos!" cried Ranir. He was very happy to see his friend. Marnos was more of a brother to Ranir, than a friend. He and Ranir grew up together, from the time they were small boys. Their parents' farms flowed into each other.

Selendt was another dear friend, to them both. She was of the same age as Ranir, with auburn colored hair. Most people in Heramor were attracted to her fair face. She had light, unblemished skin and green eyes. To Ranir, she was family, though. She was like a sister.

"W-where are we? How did I get here? How did you find me?" Ranir rattled questions in rapid fire. In an instant, the memory once again flowed over him. He was panicking. He felt lightheaded.

"Calm down! Ranir what happened to you? We've been looking for you for days," replied Marnos.

His voice was high pitched, and almost crackling. He sounded distressed and panicky. His brown eyes seemed to bore a hole into Ranir, trying to get some semblance of an answer.

"We thought- Well damn it Ranir, we thought something happened to you," cried Selendt. She seemed more worried than Marnos. Her green eyes glistened with tears of joy, that he was alive.

"What do you mean days? I was hunting just yesterday. We all left together, don't you remember, just nearly two days ago. I went towards the mountains to track down a vräel. I must have passed out," exclaimed Ranir. His head was spinning so fast that, for a moment, the bounty hunter and shifter slipped out of his forethought.

If it were even possible, Marnos and Selendt both shifted into further discomfort, looking at each other. Ranir was confused yet again. What was wrong with his friends? He felt like everything he understood was falling apart. He felt an unseen weight press against his chest.

"Ranir, we left out six days ago. Marnos and I returned four days ago, because we thought that maybe, just maybe, you had gotten a deer, and you had gone home. Then when you weren't home, we started searching for you," said Selendt, as her eyes began to glisten more, "we thought something happened to you."

Ranir didn't know what to say. This was partially because he didn't understand his loss of time, and because he didn't want to sound crazy, ranting off delusions, recalling the situation that happened with magic. Magic was still a simple myth among most. He eased himself into conversation, careful to not get overly excited.

"Something did happen to me. I was tracking a vräel towards the mountain and-"he started.

Marnos interrupted him, "you didn't go all the way... to the mountain, did you? I mean that'd explain why you've been gone so long."

"I did go to the mountain but it was- no it was only a half day ride from my hunting path. Or that's what I thought," continued Ranir, "I followed the tracks to the mountain and there was a beast there." Ranir told them every detail that he could remember. Marnos and Selendt both sat silently, staring blankly at Ranir. After a few, long and awkward, moments, they both looked at each other and back to Ranir.

"Well, say something!" shouted Ranir. The abrupt break of silence made Selendt jump. He didn't mean to shout or startle her at all.

"There was a bounty hunter, in Heramor," started Marnos. His demeanor shifted to somewhat calm, yet disturbed. A look sped across his face of someone trying to put a puzzle together. Marnos was the thinker of the three friends. He was always paying attention to details and trying to find solutions to problems most people tended to look past.

"He was asking if anyone had seen a boy," said Selendt. She had the same perplexed look as Marnos. Her voice trembled slightly.

"Detmés survived!" cheered Ranir, sitting up with newfound energy and oddly, joy. He didn't know the bounty hunter. He didn't know who he was, how he had magic, why he worked for the Emphyre, who never cared for the poor. He still had so many questions but, he was relieved to hear his savior didn't perish.

"Who?" asked Marnos. He and Selendt exchanged

more anxious looks.

"The bounty hunter. Were you not paying attention to me?" exclaimed Ranir. He felt a surge of frustration. He needed to go see the bounty hunter.

Ranir got his feet, still feeling sapped of energy, and steadied himself. He had a dull ache in his back and a throbbing ache in his head. He must have hit it on a rock when he passed out.

Ranir gathered his sack. It felt light. His bow and arrows were missing along with his blanket. He knew exactly where he left them, at Veörn Mountains.

The three of them started out towards the village. Along the way, Marnos told Ranir that he and Selendt had killed 3 deer. They brought a mule into the forest two nights ago to drag them back to the farm. Ranir was glad for their hunt because they often split the meat of their hunts.

As they were approaching the conjoined farms, Ranir couldn't help but feel lonely, even in the company of friends, for his parents had perished. His father left for battle, with the Emphyrius Guard, when Ranir was just a small boy. He barely had a memory of him and he had never returned home. His mother passed away nearly 4 years ago.

Ranir has inherited the farm. By the time his mother died, he had learned to take care of the farm by himself. Any wiser dealings that needed made, Marnos's father would help out.

Through all the loneliness, the mountain base battle was something new that peeked his interest. It was something that he knew he would never forget. Why would he? It was a once in a lifetime sight. At least, that's what Ranir thought.

As they were almost to the other side of the barn, where the deer were being butchered, a voice called out, "Ranir Trysfal! I have come to claim your bounty!" Startled, Ranir spun around to see a man, clad in near identical black attire that cloaked Detmés. This was another bounty hunter!

"You are hereby deemed murderous of one Emphyrius Bounty Hunter and therefore dangerous to all of Sythestine!" called the man who seemed to have appeared from nowhere. Ranir remembered the portal that Detmés had created.

"This must be another spell caster!" Thought Ranir. He was filled with fear and excitement. Now, he may just witness more magic, a subject that never intrigued him before meeting Detmés, but at what cost? He was mistaken for a murderer.

"Why is there a bounty after me? What did I do?" started Ranir. "And why am I deemed dangerous to the whole country?" He looked through a crack in the wall, "I didn't do anything!" h yelled, feeling his heart beating inside his tunic.

"Did you forget your bow!?" snapped the man, now walking towards Ranir, angrily it seemed."I found it lying next to my friend, Detmés. Your arrows were still in his back!" growled the bounty hunter. Something eerie and familiar resonated in his voice. Ranir felt himself walking towards the man. Ranir got a flashback of the glowing, ember like, arrows hitting Detmés in the back. The sound of the arrows thudding in the fire mage was a vibrant memory.

"I did not shoot him!" bellowed Ranir, "He was shot with glowing orange arrows. They looked like hot embers, and I didn't see the shooter but Detmés saved me from a shape shifter he was tracking. It was his bounty." Ranir finished with his alibi, breathing

21

heavily. His heart was racing.

The bounty hunter's face shifted from brooding to worrisome. Something Ranir said must have meant a sort of truth to him. This almost relieved Ranir, yet pushed worry onto him as well. The bounty hunter shifted his body, looking down at the ground, wide-eyed.

"My name is Taryn Ontaga. Detmés was my brother, not just my friend. I have come to find his killer. All signs pointed to you, at first. Now I know otherwise. I know of the shifter bounty he had." declared the bounty hunter.

Ranir glanced over to his friends. They looked at him with sympathy almost, blended with fear, as they learned that he was being truthful. They now knew that something else entirely had happened to their friend.

Ranir was relieved to know that he wasn't going mad. He was also saddened, for the man who saved his life, died just to protect him. Why? He thought of the arrows again. Magic arrows may have been why a pyromage was taken down so easily.

"If I would've had my bow, maybe I could've save your brother. I'm sorry, Taryn," murmured Ranir, remorsefully.

"It was not you who shot my brother. It wasn't your fault. And if Detmés died... protecting you, then for one, he died doing what he loved, which was saving and protecting. If he didn't fight back, though..." Taryn trailed off, wiping away a tear. He looked back at Ranir with newfound determination.

"He didn't fight. He just protected you... and that's what I'm curious about. He usually tended to end conflict, with pyromancy," said Taryn, looking more bitter now.

Marnos and Selendt looked exhausted from trying to keep their sanity. Marnos gave her a reassuring glance, that she was not going crazy and that all three of them were into the realm of the unknown.

"How did you know that it was Ranir's bow?" asked Marnos in an accusing tone. It seemed to be the one thing that was grounded in reality yet, didn't fit the narrative of Taryn.

Looking interested in Marnos's attention to detail, Taryn replied, "A tracking spell. It's simple and basic for finding possession of mundane objects, that weren't cloaked."

Marnos shifted back a little. He looked at Selendt. They mutually seemed satisfied and annoyed at the same time.

"So now what? Are you going to track down your brother's bounty? Also, do you have fire magic as well?" questioned Ranir. It seemed like a legitimate question to ask. Taryn boastfully chuckled to himself.

"Yes, I am a pyromage, as well," he said amusingly. "As far as what my plan is?" he continued in a more serious tone, "I can't track my brother's murderers because I don't have the bounty...yet. And by myself I don't know what they look like. There are hundreds, if not more, Druids out there."

"So the shifter, he is called a Druid?" asked Ranir. This question seemed to shift Taryn's focus. He open his mouth to speak, but refrained. He looked at each of them, pausing a moment in between.

"I will tell you this, I think I've already said too much. I apologize for speaking freely, of the magical world. I'm not used to meeting such uninformed people, outside of it," he said, looking poised, and standing more properly. He crossed his hands, interlocking his fingers. He looked straight into Ranir's wondrous brown eyes. "I cannot go after them," he continued. "Not without your help, anyway.

With his interest peeking, Ranir's eyes grew large. A pull of wonder started to creep up in him.

"*My* help?" he asked. "How could *I* help?" Ranir felt intrigued now, more than ever.

Taryn flashed a smirk. It faded as quick it came. He now looked intrigued as well. He assumed a citizen, of a small village, like Heramor, would either be afraid of the magical world or they would simply be inclined to keep a distance from it. He knew that Ranir was different, in that way. Magic drew Ranir in, in a way nothing did before. He wasn't sure why this was. Even he couldn't explain it, yet.

"Ranir, you are the only one, that I know, that has seen the face, of the druid," started Taryn. He spoke as if he were speaking carefully, minding the context of which he spoke. He continued in such manor, "therefore, I can use a spell that will lead, from your memory, to any location in the world. It will act as a guide."

The thought of witnessing magic again excited Ranir. He didn't even give Taryn the chance to explain how or why he needed Ranir. Without hesitation, this small token of information was enough for Ranir to jump straight into this quest.

"Whatever you need, I'll do it! Lets go!" he shouted. He nearly couldn't contain himself. He looked over to Marnos and Selendt. They looked as if they were displeased with his readiness to ride off on a magical quest of revenge. To them, he seemed like he

24

was a different person altogether.

"Splendid, Ranir. Shall we set off? I need to perform the first spell to track the location of the druid," said Taryn. He glanced over to Marnos and Selendt and realized, he too, got excited at the possibility of getting revenge for his brother.

"And your friends, would they like to join us? It seems rude of me not to ask, with all that they now know." Taryn likely was hoping for a negative response from the pair, as to partner up with more than 1 person for a ride so long.

Ranir turned to his best friend. He did not need to say anything. Marnos could read on his face, the question he was about to ask. Marnos motioned him over, with his head, shaking his shaggy hair.

"Ranir, what are you doing? You can't be seriously thinking of running off with a mage? To seek revenge for his brother?" asked Marnos.

"Of course I can," started Ranir, "that man's brother saved my life. I want to do this to help repay him, show him I'm grateful. And I want to do this to find out why he saved me, if there was another reason. I want you and Selendt to come with me. We can all watch each other's backs out there." Ranir finished in a tone that was almost crying, begging even.

Marnos looked at Selendt. She was silent, but he could tell this conversation, and thought of running off, unsettled her. Her dark green eyes were widened. As well, he didn't want to venture far, either. The forest was far enough for him. He was not a coward, but he like to keep things within the realm of what he knew. Surprises and the unknown made Marnos uncomfortable. He wasn't going to let his best friend, almost brother, go alone.

Marnos let out a long, windy sigh. "Okay," he said. "I will go with you, because quite frankly, one of us needs to keep some sense. I don't really trust this mage. I am not sure why you do, either. But we will go with you, so that we can keep you safe, as well."

Selendt walked closer to them both, within whispering distance. Ranir looked into her eyes and she returned the stare-down. "I will go with you as well. I will follow you both into danger if it means that I may be able to help keep you safe. Ranir knew that Selendt was more than capable of handling herself. She was the best archer in all of Heramor, and an amazing tracker. She was calculating to a dangerous degree. Most people in the village saw her beauty and her quietness. They would never know her like Marnos and Ranir do.

The plan was set. The three friends gathered up supplies. They horded all they could sneak past Marnos's father. The idea of everything they were doing was against the way he was raised. He knew his father would be displeased. He was old enough to leave, though. He was Ranir's elder by a year.

Nervously they walked over to Taryn. He looked nervous as well. He looked deep into Ranir's eyes, as if he were staring through him.

Placing his hands on Ranir's head, he muttered a spell that was inaudible. Ranir felt a jolt of energy surge through his temple area, almost warming. Ranir could see a fog like trail lead from his forehead into the forest. Then it vanished.

"That is our path!" cheered Taryn. He was determined to see this through. They set off into the dense evergreen forest, not knowing when, or if, they would return to Heramor. It was a gamble and a risk. In his heart, Ranir felt this was the right decision to make.

Other than his friends, he had no one to call him home, or to miss him. He felt that this was his duty. A large part of Ranir's thoughts were that he was destined to do something in this world, other than hunt, farm and grow old. Not only did he feel that he needed to do something, his life had grown stagnant every since his mother passed. Chores and menial work had kept his hours of the days busy, but Ranir wasn't happy.

Often, he had thought of selling the farm and traveling. There was a whole continent of things to see and people to meet. One day he hoped to actually venture out into Sythestine and even beyond, taking to the ocean's on the coast.

Chapter 3: The Calling of The Storm

Several days had passed by as Ranir, Taryn, Marnos and Selendt continued. They traveled on foot, making for a slow, and steady pace. They had packed up nearly all three of the deer that Marnos's father had butchered. Taryn had been teaching the three friends more about the world of magic, and living within the walls of the Emphyre, the leader of Sythestine.

Even as the nights went along, with no sign of the druid or the mystery assassin, Ranir remained optimistic. He continued to keep up his high spirits. He seemed to never run out of questions for Taryn, much to his annoyance.

"We should camp here for the night. There is a storm coming," declared Ranir. Taryn might have had magic, but Ranir had a sense of nature from years spent in the forest hunting and gathering. They began to search for usable limbs and materials to make a shelter, large enough to sleep four.

It was near dark when the storm moved in. Being spring, they were prepared to have storms. Luckily for them, the forest was so massive that they were still under the canopy of large evergreen trees, still. They had successfully created a roof over their heads and built a fire. To be exact, and to show his magic more clearly, Taryn lit the fire with magic.

He kneeled down in an open area, about an arms length from the shelter. He took a few long breaths and closed his eyes. Once again, he spoke a language that was lost to Ranir and his friends.

"*Alak atu sethika*!" Taryn breathed life into a small flame. It was much hotter, than a normal fire, with merely half the size. Marnos thought this would be very convenient whilst hunting. Taryn stood up and began pacing around the fire, as if to insure that it was done well.

"How does magic work? Where does it come from, I mean? And why do you have it and not others? Were you born with it?"asked Ranir. When he got on the subject of magic, his questions seemed to flow into each other.

"Magic is a gift from the Old Gods, to us down here on Gnariam. It is a gift, a task, and an oath," started Taryn. "I wasn't born with magic, no. It was gifted to me by Baryt, the Fire Lord. Not every mage is a pyromancer, either. There are water, earth and air mages. All are given their elemental power, from different elemental gods." Taryn finished, with a look of reminiscence on his face.

Ranir seemed as eager, to listen to magical tales, as Taryn was to tell them. He wasn't sure why, yet, but he had a feeling that Ranir was meant to know all that he was teaching him. The same could not be said for Marnos, nor Selendt, who remained quiet mostly. During most of their walking hours, the pair of them seemed to be rather quietly annoyed. Marnos seemed to be listening halfheartedly, and Selendt simply seemed to be enjoying her travels.

"So fire magic. Why Fire magic?" questioned Ranir. He wanted to know all that could be taught to him, yet he had no reason to know. He had no magic, though, he so wished that an Old God would bestow power to him. He was almost in a jealous fit about it.

"Well," started Taryn, pausing his steps, "we aren't really sure why each person is chosen by certain Old Gods. They sort of, just, step in and bestow the power. There is no reason given, nor is there a guarantee of who gets magic, and if they do what they are meant to do with it!" finished Taryn. He just realized that knew very little, himself, on the process, of one becoming a mage.

Ranir sat quietly with his knees bent, pondering what it would be like to have power like that, running through his body. He thought of all the things that magic could help make easier.

Marnos and Selendt were being rather quiet, more than usual, on this evening. They also sat particularly close to each other. Upon further thought, it made Ranir slightly uncomfortable but he wasn't sure why. Seeing them as family, he never thought more on the subject though. He assumed they were still wary and unsure of this quest, and came together as comfort to each other.

It must have ultimately became clear that it was raining to Taryn because he broke his glazed-eyed stupor as he shot a look upwards. He squinted his eyes trying to peer into the rainfall. He brought his arms outward, palms facing the sky and mutter, "*Tustik amo delathk*," and a nearly invisible fire shield emerged around him. The raindrops could be heard hitting the shield in a sound that was like water landing in a hot iron skillet. Ranir looked around the sphere of heat that surrounded Taryn. He shook his head in a sarcastic manor, still entertained by magic.

"Now that is something you could do for all of us," said Ranir, chucking to himself.

"No, a mage can only cast an elemental shield around himself," said Taryn. "If I cast it on anyone but myself, it'll simply burn them. On myself, I can dampen the spell to use it like this," he said with arms directed at the shield.

Seeing that the storm was not showing signs of calming down, Taryn let the fire go out. They say in darkness, apart of the blinding bursts of lightning streaking across the sky. The lightning on this night was particularly steady. To Ranir it was almost soothing, as he lay down on his blanket. The shelter they made was large enough to fit at least 6 people in it. Taryn was still sitting up when Ranir felt to call of fatigue take him into a smooth sleep.

"Ranir! Wake up!" said Marnos. Looking up, Ranir could barely see Marnos kneeling over top of him. It was still dark and storming outside. Not fully understanding Marnos's panic and haste, Ranir raised up slowly. He was sitting in the shelter alone. He was befuddled. Where were the others? From outside the shelter and through the storm he could hear yelling outside. He picked up his dagger and rushed outside.

"Selendt! Selendt?! Where are you?!" Marnos was screaming in a frightening tone

"Selendt?!" Ranir could hear Taryn from the other side of the camp site. He looked around, panicking.

"What happened?" yelled Ranir through the crashing of thunder and downpour of rain. The ground was saturated well beyond forming puddles. In a short moment, Ranir could feel his shaggy hair sticking to his face, water sliding down his forehead.

"We don't know. I woke up and she was gone," said Taryn. "and this was in her place," he continued, holding an arrow in his hand. Ranir's heart skipped a beat seeing the arrow. It was the same kind of arrow that flew from the dark at Veörn Mountains. It had the same ember glowing shaft as the arrows that landed in Detmés' back. He looked back up at Taryn. He was already wearing a look of understanding.

Taryn turned around and looked at Marnos, then back at Ranir. He was deep in thought. He looked down at the arrow in his hand. Ranir knew that it would be unfruitful to continue calling out for Selendt.

"I have an idea. I need both of you," said Taryn, "I can do a spell to track this arrow back to the last hands it touched. I'll need your energy though."

Confused, Ranir looked at Marnos, who was walking towards Taryn. "Why would you need our energy for a spell?" he said.

"Magic needs energy to work. Small spells I can do with my own energy without fatiguing. Larger spells, I need to absorb energy to perform," explained Taryn.

Ranir thought back to the sport all that Detmés has created to save him. He remembered being completely exhausted and passing out. He remembered seeing the Druid cower with fatigue and faint. This must have been the reason.

"Okay, just do it!" exclaimed Marnos. He was anxious to find Selendt immediately. He was willing to give magic a try if it meant bring back their friend.

"*Sethak alatu mon shak!*" squalled Taryn, without hesitating. Ranir and Marnos suddenly felt a draw of the energy. It felt cold, like a wet blanket being draped over them. The power being drawn out was more uncomfortable yet. It was as if the very force of their life was being slapped away. Ranir thought it felt like a cold hand of death taking ahold of them. Then, in an explosion of fire and bright light, the arrow shot up in the air. It began to move in a circular motion.

"What is it doing?" shouted Marnos. He was beginning to second guess his choice of trying magic. The energy tap was more than he imagined it would be.

"It's finding the archer!" yelled Taryn. It was inaudible as the spell became louder still. His eyes were glowing with an orangish hue in his irises. To Marnos, he looked like a demon performing this spell. Suddenly, the arrow shot forward, leaving a trail of glowing fire that clung in the air as if it were frozen time. It began to swirl back and forth. Ranir noticed glowing footprints beneath the trail of flames.

"There!" shouted Taryn. He put his arms down and ran towards the trail. Ranir and Marnos began to follow him through their tiredness. Ranir realized that Taryn had another secret. He was moving faster than any human he had seen run before. He must have realized that he left his new friends behind because he stopped short in his tracks, slinging mud and pebbles forward. He turned to see them at least 50 paces behind him. He waited impatiently, looking back and forth between Ranir and Marnos, and the fiery track leading to the assailant. Once they caught up he proceeded, at a normal humane pace.

Several minutes passed by as the trio hunted down whoever took Selendt. Taryn presumed it was the archer, who killed his brother, taunting him. He was almost certain and yet he was just as eager as the archer's plan, to find him and unleash his vengeance. Ranir and Marnos were uncertain what kind of messy world they stepped into. To Ranir, it was fun and intriguing until this moment. Now he was simply realizing the dark side of this magical world. He was beginning to understand the threat that comes with just knowing very little. Marnos was the most eager to find

Selendt for they had grown closer than ever on this trip.

The flaming trail stopped at the edge of another forest. Taryn realized that was uncertain how far they traveled and which forest they were about to embark into. Upon reached the edge of the tracking spell, they noticed a small niche inside the forest. It was only ambient lit from echoing lightning around them.

"What is that?" called Marnos. He saw what appeared to be a cocoon the size of a human. His heart sank. He hoped this thing in front of them was not Selendt.

"It's a transmuting shell," said Taryn, looking weary, "it's what happens when a Druid dies," he explained. It had been a very long time since Taryn saw a shell like this. In fact it was nearly two decades since he laid his eyes on one.

"Do you think-"started Ranir, but was cutoff by Taryn. He already knew what Ranir was thinking. He had the same idea.

"Maybe. Let's cut it open and find out before it dissipates," he said. Walking towards it he held out a hand forward, palm facing the cocoon. "*Estashashik*," commanded Taryn. A bright orange slice appeared in the shell. It sounded like the crushing of an insect, but much more audible. In an instant, the hide split open, ashes spraying into the air. Ranir watched as several trees around the husk began to decay. At first, he thought maybe the deceased Druid had the effect surrounding it. Then he realized that Taryn pulled energy from the trees to perform the spell. Ranir was starting to understand magic more.

From within the gap in the cocoon, Ranir could see a shadowy figure of a man inside. Taryn walked over and peeled it open. It cracked with the sound of cloth being torn apart. Inside, a man lay bare naked. He had pale skin and long jet black hair.

"That's him! That's the Druid from the mountains!" exclaimed Ranir, instantly recognizing the body and its disgust. A part of Ranir felt sick, seeing a dead body like that, and another part of him felt relieved, almost justified, that someone carrying that kind of inhuman darkness was brought down. Now he could do no more harm to people. Ranir could still imagine the sights and sounds of the Druid changing shape and morphing into a wolf like beast.

"Are you sure?" questioned Taryn. He wanted to know if Ranir was sure all the way before he executed his plan.

"Yes I am sure!" exclaimed Ranir, "How could I forget a face so grotesque, and a body so bony and leather like, nasty creature."

"Good. I just wanted to make sure," said Taryn. He held his hands toward the cocoon. "Stand back," he said, as he waited for proper space to do an incineration spell. He drew his arms upward, drawing mana from the surrounding trees. Once he had the sufficient amount of energy, he let out a bellowed cry, "*Atakult Brakat Disto!*"

The husk burst into flames, that seemed to be contained to only the cocoon. The fire began as a deep orange color. It reminded Ranir of the setting sun's hue across the sky. Quickly, the fire lost its saturation and faded to a pure white flame. The intensity of the flame grew as did its brightness. It was almost blinding. Suddenly, the flame wrapped body and husk altogether burst into an explosion. All was still, except for the rain seeping through the treetops. Through the flashes of lightning, Ranir and Marnos could see dead trees encircling them. This was a sign of a mage in the area.

35

Taryn had pulled so much energy from the trees, for this spell in particular, that it killed the trees all around them.

"Sssht!" came the sound through the black. Ranir felt his heart sink. This sound was all too familiar and too quick for him. *An archer!* Just as he instantly imagined the arrow fired from the shadows at the Veörn Mountains, an arrow came through the pause between lightning strikes. An arrow found its place in Taryn's shoulder.

"Ah!" Taryn shouted. Even in the pitch black of the forest, they could all see the glowing undertones of ember in the arrow. It was the same kind of arrow that killed Taryn's brother. He clutched at this shoulder, then reached up and ripped the arrow that was lodged in his muscle. They all ducked down as if to find cover in a rather open area of the trees.

"Either there are more than one, or they are super fast!" thought Ranir. Again, another arrow came pelting through the darkness, this time burying itself in Ranir's upper back. He screamed so loud it made Marnos jump backwards.

How could separate arrows come from two different directions rapidly and be from the same archer? As of late, the usual answer was simple: Magic. Whoever is shooting is a mage or another consorter of magic. It grew very quiet. The storm seemed to calm down for a moment. They could hear a blood curdling laugh coming through the dark. Even scarier yet came the scream from a girl. A scream that pronounced the very feeling of physical pain and fear.

"Selendt?!" Marnos yelled jumping back up to his feet, trying to peer into the dark. "Can't you light this place up?" again he yelled, this time directing his frustration at Taryn. He began to wander around, continuing to yell for their friend. He was met with only silence.

Jumping up in the air, Taryn clapped his hands in the air, this time not audibly making a spell. Instead of words, the forest was met with a resounding boom and a massive blast of fire and light erupting from his hands. In a fraction of a blink's time, they saw what they needed to. Selendt was tied to a tree not even twenty paces from them, a gag in her mouth. Hiding just above her on a branch they saw the monster of an assassin, perched with bow in hand. She had frizzy black hair and eyes that looked to be sunken. Her lips were pursed back, revealing sharp teeth like those of the Druid.

Taryn began blasting spells in rapid fire. He was overcome with emotion of rage and pain, seeking vengeance that seemed so close him now. The assassin jumped around the trees as if she were made to live in them. Taryn's spells missed over and over again. The assassin made one last daring move, jumping out of the trees doing an aerial flip. While in midair, she knocked an arrow and fired it. The arrow landed a few inches from Marnos's face, pinning itself in a tree.

Taryn began to grow weak from over exerting his magic. He paused for a moment, letting the darkness once again consume the area. Ranir wondered how this assassin could see in the dark enough to hunt someone down. He turned around to look at Marnos, but he was nowhere to be found. Taryn fell down on one knee. This scene was very exact in Ranir's mind. This is the same way that his brother, the fearless protector, died right before him. He had to do something.

He crawled over to the tree and pulled the arrow from the tree, half way expecting it to burn like actual fire embers. Strangely, it felt cold and void of energy almost, unlike the one stuck in his back which felt like pure fire. He put it in his shirt top. No more arrows were being fired. The assassin was left with only her wits and her daggers. Creeping in the shadows, she snuck up behind Ranir.

"Ranir, behind you!" yelled Taryn. Another surprise to Ranir, that Taryn could see so well even standing a few paces in the pitch black. Without hesitation, he pulled the arrow from his shirt and thrust it backwards. The tip of the arrow found its way directly into the eye of the assassin. She let out a scream that seemed to echo through the whole of the forest, then felled backwards into a tree. Taryn stumbled up to both feet and without permission this time, he sapped the energy from everything and everyone around him.

"*Talatak Figotok*!" he screamed so loud his voice broke. The pain and grieving was audible in his vocalization. A large blast of deep, red fire came directly through his palms. The seemingly perfect sphere of flames stabbed straight through the assassin, burning a hole the size of her head, directly through her body. Ranir looked back and saw her rips through the hole. He became sick. He felt lightheaded and fell down. He knew this feeling of fatigue. Taryn took his energy. He looked around through blurred vision as red and orange glowing ashes dimly lit the area. Taryn collapsed. Ranir relaxed and his face hit the mud.

This time he didn't faint. He could still see Marnos struggling to untie Selendt from the tree. She hung in the ropes like a doll, unconscious. Suddenly, the storm resumed its thunderous reign over the area. He began to black out. In and out of focus, he could hear ambient sounds of the storm and Marnos yelling for help, in addition to his own heart beating. He needed to find a way to get up. Taryn was dying from overuse of magic and bleeding. Selendt's condition was unknown.

As if it were a sign from the Old Gods, a massive bolt of lightning struck down and found its way into Ranir's chest. In the same time it took the lightning to strike, Ranir felt a surge of burning pain, coupled with feeling every muscle in his body contract at once. It felt like his heart was exploding inside him. He heard the crack of the thunder. Perhaps it was the sound of his body shattering, fragmenting under the power of nature. He wasn't sure at this point. He felt a massive increase of energy, immediately followed by the discard of all energy. He swore that, for a few seconds, the lightning held onto him, channeling a burst of death. He didn't have time to even scream, all was cold, and dark.

Chapter 4: Immersion

Ranir was exhausted. Much had happened in the last couple weeks, he almost felt numb. Everything that had happened had started with magic in the Veörn Mountains. Something that seemed amazing to him, at the beginning, was a spectacle like no other. Now, he was unsure how much good magic could do in the world. He still had so much to learn.

Lost in thought, feeling cold and afloat, Ranir called out, "Hello?" He was met with an echo followed by silence, except for a slight ambient noise pulsating around him. It was pitch black. He tried to remember the last thing that happened. Suddenly, a flash a light and bursting lightning flashes in his mind. He was struck by lightning!

"Am I dead?" thought Ranir. He thought that, maybe, he'd be afraid of death. In this moment he was content. He didn't feel his life mattered nor had he achieved anything great.

"No!" a voice erupted from the darkness. The voice was resounding and near threatening. "You are in between, another realm. You are not dead, and yet," he continued with a chuckle, "you are not alive."

Ranir was calm and still. Something about this place seemed to dissipate sinister auras. He wasn't alive, and therefore had no reason to fear for his life, or anyone else's life.

"So where am I?" asked Ranir. He knew that he was no longer in the forest nor was he anywhere close to his friends. He realized that he felt bodiless. Maybe that explained why he felt like he was floating.

"As I said, you are in between," started the deep voice. Suddenly his face appearing through the black, as if an unknown light casted a bright ray on his face. He had a gray beard and bright white, long hair. It was half braided like a nobleman. "I have prolonged your passing, to offer you a choice, a gift," he finished, disappearing back into the black. A swooshing sound was swirling around Ranir. He was uncertain of many things at this point.

"What gift?" asked Ranir. To his right, the old face appeared again.

"Life. For a price," the voice barked out again. Ranir could've swore the voice was in his head and not emitting from the man.

"That seems like an easy choice! Life! I don't want to die," replied Ranir. He didn't care, in that moment, what the price or expectation was.

"Very well, Ranir Trysfal. What do you know about magic?" asked the man. Truth was, after giving it some thought, that he didn't know much at all.

"I know it got me into a couple messes. It also saved my life. What does magic have to do with anything, though?" Ranir gave a straightforward answer without hesitating. He was bewildered by the fact that he didn't think before speaking, or perhaps his thoughts were his speaking voice here.

"Ranir, you chose to place your life, a fragile human life, in between death and a mage. It has been millennia since we have seen that kind of bravery from a mortal human. I think you deserve a second chance at

41

life because the world needs people like you," he spoke with nearly no pause to breathe or think. He stepped fully out of the shadows. Ranir wondered if this was a trick of illusion because there was no clear light around them.

"So, you're saying you can bring me back to life?" asked Ranir. The thought of the power it would take to do this would have to be immense. How could he do that? What magic user had that kind of power. It dawned on him.

"Who are you?" he asked. "Better yet, what...are you?" He tried to sound demanding, albeit knowing it was a nonachievement.

"I am Eros. I am the God of Lightning," he stated, then awaited Ranir's reply. He did not reply, not even with a thought. The intensity of this knowledge dumbstruck Ranir.

He sat quiet for several minutes, in a daze among the darkness. Drawing himself back to this version of reality, he looked directly into Eros's eyes. He hadn't noticed before, but they were completely white. No pupil or iris was present.

"So I really am 'dead'," started Ranir. "But you can fix that...because you're a God. The Old Gods are real...magic is real," he began rambling on. This was the first moment in this "in between world" that he felt human again. He was panicking as if his mind about to snap into insanity. He calmed himself down and recharged his steadiness.

"It is a lot, to take in, for you I see. This may not be the right choice, yet, I have given you the choice," Eros said. This seemed to be quite the ordeal for him as well as Ranir.

"Yes and I choose to live, if I may. Please. Send

me back. Please," begged Ranir.

"Very well. The only way to do this however," Eros began, "is with magic. And by magic, I mean in order that you will have to retain the magic, that is used to bring you back. Do you understand?" Eros asked.

Ranir understood only understood half of the information Eros gave him. He looked down, which was pointless in hindsight, because it was all darkness except Eros. He was wearing a silvery colored robe adorned with sapphire colored jewels. It looked like casual wear for a mighty and magical warrior, which was fitting.

"Y-yeah. Sorry, no, what do you mean, 'retain magic'? Like, I have to...do what exactly?" he asked.

This must have been amusing to Eros because he croaked out a loud booming laugh. It reminded Ranir of someone yelling in a cathedral, the way the echo seemed to reverberate.

After containing himself he said, "you will have to have magic in your body in order to live." He waited for a sign of clues coming together for Ranir. He enjoyed speaking in near riddles.

"You mean I will be a mage?!" yelled Ranir. He didn't mean to shout. He cupped a hand over his mouth. It was difficult to keep his excitement in check. He always felt pinging fear as usual of the unknown.

"No," Eros replied, "a mage controls and channels a certain element of the world: earth, water, fire and air. You will harness the raw power of lightning. It holds some similarities to mages, hedge witches, and other magical beings, yet it's vastly different. You will be tasked with a hard life, struggling to control your power. Know this; life with this power,

43

and death, both hold their own forms of Hel," he explained.

Ranir instantly lost his excitement, reserving for more seriousness. He would need to take on a large amount of responsibility moving forward.

"I stand on my same choice: life," said Ranir. He was no longer certain of anything else, including his future, or what burdens he would face. He knew that death would not be an option.

"Very well!" boasted Eros. He continued, "there is one more thing. You will be tasked, as all mages are tasked, to protect Gnariam. You must bear the light against all darkness, no matter what form or presence they take. It is an oath to The Old Gods. So, lastly, do you accept the Calling of The Storm?" He finished, lowering his head in a half bow.

"I accept," answered Ranir, returning a full bow to the God Of Lightning. Eros stood up, making Ranir realize in that moment that he was at least three times his size. He turkey was an Old God, a spectacle unlike any other. Eros puts his hands together for a brief moment. When he separated them, a single arc of controlled light blue lightning arched between his hands, making a low sounding hum, like that of a bee flying. The lightning grew brighter and louder. Suddenly Ranir felt a surge of energy and burning, exactly as it felt when he was struck by the lightning in the forest. He thought he would faint yet again. Instead the light grew to a blinding degree of white. Through the light he could hear Eros.

He called out, "Ranir Trysfal, you have been chosen to become the Channeler of Lightning, The Carrier of Mana. With this, I gift you my child, with my power to control the most devastating force on Gnariam, Lightning. I hereby endow you with the power...of The Lightning Rod.

The thrashing sounds of lightning and thunder in the midst of a hurricane splintered through the air. It was near deafening to Ranir. He felt the power consume every part of him. Suddenly, all was still.

Chapter 5: A New Leaf

Taryn cracked open his eyes, taking a quick, deep breath. His lungs filled with warm, humid air. The sun was beginning to rise, casting a red hue into the shelter. He started to sit up but he was halted by the stinging in his shoulder. Cupping his hand over it, he winced at the pain. Looking down, he noticed he was covered by branches and foliage.

Outside the shelter, he could hear echoing conversation. He stepped outside to find Marnos and Selendt sitting by a fire. Marnos had his arm around her shoulder. Selendt laid her head on his shoulder. Her eyes were puffy from crying.

Taryn looked around. A few paces away, Ranir was laying on his back. His head was propped up with a small boulder. He was still. Taryn got a rush of emotions recalling the fight with the assassin. He became overwhelmed with rage in that moment he took all the energy he could get in order to kill her. In that moment, he hadn't thought of the collateral damage.

He saw Ranir laying there, presumably dead, and he fell to his knees. Guilt took over as his eyes began to water. Ranir was just a boy who was full of light and wonder. He hadn't even experienced life yet his was over.

Selendt got up, and walked over to Taryn, wiping away her own tears. She held out her hands offering them to stand Taryn up. Marnos joined her. He looked into Taryn's eyes, then turned to Ranir. A smile overcame his face as he recollected how Ranir was always brave.

"When we were small boys, maybe 8 years old or so, that is when I realized how brave and special he was, for the first time. We were playing in the forest and a sleeper snuck up on us. Without even thinking, Ranir jumped between me and the snake. It but him and he nearly died then. That's just who he was," he turned back to Taryn with tears streaming down his face, "that is how he was; selfless and brave." His voice trailed off, cracking. He began to weep for his best friend, for his brother.

"And now? He's gone. Because of me! I am so sorry that I dragged you all into this. It should've been me who died," he cried out, fighting the sobs.

"Not because of you," replied Selendt. "He did it *for* you. Don't take that away from him. He stayed true to himself, always. He wouldn't regret it."

Taryn remembered his oath: To protect the world from darkness and evil. How much into darkness did he fall, to achieve vengeance? He sighed, "I thought I had more control over my emotions. It's one of the first things we are taught. I've always been short tempered. It's part of why The Firelord chose to bestow me with his element. It's meant for protection," he explained. "And yet I used the destruction nature of fire." He looked down at his hands, as if they were weapons of chaos. He said, "I need to return to my post."

He took Selendt's hands and rose to his feet. On her wrists he noticed pink scuffs from the rope she was bound with. "Here," he said, guiding her to the fire, "let me heal those." He outstretched a hand over the crackling flames. "*Atulashut*," he commanded.

A small flame slowly rose. He held it in his hand. More accurately, it floated an inch from his palm. Selendt looked scared to be touched by the fire. She still hadn't trusted magic. After all, magic caused more pain in her life than it helped.

Taryn nodded to her, reassuring that he was helping. He rubbed the dim orange fire over her wrists as if it were an oil. Instant relieve overtook the stinging ache. The marks faded slowly. Within seconds they were gone. She was healed.

"Thank you," she said, walking back to Marnos.

"I need to get you back to Heramor, then I must return to my home. The Emphyre will not take kindly to me straying from my mission," he looked around, finally realizing they were not in the same place as the previous night.

"Can you teleport us home?" asked Selendt.

"I cannot port someone who has passed. I am sorry. I can escort you back, though, offering what protection I can if need be," he started. "Once we get-"he was interrupted.

A massive light blazed down from the sky, blinding everything within nearly a mile radius. It sounded like the sky was something solid, that had just split open. When the light passed, Taryn looked around through blurred vision. He could only hear a high pitch ringing in his ears. He saw Marnos and Selendt crouched down, hands over their ears, eyes slammed shut. He looked over to where Ranir was laying. His body was gone. Taryn had never seen or heard anything like this in his life.

"Where did he go?" asked Marnos. He pivoted around to see if maybe he was disoriented, and lost his direction.

From behind them another flash of light ripped into existence. This time it contained a humming sound, and was much dimmer than the explosion of luminous power. A shadowy figure appeared in the light orb. As the glow began to diminish, the dark form in the center took form. It appeared to be a man inside.

Taryn, Marnos and Selendt held their hands before them, peering between their fingers to mitigate some of the light. Squinting, Taryn took a step diagonally forward, placing himself between the unknown figure, and Marnos and Selendt.

"Stay behind me!" he yelled. He held his hands up, palms toward the light and shadow. He was prepared, mentally, for a fight. He hoped it wouldn't come to that because of both his wound and his depletion of energy.

Suddenly the light faded, and the figures touched the ground, remaining still. It was a man. He was cloaked in a gray robe that was lined with bright, shining blue, jagged lines. He was adorned with a hooded cloak of the same color. The hood was broad and covered the figure's face. The man had his head bowed, hiding his face behind folds of fabric of the hood. His arms were out to the side. He didn't shift a hair's width. He appeared frozen in time.

Taryn looked back at Marnos and Selendt. They both appeared as confused and mesmerized as he was. The figure stirred. Suddenly a bolt of lightning cracked down from the clear blue sky, completely enveloping the figure in a bluish white light for a split moment. His body relaxed, and his feet settled on the ground. It wasn't until this moment they realized that the figure was actually floating. Arms dropping to his side, the figure looked up.

Looking into his golden brown eyes, they were flabbergasted. Ranir was alive! He didn't move. He was still rather stunned at his own resurrection. Marnos took several slow steps towards Ranir. His eyes welled up with emotion.

Marnos approached Ranir cautiously. He gazed upon the robe he was adorned with, looking for a sign of explanation.

"Ranir?" he asked, "is it really you? How-what...how is this possible?" He questioned, shaking his head in disbelief. Selendt and Taryn remained still with shock.

"It's *me*, Marnos," Ranir replied. Marnos rushed over and fully embraced him in a tight hug. He held on what seemed like an eternity. Selendt rushed over to them as well, wrapping her pale arms around them both. Ranir squeezed them both. Marnos gasped for air. Selendt let out a "woof" sound. Ranir let go of them both and took a step back.

"I'm sorry," he said looking down at his hands. The Lightning God Eros's gift must have given him newfound strength as well. Ranir looked past his friends and saw Taryn. He remained in the same place with a look of disbelief and distrust.

"How is this possible?" Taryn said, breaking his silence. His tone was darker, more serious and otherwise sounded accusing. His question took Ranir by surprise. He expect a sort of welcoming. Instead he was greeting by Taryn being rude. It was confusing for his friends too, because they both turned to face Taryn with scowls.

"I died, sort of," started Ranir. "I didn't plan on dying. I certainly didn't want to. The God of Lightning had other plans for me, though," he explained.

"The God of Lightning?" asked Taryn, again with the same tone. "Not even the Old Gods have seen him for over 12,000 years. You're telling me, he came to you, upon death?" he interrogated.

"Y-yes," said Ranir. "He came to me when I died, sort of, and gave me a gift in the form of a choice."

"And what choice is that? What gift?" demanded Taryn. Something about his manner seemed to be off. It was becoming frustrating to Ranir, who, in turn, gained an attitude.

"He gave me my life back, okay? That was the gift. Or part of it, magic was the other part. He gave me magic, I guess, I don't know, I don't feel any different. Why are you hammering me with questions. Are you not satisfied that I am back? Why are you being rude?" It was Ranir's turn to fire back the questions.

"That's why," he said, pointed at Ranir's hand. "I was just trying to provoke you."

Ranir looked down, noticing a light blue lightning arc running between his fingers, dancing around his palm, swirling around like a live string. His palm itched like a rash. He looked up at Taryn and saw a smile on his face. Now, Ranir, Marnos and Selendt were all confused. The lightning dissipated.

"You're a sorcerer, Ranir!" exclaimed Taryn. He was reinvigorated with excitement, both for Ranir's return, and for having someone and something to relate with. "What kind of sorcerer, is the question."

"Eros specifically said that I'm *not* a mage,"

51

replied Ranir. He realized he still had an attitude. He sighed, shook his head and let it pass. He continued, "He said mages are bound by the four elements, or whatever."

He noticed Marnos shift his stance a little. An estranged look came over his face. Ranir knew Marnos was not a fan of magic, but not that he'd feel differently about his best friend.

"Then what are you?" Asked Marnos. He looked concerned.

"Eros said something about a lightning rail, or rod..I think that's-"started Ranir.

"The Lightning Rod?" interrupted Taryn. His eyes were opened wide, eyebrows raised.

"Yes! The Lightning Rod! That was it," said Ranir.

"Ranir, why did he choose you? Many people die, everyday. Why did he save you?" asked Marnos.

"He said...because I saved Taryn. As a mortal human, I saved a mage. That meant something?" He was having trouble recalling the words he heard only moments ago.

"The Lightning Rod is a title, that is extremely rare. In fact, it's been endowed only once before in records, that I am aware of, over 12,000 years ago, to be exact," replied Taryn.

"So what does that mean? I'm special?" he asked, letting out a chuckle.

"You could say that, I suppose. Unique is a better word, I think. You may just have more power than all of the Emphyre's mages," he said, dropping back to a serious tone, "Just maybe, according to the stories of the old bearer of the lightning elemental."

"So what does that mean for him?" asked Marnos. He was going to have to accept this new path of Ranir's, or choose to leave him behind. He knew that the latter was not an option.

"It means," said Taryn, "that he will need to be trained properly for controlling his power, and how to use magic. He needs to go to the Emphyre, safely, so that he doesn't hurt anyone or hurt himself."

Ranir looked at Marnos for a sign of an opinion. He simply stared blankly back at him, apparently searching for the same. He turned to look at Selendt. She looked down towards her feet, then back to Marnos.

"We need to do whats best for Ranir, and I will not leave him behind. I won't abandon my family," she said. Ranir had half expected her to react the same as Marnos had upon learning that he now possessed magic.

"Well then," said Ranir with a sigh, "I don't want to hurt anyone, especially my family," he looked at Marnos and then to Selendt. "If you are willing, I'd like to go, figure out this magic thing and learn how to control it properly. It obviously ties into my emotions and I don't want any accidents to happen."

Marnos looked back at Taryn, still unsure which choice was the right choice. He connected what Ranir had said about emotions to Taryn saying that emotions were something that he was taught to control first. He thought about his options for a moment. He remembered that this was not his path, it was really no longer even Taryn's path. It was now Ranir's path to get help. Marnos missed home, his parents, his farm.

"Okay," he started, "we will go to the Emphyre.

I miss home but if I have my two best friends, one with magic, and another mage with us, I feel safe going forward.

"I second that," said Selendt. She turned to Taryn, who patiently waited for their decision.

"Good. That's settled then. We should move soon. That bright blast of power is bound to attract some unwanted attention. Hedge witches and rogue mages are always looking for energy boosts to store in gems," replied Taryn. There were many things that the three young friends needed to learn. Now was not the time for questions, though.

"Right, so, we pulled you both from the niche where we found the cocoon and...well you know," said Marnos. "But we have no idea where we are. We have no supplies and we are on foot, in the middle of a forest. Can we just teleport to the Emphyre's castle now?"

The fact of how little he, Selendt and Ranir knew of this newfound world amused him. He laughed, bellowing, "Its not a castle, its more of a keep. Its called the Emphyrius. And yes we can port there if I can muster enough energy. I don't want to take your energy again, not now. Let me go to the woods and gather enough mana for the spell." He started walking quickly into the overgrowth.

"Ranir, how much do you trust him?" asked Marnos.

"I trust that he will get us to safety and get me to the right help I need to control this magic," he replied. The answer he gave must have sufficed Marnos for now, he didn't ask anymore about the subject.

A few moments passed by as they waited for

Taryn's return. Selendt walked over to Ranir and rubbed his cloak. It wasn't until now that he really thought about his new wardrobe.

"Did the Old God give this to you?" she asked. She let her long, skinny fingers follow the blue pattern adorned. They felt like silk against the felt-like cloak.

He looked down, rubbing his hands down his chest and stomach, "I suppose he did," he replied.

Taryn returned to the group and said, "Okay let's go home, well, *my* home of course."

They all gathered in a circle. "*Orshtu Alak!*" he called out. Ranir got a flash of memory from the first teleport spell he had seen from Detmés and felt a little saddened again. A bright orange ring popped up on the ground at their feet. Looking up, Ranir could see the heatwaves distorting the outer region around them. He was prepared this time for the experience of porting somewhere.

Suddenly, the ring turned to a white color. Ranir looked over to Taryn who was gazing into his eyes. He said, " Ranir, your eyes!" They were glowing white with little arcs of lightning coursing through them.

"What about my eyes?" asked Ranir. He looked at his hands, which had the same bluish arcs jumping between his fingers. He felt a surge of energy erupt inside of him. With a bright flash of deep blue color the ring beneath them exploded knocking all of them apart. Marnos and Selendt crashed to the ground. Taryn stayed on his feet but slid backwards several paces, leaves drag marks on the ground. Ranir noticed he didn't move much and upon glancing down, realized he was hovering a few inches off of the ground, for only a second.

He relaxed as best as he could. He could feel the intense energy in his veins. The lightning power inside him was mighty. The hairs on his neck and arms stood outward. He could feel his heart pounding inside of his chest. He looked at Taryn, who looked bewildered. Ranir took a deep breath and exhaled, lowering his body back to the ground.

"I'm sorry. Was that me?" he asked the pyromage. Taryn nodded, silently. Ranir rushed over and helped his friends up. "What happened exactly?" He asked, turning back to Taryn.

With his eyebrows creased, he replied, "It seems, that your power prevented me from teleporting you. I guess I should have guessed something like that *could* happen. It happens when you try to port someone who is opposite on the element flow than you as well occasionally. I just figured lightning and fire would get along just fine. It may be something different entirely as well."

At this point, he really confused the others. When they didn't say anything, just gave him blank stares, he elaborated, "I am a fire mage, the opposite side to my element flow would be water. So if a hydromage resists me, then something similar happens to a teleporting spell. Its just the way it is, and I've never seen it react so powerfully," he explained more, "it usually just dissipates and voids the spell. I've never seen it explode like that before. Your lightning may be hard to figure out the loopholes and pinch points."

"It seems like magical ways of travel are off the table," said Marnos. He was rubbing a scuff mark on Selendt's elbow. She had been knocked back the farthest. She was average size for a girl, but she was lighter than she looked. "For now, it appears we will be walking."

"Do you know where we are?" asked Selendt, to Taryn. "Do you know where to go from here?"

"No but I can find out rather quickly. Its part of what makes me a good bounty hunter is tracking and finding directions or locations," Taryn said. He held out his hands, palms facing each other and muttered a spell under his breath. A small orange symmetrical ball of fire appeared between his hands. A white circle appeared on the ball, spinning around the flame. It reminded Ranir of a compass of sorts. The white mark spun around then suddenly stopped, facing east. Taryn pointed, "that is the way," he said. He tossed the fireball in the air and it lingered there.

The fireball would act as a guide for them back to the Emphyrius. Marnos looked to the west, he knew that somewhere, days away from them, was his home, his farm in Heramor. He turned to look to the East, finally embracing their decision to leave, now that he knew they would be gone for an unknown, but rather long time. He turned to Taryn.

"How long will it take us to get to the Emphyrius?" he asked. He somewhat hoped in was close to them, but his instincts disagreed with his hopes.

"At least 3 weeks on foot to get to Killiad, if we take the route around the mountain, which is the safest," he paused, as if to calculate time, "there we can buy horses, and ride another day across the desert to Thrast. *That* is where the Emphyrius is."

Altogether, they knew that this was going to be no ordinary trip. They were all about to change in ways that they didn't know. Taryn was used to teleporting, using magic and running missions, solo. Ranir was going to have to learn to use magic, bestowed to him, by the God Of Lightning, which was baffling in itself.

Marnos and Selendt were both going to need to push themselves, to see how much love they had for each other, and for Ranir. They were going to have to learn a lot, and grow more mature on this trip, for it was not a quest for children. At this point they nearly forgot that they were not adults yet.

They set out on this journey, each of them changed already, and about to change more. Taryn seemed to keep his eye on Ranir more than he had before. Ranir wasn't sure if he should be worried about Taryn or the fact that Taryn saw, or knew something that was worth monitoring. For now it was time for them to proceed into their journey. It was time to turn over a new leaf.

would be the same for the others. Each elemental mage would be able to create, manipulate and control their bestowed element. Of course, you would be just like that, although," he explained, "we don't know what limits you may or may not have."

"Will I be able to do the other things like mages, do you think?" Ranir asked.

"What other things?" Taryn returned with a question.

"The teleportation, and how you split that cocoon open, things like that," said Ranir.

Taryn smiled again, pausing his steps for a moment. He turned and looked at Ranir. Placing his hands on his arms, he slowly stated, "I think you are going to be able to do grand things, Ranir. I think you will become skilled enough in magic to do things that other mages only dream of. At least, if the myths of The Lightning Rod, King of Thunder, hold any truth."

Ranir looked down, trying to hide a smile of his own. This small amount of information gave him hope for being a wielder of magic. They continued to travel down a slope. It was not steep, but drove far downhill. The brush and overgrown weeds seemed to be thickening.

"You see this?" Taryn asked, gesturing with his arms spread wide. "This means moisture, this means a water source is most likely near."

Upon further examination of the area, they could hear the ambient sounds of a stream nearby. Ranir instinctively picked up speed heading downhill. His excitement increased at the thought of getting half of their quest done: Find a water source.

Around a small bend in the valley of the hill,

Taryn put his arm in front of Ranir, halting him, saying, "wait. Someone is close."

Ranir looked around cautiously. He didn't see anyone, though a tingling sensation crept through his spine. He could almost feel a shift in the energy in the air. Of course this was the powerful lightning in his veins. The magic at certain times seemed to have a mind of its own, or be aware outside of Ranir's conscientiousness.

Ranir spoke up optimistically, "hey, maybe its a farmer or someone that can help us out."

"Do you not feel that?" asked Taryn with his eyebrows pressed together.

"You mean that energy in the air? What is it?" asked Ranir.

"That is the presence of a mage." he replied. "You have been around me for a little while and awoke with magic in you when I was present. You probably didn't even notice the difference, of course." He was speaking near the volume of a harsh whisper.

They both crouched down. Ranir was desperate to avoid confrontation at this point. If his magic took control as it did against the teleportation spell, he might hurt someone on accident. He wasn't sure what the problem was, still.

"Why are we hiding?" whispered Ranir.

"Because I don't know of any mage tracking in this area of Sythestine. As far as I knew, my brother was the only one, then I came to find his killer," he explained. Now Ranir was anxious.

They began to creep more around the bend to see if they could spot the spell caster. Near the bottom of a valley, they spotted the edge of a stream. Just as Taryn warned, a woman was by the water, her hands up in the air. Ranir watched in amazement as she moved her arms around in a flowing like manner. There was a small orb of water floating before, dancing and spinning around. It reminded Ranir of watching the fireball Taryn had created.

The woman wore a long blue-green colored robe that seemed to touch the ground. Suddenly she spun around facing them. His heart skipped a beat. They were spotted!

"Worsha lay étá!" the woman called out. The once beautiful, dancing water sphere shot towards them, targeted Taryn's head. Moving faster than Ranir expected, the orb smashed against the ground, throwing dirt and grass in the air as Taryn dodged it, returning a fireball of his own towards her. She leaped to the side, landing in a roll.

Ranir hunkered down even lower, with his bottom nearly touching the ground. He covered most of his head with his hands and arms. He looked up and saw that Taryn was in a fighting stance, both arms raised, palms facing the water mage.

"Stay behind me," commanded Taryn without looking at him. The mage by the stream lowered her hands. Ranir couldn't see her face as it was hidden inside an oversized hood. Her body and stance mirrored that of Taryn's.

Another water ball was sent towards the slope, again missing them both. This time Ranir noticed heatwaves around Taryn. He must have casted a shield spell of sorts. She was not missing! They were ricocheting off of his fire shield. Desperate, the water mage casted a larger spell that was inaudible. A massive wave rose from the water the size of a house.

"She's going to drown us!" yelled Ranir. His heart was racing. He panicked. He felt a suddenly pull on the magic inside of him. He didn't know any spell, so he concentrated on forcing the power outwards, trying to give it direction. Arcs of lightning sparked between his fingers. He clinched his fists, standing up. Raising his arms up, he let out a war cry, sending lightning towards the water mage.

A tremendous force of lightning erupted from his palms, blanketing the entire area in bright blue light. The lightning bolt missed the mage, slamming into the river. It seemed to hold onto Ranir, channeling it for several seconds as it slowly crept across the water. He attempted to redirect it back towards the mage who shuffled backwards away from the ray of power.

The white-blue colored lightning made the water steam up and push waves outward, slinging river rocks and mud soaring through air. The chain of lightning whizzed past the creek and busted into the far side of the bank. A small tree fell casualty, shattering into several pieces. Ranir concentrated on releasing the lightning. The power seemed to obey his thoughts and will, and subsided.

Ranir looked for the water mage. She was huddled down by a log, just her head peering around the cover. He looked over at Taryn who was wide jawed, his body relaxed in disbelief. He had one eyebrow slightly lifted.

"What the Hel was that?" asked Taryn. "Did you do that on purpose or did it take over like at the camp?"

"I-I don't know. I...guess? I kind of just pushed it out. I'm sorry," he said. He thought that Taryn was going to be more upset than he showed.

"Don't apologize for that. You stopped her," he said. "And," he added, pointing to the mage that was still hiding, "you didn't even have to hit her to halt her attacks!" He let out a loud laugh. It seemed forcibly loud enough to reach the water mage, as if to mock her. She stood up, hands raised high in the air, and stepped out from behind her cover.

Ranir took a deep breath, suddenly feeling fatigued. It wasn't the level of exhaustion as before, when magic was done around him, but enough to be noticeable.

"We are lucky, actually," said Taryn upon further thought, "we are in her domain being that close to water, she didn't have to create water from nothing. She would have outlasted me in a duel. So thank you." He gave a quick nod.

Ranir halfway returned nod, accepting the thanks. They made their way down the hill to the bank. Taryn kept a close watch of the water mage. The approached her with caution, expecting another attack perhaps.

"Take your hood off!" demanded Taryn. She slowly grabbed the front folds of her hood, sliding it back onto her shoulders. Her face was covered with a scarf. Ranir looked into her eyes that seemed so mesmerizing to him. They were a deep, bold blue color. She had black color lined around them, making them appear slanted, almost catlike. Her hair was a dark gold color, like that of the setting sun.

"The scarf, too," said Taryn. He didn't seem as taken aback by her radiant beauty. He held onto his guard. It made sense to Ranir, thinking about how Taryn must have been trained and experienced in focusing on tasks.

She slowly lowered the scarf, revealing an

unblemished face. Her eyes flickered back and forth to Taryn, then to Ranir. "What is he?" she asked Taryn. Her voice was soft, ironically like a slow flow of a river.

Taryn looked back at Ranir, shooting him a wink so that only he could see. He turned back towards the water mage and said, "The Lightning Rod."

She puffed out air in a half laughing manner replying, "I am sure he is." She sounded sarcastic.

"Don't believe me? Didn't you see?" asked Taryn, pointing towards the black scar on the ground, extending from one bank to the other. She glanced back toward the stream, then back to Ranir. She nearly looked fearful. She stood still silently.

"Why are you here?" asked Taryn. He wasn't in any mood to waste time with queries and conversation.

"I was tracking a bounty. You know how that goes," she replied, nodding towards a pin on Taryn's cloak. Ranir hadn't noticed the Emphyrius Mark before.

"I see," said Taryn. Ranir noticed his tonal shift. He didn't seem to be convinced of her narrative. "Who are you tracking?" he asked.

The hydromancer did not answer. She had her eyes locked onto Ranir at this point. He felt his face flush. Blaming her beauty, he knew he was blushing, and looked away. He could not hold her stare.

"Hey, I asked you a question," bellowed Taryn.

Without any warning or movement, she muttered something under her breath. Taryn leaned closer to hear her. With a flick of her wrist she casted a spell. Water shot up hitting Taryn in the side knocking him several feet away. In one fluid motion she casted another spell. The same water that exploded into Taryn reeled back and slammed Ranir in the legs, knocking him down. He looked up quickly. She punted Ranir in the face yelling, "*Emphyrta alak*!" In a flash of blue light, she teleported.

"No!" yelled Taryn from the ground. He jumped up to his feet and ran over to Ranir. Helping up the boy, he said, "Damn it."

"She is fast," said Ranir. He sounded impressed.

"Yes, because she works for the Emphyre," said Taryn. He recognized the spell and knew exactly where she went.

"How do you know that?" inquired Ranir, brushing off some dirt and ringing water from his robe.

"Because," started Taryn. "She just teleported straight to the Emphyrius." His lips were pursed in an annoyed fashion.

"She's going to tell the Emphyre," said Ranir, realizing the danger he put them in.

***   ***   ***   ***   ***   ***   ***

The spring breeze brushed airy smells of evergreen towards Marnos and Selendt as they walked into the forest. They turned and gave Ranir and Taryn one last look before ascending into the wooded hillside. They both had new fashioned bows ,and arrows to match. With no quiver, they were forced to carry the arrows as well.

"We will go to the top of this hill," said Marnos, "and see if we can get another vantage point from there. Let us hope to find tracks or trails."

"I hope that have fortune on our side, Marnos. These are new hunting grounds," replied Selendt.

It took them several hours to reach the summit of the hill. From the bottom, it hadn't seemed nearly as tall as it was in reality. They were both drenched in sweat when they approached the top. Humidity was a sizable factor for this. Both Marnos and Selendt were fit from farming and hunting or tracking for years.

The crest of the hill was vast and open. Hardly any trees grew there. This was both an advantage and disadvantage. While it was nice to have an open area to scour for trails of deer or other food sources, it also meant they wouldn't be able to see above and beyond the hill. They began by walking through the tall grass and weeds, searching for any indication of game.

"How do you feel about it?" asked Marnos. Selendt knew that he was referring to their lifelong friend's new ability to use magic.

"I am not sure what to think about it. I know that I am forever grateful that he is alive," she replied. She wanted to emphasize this fact to Marnos, who still seemed torn between his opinions. He had been struggling to accept everything that had happened over the past couple weeks. It appeared that too many things have happened so soon, that it was overwhelming to think about.

"I am too," he agreed. "I just can't believe that we are here, you know?"

"I can't either but we are here for a reason and we are together. I wouldn't want to be anywhere else with anyone else," said Selendt. She shot a grin to

Marnos who returned with his own. He and Selendt had been growing closer in their relationship and Marnos wasn't sure what to make of it just yet. After all, they had known each other for almost their entire lives. Yet, now he was beginning to see Selendt as more than family or friend. He wouldn't say it out loud, though, particularly to her.

Marnos stumbled upon a small cutout in the grass. He knelt down, placing his fingers in the moist dirt. He could feel the indentation of small footprints. "Here, we have something smaller," he said.

Selendt marched over the small game trail. Kneeling down beside Marnos, she examined the footprints. They were from a fox. Normally, foxes didn't come this high on a hill. They stayed down lower in the taller weeds to give their silent feet more of an advantage to hunting. She looked out of the corner of her eye, noticing Marnos wasn't looking at the tracks. She turned her head to fully observe him. Shyly, he looked away with a quick jerk.

She felt a smirk overcome her face and in turn, she too, looked away. With this being the first time they had been alone since they were thrust into this new world, they hadn't had time to talk really. She missed their long, late- night conversations. Though Ranir was also her friend, she always had a closer relationship with Marnos. They were more similar and were drawn to each other.

With Ranir dying, then being reborn, coupled with the rush of knowledge of magic and creatures thought to be myth, things like relationship and family seemed to hold a more important stamp in her life now. She knew that she had romantic feelings for Marnos for a little while and largely ignored them because they were like family.

Marnos stood up and gazed about the opening, looking for a cutout of trees or brush, something that might hint at another path. He turned towards Selendt who was still kneeling. She seemed deep in thought.

"What are you thinking about?" he asked softly.

"Oh its nothing. Just several things on my mind," she answered, standing up and facing towards him. She had her eyes lowered to the ground. The light glistened, radiating through her dark green eyes. Marnos felt that time seemed to slow down. She looked up to him slowly, the wind brushing her auburn hair across her face.

Without thinking about it, Marnos brushed it aside, tucking it behind her ear. His heart was pounding in his chest. He felt his face flush with hot blood. It was as if something had taken over him. As he was dropping his hand slowly, Selendt caught it in mid air. She placed his hand on her cheek, leaning into it.

Marnos knew then, that the feelings he had for her were mutual and may be reciprocated. He smiled. Somehow, before this moment, he had never seemed to notice just how beautiful she was. He knew that her attractiveness was vastly known to all of the boys in Heramor. He grew closer to who she was on the inside for years. They were nearly touching chest to chest. Selendt stood up on her tip toes, still not reaching eye to eye with Marnos.

He leaned his head towards her, his heart rate increased even more. He had never felt this way toward a girl before and had no experience in romance. The past couple weeks had drawn them closer than ever before. He was her comforter, she was his anchor to all the mystical events that were playing out around them.

He was nearly touching her face with his,

feeling his brow moistening with sweat. They moved together like magnets, slowly. His stomach felt like a knot was tied inside of him. Suddenly they were close enough, he paused his movement for a small moment. Then, they embraced each other in a first kiss for them both. Marnos could almost feel her emotion adding to his own.

It was as if the world stood still and fell asleep. Yet, it seemed like he grew an immense amount of energy washing over his entirety. Her soft lips pressed against his, his eyes and hers naturally closed as if to meld into each other's mind. Marnos knew then, at this precise moment, that he loved Selendt. Maybe he always had loved her, but this was different.

"Boom!" a loud crack came from the sky. The broke their kiss and looked around frantically. It sounded like the sky was breaking apart. They knew the sound very well as it was spring time.

"Was that thunder?" asked Selendt.

"I think so," replied Marnos. He was staring at her pale face without blinking. A new hope had been thrown into him. A hope of life and light, for he was in love. "Great timing huh?" he asked her.

She looked down again, her face blushing, "yes you could say that," she laughed.

Marnos finally snapped out of his fantasy and stepped back to reality. He looked up to the skies to gauge when the storm would be upon them. He saw no sign of a storm. He turned back towards the east and saw a bright light flashing at the ground. It was at least six miles away, yet bright enough to see from their summit.

Selendt ran to the edge of the hill, breathing hard, "Do you think that's Ranir?" she questioned.

Marnos had not thought about it until then. The thought of his best friend getting into enough trouble to use magic sent him into a panic.

"We need to get down there and find out, now!" he yelled. He grabbed Selendt by the hand and pulled her down the hill, trying his hardest not to fall down the steep east-side cliff.

Chapter 7: Chaos Revealed

Ranir was still brushing the dirt off of his robe, thinking about how the hydromancer moved so swiftly. He hoped one day that he may be as skilled as she was in both magic control and combat. Taryn marches over to him. He looked like he might have sustained more injury than he did.

Laughing, Taryn said, "well it's not everyday you get your arse kicked by a healer!" Ranir looked at him with deep brows, confused.

"What do you mean by healer?" asked Ranir.

"Well, every mage can obviously fight with magic. But, some fill different roles at the Emphyrius. Water mages are just the most adept at healing," he explained. "So that's the role they tend to take."

Ranir wondered what role Eros had in mind for him. He walked over to the stream and kneeled down. Cupping his hands, he dove them into the cold water, scooping up a drink. The water bit at this throat from being parched. He felt it sink all the down to his empty stomach. He thought for a moment.

Standing up, he said, "this is ridiculous!" coming to a realization. "Why did we even go searching for food at water?

You could have teleported to a city and brought it back here."

Taryn looked amused saying, "True, but then I would have to leave you alone, and in a part of the world that magic seems to be myth, there sure is a lot of mystical activity around here."

"Oh. I guess that makes sense," Said Ranir. He didn't sound all convinced. "Do you think she'll be back?"

Taryn's face shifted darker. He let out a harsh sigh, "Yes. And I don't think she'll be alone, either. All the more reason we need to head back to your friends. The world, magic or not, isn't ready for The Lightning Rod to be revealed."

"I've been thinking about that. What exactly is the Lightning Rod and why is it so coveted? And if its so mythical and dangerous, why did you just tell that mage?" asked Ranir.

"I don't know why I told her. I was gloating I suppose and not thinking. The Lightning Rod is largely a myth because even in our magical world, there are limitations," he explained. Ranir had a bewildered look. "You know that energy is required for magic, right?" Taryn continued.

Ranir nodded, saying, "Right, that's a big limitation." He understood the siphon of energy well because he had been on the receiving end of it.

"That's partially the limitation. The other part is that it is a balance. It's a part of the Old Gods' insurance that no mage would, basically, become a "God" So to speak," he said, waving his hands around like he was drawing a picture.

"So no mage can do big otherworldly spells?" asked Ranir.

"Right!" said Taryn. It seemed as if teaching was new to him.

"Okay...but what does have to do with The Lightning Rod?" he questioned, excited and desperate to understand.

"Patience, we'll get there," said Taryn holding out a halting finger. He walked over to a fallen dead tree and sat down. Raising his eyebrows, he gestured with a hand for Ranir to join him.

Walking over to sit down Ranir started, "Eros the Lightning God said-." He was cut off again by Taryn flipping up his pointer finger.

"We will get there," he reiterated. "So. Mages need to siphon energy for complex spells, like wards. Or, more commonly, for a series of spells like in combat. It's why we're trained for combat using and without using magic."
"Well all I've ever done is fight without magic," remarked Ranir slyly, chuckling to himself.

"You're going to need more training," replied Taryn, returning a laugh. "But anyway, as I said, The Lightning Rod is mostly myth. So anything known about them is relatively just rumors and speculation."

Ranir started to speak but stopped himself this

time. He decided he would ask questions after Taryn finished talking.

"However, with that," he continued, "the rumor is that The Lightning Rod doesn't need to channel energy, or as mages call it, mana. That's what makes them so powerful and dangerous."

"That must be why He said I wasn't a mage," said Ranir. He knew that his, now official, title was The Lightning Rod but there was so much that he did not know about it or what he was meant to besides 'protect the world'.

"Maybe. Mages in general are harbingers of the four elements. Lightning is not one of those main elements of Gnariam," said Taryn, "What it is, is pure mana in its rawest form. So it would make sense that The Lightning Rod wouldn't need to channel or siphon mana because your whole power is made up of pure mana, in theory. We won't know until we can test a few things out for ourselves."

"You seem nervous about that," granted Ranir with a smirk. He was certain that he was nervous about actually performing magic. It went over pretty well for his first time using it though. That much, at least, he was happy about.

"You can say that," he replied with a chuckle, "nobody that I've ever heard of has trained a lightning wielder."

"It seems that a lot is up in the air for guesses," said Ranir nervously.

"Yes it is, but one thing we do have is time," said Taryn.

"Sure, until we get to the Emphyre and then what?" he asked.

"Yes, sure, you will need to go to the Elder Council and they will test you for where they deem you need to go to train more," started Taryn, "but that is good, because you will be in good hands there with some of the highest skilled mages in the world. For now, lets focus on what is ahead of us."

"We should start heading back to Marnos and Selendt. The day is getting darker and we still didn't manage to get something to store water in," said Ranir, quickly changing subjects. He didn't want to think about traveling to simply get to another point to travel and train. It seemed to him like training and placement were about to become a large part of his life whether he wanted it to or not.

Looking toward the west, Taryn sighed and said, "You're right. Maybe they got a deer."
As they were nearing farther to the west, Ranir began to feel an almost numbing, itching feeling in his palms. Looking down he discovered small blue lightning arcing back and forth. The hair on his neck felt like it was being tickled with a feather.

He thought maybe it was dehydration or hunger setting in. They had walked for hours before the fight at the stream, and had been walking for a couple hours since then.

"Taryn, something is wrong. I can feel it," he warned. He couldn't pinpoint what was afoot but he knew that something or someone was near.

"Why do you say that?" replied Taryn. He didn't seem to pay it no mind for he kept his normal pace without so much as a glance back.

Ranir looked down to discover his palms were lighting up with lightning arcs. It was as if his power were manifesting on its own. His instinct told him it was trouble nearby.

"Erm, look!" Ranir yelled. He had stopped walking and was locked in a stare at his hands. It felt as if he were staring at someone else's hands.

"Ranir! Taryn!" Ranir looked up to see his friends coming down a small slope. To his dismay, they didn't seem to be carrying or dragging any game animal with them.

"Interesting, your lightning warned you about incoming people. My fire doesn't even do that until someone is close!" said Taryn.

Marnos and Selendt made their way halfway between their points. Ranir was relieved to see them.

"Are you guys okay?" asked Marnos. They both looked parched and damp with sweat from the haul.

"Yes we're fine, just a little skirmish down at the stream," replied Ranir.

Marnos and Selendt shot each other a hurried look. Selendt spoke up, "So that was you?!" she exclaimed.

"Yeah, we got in a fight with a water mage! Can you believe it?" shouted Ranir.

"Did you use magic? We saw a huge flash of light and heard thunder. We got worried so we ran back," said Marnos.

"Yes I did but it was almost accident or," Ranir said, trying to think of the right word, "instinct."

The same itch crept back into his palms and neck. "Taryn, it's doing it again," panicked Ranir. The small arcs shot out again this time extending to his forearms. Ranir tried to swallow it down but couldn't control it this time. Taryn put his arms in between Ranir, and Marnos and Selendt.

"Ranir look at me," exclaimed Taryn, "just breath, close your eyes and fight for control over it. Think of it like your breathing and control it."

Ranir's eyes lit up with lighting and became bright white. He held his breath, closer his eyes and focused. Clenching his fists he felt the source of power in his veins. The magic started to suppress. After a few seconds, he managed to regain control.

Opening his eyes, he saw Taryn bearing himself like a shield to Marnos and Selendt. His friends were peeking around Taryn. Selendt had a terrified look oh her face. It made him feel like a monster.

"Are you okay?" asked Marnos, seeing a disgusted and scared look on Ranir's face. He walked over to him and embraced Ranir in a deep hug.

Ranir sighed, relieved to take control over the power. He felt like he was being torn between two different people. "I'm alright," he said, gripping his best friend.

Ranir felt tears welling up in his eyes. This was going to be much more difficult than he expected. How could he expect to control this if another threat arose? What was going to happen once they reached the city?

He didn't want to hurt anyone by accident. He released Marnos and wiped away his tears.

Taryn walked over and placed a hand on Ranir's shoulder. He said, "You're going to alright."

Ranir looked back as Selendt approached him. "Ranir if there is someone who can control this and even master it, it's you," she said with a smile. She always had a calming aura about her. Ranir nodded. They needed to keep moving, as much as they could before the night took over.

Suddenly, with the sound of an explosion, bright flashes of white, blue and red erupted before them, casting a quick purple hue around them. Out of seemingly nowhere three mages appeared before them. Ranir recognized the cat like eyes of the water mage they met at the stream.

Taryn leaped our in front of the others, with black flash of his robe, dagger in one hand while the other was instantly covered in fire. His stance was near crouched, like a cat ready to pounce.

The other two mages that accompanied the hydromancer were clad in similar robes, and scarves that covered their face. They didn't seem to care that Taryn was before them, ready to strike. Their eyes were fixed on Ranir. "That's him," said the water mage pointing at him.

The man to her right croaked a dry throated spell, "*Hiathas,*" as a gust of wind suffocated the flame on Taryn's hand. As he looked down a second spell blasted him in the chest from the water mage. Taryn landed on his back fifteen paces away with a thud.

As if unaffected by the attack he jumped right

back to his feet. "What do you want?" he demanded.

"Don't play stupid, Taryn. We serve the same Emphyre," said the third mage. Her voice was strong with confidence.

Taryn squinted his eyes and tilted his head. He had a look of one in deep thought. Looking at the third mage he said, "Omat? That you?"

The mage uncovered her face. She was a dark skinned woman with grayish eyes. "You see? I knew you were smarter than you act," she said.

Omat was a fire mage. She was also Taryn's mentor, years ago. As one of the most powerful pyromages ever, she led the council of pyromancy. Taryn looked over to the wind mage. Something seemed familiar about him as well.

"I know you as well," blurted out Taryn, taking a chance on a bluff. The man revealed his face. He was elderly, with a wrinkled over forehead.

"Ashtal Therise, head of the Seven Winds," he spoke slowly with a dry voice.

In a smart manner, Ranir spoke up, "so what is she, water mage leader?" He chuckled at his own joke.

"Actually," said the water mage, removing her scarf and hood. "Yes, Verna Malai, head of the Water Tribunal Council." She gave a quick, sarcastic bow.

"Ranir, we need you to come with us to the Emphyrius," demanded Omat. The fire mage spoke with confidence and seemed like someone you didn't want to cross. She had a commanding presence about her.

Taryn waved a hand in silence, halting Ranir's response. Rank waited. Taryn spoke up, "That is exactly where we are heading. We couldn't teleport because of...interference."

"Well, no offense to a revered bounty hunter as yourself," started Ashtal, "but you didn't have us to teleport him back. You may find we are stronger than most mages.

"You can't try to teleport him, I'm warning you!" said Taryn. This seemed to agitate the 3 head mages. Verna took a step forward.

"You May have caught me off guard with The Lightning Rod before but my guess, judging by how inaccurate his spell was, that he doesn't know what he is doing," she said. Ranir had no argument either.

"All the more reason for us to get him back and understand his power so that can train him," said Ashtal. Verna shot him a quick look.

"Furthermore you," she said as she jabbed a finger towards Taryn, "do not warn us of anything."

"Step aside, Taryn. Let us show you," said Omat.

"Taryn," started Ranir fearfully.

"It's fine, Ranir, they aren't taking you anywhere," he said as he put his dagger away. He murmured something under his breath and both of his hands ignited.

"It's a nice gesture, but a pathetic show of

force," said Omat. "You know that I can sense the energy of your fire, right?"

Taryn stood still. His resolve and bravery were impressive. He was prepared to fight, not one but three, of the strongest mages in the kingdom. He had good intentions.

"Enough of this, Omat, take the flames away, Ashtal hold him down," commanded Verna. She seemed to be the leader of these three mages somehow.

Suddenly Ranir felt the familiar itch in his hands, "Oh no," he said to himself, hiding his hands behind him. Marnos and Selendt saw his hands and slowly began to back up. They were terrified of the potential outcome about to unfold. His eyes lit up like stars in the night sky, white lightning arcing in his pupils. Verna shot a quick look to Ranir, looking more nervous now.

"Taryn..." said Ranir. Taryn turned around and saw the take over of The Lightning Rod. This time, he said nothing. He simply backed up to line himself beside Ranir. What was he planning.

Suddenly, without warning, spells began to blast through the air. Fire and water shot back and forth causing bursts of steam. Taryn was struck in the stomach by a sharp gust of wind, knocking him to one knee. Ranir could no longer hold back the power of the lightning.

Releasing his clenched fists, he looked up to the sky, hopeful it would simply dissipate. He looked back down as Omat shot a sharp red flame at Taryn, searing his left palm. Taryn screamed out in pain. Ranir was now fearful for his friends, thinking about Marnos and Selendt. They were mere mortals with no way to fight back.

He released his hold on the power. Clouds began to roll in above them, darkening the sky further. Lightning began firing back and forth, followed by massive surges of thunder and wind.

"Ranir! Don't!" yelled Taryn. It was too late. Ranir gave in to the power, trying to guide it to protect his friends. A bright blast of white and blue lightning crashed down. It slammed the ground between to groups, separating the mages with blinding light. Ranir missed again. This infuriated him.

Screaming out, feeling overwhelmed with power, he unleashed a chain of lightning again, this time it smashed Ashtal in the chest, sending him soaring through the air. His limp body smashed into the ground, twisting like a doll.

"*Astuk alo bis!*" cried Omat. A huge fiery serpent shaped flame burst from her hands. The fire landed perfectly center of Ranir's chest. It scorched his robe and skin. He hit the ground with a loud thud, imprinting the dirt.

Verna ran to Ashtal's lifeless body. She looked back to the group, tears glistening in her eyes. "He's dead!" she screamed. Ranir rose from the ground. He aimed to release the storm but it was bound to him. Lightning repeatedly crashed to the ground. A flash of orange came from an exploding tree.

Verna rushed towards Ranir, screaming a furious spell. He couldn't hear what she said but he watched as a wave of seemingly oceanic proportions conjured from her hands. The massive wave hit him and flooded the area around him. As he looked around he noticed Selendt was laying in the water and Marnos was half way in water half way in the mud, unconscious.

Ranir retaliated again with the storm, screaming, "leave us alone!" He was aiming to shut the mages down in one swift blow he focused all his rage and fear on them, sending hundreds of lightning strikes ranging in color from blue to white to red and yellow.

The storm overtook the mages, striking the other two, one lightning bolt went clean through Verna's back and burs ted through her stomach. Omat was met with a strike arcing from the water. They both died immediately. Ranir collapsed on his back, watching the storm above wash away into a clear blue sky.

He felt the burning in his chest. He tried to sit up but was immediately met with fatigue. He looked upwards towards his friends only to discover they were still lying on the ground. He was overwhelmed by the power that took hold of him, barely remembering what had just transpired. He tried to call out to his friends but he was mute. He forced himself to his knees. He crawled to where his friends were.

Horror was an understatement compared to what Ranir found. Marnos was laying on his back, unconscious. Half of his body was scorched and mangled. Tears instantly began pouring from Ranir's eyes. He started to touch him but stopped himself. He couldn't. He leaned over to his left to check on Selendt. At first glance she didn't look injured. He crawled over to her and shook her. She didn't stir at all. The worst fear gripped him. His hand was shaking as he laid his hand on her neck. There was no pulse.

Water was slowly oozing from her mouth. She had drowned. The water mage had killed her. Ranir's heart sank. He felt sick to his stomach.

Taryn stirred on the ground. Ranir rushed over to him, "Taryn!" he shouted. His left hand was seared and blackened. Ranir felt heavy as he knew this all because of him. Taryn sat up and held his burnt hand against him. He looked over at Selendt and Marnos, then hung his head.

Marnos jolted upright with a deep breath as if he had awakened from a nightmare. Looking around, he realized that this was the nightmare. He saw Selendt. Immediately he crawled over to her, ignoring his injuries and the pain.

"Selendt!" he cried out. No answer. He sat down and dragged her to him, resting her head on his lap. Tears streamed uncontrollably from his eyes, he realized that she had passed. He was in shock, and begun rocking back and forth trying to make sense of everything.

Ranir went to hug him, but Marnos gave him a hard shove, knocking him on his back. "Don't!" he screamed at Ranir, "You did this! This is your fault! You and all that damn magic! We shouldn't be here Ranir." He was sobbing harshly at this point, his love had been taken from him. He was mangled. All of it was to be blamed on Ranir.

Ranir slid back a couple paces, thinking back to the first decision he made to hunt near the Veörn Mountains. That's where this entire path started. If he never trekked there, he would've never met the Druid and Detmés. It would've never led to meeting Taryn and saving him. That brought him to rebirth and now death from his hands. He felt a rush of guilt. He took the blame.

"Taryn, take us home. Teleport us now!" demanded Marnos. The look Ranir saw in his eyes and on his face was like nothing he had ever seen before. True loss had ripped through Marnos's heart.

"I can't Marnos, Ranir-"He was interrupted by Marnos.

"Not him! He can stay as far away from me as possible," he said looking at Ranir, his eyes were bloodshot. The right side of his face was seared like the right side of his body and clothes. "You and I are done. I never want to see you again."

"He is right, Taryn, take them home," said Ranir. "I will wait for your return."

Taryn didn't argue at this point. He got up and walked over to them. Ranir gave his lifelong best friend one last look, and they were gone. Ranir sat in the water, crying. He had just lost everything good he had in his life.

Chapter 8: Repentance

Nearly two weeks had passed since Ranir lost his best friends and his world became a bleak and hopeless mess. There were so many things that he had wished he could reverse. He wished that he never took the gift of power from Eros, the unpredictable Lord of Lightning. Taryn had not returned. Ranir actually expected this. He couldn't stop thinking about the battle that costed him the only important people in his life.

Ranir healed rather quickly. Unfortunately, Ranir tried to reverse his choice. His guilt pushed him into darkness. His solitary made him bitter. His world now felt colorless. He tried to end his life by hanging himself. The sneaking lightning inside had other plans. It arced out and cut the vine. He tried to jump from a cliff. The lightning struck him in the chest before he made it to the edge. He gave up the fruitless effort.

Using Selendt's now he had managed to kill a boar. He wasn't hungry lately and so the meat was only partially eaten. He lost a good amount of weight. His muscles felt harder now than ever. His general skills of traveling began to increase. He decided a week into his suicide attempts that the Emphyrius is where he needed to go, still. They may have been the only ones with answers for him. Answers were the only thing holding hope for him now.

"Day 13, no. No,14. Yes. Definitely day 14," Ranir rambled to himself. He had been taking mental notes to retain his sanity. "Still no sign of Taryn. Not that I expected him to return. I'm a monster after all. Isn't that right, Eros?" he said looking to the sky.

"No you're not," said a voice behind him. Ranir turned around quickly. Standing there in fresh robes, with two swords mounted on his back was Taryn, the relentless bounty hunter. Ranir did not move. His face still brooding and dull.

"Go away mirage," he said coily, he hummed a subtle note while sighing, "Don't have time for you today." With that he turned and continued walking up the jagged black rocks.

"Ranir! I'm not a damn mirage! I'm real. Look at me!" shouted Taryn. "Do you even know where you are? What day it is?"

Again, Ranir wasn't convinced of reality. He turned and looked at the hallucination, and with a flick of his wrist shot a deep blue colored lightning bolt. Even as supernaturally fast as Taryn was, he couldn't dodge or block the spell. It perfectly hit him in the chest, knocking him through a pile of rocks. Ranir paused, looking confused. He took a step towards the mage. This time he didn't disappear like he did for the last 6 days when Ranir attacked him.

"Taryn?" he asked slowly.

Taryn stood up with a grunt. He brushed his

89

chest off like it was hit with a cold of dirt. He scolded Ranir and commented, " When the Hel did you gain control of the lightning?" It was Taryn! He was actually here!

Ranir ran down to Taryn and wrapped his arms around him. "You came back for me!" he cheered. Ranir found a new sense of light in the world again. He thought about having a friend again. Then he thought about the ones he had lost. "How is Marnos?" he asked shyly.

Taryn gave a half sad smile. "He is back home, recovering. I only stayed for a few days with him."

"Good, he is home," said Ranir. He couldn't help but feel guilty and estranged from the events that had passed. Much of it seemed like a bad dream. He knew that Marnos would never be the same, physically or mentally. It broke Ranir's heart and enraged him that Selendt had died. He could only imagine how Marnos feels because they were much closer. Adding to that internal pain was they fact that half of his body was scorched from the most powerful fire mage in the entire kingdom.

"I returned to the Emphyrius and explained everything that happened. The Emphyre wants to meet with you," he slowly announced. Ranir shot him a worried look. "Not like that," explained Taryn, "You see the mages that showed up, were rogue. Their lust of power drove them to you. They have already been replaced and the Emphyre doesn't hold you accountable."

"Why would I be their beacon? Because the lightning?" questioned Ranir.

Nodding, Taryn answered, "precisely. They

wanted to take your power somehow."

Ranir was unaware power could be taken. He was glad that Taryn returned for he still had uncountable questions about magic.

"How could they 'take' my power?" he questioned the bounty hunter.

"I'm not exactly sure how they do it. I assume its the same as channeling mana. It's mostly a necromancy thing. They can take power as well, not just siphon mana," said Taryn. Ranir had almost forgotten how he carried the same accent as his brother Detmés.

"Necromancy? Like raising the dead?" asked Ranir.

"Exactly. Well," he added, "that among other things. They are bound by chaos and conjure dark magic. It is forbidden and for very good reason."

"But they were mages, not these necromancers," exclaimed Ranir.

"You are correct. You see, a necromancer can only become a necromancer by either starting as a blessed mage, or being given power through other means, like hedge witches or wraiths," Taryn said, waving his hands together from left to right, as if to follow an invisible path. "Then, they choose to become a necromancer once they give in to the power lust and become darker."

"That sounds terrible," Ranir stated. "Are there still necromancers today?" he added.

"There is one that was never caught," began

Taryn, "He is the darkest one ever recorded as well. Makes sense that we didn't put him down. He was smart, cruel and cunning. He personally killed over a hundred mages and bounty hunters and is believed to have risen over another hundred forsaken bodies."

"How long ago was that? You sound like you had a hand in trying," interjected Ranir.

"He was first reported, let me see, about 30 years ago or so, but then," Taryn stopped and looked around as if waiting to makes sure nobody else was around them, "he disappeared about a decade ago, maybe a little more. And yes, when I was first hunting bounties, I helped track him. But we never found him."

This necromancer seemed like a scary story to tell children around a fire. Ranir knew that there was darkness with magic. He had seen it firsthand from the druid. He wondered if the necromancer was as wicked and vile looking as the shape shifter he met at the base of the mountains. He didn't ask anymore questions at this point.

"You didn't answer my questions, Ranir," grumbled Taryn, his eyebrows raised as if he were impatiently waiting.

Ranir looked down as if to search for the questions that he forgot. "What questions?"

Taryn glared, "Do you know where you are right now? Or what day it is?"

"Not particularly, what day it is. But I think I'm close to Alagien Lake, right?"

Taryn sniggered, "Not even close, Alagien Lake is that way," he jabbed a finger to the north, "On the other side of the mountain."

"Mountain?!" Ranir was taken aback.

"You crossed back over the forest and worked your way back to the Veörn Mountains, Ranir." He sounded mocking.

Ranir shot his head around to his left and back to the other side, reeling in his environment for the first time with focused eyes. He realized that he was vastly far from his intended course. He wondered how Taryn even managed to find him, and how far he would have been if he hadn't been pulled from his daze.

"So how far away is the Emphyrius?" questioned Ranir.

"From here? By foot at least a week. Now if you could teleport, that'd be nice. Speaking of, how did you do that spell? Did you gain some control of your power?" Taryn was hopeful for Ranir getting better at magic, even if it was small.

Ranir looked at his palm and sighed. He was reluctant in attempting more spells. He wasn't sure if he'd gain control like he wanted to, like he needed to. He had begun to feel like the lightning was part of him now, though. "I can do a small arc like I did, haven't tried much else. Afraid to really."

Taryn gleamed. "Small?" He laughed as he looked at the broken rock. "It didn't feel small."

Ranir looked saddened. "Sorry, I... er..I've been seeing things. People really. You and Marnos." He looked away to hide his glossy eyes. "And Selendt." He sniffed and cleared his throat. "I thought you were just in my head."

Taryn walked over and placed a hand on Ranir's shoulder, looking empathetic. "It's alright, Ranir. I'm here and I'm real."

Ranir nodded, accepting reality for the first time with a new outlook on life. He finally accepted his life in the magical realm and his role as The Lightning Rod. He wasn't certain where this path would take him. He knew that he couldn't go back to his old life though. It was time to move forward. It seemed as though this, and now was his true calling. This felt like his rebirth.

Taryn and Ranir agreed that the Emphyrius was their destination. They needed to get some food and water. Taryn remarked, "You look like you could use some food. You've lost weight out here starving yourself."

"I suppose I haven't really been that hungry," growled Ranir.

Taryn didn't reply. Ranir was more reserved and bitter than he had been a couple weeks ago. "Ranir, I have a question? I've noticed you can use magic without using any spells. You literally summon lightning."

"Right." Ranir squinted his eyes.

"I have only ever seen that from elder mages before. I know you're not a mage and so it makes me wonder if you can do actual spells." Taryn had been thinking about this every since he first witnessed Ranir's unleashed power against Verna by the stream.

"Well why don't you teach me an actual spell and we'll find out!" Ranir seemed agitated at the almost accusation.

"Right but I don't know any lightning spells," barked Taryn. "Well I guess I could teach you something small in the form of my fire and see what it dies for you."

"So each elemental mage has their own form of magic?" Ranir was amused.

"Yes, different forms, and different words for spells." Ranir assumed as much after recollecting the battle with mages. Their spells were similar in the way that they produced bursts of different elements, but were spoken very differently.

"So is there a general magic spell you can teach me that doesn't follow the mage's words?" Ranir felt compelled to ask as many questions as he could. He wanted full control over his power.

"Yes. Several actually. For example, *Estashashik*," he commanded, running his hand like a knife upwards. A familiar red line appeared on a rock. In a burst of energy, the rock split cleanly in half. Ranir realized that was the spell he used on the Druid cocoon. "It only words on nonliving objects. It translates to "open," roughly," he explained.

Ranir was nervous to try an actual spell. He stuttered the word, waving his hand like Taryn did. "*Estashashek!*" he bellowed. The small stone he attempted to "open" shattered, sending jet black gravel and dust flying. Taryn waved a hand to block a piece moving towards his face.

"Well, now. You mispronounced the word, shik not shek. However, it should've done nothing." Taryn rubbed his stubbly beard, perplexed. "Do it again. Say

95

it the same way."

"The incorrect way?" jokingly asked Ranir. Taryn just nodded, watching as if waiting for an egg to hatch.

Again Ranir rose his hand, "Estashashek!" Another rock exploded with blue energy, sending pieces flying. Taryn squinted his eyes, trying to think of why this was possible.

He held a finger up in the air, "say it the right way this time." He pointed at a large section of the mountain, and directed, "there."

Ranir looked up to where Taryn pointed. It was almost a cliff protruding from the side of the mountain. The section was nearly the size of a house. He looked back at Taryn with a raised eyebrow. "Seriously?" he asked. Again, Taryn nodded. His silent confirmations were frustrating to Ranir.

He turned to the area. Focusing he brought hand up, thinking slowly as to not mess up again. He felt a surge of energy in his palm this time. It was slowly building. "*Estashashik!*" he shouted at the mountain slab. A thin blue line appeared at the base and climbed upwards rapidly. It faded quickly. Ranir scowled, but his agitation was interrupted by the sound of cracking rocks. Suddenly, the place where Ranir casted his spell, split in two perfectly.

Excitement filled Ranir. He had finally casted a spell, an actual magic spell, on purpose. He clapped his hands rapidly and turned to see a bright smile on Taryn's face. He gave Ranir another nod, eyes shooting directly at the rocks before them. Ranir performed the spell again and again, perfectly splitting the rocks in half. After a few spells, Ranir felt the pull of fatigue casting its shadow over him.

"Why do I exhaust after using magic?" He felt as if he had ran for the last half hour straight through.

"That is magic, Ranir. It always comes at a price of mana. That is why mages pull mana from people or things, even animals to perform larger spells. I guess that disregards the rumor of The Lightning Rod not needing to pool his mana."

"So how was I able to cause that storm and cast lightning spells during that fight?" Ranir still couldn't figure out the difference.

"Ranir, you weren't casting spells, you were conjuring raw lightning. Its still magic, but a different form of magic. It seems like you can do spells, if we find your Elemental Language, like any other mage, and it costs mana," Taryn explained. "But it seems like you can conjure up the full power of lightning itself. That alone is almost unheard of."

"Are there mages who can summon just the elemental power?" asked Ranir.

"There are a few mages who can do that. Necromancers can do it more than mages because they are using dark magic. They use almost all shadow spells."

"I see," said Ranir scratching his head. He wondered if there was someone who could teach him a language for lightning. It also confused him because he was told that he wasn't a mage. So how could he use mage spells? Maybe he didn't have the full story. He was certain of it. He needed to get to the Emphyrius and get answers. Looking up at the mountain he asked, "How long will it take to get over the mountain?"

"Hard to say really, maybe 3 days if we keep steady." Taryn had a lot of experience in Sythestine traveling. He had tracked many bounties over the last decade. He knew the mountains were the most unpredictable terrain. "We should get a move on though. Lots of ground to cover."

"Yes we do. It's a good thing we have the day to climb," said Ranir.

The climb to reach the summit would take almost a full day to reach due to its steepness. Once they created over the peak, the eastern side was less dangerous but twice the distance to the base. Ranir was wishing he could have been given any other mage power and he could teleport to the capital, The Emphyrius. He oft wondered why the lightning didn't allow him to be transported through magical means. He thought a lot about what his limits were and vice versa, what limits others had that he didn't.

It was nearing nightfall when Taryn spotted a cutout in the mountain. They decided to take camp inside for the night. They were lucky that for the night they had cover, Taryn could make fire, and Ranir still had some rations of the boar he had slain.

Taryn told Ranir the mystery of the Veörn Mountains. "These mountains have been plagued with darkness and death for millennia. That's a big reason that most people, magical and not, stay away. Nobody knows where or when it started. The story goes that the world's first necromancer created the mountains as his throne. You see, necros deal heavily with death and shadow magic. That's why the rocks all the way through the mountains are pitch black."

"Why a throne? Was he a king?" Ranir was

intrigued by the story.

"Yes he was. King Veörn of Sythestine. It's where the name comes from. He was born into nobility, so naturally inherited the throne. Years after he ruled over the kingdom, he put himself in harms way to save a peasant woman from another King's wrath. After that he became a mage, being gifted the power of water." Ranir sat wide eyed, listening, imagining this piece of history.

"So he became a mage, after being a king? That's amazing! But what happened?" he asked.

Taryn smiled, recalling the story he learned as a boy, "King Veörn became very powerful, learning from the elder mages during his time. Then he grew greedy of magic. He wanted more than the Gods would give him. So he turned to dark magic." Ranir looked sad for the King and his turn of events.

"So he became a necromancer on purpose for power?" questioned Ranir.

"Not right away no. Dark magic needs full commitment in order to maintain it. If you begin doing shadow spells because they are powerful, that magic will consume you. Quite literally," he explained. "King Veörn was going mad from the lust of power, it needed a balance. You see mages have power of life, mana. Shadow makes them more of a warlock. The balance between them is the necromancer. Once they resurrect the first person, they become a necromancer."

The story was a lot for Ranir to take in. It was as much of a story as it was knowledge of magic and a warning.

"So the resurrected someone?" asked Ranir,

holding his hand up to the fire Taryn had made. With no wood or tinder to burn, Taryn created a fire spell to keep them warm. The higher elevations of the mountains grew colder as the night came on.

"The peasant that he saved all those years ago. She became his Queen. When he turned to darkness she killed herself, not being able to compete for his attention of magic anymore. He brought her back." Taryn but the corner of his lip as if he grew empathetic. "But she wasn't the same. She was mindless and some say soulless. She did everything he wanted as he learned, Necromancers take full control over their forsaken. Then he built this mountain, or so they say, and it is the summit where he perished, bleeding his power and corruption into Gnariam forever."

Ranir didn't know whether to take this story as factual or myth. Either case, he had learned quite a bit about the consequences of dark magic and was adequately warned to keep away from it. With no further questions, Ranir laid his head down on a rock, and let the legend of King Veörn and magic take over his dreams. Taryn snuffed our the flame, leaned against the wall and whispered, "Goodnight...Lightning Bringer."

Chapter 9: Grounded

Ranir peeled his eyes open upon hearing the cracking of rocks. The sound echoed throughout the hollowed out cave. It sounded like the frozen lake ice cracking. From the opening of the cavity he could hear distance voices from outside. He looked over to see Taryn still asleep on his back with his mouth wide open. It would've been amusing, if not for the obvious company they were about to have. Quietly, Ranir slid over on his butt, using his hands to push himself forward. He shook Taryn. Ranir thrusted a hand over Taryn's mouth who, in waking up, began his normally loud morning greeting.

"Taryn," he whispered almost inconceivably quiet. "There are people outside. Sounds like they are digging or looking though the rocks." He shook Taryn, making him snap his yawning mouth shut.

"Earth mages!" Taryn sat up with a jolt. He was certain that is what they were.

"How do you know?" Ranir shot a look towards the bright light of the entrance.

"Earth mages are almost all residents of mountains or forests, and generally are guardians of

Gnariam more than the people who inhabit it," he explained.

"So are they part of the council?"

"They are but in a much different way. They are estranged, but can be very dangerous as a foe," explained Taryn. He legitimately seemed worried that there might be one or more earth mages nearby.

Continuing a low whisper, Ranir asked, "Why are they so dangerous?"

"Because the literally have their element all around them at any time. Makes them quick and drawing mana from nature is easiest for an earth mage."

"I mean, are they all unfriendly? Are we trespassing? Why do you seem so worried about them?" Taryn's mood started to rub off on Ranir, making him uncomfortable now.

"I doubt we are trespassing. Its a mountain, nobody owns it. But no, they are usually friendly to anyone outside of their element."

Remaining as quiet as possible, Ranir and Taryn made their way to the end of the cave, in order to get some adjustment to the bright daylight pouring into the hollow. As they moved closer to the mouth of the cave, the voices seem to grow louder, almost sounding like a completely different language.

Suddenly a much louder voice seemed to resonate from the ceiling, yelling something indistinct. Ranir felt the usual warning from the lightning flowing through his veins. His hands began to itch slightly. This itch had slowly lost its boldness. His eyes began to glow white for a flash of a moment. Ranir closed his eyes and pushed back against the lightning. It was like another person or entity inside him with its own process of thoughts. He may not have known yet how to project his magic properly, but he was certainly getting control of keeping his power outbursts suppressed. After Marnos, and the death of Selendt, he felt this was his number one priority just ahead of fully controlling the magic.

Taryn gave Ranir a gesture with his head, urging him to follow him out of the cave. Ranir understood his silent command and swept over beside him. They moved together like they were tied to each other. The first step into the bright sunlight almost hurt Ranir's eyes. Squinting and looking around he could instantly make out the silhouette of a man above the cave on a small plateau sticking out like a roof to the hole in the mountain. Once his eyes adjusted, he fully embraced his vision and collected his senses to see a man, fully clad in leather that look like it had been dyed a greenish color. The man saw Ranir and Taryn at the same time and immediately casted a spell, yellowing, "Hatchul azak!"

Ranir expected a flow of magic from the mage's hand as he had seen with fire and water mages. Instead, it was as if the mage controlled the very rock they stood on. The black, jagged stones beneath them crumbled into a dust like consistency. Their feet gave way like sliding down an icy hill. Without hesitation, Taryn casted a fiery spell beneath them. A bright red light flashed from his hands. It heated the sand to a red hot material. The spell bonded the small particles of sand together like glass. Their base was solid once again. It seemed as if Taryn had experience in combating this earth mage trick. The mage above them called down to another mage several paces below them. The lower geomancer casted a spell of his own.

Ranir thought the spell was one of the most beautiful spells he had seen yet.

"Shatalak Chorlo At!" called the mage from below. A swirling ball of energy formed in his hand like Taryn's fireball. The earth mage's sphere however, was green and brown, blended perfectly, swirling with power. He thrusted his hand forward to project the spell at Ranir. In midair the sphere changed to a more drastic brown color, becoming a solid rock, moving at high speeds.

Without a single thought, Ranir thrusted his hand outwards and called out, "Estashashek!" The fist sized stone shattered in a hundred pieces before them. Small bits of shrapnel sped past his face. Taryn casted a fire shield around him just before a handful of dust and gravel smashed against him.

Ranir was ready to deliver another blow of magic when Taryn cried out, "Wait, we aren't here to hurt you!"

The earth mage from atop halted the lower mage with a wave of a hand. He slowly climbed down to match their elevation. He was careful not to take his eyes off of Ranir and Taryn. He looked at Taryn's robe lapel. Ranir followed his gaze and noticed a small pendent on Taryn's collar. Then shifting his focus back to the earth mage, he noticed an identical pin on his robe. Ranir assumed it was something to do with the Emphyrius.

"What are you doing here, fire mage?" questioned the earth mage. He sounded so clear now compared to when Ranir first heard his echoing voice. The way he asked the question was near accusing in tone. He was very straight forward and didn't have a thought to be kind about it.

"My name is Taryn. I am a bounty hunter. I-" he began before he was interrupted.

"I don't care who you are, why are you here, in my mountain?" Again, the earth mage seemed to be commanding. Taryn put his hands up in a surrendering motion.

"This is my bounty," he said, pointing at Ranir. This was the first time Ranir was aware of Taryn bluntly lying to someone. He assumed the bounty hunter was putting up a facade to keep the identity of The Lightning Rod hidden. "I tracked him for the past two weeks and found him last night. He cannot be teleported, so I am taking him back to the Emphyrius by foot. We were trying to reach the summit before nightfall. When I saw we weren't going to make it, we took refuge in this hollowed cave."

The earth mage looked deep into Taryn's eyes, then shot a glance to Ranir. He seemed to be lost in thought, perhaps trying to uncover whether or not he was being deceived. "His aura is all over the place, you know that?"

Taryn looked back to Ranir. "I didn't realize he even had an aura. Remember," he said, pointing at his own chest, "I'm just a fire mage. We cannot see auras...as I'm sure you are aware." Reading magical auras was a talent that earth mages had, and one they liked to be arrogant about.

"What is the reason he cannot be teleported?" The geomancer seemed to be getting closer to them as the conversation went along, like the rocks beneath him propelled forward.

"I don't know," said Taryn. He seemed to be

already failing at creating a bluff that was believable. It wasn't a complete lie, because even though he knew that the lightning inside Ranir protected him, he was uncertain why he couldn't teleport.

The man below them held up both of his hands and closed his eyes. He was muttering something under his breath. Ranir noticed his mouth moving rapidly in a fashion that Ranir couldn't read what the geomancer was saying. After a moment, the man stopped, opened his eyes and looked to the other mage. His eyes were glowing with bright green color. As if they were speaking with their minds the mages both bowed before Ranir and Taryn. The lower mage said, "Hail to The Thunder King!"

Ranir was bewildered first by their bow. He nor Taryn was nobility or worthy of a bow. He was also confused by the name, The Thunder King. Did they somehow know what he was? Without further words they both turned and walked away. Taryn turned to Ranir, his face showed as much confusion as Ranir felt. He wanted to inquire more, but decided to let them go. He had a feeling they would be seeing them again.

Without dwelling on the situation too long, Ranir and Taryn decided to start their day by continuing their climb. The summit of Veörn Mountains was a few hours of passing up and over jagged, dangerous black rocks. The stones shining in the sunlight gave them a camouflaged look. Some footholds blended in with each other.

When the reached the peak, the sun was near the highest point, its blazing heat beating down from the clear blue sky. Ranir began to notice his breathing stiffening with each rise in elevation. The air was growing thinner, biting at his throat. Curious, he asked Taryn, "How many times have you passed over this mountain?"

Taryn showed no sign of fatigue or slowing
down. He chuckled, "Several times, but never this way.
I've never crossed the peak before."

"Is this the fastest route, then?"

"I think so, the Emphyrius is a straight shot
from the mountains. Getting to the top will give us a
view point." Taryn seemed confident in his navigation
skills. Ranir still wished that they could simply teleport
though.

"So what spell are we going to learn today?"
Ranir said. He was eager to learn more given the time
they had to reach the capital.

"Well," said Taryn, turning to Ranir, "when we
get to the peak, we're going to test out a few spells to
see what you can do." He carried a smirk on his face.
He had a plan and was purposely keeping it secret from
Ranir.

Keeping it in his head, Ranir repeatedly the two
spells he had learned. He first cite the "open" spell,
then the "explode" spell. If there was a spell he could
that didn't require channeling lightning, he was
determined to remember it.

Once they reached the summit, Ranir gasped
with excitement. He was another step closer to getting
to the Emphyrius. Another reason that sparked his
interest was the fact that he had never been to any city
before, including the capital. He had heard many
stories while he was growing up of the capital city.
Stories flowed of warriors, and of massive buildings.

As they neared the top of the mountain, they

noticed the edge of a small shack. It looked like it had been abandoned for decades. On the last step up, noticing the top was actually a plateau, Ranir was preoccupied and missed a step, landing on a sharp rock. His forearm was the first thing that landed, cutting a deep gash. Ranir cried out in pain. Taryn rushed back over to him and pulled him up to the flat surface.

Ranir immediately felt the hot blood running down the inside of his arm, pooling up between his fingers. "Hold still," he heard Taryn say.

Taryn grasped his wrist to steady his arm, the other hand he had hovering about an inch from the fresh cut. He whispered something quick. His palm started glowing over the wound. Ranir screamed out as he felt like a hot rod was stabbing him. Suddenly, the pain disappeared. Taryn sat down, and sighed. He seemed to take a deeper breath than normal. Ranir looked down at his bloody arm. Wiping it clean, he discovered the wound was fully healed up, leaving a slightly risen light colored scar.

"Um, thank you," Said Ranir still running the scar. Taryn removed one of the swords from the sheath on his back. The blade had a bright shine to it, as if it were freshly made. In the pommel was a reddish orange gem. It seemed to be swirling with fire inside the stone. Taryn laid his hand on it, closing his eyes. Ranir sat watching, silently.

After a short moment, Taryn put the sword back in the sheath. He didn't look behind him, or feel for the casing. It was another thing that reminded Ranir that Taryn was a bounty hunter first, and he was highly trained. It was comforting to know that he was not in Taryn's bounty list.

"What is with the swords?" asked Ranir.

"They are rune blades. The Stärńet in the handle absorbs and contains energy with certain spells," he explained. "Usually bounty hunters or warriors with store energy inside them in order to perform bigger spells."

"Like healing?" asked Ranir.

"Precisely. It seems like a small thing, but healing takes more energy to do than almost any other type of spell," Taryn said.

"It seems I have so much to learn." Ranir was beginning to feel discouraged. It seemed as if he were far behind in training and controlling. Yet he was certain that he would endure all the training that he must, to insure that he was in control of The Lightning Rod.

"You do. And what you plan to do with your magic will determine how much training is required," explained Taryn.

"What do you mean?" asked Ranir.

"Well, for example, a fire mage in general goes to train for about two years or so. Their purpose is usually defense of the capital. Pyromages are the best at shields and defensive wards. Pretty straightforward. Water mages are usually healers and need more time to train, so that they don't become consumed by their water power."

"Not all mages work for the Emphyre though, right?" he interrupted. Ranir was beginning to feel that his role was chosen already.

"Right, but the best training is found at the Emphyrius. Other mages are called hedge witches a lot because their magic is far weaker and less controlled," said Taryn. He was dusting off his black robe as he stood back up. Ranir got to his feet. He was eager to have a trainer found for him but he didn't want his life bound by a job. He wasn't sure that a trainer or role could be found for him.

"What if I didn't want to be apart of the Emphyre's plans?"

"Why wouldn't you? He serves to better the kingdom," replied Taryn. His brows were pushed together. Ranir felt he might have stepped out of line. His newfound bitterness spoke through though.

"I want to embrace my magic, the way I want. I don't want to be a pawn," he said stiffly. Ranir began to recollect details of the past couple days. He thought of how Taryn tracked him down, the new energized swords that allowed him to do more magic. He wondered where Taryn truest laid his alliance. "Wait. Are you even here to help? Or you just here to see that I get back to your Emphyre?" He began to grow angry with thoughts of distrust.

"Excuse me?!" bellowed Taryn. "You think I would track you down just to take you to the Emphyrius? You aren't that special, Ranir," he snapped back.

Ranir felt a rush of guilt. "I'm sorry. I don't why I said that."

Taryn sighed, calmed his breathing and said, "You didn't. It's just your magic. You need to get in control of it." He drew both swords and stabbed them into the ground. Ranir didn't know what was more

110

impressive; The fact that the swords busted through the rock like it was dirt, or how easily Taryn seemed to perform this feat. "Let's have a look," he nodded towards the shack.

Ranir took another look at the swords and turned to the run down house. The old daub and straw were still mostly intact, the wood however wasn't. The siding was rotted allow the weather to pass through unchecked. Taryn opened the door causing a break in silence as it creaked against the iron hinges. Ranir stepped inside.

Something about the shack felt cold, like the hand of death, sending shivers down Ranir's spine. Taryn startled him. "This is an old Necromancer's home. You feel that?" Taryn knew the presence of a necromancer from the couple years that he had helped track down Seldos, the infamous Necromancer that terrorized the kingdom not so long ago.

Absolutely did Ranir feel it. "Yes I do. What is it?" His voice was trembling. As he spoke he could see the steam form in front of his face. The one room house had no reason to be cold. It was bright and sunny outside and the middle of Spring.

Taryn turned and gave a warranted fearful glance, "That's death magic, the darkest form of magic there is. We shouldn't be in here." With that they both scurried out of the cold shack. Taryn was pacing back and forth, gazing at the ground.

"So now what? Keep moving?" asked Ranir. Taryn didn't reply. "Taryn!" barked Ranir. This seem to startle him. He was in a trance, thinking of something dark and mysterious. Ranir didn't want to push the subject any more for Taryn's sake and for his own. The very feeling of the darkness that soaked into the small house felt like it was eating at his soul.

"No. This may be the last place before reaching Killiad that you can learn more control of your magic," he explained. "And you'll want to do that before traversing hundreds of people." Taryn was concerned thinking of a small city filled with people, good and bad, that might tempt Ranir's self preserving power leach out against someone.

"You're absolutely right. All those people might set it off. I-," he thought about his friends who had suffered from his magic. "I don't want anyone getting hurt, because of me."

Taryn looked down at his feet. Then he shot a sharp look to his swords. He looked up at Ranir's golden eyes and nodded. He had the determination set. It was time for The Lightning Rod to be trained. Promptly he said, "Let's begin."

Chapter 10: Killiad

A few nights had passed since Ranir had began any formal training from Taryn. They continued to build his memory of the correct words and managed to find a few words that Taryn assumed were of the Lightning Elemental Language. Using the Stärñet, they were able to continue lessons without interruption. With no sign of life atop the black mountain, the swords' stored power was their only option for mana regeneration. With each passing day and rest, Ranir was beginning to feel more energized, relying on the stones less.

Ranir had now managed to perform an opening spell, an exploding spell and an arc channel spell. Of course the only casualties were rocks at this point. Ranir was beginning to feel like he had stabilized the magic inside him. Taryn had one last test before descending the mountain top. It was for good reason that they were planning to descend the next day because their rations were nearly depleted as well.

"Again!" commanded Taryn, sitting on a rather larger boulder. He had Ranir learning balance skills coupled with magic spells in order to gain accuracy. Ranir was balanced atop a small rock with one foot.

Taryn tossed a fist sized rock in the air, Ranir shouted, "*Estashashik!*" The stone split perfectly with an iridescent blue line. He had managed to keep his footing on the small rock this time. "Ha!" he shouted. "Did you see?"

"Very good, next rock," Taryn said as he contained his excitement, camouflaging it with a serious face. He felt that he needed to be stern, as that is the only way he was taught discipline of magic. Since he had no other experience teaching, he based his teachings on how he was trained.

Ranir stepped onto a higher rock about two feet off of the ground. Another rock zinged through the air without warning. They had a pattern of spells in line, "*Estashashik!*" Ranir raised his hand with all four fingers together like a blade. With a small arc of white and blue lightning, the smaller rock shattered in the air, sending pieces soaring in all directions. This time, Ranir too contained his excitement, because the next spell was harder yet.

"Next!" Taryn shouted. Ranir dove up onto a rock three feet higher. Before he landed Taryn through a pebble in the air and to the left of Ranir this time.

Ranir spun while he was airborne, drawing his palm outward, he bellowed "*Likta Azhik!*" Like a bright blue lightning bolt moving in slow motion, an arc ascended from his palm and wrapped around the pebble. Ranir's foot landed smoothly on the rock. He drew back his arm, pulling the pebble with the arc of lightning, catching the small stone. He stepped down, and brought the pebble to Taryn.

Taryn took the rock from Ranir's hand and observed it. "No burn marks from the lightning, perfect landing, and perfect catch." There was only a hard face when he said these words. For a moment, he seemed

114

like he was not satisfied. Suddenly he broke a smirk, and said "Ranir, well done. That is great progress for such a short time."

"Thank you very much," said Ranir in a contented voice. He knew that he could perform these spells adequately enough to help do some things. The power inside him was still pulling at him, though. It was calling to him to be released in a force of nature that was beautiful and dangerous.

"Now, for the rest of today, we're going to push your control over the element inside you," said Taryn turning his back to Ranir.

"How so?" Ranir said as he cocked his head in confusion. Without informing, Taryn turned back and punched Ranir in the chest, knocking him on the ground. For a short moment, Ranir had lost his breath. Gasping for air, he looked up from the ground, Taryn was raising a leg up, charging it for a kick.

"Let's draw out fear and emotion!" Taryn roared as he thrusted a kick into Ranir's stomach. The pain Ranir felt was as much physical as it was emotional. He didn't know why Taryn would attack him in such manner. He wondered for a flash of a thought whether he had upset Taryn. Suddenly it was clear.

Ranir felt the familiar itch in his palms. His eyes lit up like the stars, lightning arcing between his fingers. This time, Ranir felt a different sensation as he felt his body lift off of the ground. He looked over his shoulder and noticed he was hovering a foot above the ground. Taryn's eyes grew larger than ever. Small rays of deep blue lightning arced from Ranir's body to the ground. With the very thought of standing up, his body rotated him in the air vertically.

Taryn casted a shield around himself. He yelled out, "Now, control it, Ranir!" He ran straight toward Ranir charging his hands with fire. Ranir focused and closed his eyes. Time seemed to drag down tremendously, as he opened his eyes, Taryn was moving in slow motion. Ranir watched as he moved his hands as if making sure it wasn't an illusion. His body seemed to move at normal speed. He realized, Taryn wasn't moving slow. In fact, Ranir was moving staggeringly fast. It seemed to give him more time to think and focus.

He brought his palms together, clasping his hands. He could feel the power of lightning building inside his hold. He was consciousness of every spark in and around his body and channeled it forward through his hands. He aimed with his mind and with his palms directly at Taryn's chest. Releasing the bolt of lightning, a bright white light flashed and time reeled back to reality. The bolt smashed through Taryn's shield, knocking him backwards 30 paces, smashing through the wall of the shack.

Ranir was standing still in shock at what he had purposely gone through with. Quickly, he snapped out of his daze and ran to the hole in the wall. Taryn was lying on his back, grunting in pain. As he rolled over onto his side, Ranir could hear a faint laugh come over Taryn. Now, Ranir was even more confused. He reached down and grabbed Taryn by the arm. As he pulled him up, he noticed that he felt as heavy as a bag of flour. He accidentally pulled too hard, causing Taryn to rack his head against the broken wall. "Oh! I am so sorry, Taryn. I don't know what happened!" cried out Ranir.

Taryn began to laugh even harsher now. "Boy! You controlled your magic inside you! That's what," he said.

"Was I floating?" asked Ranir. He was certain that he was hovering but even that seems like something absurd.

"For a moment, yes. I've never seen anything like that!" he boasted. It made Taryn realize that while Ranir may not have been more than a village boy, now his power was great. He was changing.

For the first time since he received his power, Ranir felt at peace, with no overwhelming doubt. He felt the melding of his spirit and the lightning. He had finally became one with The Lightning Rod. "Are we ready now?" Ranir said reluctantly. He was enjoying his time with Taryn, and he knew that soon they would have to depart. It saddened him.

Taryn looked at Ranir with admiration. "I think we are ready. If I may say something, I think you were meant to become The Lightning Rod, Ranir. I've never seen someone attach to their magic and control it the way you have in a matter of weeks."

"Thank you, I think." Ranir wasn't used to Taryn being overly kind enough for compliments.

"Well," said Taryn looking down the mountain side, "Killiad, here we come." He turned to his swords and cloak laying on the ground. Picking them up, he said, "So the plan is to get to Killiad, find a stable house for horses, maybe spend the night above the tavern, and head straight for The Emphyrius. On horseback it'll be less than a day's hard riding." He sung both swords behind him, landing them perfectly in the sheaths that were harnessed on his back. Pulling on his cloak he continued, "we don't want to stop in the desert pass."

"Oh yeah, I have heard stories of the desert. Is it as desolate as they say?" Ranir recalled stories from traveling merchants of the Drâgok Desert. They described it as blazing hot and dry, with no water or food.

"Every bit, maybe even worse," explained Taryn. "You have to ride straight through it to avoid the dune pits and the Skorn Serpents, large, hateful, snake creatures that will kill you for entertainment." Ranir decided to tryst Taryn and not question him further. He had enough to worry and wander about. They began their descent of The Veörn Mountains.

It was nearly sunset when they arrived at the front gate of Killiad. Ranir was immediately put off by the massive oak barrier surrounding the city. The front gate was compromised of oak with iron bindings. On each side of the gate stood a tower with an archer in it. These were the guards for the southern entrance. It made Ranir wonder what they were guarding against since they came from the south.

"Halt! Who are you and what business do you have in Killiad?" roared one of the guards. He had a large red beard and peered out through his horned helmet. He was clad in a leather and chain mail vest.

Taryn looked at Ranir and seemed to share the confusion. "My name is Taryn Ontaga. I'm a bounty hunter from The Emphyrius," he said with a sarcastic bow. Pointing at Ranir he said, "This is Ranir Trysfal of Heramor, a friend of mine. We just want a couple horses, some food and rest. We're only passing through."

The guard looked down at something unseen inside the gate. He appeared to say something. He gave a nod to the other guard and they released the latches for the gate. The giant gate swung open with a loud creak. They only opened it enough for them to pass through.

Before they advanced into the city, a woman appeared from within the walls. She looked stunning to Ranir. Her hair was black and she was dressed formally in a blue dress. Ranir looked at Taryn who appeared to recognize the woman.

"Sora, I-" he began. He was interrupted with a wave of her hand. She held a hard gaze on Taryn's face.

"You have the nerve to come to my city?" she said coldly. "You must have known that I would've caught you before you left."

"I wasn't sneaking. I wanted to confront you. That is why I decided on pushing through Killiad," explained Taryn.

"Confront me? Like you did my sister?" said Sora, forming a water ball in her hand. "*She's a water mage!*" thought Ranir.

"I didn't confront Verna, she came looking for the boy, lustful for power." Taryn's tone shifted to a begging sound. Ranir knew exactly who Verna was. She was part of the reason that his friend was dead and his other friend had abandoned him. He instantly filled with rage and disgust for Sora.

"Liar! She was the Head Hydromancer!" shouted Sora, forming another water ball in the other hand. Ranir's first impression of her was that she shouldn't be too difficult to handle. He second guessed his instinct when he saw the way Taryn had cowered in her anger. Something about her now seemed powerful, intimidating even.

"She came with Omat and Ashtal, to take him back to the Emphyre. He can't be teleported, and she wouldn't listen. They attacked us!" Taryn was trying hard to convince Sora.

Ranir had enough of the references to him. He let his bitterness overtake his nervousness. "Excuse me. Yes, hello, boy here. My name is Ranir. I killed your sister," said Ranir, letting the words loose without thinking them through. On second thought, Ranir didn't regret it and made a pact with himself to stand up for himself in the face of fear. He was no longer going to be a pawn, or allow himself to be pushed around.

"You?!" Sora barked and released both orbs of water. Instantly, Ranir understood why Taryn had some fear from her. The two crystal clear orbs stabbed Ranir directly in the stomach. His feet went backwards causing him to land on his stomach with a loud thud.

"Sora! Stop! I am warning you!" barked Taryn, igniting his own hands in glorious orange fire. Without hesitation, Sora slammed another spell through the air, like a sword blade it cut straight through Taryn's robe, landing perfectly in his knees. He had the same effect as Ranir did, landing harshly on his stomach.

Ranir felt the familiar sting of power in his palms, but pushed it aside this time. He had been practicing spells for several days and he wasn't sure if he was ready to reveal to the world that he was The Lightning Rod. He closed his eyes and felt the draw of magic subside. He thought of the three spells he knew. Taryn said that the Opening Spell and Explosion Spell were only able to be casted on non living objects. Which left his last spell, which he promptly called

Tethered Lightning. Then he thought the obvious, that the group of people now standing behind Sora would see the lightning.

Recalling how he was able to slow time by giving in to the lightning, he attempted to do the same. He drew back the magic of lightning, feeling it course over and through his whole body. He let it rush into his eyes and his palms. The energy was warm as it washed over him, giving him the ultimate rush of power. He opened his eyes. Sora was standing still. He turned to look at Taryn who was barely moving. It had worked! He jumped up to his feet and rushed Sora like a cat after a field mouse. As he was just about to touch her, he planted his feet into the dirt and leaned forward. He tipped his shoulder first to the side and slammed Sora in the chest with his full force. Ranir noticed a shock wave ripple through the air and a surge of pain in his shoulder.

Regular speed resumed. Ranir slid backwards a couple feet. He looked up to see Sora flying through the air backwards. She soared every bit of a hundred paces and smashed into the eastern pillar's post. The old timber was the size of a century old tree. She cut straight through the pole, causing it to topple. The guard at the top was sent falling to the ground. The rest of the guard toward followed the crumble, sending splinters of wood and iron gliding through the air. As the debris landed, dust was pushed through the air like a thick fog.

It happened so fast that Taryn was still lying in the dirt. Ranir walked over to him and lending a hand. "You okay?" he asked Taryn, who passed glances from Ranir and then to the fallen tower and back again.

"What the Hel happened?" he asked in disbelief.

121

"I hit her." Ranir gave a short answer because he was still in shock that he could accomplish a feat whilst still hiding his powers.

"With what?" Taryn's eyes were opened wide, his breathing heavy.

Ranir looked back at the mess, Sora was standing back up, dusting herself off. He couldn't believe that she could stand after a hit like that. This gave Ranir another reason to admire or fear the water mage. She drew water to her hands and healed several scratches as the water ran over her body, soaking her dress.

"M-my shoulder," said Ranir without looking at Taryn.

"You did that super speed thing again didn't you?" Taryn remembered how fast Ranir had moved on the mountain top, knocking him back with a spell in a similar fashion.

"Yes, I didn't want to show my magic and I had to do something. Her sister killed my friend and she had the nerve to blame me for killing her?" Ranir's heart was racing.

Taryn nodded, "that was smart, Ranir."

Sora walked over to them, cracking her neck. The loud popping sound combined with her no longer having a scratch after smashing through a wooden tower gave her a tough presence. "We need to talk," she said looking at the crowd standing by the gate, mouths gaped open, "in my hearth. Come now!" she demanded.

Ranir and Taryn exchanged looks before trailing Sora without question. She proved herself a strange adversary. "Sora, why the gates and towers?" asked Taryn. He had history of operating in and around Killiad. It was also known that somehow he and Sora had their own history.

"Rumors were spreading," she stated without elaboration.

"Of what?"

She didn't answer. She resumed walking at a quick pace, glancing around at passersby. After a few moments they reached a large building that was adorned with clay tile roofing. Ranir had never seen such craftsmanship in a house before. The structure seemed similar, of wood and pegs. The outside, however, was lined with bricks, cut perfectly and laid out overlapping each other. As they passed through the large door, Sora turned and pulled a sizable log that was ripped down to latch inside iron hooks.

"Alright, now we can speak," declared Sora. "Rumors were spreading about Seldos returning to the area and continuing his spread of fear and darkness."

"Those rumors always persist, Sora," said Taryn, shrugging his shoulders.

"That is what we thought. Then one night, a forsaken stumbled into the city from the south entrance. He killed 13 citizens before he was destroyed."

"Forsaken? And you're sure it was a forsaken?"

"Taryn, you know that I know more than you about combating the dark magic, right?" snarled Sora.

Taryn pursed his lips. "Seldos. I haven't heard anything about his whereabouts in a long time. Lets hope, if it is him, that time has weakened him."

Sora turned to Ranir. Her eyes examined him up and down. "How did you do that outside? Why was Verna after you?" She was demanding.

Taryn spoke first, "Go ahead Ranir. She's the Lord of Killiad and an old...friend." There was something smooth and sensual about the way that Taryn say this. Ranir thought it best to leave it alone. He wasn't sure yet what Sora's relationship with Taryn was and indirectly how her hospitality would continue with him if Taryn wasn't around. After all, he did kill her sister.

Ranir cleared his throat as if he were about to give a presentation. He had another idea. Bowing, he closed his eyes and drew the lightning forth. It was becoming easier to summon each time.

Ranir stretched his arms out and opened his white eyes. They were glowing bright. Lightning arcs raced between his fingers, dashing up around his forearms like bracers. "I am The Lightning Rod."

Dora's jaw opened up as she took a shirt gasp of air. She was stunned. "But," she shot a look to Taryn, "How? That's supposed to be a myth!"

Taryn puts his hand on Ranir's shoulder. "Yeah, well now it's real." Ranir relaxed his hold on the magic. The lightning subsided. "Your sister wanted his power. Many people are going to want his power or to see it be used as the prophecy says." Ranir hadn't heard anything prophetic from Taryn. Knowing this,

Taryn looked at Ranir to elaborate, "There is a prophecy of The Lightning Rod returning to Gnariam to fight the darkness. It's always been assumed to be a myth because there is always darkness in the world."

"I am sorry about your sister. Taryn is telling the truth. She attacked us, killed my friend and that fire mage scorched my best friend." Ranir was empathetic to her loss. Sora turned her back to them and bowed her head for a moment.

Turning back, she said, "Thank you for the truth. I'm sorry for her blood lust. I'm sorry sorry for your friends." She has glossy eyes. Wiping away a tear forming, she said, "You can't stay here. Too many people witnessed you attack the Overlord of Killiad. That's an offense usually punishable by hanging."

Ranir had thoughts of sleeping in a bed and enjoying a full meal. It had been weeks since he was among civilized people and normality. Now they were about to be thrust into the wind once again. At least this time they may have a better journey to The Emphyrius.

Taryn sighed, "Well Sora, I wish that we had met up again on different circumstances. It seems that we have several things that we should catch up on. Right now is not the time obviously. I will come back to you once we reach The Emphyrius. For now, we will be on our way. We are going to need some things," Said Taryn desperately.

"I wish so as well. And I saw you walked here, now I understand why, but you can't traverse the desert on foot, right?"

"Precisely. We'll need horses and rations to get us through. Maybe some blankets and water," said

Taryn. He was trying to think of different scenarios and what they may need should their trip go awry.

"Come with me," said Sora. With that she sped off down a long corridor that was adorned with torches, cast dancing shadows down the tunnel looking hallway. She led them to a large pantry where they gathered some bread and fresh meat. Once they decided it was enough, they followed her to the stable house. Inside the massive hall of the stables the sounds of whinnying echoed about. Sora have Ranir and Taryn two black horses. "Black will be better to cover you in the night shades," she told Taryn with a wink. He gave a short smirk.

Once they were ready to begin again, Ranir thanked Sora several times. She was patient and kind, the opposition to her sister's characteristics. He mounted his horse and waited for Taryn by the northern gate.

Ranir watched as Taryn and Sora conversed for a moment. He could tell by how they were acting around each other they had known each other for awhile. There was some romantic tension between them. It made Ranir wonder how they knew each other. He speculated they were intimate once. After a couple minutes Taryn mounted his horse. The night was warm. The moon was dim. Looking to the north, Ranir got discouraged seeing the black background. It was time for him to reach the Emphyrius and become who he was meant to be. They kicked off, another journey into the unknown.

Chapter 11: The Emphyrius

After a few hours of steady riding, Ranir's legs were throbbing. He had ridden horses for years around Heramor, but never for hours at full speed. Taryn didn't seem to tiring or hurting. "I wonder if I'll ever be that tough," Ranir thought. He imagined what training it would take to strengthen a body like that.

"Can we stop and rest for a moment? My legs are killing me." Taryn looked into the black surrounding them. Only small distinctions could be made from deeper shades.

"Not just yet," he stated as he pressed harder in his saddle and picked up speed. Ranir was agitated. His legs burns with fatigue of gripping the sides of his horse. He closes his eyes and summoned the lightning within. The full rush of power overwhelmed him and calmed him simultaneously. His legs immediately lost their pinging sting. It was like he was healed. He let the magic fade, feeling refreshed and calm. They pushed on through the night without any stops, much to Ranir's surprise.

The sun rose from the bleak background. Ranir was delighted to see silhouettes from a city on the horizon. They had just a few more hours left. Ranir's legs were throbbing again but this time he didn't care. They were so close to finally reaching The Emphyrius.

Ranir began to noticed a dark cloud rolling towards them. When he was young, his mother used to tell him stories of massive sand storms that crossed the deserts. "Should we be worried about that?" yelled Ranir.

Taryn began to slow down as he squinted toward the dark brown cloud. Suddenly his eyes grew wide. "Stop!" he roared. His horse buried its hooves in the sand coming to a quick stop. "That's not a sand storm, those are Skorn Serpents!"

"How can that cloud come from snakes?" asked Ranir. He steadied his vision attempting to see any sign of life. Nothing but dust was visible.

"They move beneath the surface and they aren't your average field snake. Get off the horse now!"

Ranir topples off of the horse and planted his feet in the soft sand. He could feel the heat of the desert floor even through his leather boots. Taryn casted a spell that Ranir couldn't hear. Spinning in a circle, fire blazed from his hands creating a perfect circle around them. "This will burn anything beneath the surface. But it won't keep them back for long. They are stubborn and resilient."

"Should I do anything?" asked Ranir. His heart was thumping for he didn't know what to expect.

The cloud moved at a steady pace and was soon upon them. Once it reached the ring of Fire, Ranir heard one of the most terrifying screams ever. It reminded him of a screaming eagle and a wolf's low growl blended. Suddenly three creatures bursted from the sand. They were serpents, like cobras, but at least 20 feet long and the girth of a full grown man. Spikes ran along the spine stretching all the way to the tip of their tails. The eyes of the Skorns were glowing yellow, giving them a menacing stare. Their mouths were wide open, baring multiple rows of jagged teeth.

Each of the serpents took turns snapping their powerful jaws in the air, hissing all the while. Ranir stepped closer to Taryn.

"*Artul askat*!" cried out Taryn. The ring of Fire stretched out in diameter scorching the Skorns. They riled up in the air screeching. Ranir was busy thinking of how he could help. The fire was going to stop them much longer. Their scaled were like that of ironbark. Suddenly it became clear, the path to take.

"To Hel with this! *Likta Azhik*!" A blue arc of lightning coiled from his palm and wrapped around the neck of the left Skorn serpents. Like a rope Ranir tugged with all his Lightning Rod power. The chain lightning ripped clean through the serpent, decapitating it. The head rolled into the flames and seared. Ranir felt the fatigue of magic usage. It was even less tiresome than before. He was getting stronger! The other two serpents reeled back, hissing and shaking. Ranir shot a glance to Taryn who seemed shocked. He lifted his eyebrows and nodded his head sideways, giving Ranir permission to proceed.

Ranir turned back to other snakes and summoned the might of lightning within. Using the same bolt of lightning that he used against Taryn after he was isolated, he aimed for the heads of the Skorns. He bellowed out mustering as much power as he could, burning a hole straight through both skulls. The serpents fell silent, then dropped to the ground with a thump. The ring of fire extinguished. The desert was quiet again, the horses relaxed.

Taryn was impressed. "You are getting rather

good at this magic thing," he said chuckling. Ranir was satisfied with his efforts. Without any discussion they mounted the horses. He thought, "I'm not the same as I was when I left home. Let's hope it's for the best."

The rode on into the sunrise. The remaining ride was much farther than Ranir thought it would be. From a distance he could see glistening buildings and a wall around the southern side. He soon realized why his guess was wrong. The capital city was massive.

"You see the tallest tower?" Taryn said, pointing at the largest building in sight. Ranir could easily guess what it was. "That is the Emphyrius. That's where we're heading."

They rode for another hour before reaching the gate. It reminded Ranir of Killiad's gates. These gates however, dwarfed Sora's city. The giant walls surrounding the city felt like an omen. There were 4 towers fairly close to each other overlooking the wall and peering out to the south. Each tower was manned with four archers. They jumped from their horses. Ranir instantly began stretching his legs after the long ride. Taryn was once again not showing any signs of pain.

"What is the actual city called?" asked Ranir. Taryn put a hand on his back and turned him to face the city.

"Ranir, I give you," he swung his arm forward towards the city, "Thrast. The city of silver!"

"How could anyone build something so immaculate? Where would you even begin?" Ranir stood before the craft of great builders. He knew that before he even stepped foot inside the walls. They proceeded to the front gate, which was open, unlike the gates of Killiad. A man met them at the opening to check them. He allowed them to pass without hesitation. He must have either know Taryn or at least saw his Emphyrius bounty hunter cloak. Ranir thought that the city must have more protection or guards hidden somewhere.

"This city was built nearly five centuries ago," explained Taryn, "Many Kings ruled it before the great Emphyre took control and became the first Lord of Sythestine."

A vast variety of sounds could be heard echoing and bouncing about between alley ways and brick structures. Ranir had never experienced building technology or skill like was used to build Thrast. They passed by what seemed several layers of economy, ascending to the great Emphyre's keep. By the gates and exits of Thrast were mainly peasants, farmers and merchants looking for passersby. Moving further into the city, making a straight path towards the massive building, were increasing classes of people. Next were groups of blacksmiths and weapon forgers, leather workers and tailor workers.

By the time they had finally reached the mage headquarters, the keep of the Emphyre, The Emphyrius, Ranir was exhausted from such a ride. His excitement to finally reach a place of learning, had almost all but faded. Taryn led him through a set of marble doors that seemed to carry the weight of an entire house. "This way, Ranir. I want to take you to first see The Emphyre, then straight to your room and you can get plenty of rest and recovery. You will need it," said Taryn.

"What do you mean I'll need it?" Ranir was calm before this statement was cast into the wind. As they passed corridor after corridor, people after people, most of them Taryn seemed to know fairly well, they arrived at a monolithic black door. It had golden painted iron hinges and large rings for handles.

Taryn turned to Ranir and halted, looking down as if searching for the words to use, "Ranir, this is The Emphyre. I know that you are excited, and all of this magic is still new to you. But you are still a boy, and never having dealt with politics and nobility, please, let me do most of the talking."

"Certainly. I wouldn't know what to say anyway!" said Ranir laughing. Taryn gave him a stern look. It was time for Ranir to mature more if he was going to be in the presence of nobles and the Lord of Sythestine. He nodded to Taryn that he was ready to proceed.

Taryn knocked on the door. It carried the sound of cracking ice. The door swung open to reveal a small woman. She had large green eyes looking up at Taryn, "Ah, Taryn. The great Bounty Hunter returns," she said with a bow. Something about her greeting was sarcastic.

"Nice to see you too, Erelta." Taryn returned a half bow and pushed passed her. Ranir stayed in tow. The woman shot a scowling glance to him.

Taryn slowed his pace and looked over his shoulder at Ranir, giving a cautious reminder to speak only when spoke to. Taryn led him up a flight of coiling stairs. At the top of the landing there was a large balcony on which stood a tall man.

The man had his back towards them as they approached. He wore a long cloak that reminded Ranir of a snake skinned tunic that a merchant brought to Heramor once. Turning around, he seemed overly collected. He had dark colorless eyes and a long face. Speckled along his sharp jaw were silver stubs of hair.

"Taryn," said The Emphyre with a sideways nod. "I was wonder if you were coming home or not." His voice was smooth like silk but it carried a deep weight.

"Your highness," replied Taryn. This time his bow was deep and long, full of respect. Ranir was still, contemplating if he should follow. Out of respect, he bowed as well.

"So you are Ranir. Taryn came to me and told me what my head mages did. I am sorry for your loss and I want you to know that they were not following my orders," said The Emphyre.

"Thank you, uh, your Highness." Ranir and Taryn stood up. From the height of the balcony, Thrast looked much smaller.

"So. Your the Lightning Rod, yes?" asked The Emphyre. He walked over to a high, white chair, and brushed his cloak behind as he sat.

Ranir gave a nod. He knew that with all his power, The Emphyre shouldn't be a threat. He couldn't help but feel intimidated. The way The Emphyre carried himself was a testament to his age and wisdom. He stared at Ranir without blinking, tapping a finger on a small marble table beside him. What was he thinking?

"Taryn, you are released to continue your next bounty. Erelta will see you out," The Emphyre commanded. Ranir expected a form of argument or side note from Taryn. Instead, he shot a glance to Ranir and marched through the door.

133

"You are seeking training yes?" he asked. Ranir thought hard about his next few words.

"I do," he paused. "And a purpose I suppose."

The great Emphyre was amused. "A purpose? Why you're the Lightning Rod of course. You have a purpose. You are the guardian of Gnariam." His tone seemed almost untruthful, as if disappointed in who became The Lightning Rod.

"I am still not sure what all that entails," Ranir admitted. The only thing he knew is that he was meant to protect the world.

"We have trainers assigned to help you. In our Great Library, you will be given all of the books collected on the The Lightning Rod. If the prophecy is true, you're going to need as much knowledge as you can get." As if by some unspoken queue, a man entered through the large door. He was lined with pure white robes. He was elderly. "This is Ramshi Jut, our eldest mage within Sythestine. He has more knowledge than almost any other person on magic and," he pointed at Ranir, "The Lightning Rod. He will be assisting you for the next several months." He waves his hands in dismissal of Ranir.

Months! Ranir knew that his training would be long. He simply wasn't ready to dive into tuition just yet. Over the last several weeks he had taken in so much information already and had his world flipped upside down. Now he was about embark deeper into the world of magic.

"Your highness," Ranir said with another bow and turned to Ramshi. Without a word, the man turned and walked back through the door. Ranir waited for a moment, thinking. He wondered why someone of such power, politically, would want someone so powerful, prophetically, just to show disinterest upon introductions. He made no connections. He turned and followed the old man who he would be spending much time with.

Ramshi took him down and about corridors left and right. Ranir was lost by the time he was shown his living quarters. His sense of direction from a compass stand point was voided. He figures in due time this would feel like home, and he would soon learn his place. Tomorrow is a new day and the beginning of vast training but for now Ranir needed to rest and recuperate.

****

Chapter 12: Upon Further Examination

"Chain lightning!" called out Ramshi. Ranir was getting quite decent at casting his spells now. The targets were familiar to him. The books he revived from the great library nearly four months ago had brought a lot of light to his knowledge and Ramshi's as well. In the time since he started his formal training, Ranir had grown more stern and steady. His resolve had strengthened. He had only seen Taryn twice since his departure, a fact that saddened him slightly. He had not made any real friends besides Ramshi. Even Ramshi himself wasn't a friend, more of a strict guide.

Back to back, Ranir casted various spells on targets. It reminded of the first training he received in The Veörn Mountains. Over the past months he had grown stronger in his resistance to the cost of magic. Fatigue only came around after ultra heavy spells, which were rare in training. He likes to mix up magic with elemental power to build instinct in combat. His examination from The Emphyre was approaching fast, and from the other mages around the keep, it was crucial to becoming a bounty hunter, a career Ranir decided on taking. He didn't know how he would be tested, but intuition told him to be prepared for heavy combat challenges.

Thus far he had learned Lightning Bolt,

Thunderstorm, Sundering Skies, Polarity Shift, Chain Lightning, Static Healing, Opening Spell, Explosion, Lightning Shield, and Temporal Rift. He had hoped that his concentration and control over his power to master his texts. His most frustration came from not learning to teleport, which is vital for Bounty Hunting.

After combat training that night, Ramshi summoned Ranir to The Great Library. The steps to get there, and around the entire keep, had become natural for Ranir. He curved around one last staircase before ascending to the top. The entire library was encased in stained glass windows. Since the first time Ranir saw the red hue lighting in the library, it was one of his favorite places to be in The Emphyrius.

Ranir open the pale door and entered the library to find Ramshi sitting in a large chair. A haze of smoking lingered from his pipe. The aroma of sweet tobacco filled the air.

"Come. Sit with me, I may have figured something out today," he said, gesturing with his pipe to another chair. Ranir politely obliged. "I may know why you can't teleport like a mage. It has to do with your surging speed." He sound almost careful to speak too loudly, even for a library.

Ranir leaned it, intrigued. "What about it? That only lasts in very short bursts. It won't help traverse cities for bounties."

"Here's my theory," he said leaning closer, looking around the room. He seemed paranoid of anyone hearing his discovery. "I think that in time, you can become raw energy and move that fast. For great distances." He demonstrated by waving his hands apart. The theory sounded interesting. There was no evidence to prove it. Quite frankly, Ranir was more disappointed by the words 'in time.' He was out of time, in a sense, for learning new spells or elemental tricks.

"Maybe. We can revisit this theory once I have free time, like after failing the bounty hunter exam for not being able to port," Ranir said as he dropped back in his chair. Ranir asked several bounty hunters what the final exam consisted of and never got them same answer twice.

Ranir has trained in both magic and in non-magic arms. His skill with a bow, sword and daggers increased. Sometimes he felt more like a weapon than a bounty hunter. He thought of it as a bounty hunter being Sythestine's weapon against the accused. Many nights Ranir fell asleep reading in The Great Library, in an effort to get as close to passing an exam as he could.

"Ranir," said Ramshi as he laid his pipe down. "Many mages have passed the exams without a single port ability. It's not as big of a deal as you think." He scratched his scrubby beard, "Most bounties don't have a time limit priority."

"Yeah well I'm not a mage, remember?!" Ranir snapped back. "I'm supposed to be some chosen one nonsense and they are going to take it harder on me, I just know it." Ranir was having a difficult time trying to calm his nerves. The weight of importance that he passed the exam was heavy.

Ranir had no sense of direction of the world. He was confined for the last four months to The Emphyrius and its grounds. He more than often thought about Marnos and Selendt, and the quiet life they used to live together. He didn't regret having magic. Life was just more simple before he was given the role of The Lightning Rod.

Ranir left Ramshi in the library and returned to his living quarters. Since moving into the massive building centering Thrast, he had made several rearrangements and accommodations to his room. The Emphyre provided him with all things to suffice for living, so long as he give his word that he would join The Emphyrius. The decision was made easier for Ranir once Taryn left. He was alone, with magic that needed taming and nowhere to turn. He did not like the fact that someone else could tell him where to go and what to do for the most part. He felt like a prisoner some days. The alternative, though, seemed harsher yet, and with larger risks.

Ranir now had his own living quarters that were bigger than his entire farm house in Heramor. The food that was served out shined every ration he used to obtain. His clothes were always washed. Dirt didn't cling to everything like it did at the farm. His bed was much more comfortable here as well. After thinking about the advantages, the decision seemed easier yet.

Sitting on his shelves were stacks of books that he aimed to read. He remembered his mother teaching him to read when he was a young boy, a luxury that most peasants did not have. This helped speed up his training as he spent many late nights, sometimes into the waking hours, reading his texts and history of The Lightning Rod and the responsibilities as well as spells and the prophecies.

It seemed as if several people had written these books together, clashing ideas jumped around, and the prophecies were never aligned. Some of the records tell of The Lightning Rod coming to cleanse Gnariam of evil. Other entries simply state that The Lightning Rod will bring balance and peace to the world. Others were ramblings of mad men who spent their lives studying a subject that they had no evidence on.

As the night climbed through Ranir's windows, the late Summer air was warm and dry. A fair breeze cascaded around the room. He laid on his bed, reading The History of The First Bringer of Lightning.

'And in the twelfth month, The Bringer of Lightning shall be reborn. The elemental power of Lightning and The Lightning Rod shall become one.'

"Ugh, okay? I guess that is when I'll teleport huh?" said Ranir to the book jokingly. He continued reading on into the night, falling asleep as the wind brushed his now shagged hair across his face. Wicked dreams filled his mind at night. Memories of being near death, and his friends suffering because of magic. He often awoke with tears streaming down his face. His dreams were the only place he let emotions flow these days. Bitterness had driven further into him, making him difficult to be around. He liked it that way because it helped keep him from getting attached to people. He didn't want to feel loss like he has several times in his life.

Ranir spent the next three days in the same fashion as he did the last four months. The cycle seemed never ending and always repeating. He would wake up, eat breakfast, go to the court yards to train hand to hand combat and weapons with various teachers, most of which couldn't beat him with his Surging Speed. That is what Ramshi called it. He said the speed only occurs when Ranir focuses enough to surge lightning into his muscles. Ramshi taught Ranir as much as he did studying him and his abilities.

The day was upon him. His future could be decided and set in stone. Ramshi asked to see him before the exam. Ranir found him after a large breakfast, sitting in his room. Walking in, Ranir noticed a large wooden box sitting on Ramshi's lap. "What's that?" Ranir asked. Ramshi had grown numb to Ranir's rudeness of late. He ignored it most of the time now.

"This is a gift for you, Ranir," he said setting the box down on a table. When he got closer to the container, Ranir noticed a symbol he had seen on one of his books. It was familiar and yet unknown to him. He ran his fingers across the symbol, finding it etched and filled with silver. The wood was finely crafted as well.

"The box is very nice!" said Ranir. He picked it up and was surprised how heavy it was.

"I had one of our wood workers make the box special, for you. Ranir, I want you to know that I am proud of you, and how far you've come, especially for how young you are and the life you have already lived." Ramshi was never sentimental before so it confused Ranir.

He cracked the wax seal on the lid and opened it up. Inside was a neatly folded robe. Ranir pulled it up and saw that it was freshly made and tailored to his size. It was a silvery blue color and adorned with a hooded cloak to match. White and blue streaks ran down the torso of the robes, giving the illusion of lightning. It was specially made for him, The Lightning Rod. Without a word, Ranir ripped off his tunic and put on the robe. It feel magically perfect. It was light yet, felt durable. Inside the box was a smaller container. It was about the size of a small book, built with similar wood and sealed exactly the same.

Ranir reached inside and picked it up, realizes what made the box so heavy. The smaller box carried more weight than his new robe. He was intrigued to see what it was. Opening it up, Ranir found two bracers inside. Each was fitted with gold lacing intertwined with silver. A blue crystal sat center of both bracers. Ranir looked to Ramshi, who say still with a smile. He returned the smile and asked, "Are these mana stones?"

"Close, but no. You see, I learned something that you don't know, about your powers and wanted to wait until the right time to tell you. I know now, why you aren't a mage like the rest who are endowed with power," he explained. This peaked Ranir's interest even more than the gifts. "When you are using Elemental Power, you charge the air and ground around you with static lightning. You can harvest that static and use it like mana, fueling your magic spells. These," he grabbed the bracers and slid them onto Ranir's wrists, "are stones that can hold the charge, and I've gathered weeks worth. When you do your magic combat on the exam today, or if you do, use these stones. Your lightning is ferocious, and everyone that has seen it knows it. Its time to show the world what your magic can do as well. Go big, Ranir."

Ranir was overwhelmed with different emotions. He never thought that Ramshi cared more than any other person assigned to help him from The Emphyre. By instinct, Ranir hugged Ramshi. In that moment, he felt like the closest person to him in a long time.

At midday, Ranir was assigned a guard and a guide to take him to the exam. Their job was simply to make sure Ranir wasn't going to cheat on the exam. They searched him before taking him to a small court yard he had never been to before. They obviously didn't know about the bracers and assumed the colors matched his brand new robes.

Upon arrival, Ranir first noticed, sitting atop a high throne, was The Emphyre. Beside him was Erelta as well as the new heads of the mage councils. On either side of them sat the elders, including Ramshi, who was the oldest. On the end of the rows were several of the best bounty hunters. On the very end, standing out in red and orange robes, was Taryn Ontaga. Ranir wasn't sure if this made him more determined or more nervous. He knew that they would all be judging him and his exam. Ultimately, however, it was The Emphyre's final verdict that mattered.

The guide brought him to the center of the assembly. Standing in the hot sun, Ranir was already sweating beneath his brow and above his lip. "Are you nervous, Ranir?" asked The Emphyre in his smooth voice. It reminded Ranir of a snake.

"No, your highness," Ranir said with a bow. "I am determined and committed." The group before him chuckled quietly.

"First of all, I would like to thank all of the witnesses who came today in judgment of Ranir Trysfal's Bounty Hunter Examination and Demonstration of Key Magic," he said, standing up and giving a bow of his own. The rest all followed a deeper bow, yet.

"We shall begin. Ranir, we are going to give you several tasks today and see how you handle them, or if you can handle them. You are given a bounty, and the first thing you get on your hunt is a lock-box." A couple men brought forth a large stone cube. Ranir knew this cube well. It wasn't a solid piece at all. It was an illusion. "What do you do?"

Without hesitating, Ranir casted his first spell, "Estashashik," he said calmly. He had learned that each spell had different intensity that could be controlled. Slowly, he worked the opening spell around the fine crack at the opening. The line followed around horizontally, successfully revealing a lid.

"Very good. Proceed to your next clue inside," The Emphyre commanded. Ranir didn't know what was going to be in the box, but his choice was obvious, open it and find out.

Ranir stepped forward and pushed the lid from the stone box. His physical strength had increased as much as his skill in magic did. From inside the dark box, Ranir could hear a noise. He peaked inside. Just as his face was over top of the opening, a creature leaped from the box. A mörcat! The fury beast sped around and circled behind him. Normally mörcats were calm and content. Something had this one rabid. They usually were like a normal farm mouser, except about twice the size and lived for over 50 years, growing until they died. He had heard stories of mörcats reaching the size of larger dogs before. He hadn't expected this to be a part of the testing. He shot a look to The Emphyre, who said nothing but motioned him to defend himself.

"*Likta Azhik!*" shouted Ranir, forming his chain lightning spell. The spell wrapped around the feline, stopping it in place. It thrashed against the magic leashed around its neck. Ranir held onto the lightning. It was like roping a small steer. He wondered why the mörcat was so angry. It screamed out a noise to Ranir that sounded very familiar to him. From the corner of his eye, he noticed Taryn moving toward The Emphyre. He approached him angrily it seemed, asking a heated question. With a wave of his hand, The Emphyre sent Taryn back to his place.

Suddenly, Ranir understood the meaning of the beast from the box. The mörcat began to shake wildly and its body looked like the bones were breaking from within. Ranir had seen movement like this before. In a quick flash, the cat transformed before their eyes into a man. It was another druid! Ranir's heart began to race as he remembered the first magical creature he encountered was the same kind of beast.

Ranir shot a look to The Emphyre. He suddenly realized something. He wasn't looking to test Ranir like normal. He wanted to put Ranir in a stressful state and force a decision on him: Kill the druid, or fail the test and indirectly, lose the loyalty of The Emphyre. Ranir knew that Druids were dark magic and therefore threatening to anyone around them. If he was really meaning to pursue being a bounty hunter, this decision was going to be formed sooner or later. He turned back to the Druid.

He had similar teeth as the first monster he witnessed. The creature stirred in the chain lightning, but quit thrashing about. He smiled at Ranir and leaped in the air towards him. Ranir let go of the spell, releasing the Druid. While he was midair, Ranir charged his Surge Speed in a short burst. He ran towards the Druid and slid underneath of him. The beast was frozen in time and against gravity. Ranir reached up and grasped the long black hair. Giving it a hyper-strength pull, he snapped the Druid's neck. Normal speed resumed. The body landed with a smash against the stone box. The crowd all stirred together, as if trying to get a better look.

Ranir felt a small sense of guilt, having executed the Druid in such captivity. He was still satisfied with his decision. The Emphyre stood up, "Sometimes in the open you may run into more trouble than say, one Druid."

With his last word a gate to Ranir's left swung open. From behind the hidden wall came a group of men. Each of them armed with swords, battle axes and bows. Ranir contemplated on giving them the same treatment that the Druid received.

He decided against it, imagining they were a group of angry drunkards from a tavern. This seemed to be a viable situation that he may find himself in. Thinking quickly, Ranir began to pull the static mana from his bracers. His eyes emitted bright white light and his hands filled with arcs of blue lightning. He rose from the ground, slightly floating in static electromagnetism. Looking up to the sky, he could feel the lightning forming all around him. He pulled it all together as much as possible. Looking back to the group of men, some of them angry, some scared, he dropped a thunderstorm directly above The Emphyrius. He counted the men, feeling each of their energy levels. 17 men total. He looked back to his conjured storm. 17 bolts of yellow and blue lightning struck down, perfectly incapacitating the group.

The group of judges and witnesses looked closer at Ranir. He thought they were waiting for him to faint from such a large spell. Some of them even looked fearful. The Emphyre gave a slow but loud clap.

"That is all, Ranir. You passed"

"Wait, that's it?" Ranir fired back without thinking.

"That is all," he exclaimed. The group of mages and bounty hunters had risen to their feet and gave an applaud for Ranir's demonstration of Lightning. He felt as if he wasn't being taken seriously. They all just wanted to witness The Lightning Rod, and The Emphyre just wanted to show his prize! For now, he let it pass and accepted his approval that he had worked so hard for. If not for The Emphyre's test, Ranir wouldn't have pushed so hard to learn, and he wouldn't have the control he has now.

"Thank you, Your Highness," said Ranir contently. He bowed his head low.

"I give to you, The Lightning Rod, Ranir Trysfal, Bounty Hunter!" shouted The Emphyre.

Taryn ran over to Ranir and said, "Congratulations, old friend. You did well. You look well. I am proud of you. Now, you can show the world what kind of power The Lightning Rod has!"

Taryn couldn't stay long before he was pulled back into the fray of working. Ramshi walked over to Ranir slowly and bowed his head. Ranir thanked him for the brilliance of the bracers. With that, Ramshi left the courtyard too.

Ranir could finally relax and rest, knowing that his hard work training and studying had paid off, sort of. It was time for a new chapter in Ranir's life. One of adventure and mastery. It was time for Ranir to become a protector of the world.

Chapter 13: The Wanderer

Ranir returned to his room awaited further instruction. He wondered where he would go now for his first bounty. He dreaded setting out on long distance rides. Teleportation would make everything better. That night nobody came to him, which built up his anticipation even more. He wondered if it was planned that way. Turning his attention to his books, he decided that he would continue to learn and train, even if only for himself.

He fell asleep on one of his smaller texts. Scrolls and quills scattered his bed and the floor.

Ranir woke from the rapping of knuckles on his door. He jumped up, spilling ink over his floor. He stabbed a glance to the window. It was still black outside and the air was humid rolling through. He ran to the door, straightened his robes and swung it open to find The Emphyre waiting patiently. Ranir performed an exhausted but quick bow.

"Stand up, boy. There's nobody around," commanded The Emphyre. Ranir was befuddled.

"What may I do for you, Your Highness?" Ranir said innocently.

"First of all, stop calling me that. I very much dislike that title. You may call me Credin. There's no need for political formality any more. I have your assignment."

Ranir contemplated if he was still asleep or not. The Emphyre never acted like this before. "Is it my first bounty?" asked Ranir. He was finally going his hard work bloom into his goals.

The Emphyre, Credin walked over to a chair and sat with a long sigh. "No, Ranir. I don't want your power wasted on hunting bounties." Ranir joined him in the other chair, becoming agitated, feeling like his goal of becoming a bounty hunter was slipping away.

He looked at The Emphyre and noticed his skin was shining in the candle light. He was sweating. The Lord if Sythestine was nervous and anxious about something. "What would you have me do then?" asked Ranir.

"I know that you have been secluded from the world during your training, but something dark has returned to the world," stated.

"Returned? Do you mean The Necromancer?" Ranir recalled the story that Taryn told him. Judging by The Emphyre's attitude, this threat seemed to be more serious than he thought.

"Yes. I assume you've heard the story. He has been gone from the world for years. Disappeared to somewhere. We thought he had died," Credin looked down at his hands, "Guess we should've known better. And now he has taken The Veörn Mountains all the way to Killiad. His Forsaken have slaughtered thousands."

"Why was kept in the dark about this?!" cried Ranir. He leaped to his feet and started pacing.

"I ordered everyone to keep you out of while you trained. When you first came here you weren't ready to face him," he explained. "The reason my council was so happy to witness your power was because we've lost over a hundred mages trying to combat him."

"You could've told me and I could have trained harder, for this," fired back Ranir.

The Emphyre raised his eyebrows. "Would you have stayed here, or try to be the hero?" Ranir's silence told his answer. He knew that they made the right choice but he was defiantly upset. Now more than ever he was ready to prove to the world what he was capable of. He was ready to prove it to himself.

"Why wake me now? What's the plan?" asked Ranir.

"The plan is for you to get into Killiad and stop that bastard!" The Emphyre was up front about his intentions for Ranir.

"So just ride into town and kill him? That simple, huh?"

"Not simple. He has a small army of Forsaken that are immune to most forms of death or magic. His power is great and is not to be underestimated. We will sneak you in the northern gates and the rest will be up to you," he explained.

"Something I should probably tell you. I can't teleport. No mage can port me either."

The Emphyre laughed. "We know all about you grounded abilities, Ranir. We've watched you from the

150

day you arrived here. We have a solution."

"If it's Ramshi's theory, I'm not ready," barked Ranir.

"No," said The Emphyre as he squinted his eyes. It was clear Ramshi truly kept his theory a secret. "One mage doesn't have the power to combat your static magic. But a group of mages is different."

"You think a few mages together can port me there?"

"It's a working theory that's obviously not been tested. Only one way to find out. Gather what you need for a day and head down to the armory. You'll want to save your mana for The Necromancer." With that he swept out of the room with blazing speed. Ranir was surprised he could move as swift as he did.

Ranir's heart was racing and his breathing was heavy. He gathered another robe, cloak and his two bracers. Once he got to the armory, it seemed he was the only one hidden of the plan. The entire council was in the armory waiting, including Taryn. He was glad to see him. Maybe he was away so long because The Emphyre didn't trust him to lie to Ranir.

"Ranir, grab yourself a sword, bow and quiver," said Taryn. He was away so long that he didn't know how Ranir's training had proceeded.

Ranir chuckled. Finding himself suddenly not a part of the political titles, he spoke freely. "No, Taryn. I will take my daggers, and the bow," he looked at Windeb, his combat arms trainer, who smiled.

"Ranir, haven't you been training with swords for months?" said Taryn.

Windeb spoke up before Ranir. "If you would have around more you would know Ranir put the sword down fairly soon after he started training with it it. He is very fast, and as such needed faster weapons, hence the daggers." He walked over and handed Ranir a black leather belt that had two silver daggers sheathed. Each dagger had Stärnets fashioned to them which was a new touch.

Between the mana stones and his bracers, Ranir understood that the entire
Council expected him to need back up power. Once he was set up with his weapons, and his bow was strung across his back, the mages of the council gathered around him.

Taryn places a hand on his shoulder and stood beside him inside the circle of mages. "What are you doing?" asked Ranir.

"You didn't think you were going alone did you? You are powerful, not very experienced though," he replied. Nodding to the council and bowing his head, he gestured for them to proceed. Ranir wanted to argue, but he knew he could use backup and Taryn was one of the best combatants.

Altogether the mages began casting their own elemental language for a teleport. A purple circle appeared underneath Ranir. He closed his eyes, anticipating a backfire of exploding lightning. Suddenly, a cool sensation overwhelmed him. It felt like he stepped into a frozen tundra. Snapping open his eyes, he realized he standing before the Northern Gate of Killiad. He was surrounded by silence. He turned to his side only to find that he was alone. Taryn was not with him. This fact made him panic inside. It didn't matter at this point. He had a mission to do and there were people who needed saving. The air around Killiad was so cold that he could see his breath forming in the air. He wished that he had another way into the confines of the city. The walls and gates were too high to climb.

He thought for a moment, "Maybe I could just break through the side a Lightning Bolt. No, that'll be too loud. Think. Aha!"

Ranir backed up. He channeled his Lightning Element. Using his surging speed and lightning strength, he ran and jumped. He had never tried this before and had no way of judging his distance. He didn't want to undermine his attempt so he pushed off of the ground with full power. Not only did he clear the gate, he flew past the first three rows of houses and smashed through a wall of a small shack.

"So much for silent surprise," he thought. Standing up he felt a sharp pain in his side. Upon examining himself in the dark, he discovered a piece of wood sticking out of his rib. Wincing, he gave it a quick pull and fell onto one knee. The pain was strong. He charges up his hand like he learned to do months ago, creating static lightning in his hand. "Satik Akar," He said. Running it over the wound, he healed himself. He immediately felt the draw on his energy.

He slid his sleeve up, and pulled static mana from his bracer. From outside the shack he could hear chanting from a crowd of people. He peaked out from the hole his body made in the wall but he couldn't see anything besides silhouettes of houses and occasional moonlight peaking behind clouds. He needed to move.

Clambering out of the small shack, he made his around a few houses and down an alley. He was moving toward the sound of people. His hands were near numb running along the building as a guide. Between the shadows of the houses was pitch black.

Just as he was about to step out in the street, a group of Forsaken passed him and he leaped back into the shade. They were human but different. Their skin was wilted and yellowish. Many of them walked with a limp and had flesh peeled back to bone. Some of them were missing arms. One small Forsaken was missing his entire bottom jaw. It made Ranir sick to look at them. They seemed fairly harmless but Ranir remembered Sora telling him of the Forsaken that crept into Killiad and killed several people. This group was every bit of a hundred strong. It seemed like they were patrolling the city, looking for signs of life.

In his peripheral, Ranir noticed a flash of purple light around a building. He darted back the way he came to avoid the horde. He began hearing a pulsating noise across the air. The cadence of the chanting matched the tempo of the ambient pulse.

He followed the sound as it led him to the Town Hall. This was the very place Sora had brought them. It seemed like so long ago now. The stained glass windows were vibrant as they filtered the bright light. Ranir gave a hard look around the entrance, then to the road. There was no sign of The Forsaken. He ceased the opportunity to run to the door.

Squeezing through the doorway, Ranir was met with another wave of cold that made him shutter. From upstairs somewhere he could hear the chanting continuing from a single voice. Ranir made his way up the flight of stairs. The purple light was creeping out from the bottom of a door at the end of the corridor. Ranir crouched and drew his daggers.

Moving as quietly as possible, he made his way

to the dark magic. Just as he was about to reach for the door knob, the door swung open and deep purple energy ripped the daggers from his hands. He couldn't see where the spell came from, but he could feel the energy of someone powerful. The power felt like negative energy, as if it were sapping him.

Ranir took a step backwards and braced his foot against the hallway wall, channeling the elemental power inside of him. Without a pause he launched into the room performing a front flip, and threw two lightning bolts in random directions. They made contact with nothing but the walls.

As he rolled to his feet, Ranir saw The Necromancer in the strobing light. He was clad in black and purple. A mask was sitting upon his face. It reminded Ranir of a picture of a demon from Hel. The eyes were sunken and blacked out, set behind sharp cheek bones.

Relying on instinct Ranir threw out chain lightning hoping to bound him like the Druid that he executed. Even as fast as lightning was, The Necromancer caught the chain of energy, like it was a thin rope. Wrapping it around his hand, he jerked Ranir across the room.

Before Ranir could think, the dark sorcerer planted a foot in his chest. The shear power of his physicality surprised Ranir as he flew across the room smashing through the room's wall, hitting the second wall in the hallway. He could hear the bricks break behind his back. As he stood up to recharge his attack a purple shadow bolt slammed him in the same spot as The Necromancer's foot, knocking Ranir through the load bearing wall.

Ranir was sent tumbling outside in an alley,

landing on a small rooftop on his stomach, cracking the clay tile. He could instantly taste the hot iron flavor of blood in his mouth. His vision was even more impaired as it became fuzzy from the damage he incurred. He laid still for a moment too long. He heard the sound of bricks breaking. Rolling over in his back he saw the Necromancer leap from the hole in the wall. He landed perfectly on Ranir's stomach, finishing the breaking of the rooftop. Ranir hit the ground with a thud, losing his breath. The sorcerer picked him up with one hand by his robe.

Ranir knew that his rip was broke because it was almost unbearable to take a breath. He felt his feet hovering. The dark caster held him in the air with one arm.

Behind the mask a voice called out, "It has come to my attention that you," he said looking up and down Ranir's near limp body, "are The Lightning Rod." He chuckled. His voice was menacingly scratchy and muffled behind the mask. "As in the savior of Gnariam?" He pulled Ranir's face to his mask, "Color me unimpressed." He ripped Ranir sideways, slamming him against the wall across the alley. Ranir landed on his side, further gushing pain through his rib.

Ranir felt himself fainting. His sight was pulsing between black and The Necromancer walking towards him. He watched as the evil man kneeled before him and said, "I'm not going to take your power just yet. You aren't strong enough for what I need." With that he planted a boot in Ranir's face, knocking him out.

Chapter 14: Transmutation

"Are you ready to try again?" asked the witch doctor. She wore the same white robe and pointed white shoes that she did every day. Ranir laid in the infirmary wing bed, burdened by the unhealing mark on his chest. At first glance, it looked like the inside of a plum. Discoloration around the mark left it graphically like a disease.

"Its pointless, nothing you have done for the last two weeks has worked! Why do you want to keep trying?" screamed Ranir. He was overly frustrated by his bed rest. A dark shadow was growing on Ranir's face as he hadn't been shaving since his defeat by the hands of an evil sorcerer.

The last two weeks had shown him that even through the hands of over a dozen healing mages and six witch doctors, the shadow bolt that the Necromancer casted on him cursed him. As if it were not meant to heal. As far as Ranir knew, Taryn was still missing which worried him and made matters worse.

The witch doctor stormed out of the large room. The infirmary was one of the most open rooms in the Emphyrius. Ranir was brought here by Sora. After defeating The Lightning Rod, the sorcerer had left Killiad, taking his army of undead with him. Sora had managed to escape with hundreds of citizens.

She saved many. Sora is the one who found Ranir in the alley unconscious and healed his broken rib. He remained in that state as the cross the entire desert. He woke up in this very bed to which he was now confined. He had only one visit from The

Emphyre who was mostly just disappointed in Ranir for not stopping the Necromancer. Sora visited a couple times to check on him. She was mostly busy rebuilding many parts of her city.

On her way out, the witch doctor ran into Ramshi. Ranir's old trainer had come to see his apprentice.

"Ranir, I am so sorry what you went through. I would have came sooner but it seems I was kept on a tight rope and informed that you had set out to track your first bounty."

Ranir was starting to get the feeling that not everything was as it seemed in The Emphyrius and more strings were being pulled behind the curtain than he ever knew. He didn't like being lied to or kept in the dark about choices and information. "It's okay, Ramshi. I know exactly how that is," replied Ranir.

"I have something to offer, a tidbit of knowledge for my once disciple," Ramshi began. Ranir was intrigued. He hadn't been given his books to study since being sent here. "Something that may be of use to you since your here."

"Please tell me you know how to heal this," said Ranir as he pulled his blanket down to reveal the cursed mark. Ramshi winced at the sight of it.

"Actually yes," he drew out Ranir's static mana stones from his pocket.

"Ramshi, I don't think I can do magic even with those."

"Just try it out. Humor me. Remember that I am always a student of magic!" Ramshi handed the stones

158

to Ranir.

Without even siphoning the static lightning, he instantly felt rejuvenated by touching them alone. "Now, I feel better, but it still hurts so damn bad. What is it?"

"Its the mark of your body resisting a shadow bolt mark. Usually, that is a kill curse and takes quite the power to do it. Was there a group of Forsaken and a totem in Killiad?" asked the teacher.

"There was a whole horde of Forsaken and I didn't see any totem. Why?"

"Well, that is what Necromancers need to perform a death curse like this. Seems while you think you can't do magic, that Lightning Elemental is keeping you alive, Ranir!"

"So what do I do with these now?" he held out the stones. They began to cool down as he felt the power drain from them.
"Heal yourself, Ranir," said Ramshi. He crossed his arms, reaching with one hand to tug on his beard.

"Ramshi, I-" Ranir was interrupted.

"Just do it! Try!" yelled Ramshi. Ranir had never heard this form of desperation in his teacher before.

"Okay, okay just relax and watch. Nothing!" Ranir focused like usual, finding the Elemental within and charging it to come forth. "*Satik Akar*," he called quietly. His hands lit up with a vibrant blue color and small arcs of lightning. Ranir sat up against the pain in his chest. He slammed both hands against the mark.

159

Right away Ranir felt the dissipating of the cursed mark on his chest. It felt like a massive weight was lifted from him and he felt his energy surge throughout his entire body.

"Ah there you are, my boy!" cried out Ramshi. Ranir felt like he was ready to sit up when a sharp pain stabbed in his chest. He screamed out, rolling over to his side. It felt like his sternum was cracking. Suffocation set in as he couldn't breath and his body began thrashing in shock.

"Help!" Ramshi screamed as he grasped Ranir's body to steady him. The witch doctor bursted into the room.

"What happened?" she asked sharply.

"I- I don't know. He tried to heal himself."

Suddenly Ranir was still and the pain subsided. He heavily breathing as he ripped the blanket back to look at the mark. It was gone! He wiped away the tears streaming down his cheeks. "One last reminder that he beat me," he said dryly. He let his head sink back into the pillow.

"When you are ready to train for that evil bastard, let me know," said Ramshi. He gathered the static stones.

"Thank you, Ramshi." In that moment Ranir realized that his teacher actually cared about him. He decided that, from now on, he trusted his knowledge and instincts to the fullest now.

Ranir laid in bed for several hours. Thoughts of the Necromancer passed through his mind several times. He thought of how fast and calculated his techniques were. He wonder where he learned to fight with such skill. He thought of where Taryn might be and why no mage had tracked him down yet. He wondered the real motivations of The Emphyre's decisions. He thought of how he would begin training to fight the Necromancer. He knew that he needed to start being more careful with decisions and let go of emotional tugs of interest. If he was going to be anyone's savior, he would need to be smarter. He needed to get his texts and find more texts on Necromancy. There had to be a weakness for the sorcerer.

Ranir waited until the monitors were gone, and slipped out of the infirmary. His plan was to reach his room without notice. When he stepped out of the large room he realized that he had never been to the west side of The Emphyrius. He didn't know which direction to go. He looked down the left corridor, then to the right. He randomizes his choice and darted to the right. The long hallway was dark. Ranir discovered that he hadn't been aware of the time of day. He assumed it was around midday but he hadn't calculated the extra hours he spent laid down thinking. This particular hall was lacking the normal torches that lined nearly every corridor of The Emphyrius.

Summoning a small amount of power to his palm, he made a single arc of lightning, casting a flash of blue light into the darkness. For an instance he could see small tables and shadows of unknown objects. It was ominously quiet. Ranir figures it was because everyone was probably asleep or at the least, in their rooms.

For several minutes he continued blasting light as he made his way out of the long hallway. For a moment he thought it was an endless aisle. Finally he spotted some dim light creeping around a corner.

Before he reached it, Ranir saw the shadows of two people. He could hear slight whispers.

"Why would anyone be down here in the dark whispering," thought Ranir. He crouched low, sneaking along to get a better eavesdrop. Running hands along the wall, he got within steps of the couple conversing.

"Yes well he failed. And now, that monster is lose and chasing havoc who knows where?" said the first voice he could understand. Her voice sounded very familiar to Ranir.

"You know the plan, and that sorcerer is just a pawn. Keep your head down and your mouth shut. While you're at it, keep your damn thoughts to yourself," whispered the second voice, a man.

"You mark my words, we are the pawns and are going the ones at the receiving end of the sorcerer," replied the first voice. She sounded paranoid and angry. Ranir wondered who they were talking about.

Abruptly, the couple walked away without another word. After peaking around the corner, Ranir noticed a spiral staircase that he knew all too well. It was the library! From there he had memorized the main route and other routes back to his room. He was curious as to whom he would find awaiting him. It was several minutes later when he finally reached his room. He began to recognize the fatigue setting in. He was exhausted from lack of sleep.

Ranir was slightly surprised that his room was exactly as he had left it. It looked like not a single person even stepped foot inside. The quills were still scattered about and the ink had dried, staining the hard wood floor. He began to pick up the mess that he made in his haste.

He was still momentarily lost in thought as he tidied up his room. The memory was so vivid of The Necromancer and the attack that landed him in the infirmary. What stunned Ranir the most about the scuffle is that he didn't land a single spell or punch on the dark sorcerer. *"How could he be so fast and skilled?"* he thought.

For whatever reason the Shadow magic wielding Necromancer was able to defeat him without breaking a sweat, Ranir knew that he had to change his training. He was being forced to use his creativity to maximize his skill. How could he, though? There wasn't a single mage within The Emphyrius that could beat him. Nor was there an arms combatant who was better with fist or sword. He decided he would sleep on it and talk to Ramshi first thing in the morning. He lay down and instantly drifted to another place in his mind.

Unlike most nights, his dreams this time were pleasant and filled with memories of Marnos and Selendt running after him when they were small children. This dream gave him joy to bathe in. Such a time was simpler and innocent. Of course, magic swept in and just like the thunder storm it rode in on, his world was flipped upside down and spiraled into chaos.

His mind raced all through the night of joyful memories and love. Happiness filled his bitter heart. He wishes that he could go back in time and choose not to follow that vräel to the Veörn Mountains. Such a thing wasn't possible.

He woke the next morning rather late. The sun had been in the sky for hours and the room was baking hot already. The late summer was even hotter than midsummer. The air was dry and missing it's usual breeze. Ranir sat up and yawned. Stretching his arms up in the air, his back cracked like an elder.

He felt as if he need not be in a hurry this day. He decided that while he would push to become faster and stronger, to strive to defeat the Necromancer, rushing it would only burden his progress. He walked over to his full bodied mirror and noticed that his build was much sturdier than when he left Heramor. His muscles were bigger and more refined. A fuzzy beard clanged to his cheeks. Normally he would have cut his hair and shaved off the stubbles. On this day, he chose to let it go. His brown hair was shaggy and flowing over his ears. His golden eyes were steady as ever, though.

After getting dressed, he made his way down to the dining hall to eat. It seemed like a long time had passed since his last good meal. As he made his way into the vast room, he could feel eyes upon him from every direction. He decided to take his food with him to the library and begin his studies.

Hours passed in the Great Library as Ranir read page after page of information and history texts of Necromancer's in the past, dating all the way back to the first, King Veörn. He planned to put the book down just when he read the line that he had been looking for.

"...and so King Veörn had grown the mountainous throne, so that he may sit and monitor his Forsaken disciples, from whom he drew his power to balance the Shadow Magic."

Ranir dropped the book on his lap. Finally he had leverage and knowledge. "I have to find a way to separate him from his Forsaken," he said.

He slammed the book shut and ran out of the room. He made a straight path to the small office of the magical information keeper, his trainer Ramshi. Bursting the door he yelled, "I know how to beat him in the end!" He didn't peak inside the room as he should have. The Emphyre was sitting in a chair in a corner.

Standing up, he put his hands behind his back. "So good to see you up and healed, Ranir." His voice was always so serpent like, smooth and haunted at the same time. "What's this now?"

Ranir looked over to Ramshi for permission to speak a new secret. With a nod from his mentor, he proceeded. "I have to find a way to get him away from his risen army. That is where he is drawing his power from. He is very powerful, but he needs that darkness to sustain his attacks." He wasn't certain that he wanted The Emphyre to know this. Something ate at the back of Ranir's mind about Credin. He couldn't quite figure out why, but he felt like The Lord of Sythestine was hiding his own agenda.

"Very good theory, Ranir. That actually makes sense. When I was simply the Lord of Thrast before uniting the cities under one kingdom, I had a plan to stop him before. I sent mages to cut him off in the small village of Gornine. He was boxed in. I sent mages to surround the entire town and destroy all of his horde of Forsaken." The Emphyre began walking around the room, waving his hands as he talked. It seemed like he was recalling the story in his mind as he spoke, "Once they trapped him in the center of town, he was fairly easy to defeat at that point. He would've been imprisoned too if not for a water mage that helped him escape, killing a few of the mages under my command."

Ranir agreed with The Emphyre's disgusted hate for The Necromancer. His testament gave hope to

Ranir's plan as he set to destroy the Forsaken first now. He needed to weaken the dark sorcerer if he was going to defeat him in battle.

"Ramshi, are you ready to help me?" Ranir asked.

"Of course!" said The Old teacher as he jumped up.

"Emphyre Credin, May I borrow some of your best mages?" he asked. He wasn't sure if he would allow it. He also didn't want to inform anyone of his plans right away.

"If it will help you achieve a victory, absolutely!" Credin seemed joyous that Ranir was pushing himself to defeat a threat of the world.

"Ramshi, I'll be in the mage court. Gather your top ten weapon combatants and meet me there please," requested Ranir. As he was exiting the office, he turned slightly and saw The Emphyre whispering something to Ramshi, further driving Ranir's paranoia.

Ranir made his way back to his room. He grabbed a large satchel from under his bed. He began grabbing various weapons and items that he thought could help. A few important pieces included his daggers. He realized that the static stones were still inset. He picked them up for a moment. "Ramshi must've made another pair."

He rushed to the mages and warriors that were supposed to be waiting for him. Turning one corner to sharp, he lost his footing and slammed into a wall. He quickly pick himself and made it to the courtyard.

Awaiting patiently was a large group of mages and warriors. The Emphyre was sitting beside Ramshi with his bare arms crossed. He was dressed like the other warriors in mail armor. A pair of swords were laid across his back and a pair of daggers clung to his hips.

Ranir walked over to him hastily. "Are you training with us," he asked The Emphyre. His tone was inherently doubtful.

Credin The Emphyre rose to his feet. "I'll have you know, before politics I was the best warrior in Thrast. I've never tasted defeat. "

"Good, I'm going to need all the help and practice I can get," Ranir said as he turned to the others. "Thank you all for coming. How many mages do we have?"

"There's 14 of us," a short air mage piped up.

"Good. I need two of you to go track Taryn down. He's been missing and honestly I don't why you aren't looking for him." He felt his temper straining but he decided to brush it away.

"Jairt and Florn, do as The Lightning Rod asks," called out The Emphyre in the back.

Ranir recognized that he was stepping into a commanding position. "Okay, here is what I have planned. I want you all to attack me. If I can't beat you, then I'll heal up and we will reset. You see, The Necromancer is highly skilled and highly powerful. Even with my power and speed, I couldn't touch him."

"You want all of us to attack you at once?" asked one of the warriors.

Ranir nodded slowly, determining if he was making the right choice. "Yes, but I want you all to train as well as a team. This fight is not going to be one on one. He has an army of Forsaken that I will need help with. From what I hear they are resistant to most magic."

"As mages how are we supposed to fight them then?" someone asked from the group of robed mages.

"I have an idea and it's going to take all of us together. This may take days, so if you want to sit out, you may leave." Nobody moved. He was excited that the entire group was ready for a battle. "Very good. Now, mages I want you to teleport the warriors back and forth around me so that they can get in closer. I have these," he said as he pulled out the mana stones. "We'll figure it out as we go. Okay, give me your best!"

Again nobody moved. "Now!" screamed Ranir, channeling his lightning into his eyes for show of force. The group flinched for a moment, then let loose the full force of magic and blades.

Ranir wasn't nearly as ready as he thought, just as he was over confident going against the Necromancer.

A bold blast of wind slammed him in the chest forcing him to backpedal, tripping over the leg of a warrior. As he hit the ground another wave of fire blast pelted him in the side, sliding him across the ground. He leaped to his feet with lightning speed. No longer than it took him to gain his balance, another water spell smashed him in the legs. He would have been alright if not for the warrior who slashed him across the back with a long sword.

Ranir felt like ultimate defeat was repeating itself. He yelled out, "stop!" Rising to his feet, he reached his hand underneath his opposite arm and healed himself, taking more mana from the stone to do so. He needed to reset the pieces and players of his new game. This game in particular was a long game, and it was inevitable that he was going to suffer physically to get better at the endgame.

"Again!" cried out Ranir. This time he started with offense, casting a lightning bolt at the first warrior who ported behind him. Secondly, he thrusted a chain lightning at one mage, pulling him towards the center of the combatants in an effort to use him as a shield. It worked well, surprisingly.

Suddenly another wave of spells buried him in an overwhelming force. He wasn't able to stop the powerful blasts of the large amount of mages, and was knocked to the ground again. He continued thinking of different teaching techniques that he could implement into his training. He realized very quickly that it was his defense that needed tending to, not his offense. If he were to attack them, given that they let him, he had no doubt that he could destroy the entire group with lightning alone. This was not the case, though. He now recognized that this would not be how the situation will go with the Necromancer either.

"Okay," he said rising to his feet. "I am going to try something different this time. Just do what you were doing and don't let up." He stretched his back and cracked his neck. *"Lets try this once,"* he thought.

Bracing his feet into the surface of the dirt, he casted a lightning shield around himself as a red fireball streamed towards his face. Once it reached about an arm's length away, the blazing sphere smashed against his shield. It was immediately followed by a huge gust from one of the air mages, knocking him sideways. This time Ranir used to force and lifted off of the ground with incredible balance. He spun midair and planted his feet once more, dragging foot marks in the soil. A sharp water dagger stabbed at his shield from behind just as another warrior was teleported to his left side. This was the exact buffer that he needed to buy him time and think.

As the warrior to his side bounced away from his shield, Ranir planted one foot behind his other, spinning, he swept his leg low as he traveled full circle, tripping the warrior. Before regaining his full height as he stood up he casted a lightning bolt at the air mage, knocking her to the ground. From the corner of his eye he saw two separate fire balls, varying in color slightly, casted directly at him. As they smashed against his shield, he felt the heat of them this time. Suddenly another water mage blasted him in the chest. *"The shield broke!"* he thought.

Ranir watched as more spells and warriors danced all around him. Moments passed by as he recasted his shield, fending off round after round of attacks. He almost thought it was fun even. He wanted to amplify his ability in defense, only casting offense sporadically. He had almost forgot that The Emphyre was geared up for training until he saw the double swords slashing at his shield from behind.

"Come on, Lightning Rod!" called out The Emphyre between deep breaths. "Fight back!"

Ranir ignored the taunts from him as he recounted his spells in his head. Without casting, he often thought which attacks could be used in between defensive coordination.

Suddenly The Emphyre broke through the shield. It must have been his full intention because in an instant, he sheathed both swords and grabbed Ranir's cloak. Like a leash, he was able to rip Ranir backwards. The Emphyre turned his back towards Ranir. Giving the cloak a harsh pull, their backs met. He ripped downward on the cloak, sending Ranir into a back flip, landing on his stomach in front of The Emphyre. "Ha! Didn't see that coming did you?" cheered Credin.

For the Emphyre, boasting was normal in political affairs. It did not belong on the battlefield. That was a lesson that he must have forgot. Having extraordinary strength gave Ranir the edge. He pushed off of the ground, raising directly to his feet. Cocking his hips sideways, he charged his hands with Static Shock. The Emphyre reached for his swords but he was too slow. Ranir planted both hands into the leader's chest, knocking him backwards several paces into a mage the was midcast. The Emphyre felt the full force of a water blast. It sent him soaring through the air, positioning his face in a small pool of muddy water.

The recitation repeated for the next two days in the same fashion. Ramshi would make sure that the static stones were fully charged each night so that everyone may heal up. At this point, it began to feel more like routine than a process of thoughts. Ranir became bored with defensive techniques. "You ready?" he yelled out over the eruptive sounds of magic and blades on the third morning. "It is my turn!"

He began blasting lightning and using his elemental magic in turns with defensive spells and moves. Suddenly he realized that he was swiftly taking out each of his practice targets one by one. As he was spinning under a sword he noticed nearly all of them on the ground. Within seconds, there was only one mage left standing in front of him. He was a tall fire mage. Both of his hands were surging with fire as he was ready to attack. Fear or something else caused him to hesitate. Ranir knew that hesitation was the enemy of surprise and a swift victory. He charged his own hand with lightning and bull rushed the man. The both casted at the same time. Between them, the lightning and fire were channeling into each other. Like a game of tug-o-war, the center was rolling between them. Ranir looked up at the fire mage who was barring his teeth and sweating profusely. He smiled because he knew that the fire mage was giving it his full force whereas he wasn't pushing very much. Suddenly like a game, Ranir gave more force, sending the mage flying through the air like a ball. He smashed through a small statue, sending pieces of clay in every direction.

Ranir realized something in that moment. He hadn't thought about the environment and how it could help in a fight. "Wait!" he cried out. "Line up please."

One by one each of the mages and warriors lined up, clenched different parts of their bodies. Ranir pulled the stones from his belt satchel and held them out. The last fire mage to attack stepped forward, taking the stones and began healing the rest of the group.

"I have a question for the mages," started Ranir. "Have you ever used non-living spells in combat before?"

They all stared blankly at him. Someone to his right spoke up, startling him. "I have," called the familiar voice. Ranir shot a look to his side and noticed that Sora had joined them in training. The Emphyre hadn't shown up this particular morning. If he had, Ranir was sure her visit would have been announced prior.

She walked over to Ranir and gave him a short bow, surprising everyone in the mass. She was the Lord of Killiad after all, so Ranir should have bowed first. This gave a new sense of power that Ranir carried and the importance his role would be in the inevitable battle. "What are you doing here?" asked Ranir softly.

"Well, it seems, helping you out," she said through laughter.

"You will be a very nice addition to the group!" Ranir was excited thinking that she had volunteered to join the fight.

"Oh, sorry. No, I won't be heading off into battle. Unless it comes to Killiad again. I've began gathering my own mages to fortify the city. I am worried it won't be enough, though. Oh and did I mention that I found Taryn?"

Ranir was not expect a bombshell like that. "What?" screamed Ranir. He was ready to call training off for the day and go see his friend, but he knew that too much was at stake. "Where is he?"

"He is in the infirmary. He'll recover soon, though," Sora replied.

"Why is he in the infirmary? What happened? Where was he? How did you find him?" Ranir began to get worked up, realizing that he still cared very much for the fire mage.

"For now I can tell you, he got separated from you in the teleportation. After you, well you know-"

"After I got my ass kicked you mean?" said Ranir shyly.

"-yes. After that, The Necromancer found Taryn and siphoned near all of his power. He left him alive to be a messenger," she finished.

"What message is that?" Ranir grew more concerned that The Necromancer could have killed Taryn. Instead he left him as another pawn in his game.

"He wants you, Ranir. He says that all the damage he does, is for you. He wants you to grow to your full range of power, so he can take it."

"Well, nothing new there. He told me that as well. That's why he let me live," said Ranir. The others in the group may not have known the full story of the first conflict Ranir had with The Necromancer because they started conversing among themselves.

"Well, then. He must be at some other plan. Anyway," she said, changing the subject, "I can help you with your question. The answer is yes, you can use nonliving spells as defense or offense in combat. For example, if you aim for the environment around someone, and you are controlling enough to give the spell direction, then you have yourself a new edge."

"Thank you very much for the advice, Sora."

"You are welcome, Lightning Bringer," said Sora. With that, she turned and headed back towards the keep.

That is the answer that Ranir had been looking for, more or less. He knew that it was now a viable choice if he needed it to be. For now, he decided it would be best if he let Taryn rest and recover. It was time to try something new.

"Alright, you heard her. Mages, you can all use

these nonliving spells. You have all been taught the Opening Spell, yes?" All the mages' heads were nodding through the hums of confirmation.

"So what? We just open the ground beneath you?" said the tall fire mage in the front.

"Sure, if that is how you would like to try it," said Ranir. He reset the battle training and began the attack. He knew that the Opening Spell would be of use. The spell he was more likely to test was Explosion Spell. As far as he was aware, he was the only one that could do this spell as it was Lightning Elemental.

"Lets do it," said the mage, starting an uproar of fighters.

Just as Ranir had expected, the first spell used against him was Opening Spell. The ground between his feet opened up like a book, revealing stone and root. Suddenly Ranir felt the old sting of power in his palms, his Lightning was acting on its own accord again. "Oh no," said Ranir as he braced for the unknown.

Without a warning, Ranir felt a surge of power. His eyes glowed white and arcs of blue lightning glided down his arms and legs, dancing back and forth across his fingers. He looked down to reveal his feet were hovering above the crack in the ground. Suddenly the spells and warriors stopped and backpedaled.

Ranir closed his eyes, demanding control over his power like he had done when he began training with Ramshi. He had a feeling of resistance against the ground. It was as if he was still touching the ground, but in the sense of floating in water. With his mind, he pushed forward and opened his eyes. He was able to move several steps forward without touching the ground. It was as if he was flying!

Ranir gathered full control of movement in this form. He allowed himself to touch back down to the ground. The warriors all began to talk among themselves and the mages simply gawked at him.

"I'm sorry, I didn't know that I could actually do that. I mean I've done it before by accident but not like that," Ranir explained.

The rush of excitement that took hold of the mages faded as they realized that they couldn't drop Ranir into the ground now. They still didn't know what Ranir could do back to them though. "Alright, lets begin again. Give me your full force."

He was hit with the unexpected again. Suddenly the mages all teleported with the warriors in a tight circle around him. He instantly put a shield up. He knew it wouldn't last with the amount of damage it was taking rather quickly. This was his moment. Without waiting too long, Ranir spotted his targets, the shields. Drawing on his energy from one of the mana stones in his pocket, he blasted, *"Estashashek!"*

The shields shattered in thousands of pieces around him. The spell worked better than he had planned. The concussion was large enough to knock everyone away from him. Most of them were pelted with shrapnel of flying metal and wood.

"Ranir!" one of the warriors called out angrily. "We're done. You can't go full power when we're training!"

Ranir stopped training for the day as he used all of the mana in the stones to heal everyone. One by one, he went around to the casualties and helped pull pieces of metal and wood splinters from their torsos and legs. For each new person injured, he gave them a deep apology. He hadn't meant to hurt all of them in that sense.

What worried him the most, and yet gave him the most hope, is that he did not use his full might for the spell. He knew in that moment that he was ready to fight The Necromancer again. His skill had increased, his arsenal of spells and techniques had grown and his reflexes were faster than ever before. His magic and elemental power would be enough to stop him this time.

He knew that he needed to wait for Taryn to heal before going to see him. He decided that it would be best to begin talking to mages that could, or even would, join him in tracking The Necromancer down. He didn't know where to begin. As far as he knew, a mage needed some item that belonged to the person being tracked. Nobody had an object like that. The Necromancer was too careful for something so trivial.

Ranir wanted to wait before his friend was healed all the way. He was going to need his help as well. For now, he would return to the library and begin his plan to accurately and efficiently execute a full assault on The Necromancer.

Chapter 15: Heritage

It didn't take near as long for Taryn to recover as Ranir had expected. The next day he back to full health. Ranir made his way back to infirmary. During the day, the corridors were brilliantly filled with color that bled through the stained glass windows. It seemed like an entirely path than he had taken in the darkness. Twice Ranir opened the wrong door, assuming he was confident in his memory.

After he finally reached the infirmary door, he stepped inside to find it empty with the exception of The witch doctor. Ranir bellowed our, "Where is Taryn Ontaga?"

He must have startled the woman in white because she nearly jumped off the floor. "He was dismissed already. He made a full recovery. In fact, I believe he went searching for," she said.

"Ah. Alright, well I guess I will try to find him then." Ranir turned and exiting to the left this time. He made a straight path to Taryn's quarters. Taryn stayed in a separate wing of The Emphyrius with the other fire mages. He wasn't sure they had segregated in such a manner. Perhaps it was because they had something in common.

Ranir realized that he hadn't went left from the infirmary before, and found himself turned around again. Every turn looked as foreign as the last.

It seemed like an hour had passed when he

finally fell head on into the dining hall. "How big is damn place?" he asked a man passing by. He laughed and shrugged his shoulders. Ranir thought it was amazing that he had been traveling in and around the keep for nearly half a year, and was still getting lost. It was a true testament to the design and the workers that built the place.

From the dining hall he knew which hallway to jog down. He finally reached Taryn's room and found him sitting in a chair, staring blankly out the window. "Taryn?" Ranir approached cautiously.

The fire mage leaped to his feet and rushed to Ranir. He grabbed him in a deep hug and squeezed. Laughter filled the room as two long lost friends were reunited. "Ranir! Am I glad to see you!" he yelled.

"Taryn what happened to you? Where have you been this whole time? Are you alright?" Ranir hammered away with questions.

Taryn pointed to the chairs and said, "Sit. I have much to tell you."

As they seated themselves, Taryn threw a fireball under a kettle in the fireplace. Ranir realized instantly that he didn't speak a word. "How did you do that? You didn't cast a spell!"

Taryn simply smiled. "Like I said, I have much to tell you. Where to start?"

"How about getting lost in the teleport," said Ranir sharply.

"Right, well when I came through the port, you were gone and I was lost for a minute. I figured out quickly that I was at the South Gate of Killiad. I tried to get in but it was sealed. Some sort of ward blocked me from burning a hole into the walls."

"I noticed. I jumped over the wall Nd crash landed," said Ranir amusingly.

Taryn raises an eyebrow, "Of course you did. Well, little fire mage like me, couldn't do that. I started working my way around the city and after a little while I heard what sounded like a building coming down. I've been filled in a little so I know what is was but moments later The Necromancer and his Forsaken showed up."

Ranir could almost feel what it would have been like standing in front the sorcerer again. "He's powerful, Taryn," Ranir said sadly.

Taryn nodded. "You're right about that. I couldn't hardly get a single spell off. Soon I was unconscious and woke up in the mountains. You remember that little shack at the summit?"

"Yes I do. That cold wave was all around The Necromancer as well."

"Well I learned the hard way that that was his place. And it is once again. He siphoned my mana and power so much I couldn't even get out of the chair. He knew it too. Untied me just to taunt me more.

Ranir was trying to imagine Taryn's dark recollection. It was horrifying. Now he thought the damage he took by the hands of the sorcerer seemed trivial compared to taunting torture.

"For days his Forsaken would come in and beat me nearly to death. Then that sick bastard would heal me so they could repeat," continued Taryn. "I counted

11 days that this went by."

"I'm going to look into why no mage tracked you down, Taryn. I'm so sorry you had to endure that."

Taryn chuckled. "That's kind of you, Ranir. Unfortunately the necro put an anti tracking runelace around my neck. They most likely did look for me and failed."

Ranir sat quietly for a moment. He realized that some of his paranoia might have been misplaced. This relieved some stress yet added more fear. "What did he say to you?"

Taryn rose to his feet and moved to his bed. Ranir didn't see what he was pulling from a satchel until Taryn returned to his seat. He was holding a small book. It was bound in leather and had symbols that Ranir hadn't seen before. "He only spoke to me once. Just before he let me go."

"Ranir was dumbstruck "He let you go? He let me go as well. What game is he playing?"

Sighing Taryn replied, "The long one it appears. Anyway he filled me with a huge amount of and gave me a choice. Fight him or return and give you this book," he explained as he passed the ancient looking book to Ranir.

Ranir opened it and was unsure of the symbols he was looking at. "What is all this?"

"He said to...look with your eyes of thunder. I'm not what he meant by it," said Taryn. Ranir thought for a minute.

"Maybe I know what he meant," started Ranir.

He searched within his mind and soul. Summoning The Lightning Elemental power, his eyes glowed with a bright white. He could feel tiny arcs of lightning passing through his pupils. Suddenly, looking at the book, the symbol changed. Rather, Ranir was able to read them now. The cover read:

'Memoirs of The Thunder King'

As Ranir flipped through the pages, most of the symbols shifted into letters, some into pictures. "Taryn, do you know what this is? It's a journal." Taryn rises his eyebrows as he shook his head. "Of the first Lightning Rod. Or Thunder King is what he was called I guess. That is what the earth mage in the mountains called me! Do you think they serve The Necromancer?"

"I don't think so. They serve Gnariam. That's it. Well, what, what does it say?"

Ranir flipped to a random page. "It has spells and techniques. It's all Lightning Elemental Language!" He was beyond excited to test these spells and read this journal. It could be his key to mastering his powers, fully. He knew that he would have time so he shifted his focus back to Taryn. "Speaking of power, how can you summon fire now. I thought that is extremely rare."

"Well, as embarrassing as it is, I died." He was sharp with these words.

"What?!" shouted Ranir.

"It's embarrassing because I acted like a child. I had so much more mana and power than ever before. I don't know how he gave it to me, but it was dark magic. I left the mountain and wanted to get far enough

182

away on foot so he wouldn't track me through the teleportation spell and break through our wards." Taryn got up and began pacing, waving his arms about. "So I was about to Killiad and I started testing spells, just in the air, you know. Seeing what I could do. I began to feel pull to get more power and I knew that was trick of The Necromancer. So I burned spells as much as I could into the sky, trying to rid myself of the magic lust. I pushed too hard and my magic consumed me. It was a price I was willing to pay." Ranir sat quietly and listened carefully. "But then, I was...standing in front of The Firelord. He gave me my power back, plus more! He understood my struggle with magic and knew that I would rather die than join the darkness. He also had a message for you."

"For me? Why would The God of Fire have a message for me?" asked Ranir.

"Simple really. He said that you are The Bringer Of Lightning and, as so, you are responsible for the balance of power in Gnariam. It was pretty vague." Ranir wondered if it meant he was supposed to defeat The Necromancer, or all dark magic. If felt like a heavy burden. As each new conflict rose, he felt more and more compelled to help.

"Sounds like I'm supposed to do more than be a rare elemental," said Ranir.

"Well you'll have to read that book I suppose. Maybe that is where you'll find the answer you've been seeking all along," exclaimed Taryn. "I'm here now, and I'll be here for the fight. You're going to need all the help you can get."

"Thank you, Taryn. It'll be good to have you by my side when we go to fight him again. Plus now you're, well what are you now? Super-mage?" said

Ranir jokingly.

Taryn laughed boastfully, "the term is Archemage, thank you very much." He bowed sarcastically. Ranir chuckled and stood up, rubbing the engravings on his book.

"Well I'm going to go back to my room and read. Maybe I'll learn how this magic stuff works," blurted Ranir.

"Tomorrow I'll be in the courtyard for training," said Taryn.
Ranir was excited to have Taryn to train with, not only because they were friends, but now that Taryn was more powerful, it would be more challenging yet.

Ranir scurried back to his room. He tossed the book on his bed and grabbed his ink and quill. He glanced out the window and saw that it was past midday. He knew that he would have several hours to read and learn. He cracked the old book open slowly.

'If you are reading this, then you are The Thunder King for only your eyes can see the truth. The contents of this script are my personal findings and adjustments to the path of magic.'

"Whoa, he wrote this for the next Lightning Rod," Ranir said. "Thunder King...hmm, that's different. I like it. Sounds like he was a bit more powerful."

As Ranir continued to turn page after page, he learned that the first Lightning Rod was the ruler of mages for centuries. He maintained order all across Gnariam. He began to understand different ways to channel his power. Every once in a while he would attempt a new spell. Something that was still not fully controlled was his level of power in each spell. Sometimes the spell was too weak and wouldn't work. Other times it was overpowered. In attempting to use a spell called Temporal Shift, a spell that was supposed to create a floating lightning orb that he could move through Elemental power, he made it to massive and smashed one of his small tables.

Ranir spent all night learning new spells and techniques. The hard part was going to be memorizing all of his spells. He scratched his head, "how do mages keep all of those spells in their head?"He thought it best to keep the book with him and practice when he could. He wanted to read more of a section referring to heritage.

Heritage

By all accounts if you are The Thunder King, then we are connected. Our heritage goes back to the first God Eros, Ruler of The Skies, Lord of Lightning and Thunder. He first created his children:

Baryt, The FireLord

Seli, The Queen Of Water

Pados, The Conjuror Of Earth

Haithis, Master of Winds

After his 4 children were created from his power of lightning, they ruled the elements of Gnariam. As they began selecting their own champions of magic in humans, darkness was born out of the nature of man. Shadow Magic was born of the consequences of the Gods. It was created as a balance of power by Gnariam itself. To counter the overrunning dark magic, Lord Eros Crete's his own champion, The

Thunder King, The Caller of Storms, The Lightning Rod, The Bringer of Lightning. Many names have been thrown out in my time. The purpose of this gift is to maintain balance. For good or for bad , balance must remain. My time is nearing. I can feel it. I've been maintaining balance for nearly 400 years. It is now your time. Protect the innocent, and keep the balance.

It was all nearly too much for Ranir to take in. He hadn't realized so much. He wondered if anyone else knew the lineage of the gods. He wondered what it would take to keep the balance of the world. He couldn't even teleport across a room, let alone places he's never been. How could The Thunder King live so long? Ranir thought it sounded optimistic that he could live for so long. He had so much to take in. There was a level of responsibility that was now his. Why didn't the Lord If Thunder Eros tell him this himself. Maybe he was out of time? That didn't seem like it would be an issue. He decided to sleep on it.

The next morning was humid and the sun was driving down harshly. Ranir found his usual group of mages and warriors waiting for him. He had partially feared that they would have left him alone for training to rough and injuring many of them. Ranir found them in a strange triangular formation with Taryn at the point.

As he was approaching he didn't have time for his normal greetings, Taryn screamed out, "Now!" At once they attacked. Instantly Ranir threw a shield around him and braces for impact. Five warriors were ported around him in a star formation and started hammering his shield. The mages split around him and began casting spells back to back. The tip of the attack was Taryn with his newfound power, rushing a spear of fire into the shield. Within seconds the shield busted, Ranir was cut three times by swords and slammed with

186

elemental spells repetitively. Taryn's flame smashed
against Ranir, knocking him fifty paces away. He
landed with a loud crash into the ground, dragging a
deep mark into the ground. His air was locked from his
chest.

He thought this must be a lesson for him
hurting them last session. It was deserved. It was also
fun and exciting in a twisted way. He thought for a
moment that they would pause but he heard Taryn yell
out, "Get up! Full force go again!"

While he was still on his back he watched as
more warriors rushed him and the mages teleport
around him. A full force attack now would land him in
the infirmary. Immediately he kept to his feet with
lightning speed and casted Temporal Shift, purposely
making the orb of lightning massive in between the
circle of mages.

"*Zhinik Alok!*" he cried out as he spun around
to direct the spell. The orb formed perfectly in the
middle of the mages and blasted outwards, sending the
magic users flying backwards several paces. They all
landed on their backs. Ranir sounds around to meet the
face of 5 shields. They slammed him and circled
around, jabbing with their swords. He casted a shield
around him. Channeling his elemental power, his feet
rose from the ground and he casted open spells on their
sword handles. The men all backed up with no
offensive weapons.

He could see the regret in their eyes. He casted
chain lightning and hooked the whole group together.
Giving a hard pull he threw all of the warriors in the
air. They crashed to the ground with groans and sounds
of metal clanging together.

From behind him, Ranir heard the war cry of

more warriors. He spun around to find them with their swords raised in the air. Ranir smiled. Just as he was about to smite them down, Taryn leaped up from behind them. He was using his fire elemental power to push himself off the ground. He rose up twenty feet in the air, blowing hot air everywhere. Suddenly he let go of the fire. As he was falling, he pulled back both hands to his right side and blasted a deep red wave of fire.

Ranir held his shield steady and tried to mimic a wave with lightning. It worked fantastically, blasting blue and yellow lightning in a wide wave that reminded Ranir of water. Taryn was sent flying backwards into the shielded warriors. Suddenly it was quiet. It was the best training session for the entire group. He had no doubt that Taryn coordinated it.

After everyone was healed up and resting, Ranir said, "I just want to say that I am happy to have all of you here to help me train. I know it's been rough but I hope you got more training out of as well. This fight..." he sighed. "this battle is serious and is going to have a lot of casualties if Seldos The Necromancer has anything to do with it. This is a fight we can't afford to lose, else we lose the world. I need everyone on this."

"Especially," Taryn chimed in, "since were receiving word that he his hitting the towns around the lake with the force of over a thousand Forsaken now. He is killing without mercy to build himself an army."

Ranir, again, had not been told the whereabouts of The Necromancer. This time, he knew why, though. "I think we are ready," he said. Taryn nodded in agreement. To Ranir it was still baffling how much more powerful Taryn was.

The group was dismissed and returning to the

keep when Ranir halted Taryn. "I need your help."

"With what?"

"Teleporting. Or more like traveling. I discovered something in that book. Many things actually but one in particular, talked about traveling through lightning. I'm assuming that's like teleporting right?"

"Maybe," said Taryn. "Teleportation is a spell usually. Several things about your power is different though, Ranir. I'm not sure that I can help you really. For now, we need to start preparing for the retaliation. There are enough mages here to teleport you."

"You are right, I just wish that they didn't have to use so much power in order to teleport me. I know it takes a lot and we're going to need all the energy once we get there," replied Ranir.

"That is something I've been thinking about actually, now that you mention it. You have those static stones and then the Stärnets, right?" asked Taryn.

"Yes but very few, why?" Ranir was trying to understand where Taryn was coming from.

"Well, if we could have more of them made, since you can use elemental magic, you could power the stones, and some of us mages can absorb some energy from the forest for the Stärnets." Taryn was onto a great idea. It would give them the power they needed to perform large scale spells and attack without burning down the mages.

"Ah, I see," said Ranir, "that is a very good idea indeed. I can ask Ramshi where he got the stones or how he made them or whatever."

"Good, I'll gather some mages tonight after dinner, and we'll head to the forest," said Taryn.

"Sounds good, meet back here first thing in the morning, then?" Ranir was welcoming to new ideas, especially from one so adept in combat and strategy as Taryn. They had at least the first part of the plan. Tomorrow is a new a day, and the first of many to come on the assault.

If Ranir was meant to be the balance, than the evil Necromancer, known as Seldos, was going to be his first task, and his test. He was about to lead a small army to attack an almost omnipotent evil sorcerer seemingly Helbent on conquering Gnariam. Ranir chuckled on his way back to The Emphyrius, thinking how he would've reacted to all of this information had he been told six months ago, when he was a simple farmer and gatherer. So much had changed that it felt like a distant memory now. Presently, he had bigger things to plan and focus on.

Chapter 16: The Harbinger

The day was upon them. There was an ominous aura about the group. Ranir and Taryn had managed to gather many more for their battle. Total, they now had 37 mages and 232 warriors, including several of the high wall archers. They all gathered in the dining hall to cover the plan. The Emphyre stood before the group as did Ranir and Taryn. "Taryn, let us begin shall we?" said The Emphyre.

"Thank you all for coming and joining us in this fight. This is no ordinary battle as I'm sure all of you know by now, this is Seldos The Necromancer." he paused as the room hummed with whispers. Putting his hand up to halt the chatter, he continued. "That filthy sorcerer has prepared an army of his own. We're being told its over a thousand Forsaken from our scouts across the mountains."

"Thousand? How are we going to stop that?" one man cried out from the back.

"Yeah aren't they pretty much immune to normal fatality?" another spoke up.

"I know that seems like a huge number, but bare with me here. Forsaken are dead already. But if you can manage to damage them like a living body, they will cease. I helped track Seldos down a decade ago and killed several of The Forsaken myself." The room was silent again.

"We have prepared some mana stones for the mages so that they may use a larger scale attack without fatiguing," said Ranir.

"And what about us non magic folks?" another warrior chimed in.

"The stones will help the mages keep you alive longer than any miracle could. Let them take the front. We're expecting the Forsaken to travel in one vast army like a shield for that coward. Mages can scatter them and everyone using a sword or shield can pick them off one by one. Ranir will take the front of the fight to Seldos himself. If he manages to take out The Necromancer, The Forsaken will return to death." Taryn seemed like he had prepared his speech. He was meant to be a leader and Ranir admired that.

The Emphyre stepped forward, "If Ranir should fail, all is not lost. Killing The Forsaken will weaken Seldos. If he is weak, his dark magic will be weak and we can still get to him." his words were reassuring to those fearing losing the battle in vain.

"Exactly, I'm not the only hope Sythestine has. But if we do fail, and he manages to get stronger, he will conquer, not just Sythestine, but all of Gnariam. I believe that the good will always triumph over evil. He is powerful, but he is still a man. He still bleeds and he can still die! The smallest glimmer of light will always cut through the darkest of nights, so lets show that Necromancer who we are!" said Ranir. His last words clung in the air with an echo.

The room was still silent. Suddenly they all started looking at each other with approval and nodding. After a moment of short whispers the room erupted in applause. Ranir felt his face flush and looked over at Taryn and The Emphyre. They were both clapping their hands with a smile on their face. Ranir couldn't help but smile from the speech he didn't know he could say.

After a few moments of ovation, Ranir waved his hand to the army before him. The noise slowly died down. "So, we have a scout with us from Alagien. If all the mages would gather around him, I'm told that he can guide you all where to teleport, correct?" The scout nodded his head. He was an air mage that had been scouting for The Emphyre since before Credin was The Emphyre. If there was anyone that could guide them, it would be him.

Taryn walked over and joined the mages. The Emphyre looked at Ranir and said, "Are you ready for this? Don't let what happened last time cause you to hesitate. You see him, you give him all you got."

"I won't hesitate, it's my responsibility to stop him and this time I'm not alone," replied Ranir.

For several minutes the small militia gathered various supplies and weapons. Ranir distributed the Stärnets to the mages. They all huddled together and the chants of the mages began. Suddenly a massive circle of shifting colors formed beneath the group. Ranir always disliked the feeling of teleportation. It seemed like your body was getting pulled in every direction as you passed through it.

Ranir came through the portal to find bitter cold darkness. He opened his eyes wider to adjust them to the lack of light. Suddenly he realized he was in a room. He should've teleported outside of the village. He spun around to ask a question only to discover he was alone. It was so silent that Ranir could hear his heart beating inside his ears. He focused on any noise he could find. Suddenly he heard slow breathing in the shadows. Aiming for direction of the small sound he blasted two lightning bolts straight forward. His heart twitched. The blue light from his lightning revealed a large room with about 50 Forsaken in front of him. Out of instinct Ranir casted Temporal Shift. The orb lit the whole room, proving the numbers were larger than he first saw. There were over a hundred in the room with him. They rushed forward at an alarming speed. The orb exploded in raw energy, instantly vaporizing about 30 Forsaken. Blood and pieces of the bodies scattered about the room.

Ranir didn't have time to think about the horrifying sight. The rest of the group pushed forward fearlessly. They had no thoughts or morals. They were monsters born of darkness and death. Ranir channeled his lightning, hovering off the floor about knee high, and blasted with full intent on ripping apart every Forsaken beast before him.

He was nearly blinded by the overwhelming sense of power that flowed through him this time. Throwing both palms forward he aimed to hit the entire room. Instead of two lightning bolts being conjured, this time one large beam surged from his body, cutting down every Forsaken that rushed towards him. The Lightning cut through the entire room and ripped a hole in the other wall. He felt as if he was the lightning bolt instead of throwing it. He relaxed, letting the Elemental Power subside. Instantly he heard a low clap from the corner to his left. Fear blazed over him as his stomach sank. Immediately he charged a hand with lightning and casted a shield on himself as he was turning. Before he moved a couple inches, a bright purple orb smashed into his shield and sent him rolling sideways across the room. Maintaining focus he recalled The Elemental Power whilst midair and stopped by hovering again. He was staring face to

194

mask with The Necromancer once again.

"Well it's good to see you so soon and with so much more...potential," he said in the creepy rasp that haunted Ranir for the last few weeks. "I see you've learned some new tricks. Did you get my book, Lightning Rod? Or should I say...Ranir?"

Ranir felt like someone was twisting his stomach. "He knows my name?" he thought. "Why did you send it to me?"

"Did you read it?" Seldos began pacing back and forth tauntingly. Ranir wasn't falling for any trick this time nor did he actually want conversation.

"I did and I -*Estashashik!*" Ranir rapidly casted the Explosion Spell at the floor and aimed it from the underside. Wooden shrapnel flew into The Necromancer's mask and torso, sending him flying into the wall behind him.

Without hesitating Ranir blasted another wave of lightning forward similar to the wave of water from Verna The Hydromancer. He pushed his power with full might, filling the room with lightning. The windows shattered and it sounded like the house was tearing in half. The back wall exploded from the pressure. The Necromancer went soaring from the building. It was then Ranir realized they were in the top of a church tower. Seldos blasted a near black shadowy wave from his palms toward the ground, slowing his fall. He landed smoothly on his feet without further injury. Even after taking damage, it was impressive how quick The Necromancer was.

Ranir dropped to the floor and sprinted to the hole in the tower. As soon as he looked down to the ground The Necromancer blasted a huge black and purple spell upwards, exploding the top half of the tower. Ranir could hear the sound of busting boards and the giant bell being slammed around. The top three floors were decimated. Ranir was falling.

*** *** *** *** *** ***

As the teleportation spell closed, Taryn found himself with the group just outside of Alagien, the small village outlying the Alagien Lake. The air was cold around them and the sky was blacked out. He looked around to make sure his army was still intact. He panicked. There was no sign of Ranir or The Emphyre. "Ranir? Ranir!....Where is Ranir?" he called out to the group. Everyone else looked around as well. He could feel the panic of the group. "We'll find him, and The Emphyre. For now focus! Mages, get those stones ready!"

At first they didn't notice anything besides the darkness out of normal. Then, as their eyes adjusted to the shadows, they could make out an army guarding the outside of the village, rapidly advancing toward them with an evil war cry. Taryn assumed that The Necromancer was inside the village somewhere, pulling the strings on his horde of reborn puppets. As the Forsaken began to get close, he called out "Mages up front, hold your spells until I say go!" His heart was pounding. He wasn't sure what a thousand Forsaken was supposed to look like, but the group before them looked much larger.

He almost had no time to think, and yet it seemed it this small army that he was apart of was in

196

his control. He channeled the blazing orange elemental power of fire into his hands. The heat that resonated from the flames seem to give him an extra sense of energy. He held out both arms to his side, as if holding back the troops behind him. "*A little closer, just a little more,*" he thought. Just as the Forsaken crowd was about fifty paces away, Taryn let his fire and his elemental force release chaos and destruction, signaling to the others for attack. "Now!" he bellowed with all his might, fanning a massive wave of fire into the monsters before him.

As Taryn watched through the carnage of fire, water, air and arrows, the ground troops were as driven as the mages. They seemed to stay directly under the archers bolts and the magic around them. Taryn was proud of the number of people willing to potentially sacrifice themselves to stop an evil tyrant. The display of spells was as impressive as the warriors' courage. Destructive colors of blue and orange cascaded around the Forsaken. He released his wave of power and began casting spells in a rapid fire style. First, he threw several fire bolts, blasting a couple rotting Forsaken in the chest.

As soon as the front lines of beasts fell, another wave was leaping over the bodies. It seemed almost hopeless. Within seconds the massive army was upon them. "Start falling back!" Taryn screamed out. He switched between elemental power and magic spells to reserve his energy. The other mages were not so lucky to have the luxury of choice. He could see fatigue setting in to them already.

Suddenly Taryn watched as a massive bolt of lightning bursted from one of the towers in the village. "*That's Ranir!*" He was certain now that The Necromancer was inside and more, he was in battle with Ranir. Thinking of a diversion as fast as he could, he yelled out to some of the mages, "Give me your stones!" They gave him a look of disbelief. "Now!" he screamed louder.

Taryn grasped two more stones and added the power to his own stones. He turned his back to the horde and sprinted, siphoning his mana stones on the run. With each stone drained, he felt an overwhelming sense of power. When all four stones were finally drained, and he could hardly contain the fire within, he locked his feet into the soil, sliding several feet as he turned around. All of a sudden, his eyes glowed fire red. He knew this had to be the right choice. As he was about to release the full force of burning, he watched a purple beam of shadow power blast the top of the tower. From his point of view, Taryn thought that it looked like an explosion of magnificent color and power.

He needed to hurry if his plan was going to help Ranir. He opened both of his arms backwards, and let out a war cry, clapping his hands together and releasing the element power and casting Searing Beam at the same time. The light from the flames lit up the entire village and valley behind them. In an instant, Taryn destroyed over a thousand Forsaken, clearing a path at least 200 paces wide all the way through the wall of the village and into the first house, exploding it into shreds. A shock wave rippled through the air at the same time, knocked down hundreds of Forsaken that the beam scantily missed. Taryn fell to his knees, exhausted. As he looked up The Forsaken were still advancing a thousand strong. However, they moved at a fraction of the speed and tenacity as they did before. "It worked," muttered Taryn.

***   ***   ***   ***   ***   ***

Ranir was well aware of the exasperatingly loud noise from the brick and wood being shattered around him as he was falling. He channeled his Surging Speed to slow things down and control his fall, blasting bolts of lightning into pieces of debris around him. After a fraction of a second, which was several seconds in Ranir's perception, he heard a louder explosion from outside. From the corner of his eye he caught a glimpse of a reddish orange beam lighting up what appeared to be a battlefield. He knew it was Taryn.

Ranir flipped upside down diving headfirst to the floor of the tower and yelled, "*Estashashik!*" The floor exploded in a blue lighted fashion. Mundane time resumed and Ranir went through smaller opening in another level of the tower. He managed to do a perfect front flip and landed on his feet in a cracking sound. Immediately he dove toward the doorway, smashing through the solid oak door, landing on a balcony. As he heard the crashing of the tower, he leaped down from the second floor landing in the alley.

Ranir took a short moment to catch his breath, disbelieving that he managed to escape the crumbling building nearly unscathed. He waited too long and a large section of brick pillar hit him in the shoulder, knocking him to the ground. It all seemed quiet except the distant cries from the battlefield. He heard the scuff of a boot on the brick path and looked around to find The Necromancer in the alley. Pieces of wood and brick randomly fell between them. Even with his amplified strength, his arm was pinned. He relaxed his body and went limp.

The Necromancer slowly walked over to Ranir's trapped body, swinging his arms in a cocky manner. Something about it seemed familiar to Ranir. "You make it to easy Ranir," he said with a hiss. "To think that I could end you now, take your power and destroy this world. Sounds so sweet doesn't it?"

Ranir pretended to be unconscious. He hoped that the Necromancer would get close enough that he could hit him, if only one last time with Lightning.

"Well, it seems I'm playing the hero. I'm going to let you live a little longer." He began pacing back and forth with his arms behind his back without fear. "I want you to build yourself up. I want you to unlock your full power, Lightning Rod," the Necromancer chuckled irritably. "And just when you are happy, and comfortable, and you feel like you can't get any stronger, I'll be there. I will take everything from you. And when I'm truly unstoppable, well, nobody will stop me from taking Sythestine for myself. Its about time we see another Necromancer King, isn't it...Ranir?"

Ranir cracked his eyes open just enough to see through his bushy eyelashes. The Necromancer was close enough. He waited until the arrogant sorcerer turned his back towards Ranir and he blasted an arc of lightning clear through his hand. He missed The Necromancer's back, which is where he was hoping to hit. "Ah!" The Necromancer screamed out in agony, clutching his hand and bending over. Suddenly a mage appeared through a teleport. He looked at Ranir then rushed to The Necromancer. Ranir knew that the mage was one that was supposed to be in the army with Taryn. Ranir's eyes grew wide as he realized. "Traitor!" he cried out.

The mage blasted a spell of wind gust at Ranir, causing him to crack his head on the ground. The teleport opened beneath the The Necromancer's feet and he disappeared. Just as the mage was about to step into the port a fire ball soared over Ranir's head, planting the mage in the back. It knocked him in the air far away from the teleport circle, smashing him into a wall. Suddenly the white ring disappeared. "Ranir!" came a welcomed voice. It was Taryn. He grunted as he lifted the brick off of Ranir's shoulder. The mage picked himself up and began to run. Ranir rolled to his side and, this time with excellent vision, roped him in Chain Lightning around his neck. He gave a pull and ripped the aeromancer's feet from the ground. He landed with a clunk on his back. Taryn ran over to him and seated his heel into the mage's face, knocking him out cold.

Ranir relaxed him arms and head on the ground. His body was hurting. It was infuriating that The Necromancer managed to escape by means of traitorousness, but he was gleeful that he managed to actually damage him this time. Taryn returned to Ranir and helped him to his feet. He could hear the footsteps of some people behind him. As he turned he saw about thirty people of the Thrast army. They looked weary from battle and most of them were covered in dirt and blood. The darkness of the sky immediately dissipated, returning the bright sun and blue sky. This seemed to discombobulate Ranir even more. He hadn't realized that it was actually around evening. The sun hadn't even set yet. *"Another trick of that bastard,"* thought Ranir.

"Is this it?" asked Taryn. Most of the small group nodded and looked at the ground. It was a sad day. So much lost to barely gain an ounce of pressure on The Necromancer. Ranir felt guilty for leading them into a battle of such magnitude. All of the mages and warriors that had died were supposed to be under his responsibility.

How was he supposed to lead people in battle if it simply meant they were going to die? He couldn't cope with the idea of that. Yet, he was not strong enough to beat the dark sorcerer alone. The world seemed to be in slow motion as he gathered up the remaining members of people and began healing them with his static stones' power. He couldn't help but cry as many of the group did, realizing that The Necromancer was only going to retaliate and kill more people in his name. What did he have against Ranir and the lightning? Did he simply want to be omnipotent? Ranir knew that The Lightning Rod was meant to bring balance to the world but how could he bring balance if dark sorcerers were going to be the destroyer of the world trying to get to him. Was he supposed to die in his efforts, returning magic back to the four elements?

After all of the men and women were healed up, they gathered around in a circle to mourn for the loss and honor them with a short ceremony. One of the water mages was a priest and said a few words of observance in their name. Taryn casted the fire to burn the bodies. Tears streamed down his cheeks and he channeled the flames.

Many of the people that survived in the town of Alagien had similar, more declaring ceremonies for the hundreds of deceased. They cheered for the troops that saved them, though. This gave a small amount of hope in Ranir's heart knowing that they managed to save some. It seemed in that moment, that this was going to be reoccurring. At what cost, though? He couldn't ask people to lay down their lives to save others. He knew that The Emphyre had an army, but they were nowhere near equipped to handle the shadow magic within the Forsaken, let alone The Necromancer.

After several hours, just before sunset, one of the air mages, who was highly trained in illusion of the mind, wiped away the memories of the townsfolk.

Magic was still meant to be secretive to the world. Ranir didn't understand this before. He now understood that curiosity of the mundane could lead to the cursing of their souls and turn good men evil. The world of magic was beautiful and full of miracles. It was also cruel and potent.

Taryn and the leftover mages had enough strength left to teleport them all back to Thrast. Ranir had almost forgot one lost person. "Where did The Emphyre disappear to? Wasn't he supposed to come with us?" he asked Taryn.

"I don't know. If my gut tells me anything, that coward skipped the port and is hiding on throne. He's not the man he was a decade ago."

Taryn's response only further expanded his paranoia of The Emphyre. Something didn't sit right with him. For now, they need to focus on getting back and questioning the air mage that helped The Necromancer escape. The group teleported back to The Emphyrius as the red sun set in the sky. Many lessons were to be learned on this day. Resentment was sure to grow into the souls of the men that survived the battle.

Chapter 17: Consequential

The crisp blood red hue masked the Emphyrius and passed through the stained glass windows. Ranir and Taryn proceed to transport their prisoner to a holding shack. The survivors of the Battle of Alagien were in no form to do anything but sleep. So rest they did. It was nearing midnight as the dark sky casted flashbacks in Ranir's mind of the blackened atmosphere that was The Necromancer's spell.

After the air mage was sent to his cell and bound with chains to a chair locked to the floor, Ranir and Taryn sent for fire mages that were adept in defense. Immediately the set off to track down The Emphyre, who chose to live a coward, than to fight like a hero, like a man should. Ranir thought they he may be hiding in the massive keep somewhere and that they might have to resort to magic to track him. It was more simple that that, though.

The first room they aimed toward was The Emphyre's Throne Room. It was a gigantic open room with huge statues of Thrast, the King that founded the city millennia ago. Like a child, The Emphyre pouted and gazed upon the floor immediately after discovering Ranir and Taryn approaching him.

"Where were you?" Ranir asked without a proper bow or respect to the throne. In that moment he did not care for technicalities of politics.

"I was here, where I am meant to be," said Credin The Emphyre. "You didn't expect me to go to battle did you, Ranir? And I expect a proper greeting next time you barge into here before the throne!" His words echoed in the great hall.

Ranir snapped back angrily, "You should have been with us! Oh I thought you were some excellent fighter, huh? Where was your skill while our mages and warriors were being slaughtered in Alagien?" He took a deep breath and The Emphyre sat in silence. "On your stupid throne, like a coward. That's where." Ranir turned up his heels and bolted from the room, slamming the huge oak door behind him. The sound clanged so heavy that it ricocheted down the corridors of the keep.

He couldn't believe that someone who was suppose to stand for good, and someone who fought so hard a decade ago to fight the darkness would sit back and do nothing. Ranir stormed down the dark hallways back to his room. He lit a couple candles and a torch, brightening up his stale room. The humid breeze buzzed through his open windows. Ranir picked up The Thunder King's diary and began skimming through the pages without actually reading anything. He had too much on his mind. He decided to sleep on it and let his anger subside. Tomorrow was another day, and he planned to get answers from the air mage. He wanted to know who had helped the mage sneak around. Ranir was convinced that the traitorous mage didn't act alone in this concealed disloyalty.

Another burning, bright day passed as Ranir and Taryn took turns with a couple mentalists attempting to get information from the air mage, Balor. Several guards were placed around his room. Baylor's imprisonment was inside an old brick shack with one open room inside. Many fire mages had placed layers of defensive wards on the door and walls to prevent him from blasting through it. His resolve was strong and he was stubborn in his hold.

After repeated failure to draw a reasonable response, Ranir decided that he would go visit the traitor alone. Maybe he would try other methods to apply some leverage. As he walked up to the prison cell, two of the guards standing before the door step to the side to let him pass. "Think he will talk today?" asked one of the fire mages.

"Well I guess we'll see. I doubt it," Ranir shrugged and nodded for them to drop the wards. Each night, different wards were set in place by Taryn and the mages changed positions constantly. They wanted to insure nobody helped break him out as well. The Emphyre was overseeing the entire processing.

As Ranir passed through the threshold of the door, he felt a hot rush of wind. Somehow the mage still had enough energy for casting small spells. Ranir was disgusted by someone who would betray his own people. Instantly he bellowed out Chain Lightning. Wrapping the blue arc around the mage's neck. The wind stopped. A part of Ranir wanted to end him for causing so much destruction and the death of so many good people. He released the mage who gasped for a deep breath. Sweat had begun beading on his forehead.

Instantly, Ranir recognized a hint of fear in his eyes. He decided to forward that in his technique. Ranir has never thought to torture someone, but now it seemed like a viable choice to get the mage to actually talk. "Where is The Necromancer? Who else is working with you?" The more he questioned, the more he thought about the casualties and the treachery and grew angrier. He grabbed the mage by his robe and lifted him up off the floor, the chair still chained to him.

Balor wriggled back and forth in the clutches of
The Lightning Rod. Ranir lit his eyes with lightning.
The aeromancer gained a new face of fear. Ranir
dropped him, smashing the chair in several pieces that
slid across the floor. Balor began laughing maniacally.
"You know why you're going to lose? Because you
fancy yourself as a hero...Lightning Rod." He blasted
another cackling of laughter.

"Do you think that I won't execute you? Given
all of the things you've done." Ranir was standing over
top of Balor, his eyes still glowing. Small cracks of
lightning jumped around his hands.

Balor pulled himself to his feet with a grunt.
"No, you won't. You need answers. I'm not going to
give them but that won't you from trying will it? After
all, you've nothing left but your responsibility as
Lightning Rod right?" Ranir realized that The
Necromancer must have told Balor things about him.
How could he have known?

Infuriated, Ranir blasted him with wave of
lightning again, knocking him across the room
smashing through a table. "So what? You're evil like
him, and it's responsibility to rid evil right? You talk, I
let you live it's simple really." Ranir tried to make
voice sound as threatening as possible, still hoping fear
or leverage would bleed the answers out of Balor.

Suddenly the door bursted open and Taryn
sprang into the room. "Ranir," He said as he raised his
ha damn in a surrendering gesture, "what are you
doing?" His words were slow and cautious.

Ranir thought about how threatening he looked
to Taryn and the fact that it had no effect on Balor. He
was beginning to wonder if they had a tactic to break
him. He released his elemental power and took a deep

breath.

"You see. Hero. That's why you'll always lose," groaned Balor standing himself up again. His characteristics reminded him of The Druid that he first encountered.

"Shut your mouth! You are a worthless scum who allowed a coward to enslave you. You're going to die here mage," bellowed Taryn.

"Ah yes," started Balor. "Like your pathetic brother."

"Keep my brother out of it," said Taryn coldly. Ranir noticed both of his fists clenched quickly.

"He took the bait so quickly, the famous Detmés Ontaga, best bounty hunter in Sythestine. Master was genius in that set up." Taryn's eyes began to glow and Ranir could see an aura of heat waves rippling from his body.

"Ignore him, Taryn. He's just trying to get into your head." Somehow the roles were reversed and Taryn need to be calmed.

"Oh and it's working isn't it?" hissed the air mage. "Tell me did you get your revenge on the Knight?"

"What are you talking about? What bait and what Knight?" asked Ranir.

"Another great point, Lightning Rod. How can you be the savior and the balancer if you know so little?"

"Just answer the questions!" screamed Taryn.

"You're so called vengeance was a lie! And now the path is cut because we've been betrayed!" Balor began rambling on in riddles and his eyes rolled backward. After a few sentences, his words turned in scrambled sounds. Ranir and Taryn looked at each other with concern.

"You ever seen that before?" Taryn nodded his head. "Well what is it?" demanded Ranir.

"I've seen it once before. A mage's Power Lust. You remember the story of the King?" Ranir nodded. "That's the first sign that a mage has killed an innocent and is being consumed by the shadow magic that he let into his soul."

"What can we do?" asked Ranir?

"Let it consume him, and then execute him." Taryn's eyes became glossy from watching the curse consume Balor, without blinking.

"No, we can't just let him die." Ranir turned his back toward Balor and started to reach for the door when Taryn let out a growl. As he turned around, Ranir saw Taryn draw his palms outward with flames engulfing both hands. "*He's going to kill him!*" thought Ranir.

He spun back around, whipping his cloak through the air with tenacity and blasted Taryn with Chain Lightning. The chromatic arcs wrapped around both of Taryn's wrists. Ranir pulled back as if to pull the reins of a horse. "Taryn, I said no!" he yelled.

"This monster had a hand in killing my brother, or at least helping the necromancer who had something to do with it!" he began twisting and pulling forward against Ranir. He was no match physically for Ranir anymore and yet he continued pulling with loud grunts. "He needs to die, Ranir! And you damn well know it!"

"No! We will find another way, Taryn. Now, stop! I don't want to hurt you!" he was nearly screaming at the loudest he could project. This must have enraged Taryn more because he twisted around and faced Ranir, giving him a chest full of flames.

Without even thinking, Ranir casted a shield around himself. He felt his back pressing against the wards and the door.

"Are you insane? You really wanna go there, Taryn?" bellowed Ranir.

Taryn stared at Ranir for a moment, contemplating his odds against The Lightning Rod. He closed his eyes and let the fire elemental withdraw. Ranir dropped his shield and straightened his robe.

Taryn sighed, "You're right. We're supposed to protect people." He opened his eyes and turned around, seeing Balor now on the floor babbling nonsense. Looking over his shoulder, Taryn muttered, "How is it someone your age can be so wise, Ranir?"

Ranir hadn't thought about his age in a long time. The world he used to live in was changed. He had so much loss behind his bitterness that he filled his thoughts and time with focus of his tasks and responsibilities. "I don't know, just trying to do the right thing."

"Well you make it look easy in your position."

"Thanks. I think." Ranir's heart was still racing

from the slight confrontation. He still had no idea exactly how he was going to help Balor, and if he did, would that change him? Would it let him open up? Had the darkness already taken ahold too deep that it was irreversible?

So many questions that Ranir felt responsible to answer that he felt overwhelmed at times, but he wasn't going to run away from it.

Ranir and Taryn left the small building. As they exited Ranir smelled a change in the air. The temperature had dropped. He immediately recognized the signs of a storm approaching. "Looks like rain is coming," he said as he gazed upon the sky blanketed in gray clouds. It produced the illusion of the drawing its end. The raging sun had ducked behind the cover of the clouds. Ranir welcomes a storm. It had been months since the last rainfall.

"Good, Gnariam is cracking from the drought. I'm sure the farmers will praise it," said Taryn.

Later that night, Ranir set out to the dining hall for dinner that night. It seemed he had gone a while without a good meal. As he began to eat, monstrous thunders rattled the city. Even as large as The Emphyrius was, Ranir could feel the quakes in the floors. After a moment, he began to feel like something was pulling on his mind. It was as if a force was reeling him. He thought about what it could be as it intensified. He decided to follow the call.

Soon Ranir was at a door leading him outside. He discovered what had gripped him. "The storm!" he thought.

Grasping the oversized handle, Ranir shoved the heavy door open, getting a blast of cool, misty wind in his face. He stepped out and at once noticed the difference in temperature from inside to outside. Suddenly he felt something he hadn't felt before. Inside the storm, lightning flashed furiously, revealing the dark layers inside the clouds. From within the dark abyss, Ranir could feel the buzzing of static charge. It felt familiar, almost as if it was his elemental lightning.

Ranir wanted to see if he could control the storm the same way he manipulated his magical lightning. He drew his palms upwards, raising his face to the sky. The cold rain drops pelted his face, nearly stinging. His eyes shined bright in the darkness. Feeling his power connecting to nature, Ranir drew the power towards him.

Suddenly with an over rush of power, a monumental arc of lightning stabbed Ranir in the chest, knocking him on his back. The raw lightning was siphoned from the storm. The burning rush of power last for seconds as the blue and white arcs poured into his body, leaving him paralyzed. He had never felt this much power seemingly coursing through his veins. It felt like every muscle in his body was contracted and about to explode. It was painful and yet the feeling of the physical phenomenon made it almost appeasing. Suddenly the lightning halted and the rain slowed to a drizzle. The air was calm as the wind died. Ranir had siphoned the energy of an entire storm cell, completely dissolving the gloom and pelting downpour.

Everything was restful, a harsh contrast to the deafening roars of the violent storm. Ranir's body relaxed, tardily sinking into the muck. His eyes' luminescence shined no more. He twitched his fingers to check if he was still paralyzed. The storm had dissolved yet the vast power still flooded his body. The pressure was nearly too much to comprise. He leaped to his feet and looked back to where the storm had existed moments ago.

Without a second's wasted time, he returned the lightning back to the sky with overflowing force. The arc that ascended was deeper blue than ever before, exploding into a glacial color upon The Emphyrius and the grounds all around him. Also, the girth of this lightning bolt had superseded any flash he had produced before. The ground beneath his feet trembled from the concussion. The sounds of the sky absorbing the bolt were so strenuous that a few windows above the dining hall shattered, sending shards of glass raining down. Ranir held tight to his stream of power, bleeding out all of the extra power that he had absorbed.

Within seconds he felt normal again. He gazed into the clear sky. The stars shimmered in the great distance. Deciding he should go check to see if anyone was hurt from the sonic blast, he turned and headed towards the door. In an instant the storm surged again with a deeper passion than before. Within a couple seconds the clouds blackened the night sky again and a great deal of lightning bolts wildly blasted across the sky, grounding into the mud and the keep. Ranir reached his hand upwards to regain control over it again. Panicking he slammed his eyes shut and pulled the lightning with every ounce of elemental power he could. Suddenly a bright, thick bolt of lightning pinned him to the ground. The only thing Ranir could see was white and everything was silent. He could feel no wind, nor his own body.

Chapter 18: The Lightning Rod

"Ranir," growled out an impressive voice that seemed to radiate from everywhere and nowhere. It was an acquainted vocalization. "*Eros,*" thought Ranir.

"My Lord, Eros." Ranir decided to show more respect and restraint this second intervention from The Lightning God.

"Do you know why you are here?" Eros appeared before Ranir in all of his glorious divinity.

"I'm assuming I died again?" It was more of a question than an answer. "I- I pulled too much power in that storm didn't I?"

"No, that's not why you're here. I made the storm, and called you to it. I didn't think you would react as you did, but alas you seem to continue surprising me.

Ranir thought about which choice he was referring to. In last nearly 7 months, he had grown as The Lightning Rod and made many choices. "Which is that? Going after The Necromancer? Speaking of which, you watch us right? Where is now? That would be helpful," said Ranir.

"Yes, we observe, we don't interfere, apart from The Old Gods giving magic to the world and the mages were created. The balance of light and darkness is your responsibility. We simply sense the balance of the world: good or evil," said Eros. He was patient in getting to his point of summoning Ranir into this void.

214

"I watch you, Ranir."

"Then what choice? Because I've made many, none thanks to your help, by the way. No guide, nothing from you since I got this power." Ranir began to feel his temper shorten.

"The mage you chose not to kill. How do you plan on saving him, as you say?"

"I don't know. Again, I'm still learning the world of magic without any guide."

"You have many guides around you, Lightning Rod! You aren't a god, no matter how unique your power may be. You are still human and as such, you need to let your guard down and trust people. You're young, wisdom will come to you yet."

Ranir sighed. Eros wasn't teaching him any lessons here that he didn't already know. "So tell me, please. Why am I here? Are you going to help me with the situation with the air mage?"

"He is no longer an air mage," said Eros, he began pacing back and forth in the white fog. "He is a shadow mage right now, the darkness has taken him. You can't save him from the dark magic but you can take it away."

"Take the magic away? How can I do that?" Ranir hadn't thought there would be a way to remove magic from someone. He wondered if it was similar to how a Necromancer could take power.

"As you are The Lightning Rod, you are the keeper of balance. You alone have the power to strip away all magic in someone, good or bad," explained The Lightning God.

"Strip away the power? That magic is a gift from the Old Gods, your children," Ranir emphasizes his hint that he knew about Eros's paternal connection.

There a pause in silence for several seconds. Eros glared at Ranir. He spoke slowly, "That book you received isn't factual, it's the diary of a dying man. The Thunder King, a name he gave himself by the way, regretted his decision to carry the balance as The Lightning Rod."

"Well, the spells and tips that were written down were correct. They helped me more than anything else. Why don't you tell me through truth? I can handle it."

"I will tell you this, the chronology of my offspring is correct. The spells are correct. The opinions that he gave about controlling the power were just that, opinions."

Ranir paused to think before he spoke again, "Did you teach him?"

Eros looked down, reminiscing thousands of years that had past, "Yes. I trained him. And I vowed never to do it again. He was betraying to his role in the world. I broke my oath to The Old Gods when I gave you the power. The Thunder King used vast amounts of power to end his life, magic had consumed him, and instead of evolving and growing, he was free of the world and never returned. In doing just that, he disrupted nature furiously. Mountains crumbled under earthquakes, water evaporated in some places, like Drâgok-"

"Drâgok Desert?" interrupted Ranir.

"-it wasn't always a desert. The forest of Alagien that is now a lake is another example. He nearly destroyed Gnariam by reforming it. After he died, The Old Gods made a rule that magic was meant to be secretive to prevent mundane humans from trying to achieve more than they should."

"So why me? Why did you choose me to bring Lightning Elemental power back to Gnariam?" asked Ranir. He still had so many questions.

"Some things you aren't meant to know yet Ranir. Just know, it wasn't a mistake."

"That tells me nothing, again."

"How about a tell you something helpful!" boasted Eros.

Ranir nodded and shrugged his shoulders. He nearly didn't believe that Eros would be helpful now because he hasn't been helping Ranir's journey yet.

"Stop trying to teleport. I told you, you are not a mage, Ranir. You can do magic, but you're closer to a shaman than a mage."

"What's a shaman?" Ranir shouted. He was instantly excited to hear some answers.

"It's a user of magic that has power over nature. Like the earth mages, they are more shamans with limitations."

"So how can I protect the world if I can't get across it in time?" This was one spell that had burdened Ranir since he first obtained power.

"Ride The Lightning."

217

Ranir was confused. Riddles tested his patience. He left the void quiet, awaiting an elaboration.

"You have summoned a thunderstorm before. You have felt the power within in. That power in the storm isn't magic, it's nature. You can transform into that very nature and extend across the skies. It's better that teleportation you see. You can change direction and guide yourself much more accurately."

Ranir was flabbergasted. "How can I do that?"

"Again, if you don't know it yet, you aren't meant to," said Eros. "It is something you are going to have to learn as you gain more control. You have barely tapped into the full power of the gift I have gifted you with."

"So you won't intervene, you won't tell me where to find The Necromancer. You won't help balance the world. So...it's all on me?" Ranir felt overheated and flushed. The fate of the entire world could potentially be in his hands.

"The reason we are here," he said as he gazed into the bright, colorless fog, "is because I can talk to you here. We cannot go to Gnariam. Nature itself will rip us apart. And if The Old Gods could get their hands on you, they'd destroy you. They want you to be responsible with the balance of light and dark, but if they could touch you, you would be no more. "

"They want me gone because they're afraid I'll ruin the world as The Thunder King did. That's great," said Ranir sarcastically. "I'll just have to prove them wrong," he paused. "I wish you would tell me more. I get it though, I need to learn control first." Eros

nodded. An awkward silence blanketed the
otherworldly dimension.

"I must send you back, remember what I told
you about Riding The Lightning, and nature. In time
you will perform miracles."

"I have more-," Ranir didn't get to finish his
thought. In an explosion of blue and yellow lightning
reminiscent of being inside the storm. He landed on his
chest in the mud once again, knocking his breath away.
He rolled over on his back, peering into the black sky,
as raindrops tattered the surface of everything under
the clouds. He caught his breath in a deep sigh. "Damn
Gods," he muttered under his breath as he sprung to his
feet.

Ranir had many revelations to think about as
the quest to stop The Necromancer commenced. The
thoughts of controlling the storm and various aspects
of nature danced about in his mind as he ascended The
Emphyrius. He found his dry room comforting.

Picking up The Thunder King's journal, Ranir
glided to the fireplace, dragging a chair with one hand.
He sat the book down on the chair and started to head
for a torch to ignite the fireplace. The air was warm in
the late summer, but this night held a storm that blew
cool air into the night sky. His clothes were sipping
from the tempest outside. Changing his mind about the
source of fire, Ranir thought about testing his control
of lightning. He stripped off his grey and blue robe and
laid it on the mantle.

Kneeling down, he could feel the element
drawing from within, filling his veins and muscle with
power. Ranir creates static shocks between his hands
that were clasped together. Slowly, he drew his hands
apart, focusing all of the energy between his palms. For

the first time, Ranir noticed a small orb of swirling lightning between his hands. Arcs jumped from his hands into the ball.

The further he drew his hands apart, the larger the blue sphere grew. The room flowed in a deep blue color. His hands were tingling like they did the first time his power manifested.

With his mind, he guided the orb slowly towards the tinder inside the fireplace. At first the tinder grew darker as smoke slowly shifted around the fireplace. Suddenly the lightning ball started shivering rapidly as Ranir's control started to slip. He dug deep in his mind and reached out with his elemental power, regaining a hold of the lightning.

Pushing the elemental globe of blue lightning forward slowly with his mind, white smoke began to build, clouding the base of the pit. Within seconds of sizzling and cracking, the small spears of wood ignited and spread to the other tinder. He did it!

Even as small as the magic was, Ranir wanted to test his control. It was much harder than he imagined. The stress of maintaining a grip with his mind proved to him that he needed to be conscious of how much he could actually do.

For several hours, Ranir practiced in his room. He started with the orb, working his way into accuracy test with lightning candles, which proved as hard to accomplish. He walls were littered with small burn marks from missing his targets.

Ranir developed a new technique of guiding the bolts of lightning with his index and middle finger pointing at the black wick of the candle. He began by guiding the power through his hand, aiming like he was throwing a knife. Rather soon he understood that it wasn't the correct way. He reached out with his mind, like with the orb, and controlled the flow of the arc. He learned to direct it through the tips of his fingers and outward. After countless fails, he finally reached the level of his attention to the control the lightning. He gained a new perspective, that the lightning could be strong and minuscule. It was in the control of the magic and the elemental that allowed him to overcome an obstacle in his mind.

Ranir began to feel exhausted and had a throbbing headache. He hadn't notice that the entire night had passed until the rays of the sun brushed his face. He decided that he would use the static stones to regain his energy. For now he had several tasks to dive into. He was The Lightning Rod after all, the world wouldn't stop for him to sleep.

As the sun came up, Ranir realized it was fall now. That didn't make the days any cooler. Thrast's environment was vastly different than that of Heramor. On his farm back home, the leaves were certainly about to dye their colors and the cooler winds would be ripping through the evergreen forest, bleeding an aroma of pine that would linger for months to come. Thrast still managed to keep ahold of its blistering heat. It was much closer to the desert than Heramor as well.

Ranir decided he would wait until Taryn and others awoke before he would share his experience and attempt to correct Balor's path, and stripping the magic with him. "Today is a new day. It's time to step up and be what I am meant to be," said Ranir to himself. He sat, and waited for dusk to clear away into a red and golden sunrise.

Chapter 19: Arise

Ranir set out for the day to interrogate the mage only after, with success, he completed the removal of his inner magic. If The Lightning God's treat of knowledge was fruitful, then Ranir knew of a way to scale the world between light and dark without resorting to killing masses.

Ranir knew that he required practice of his new technique. Nobody, within Sythestine, was more equipped to answer questions about magic and the removal of such than his teacher, Ramshi. Not only would he have to explain to Ramshi the meeting with The God Of Lightning, but also inform him of how he came to the conclusion that this was the right path to save Balor.

As he made his way through the gargantuan building searching for the old man, Ranir was lost in thought. Lately, he had so much going through his mind about who he should be and the journey that he is on. So much had changed that he barely remembered what it was like to be a normal farm boy. He thought about he age and realized. He forgot about his birthday! His 17th birthday had passed and nobody even knew. Realizing this made him recognize the fact that nobody, including Taryn, who he considered his closest friend now, knew much about him at all. In turn, he didn't know much about the mages or staff in The Emphyrius either. That was something he planned to remedy as well.

After several dismal hallways, Ranir reaches Ramshi's room. Usually, he would just proceed to enter. However, he felt like this day a new day and it was time to start acting according to his role in the world.

He knocked hard on the black solid door. "Ramshi, it's Ranir. May I come in?" The door ripped open and the elder was standing before him, sweat on his brow already.

"Ranir, what are you doing? You don't have to knock, you know this," said Ramshi. He was wearing an unusually casual attire. Stretched down his entire body was a dingy brown robe splattered with moth holes. The neck hole revealed his hairy chest. He wore no tunic underneath his garb. Looking down, Ranir noticed his feet were nice on the hardwood floor.

"Feeling comfortable?" Ranir teased. Ramshi's eyes were bloodshot and puffy.

"No," he said sharply grabbing Ranir's robe, pulling into the room. He slammed the door shut and slid the iron latch over to bat the door shut.

"What are you doing?"

"We need to talk!" Ramshi said as he moved over to his desk. The long wooden table was scattered with papers of various sizes. Inks and quills lay about. "I haven't slept because I'm into the traitor."

"That's why I came to talk with you actually. I think I found a way to save Balor's life and -"

"I'm not talking about that traitor! Someone else has been pulling strings around here. I suspect it's one of the mages, but last night one of the fire guards was killed in his sleep, throat slit. Another was poisoned."

"Why did I not hear about this til now?" Ranir felt out of place again. It seemed like people didn't trust him.

"I found out through a couple whispering down a corridor in the infirmary wing last night. I cut my hand see," he held up a bandaged hand.

"They were whispering about The Fallout, whatever that is. And something about getting the air mage back to The Point. Now," he said as he scratched his greasy head, I don't know about you, but that sounds like some secret wording to me. Somebody here is making plans." His breathing was heavy.

"Ramshi, I have something that may just halt that yet, whatever that may be. The God of Lightning summoned me last night in the storm." Ramshi's eyebrows raises, contorting his forehead into folds of pale skin.

"Oh? What did he want?" He continued shuffling the papers on desk.

"He wasn't happy with me stopping the execution but he said that I alone have the power to strip magic from someone."

Ramshi paused with papers I'm still in his hands and stared at Ranir. "The Lightning God, Eros told you this?"

"Yes."

Ramshi sat down the papers and rummaged his fingers through his white scruffy beard, sliding his hand up through his hair. "Hmm. Just like The Thunder King."

"What's like the Thunder King?" asked Ranir.

"Ranir, do you know why The Thunder King died? It's come to my attention you have his journal, yes?"

"Yes but it doesn't say anything about his life or death really just some spells and tips on the elemental power and a brief history of Eros's lineage," answered Ranir.

"All of his lineage?"

"Yes the four Old Gods, why?"

"I thought as much. He had another son. He was dark, unlike the others. Out of control, Eros banished him to one of the 5 realms of Hel," exclaimed Ramshi.

"Five realms? I thought Hel was just Hel!" Again Ranir realized there is so much that he doesn't know.

"Well, after this mess is over with The Necromancer, I'm gonna have to teach you the truth of this world Ranir. For now, the point is this, Eros wants you to strip the power of the mage and others that you'll come to confront, so he can slowly remove the power that his children have on him. After The Thunder King was banished from this realm by The Old Gods, they locked their father in a void." Ranir's eyes grew wide thinking of the deceit that Eros had let him to believe. "That's what makes you so special Ranir. Nobody knows, and I include The Old Gods presumptuously, how you came to possess the power of Lightning."

"Am I feared or what? Everyone around seems like they are distant to me except you and Taryn." Ranir could believe that if they thought he would follow the same path as The Thunder King in Ramshi's version, it would be a hefty reason to not trust him.

"Yes you are! Many will always fear you from the horror stories of The Thunder King. Earth mages praised him because he terraformed Gnariam and it benefited them greatly." He paused with a long sigh, "but you can change all of that, with time. Prove to them that you are different. And don't trust Eros. He is a power hungry snake."

"Well damn it! How can I know who to trust. And now how am I supposed to save Balor?" begged Ranir.

"You're not! It's the circle of magic. Life into elements, elements into power, power into darkness...and darkness into death. It's part of the balance. You would do well to remember that. The Old Gods are the ones to follow, not Eros." Ramshi sat down with a thump.

Ranir felt he needed to sit after being thrown into a whirlwind of lies and truth. He slid Ramshi's second chair away from the desk, and eased himself into it. "So Balor has to die? No other way?"

"Ramshi turned in his chair to square up with Ranir, slowly he said, "yes. Either that, or he becomes a Necromancer. And we know where that leads."

"Yes we do, and that won't help balance the world." Ranir leaned his elbows on top of his thighs, smashing his face into his hands. He didn't want to take the life of anyone else. Forsaken were the only exception because, though they looked human, they were already deceased, soulless.

A long time passed before Ramshi spoke up hurriedly, "Oh! I nearly forgot in my daze, the reason I've been up so long. I think I have an idea how to flush out the other traitor!"

"How?" Ranir piped up.

"Let Balor go. Shadow mages can't teleport! Let him go then follow him," Ramshi explained.

"Catch both traitors in one swoop. That's a great idea, Ramshi!" boasted Ranir.

"Of course it'll have to go through The Emphyre. Balor is technically a prisoner of The Emphyrius, magic or not."

"Yes, of course," said Ranir. "I'll fill in Taryn, you can notify The Emphyre." Ranir trusted the Archemage more than anyone. If he was going to get help, it would be from Taryn.

"Don't tell anyone else the plan," Ramshi stated cautiously.

"I won't." Ranir exited the small office and made his way through the long corridors to Taryn's quarters. Finding the room sparse, Ranir trekked down to the grounds in search of his friend. Ranir had scaled down to the east and then to the west. An hour had passed as he continued the sweep. "All of this would be so much better if I could teleport," he said with a huff. "Oh no! Ride the lightning!" He mocked Eros's deep voice by tilting his chin downward.

He wondered if anything The Lightning God was truthful. Ranir sat down on the ledge of a brick flowerbed, and admired the craftsmanship of the masons in the building. He began to lose his surroundings as deep thought swept over him. "Couldn't hurt to try, right?" he asked himself, thinking of how he try to ride the lightning and guide himself through the air. An image of a falcon swirling in a windstorm flashed across his mind, making him chuckle out loud. For now, he would continue looking for Taryn.

After a few more hours, Ranir decided to pause his seeking. He assumed Taryn teleported somewhere. Lately, Taryn hasn't had any bounty hunting duties per Ranir's request. This seemed to free up a lot of Taryn's time yet make him stir crazy.

The day was slowly dragging on as Ranir sat in

his room practicing control spells again. Physically, it seemed easy to draw forth the Lightning. Mentally, however, it was exhausting attempting to steady his hands and the element. He could feel progress with each arc. Every now and then, Ranir would crack the ancient journal open and try something new. He recognized that he relied on magic spells as much as lightning elemental power. He was intrigued by the fact that spells were designed for a single purpose generally. The Lightning could be manipulated in many ways to accomplish similar goals. As well, magic drew on his mana, fatiguing him more and more with each spell.

As the darkness blanketed Thrast, Ranir was becoming bored with practicing the same spells and maneuvers. Under the cover of night, he made his way out of the keep sneakily. He had decided it was time to try riding a storm. He walked for nearly 10 minutes away from the building for a safe cordon. Digging deep within, he thrusted the sapphire colored elements into the black sky. Instantly clouds formed from nothing. Blue and yellow explosions illuminated the open field. From a distance, the large panels of glass, set in the towers of The Emphyrius, glistened like stars.

Ranir could smell moisture in the air, a musk in contrast to the pine and cherry trees of the forest. He could feel the power of the storm. Not a single drop of rain fell from the monstrous cell. Instead of siphoning the power, Ranir elected to give in to the magnetic pull. Like controlling the small orb, Ranir reached out with his mind, one palm skyward, and imagined literally riding the storm and exiting on top of the keep. As he pushed forward, the storm seemed to pull more. Then suddenly he lifted from the ground at incredible speeds into the sky. It felt like a rope was tugging on his entire body. For a second he imagined flying to The Emphyrius.

In an explosion of lightning bolts, he was thrust towards the building. Before he could comprehend the events, he smashed through a window, punching a hole through the floor, then another layer of wooden flooring and finally crashing through the ceiling of the dining hall. The hall was at least 20 feet high. He flew in at a sharp angle, breaking multiple chairs and skidding to a halt on his back. He felt the angry rush of pain in his spine and neck. Rolling his head to the left, he noticed a bright white bone sticking through his forearm. Through the adrenaline, the almost felt nothing of his forearm. He laid his head on the floor, hearing the buzzing of people around him. He did it. He rode the lightning, He Traveled for the first time, and though he failed to land where he wanted to, he was happy about his power once again.

A face appeared in front of his, someone unfamiliar. Ranir couldn't hardly perceive the features of the stranger's face as it was upside down. "Lightning Rod, don't move, your arm's broke." She scurried off out of view.

A couple minutes passed by. Ranir's shock began to wear off and the shearing pain started to bite at his arm and pound in his back. He was certain that he broke his back as well. Even with all of the power that he had, his body was still as fragile as humans.

230

The stranger returned to his view with the infirmary witch doctor. Per usually she was garbed in a bright white robe and shiny white shoes. "Don't move!" she bellowed to Ranir, not that he could even twitch in the first place. "Okay bring it here." She has her head cocked over her shoulder talking to others outside of view.

In an instant four large men spread out around Ranir, two of them with a long sheet tied between two poles about 7 feet in length. Setting the stretched canvas on the ground, simultaneously the four men crouched and grabbed Ranir under his back. Just the sliding of their hands underneath him sent an excruciating pain through his back and hips. He screamed out in pain with tears welling up in his eyes.

Ranir's only sight as the four large men carried him smoothly was the textured ceiling in between the auras of passing torches. The witch doctor trailed behind them without losing a single step in distance. "What happened exactly?" she questioned Ranir. He didn't want to tell his tale of soaring through the sky. Part of him thought she wouldn't believe him, otherwise he thought it would only incite more fear.

"I don't know exactly," he lied. He was in agony, yet thankful that he landed in The Emphyrius. The traveling could have ended much worse If was thrust into the forest and alone. He remembered thinking of the bird flapping its wings heavily in the storm and chuckled slightly, reminding himself of the stabbing pain in his spine.

After several long minutes they reached to infirmary. The quartet of burly men laid Ranir down on a fresh bed. As the four bearers exited, Ranir heard the metallic clanging sound of the witch doctor fumbling her instruments. "Ah, there you are!" she exclaimed. Her hard soled slippers clicked with every step as she walked around to Ranir's left side. That was the side where he suffered a broken and piercing bone. He rolled his chin downward to get a sense of the damage now that he was in a well lit room. One part of The Infirmary that Ranir was partial to liking was the 12 large mirrors that were placed around the room. They reflected the light upward, illuminating the room to a higher degree.

The forearm bone looked like the tip of a broken stick, but bright white. Not a stain of blood held onto it. The skin surrounding the puncture was purple with faded splashes of yellow.

"Bite down on this," the witch doctor shoved a leather strap into his mouth without giving him time for questions. "Hold your breath, it's gonna hurt."

Taking a deep breath he watched as she pulled a pair of pliers into his view. His eyes grew wider and his breathing quickened. The witch doctor grabbed the bone with the pliers and, placing a hand on his wrist to steady his arm, gave a rough push. The pain was nearly unbearable. Suddenly he felt a surge of elemental power take over him. A flash of Verna and Omat getting killed by his power crossed his mind, "stop!" he yelled. He steadied his breathing and pushed the power away.

"Of course, I'm done with that part anyway," said The Witch doctor as she stuffed a white cloth against the hole in his arm. Instantly the white faded to a crimson color and glistened as blood pooled up on the surface. She glided across the room to a small cabinet.

To his right, the door burst open. Ramshi came stumbling in the room. "Ranir! What happened?" he cried out. Ranir glanced to his nurse still searching through her cupboard.

"Not here," he whispered. "Did you find Taryn?" Ranir knew that he needed magic to heal his back.

"I did. He got back about an hour ago. He ported to Killiad."

"Why did he go to Killiad all day?" Ranir asked.

"My guess is for Sora. He may be trying to recruit her for the fight against The Forsaken and The Necromancer."

Ranir thought of the way Sora and Taryn had been around each other when they were passing through the small city. He smiled, "I'm sure that's what he's doing...can you get him for me?"

"Sure. Yes. Right away," replied Ramshi shakily as he turned up his heels and sped out of the infirmary.

The witch doctor returned to his aide with a

small bronze colored dish. She was masking something red inside, transforming it into an oil. "This is Nuravé Root. It's from a magic tree born in Gorûn. It'll help speed up the healing in your arm."

"Where's Gorûn?" asked Ranir. He had read maps and saw many names of places, but never Gorûn.

"It's way on the other side of the world, my dear boy. Now don't move, it might sting at first, but it'll go numb." She pulled the sopping cloth from his arm. For a brief moment, the wound was dry. She then scooped the thick oil and pushed it into the hole. At first she gripped the bed sheets with his right hand as it felt like someone stuck a hot iron into his flesh. For several seconds he held his breath and clinched his eyes shut.

A cooling numbness filled the void where there was pain. Ranir let out a long breath and released the cloth in his hand. Slowly, the witch doctor slid about her gauze under his arm, wrapping it on top with a tight knot. For a moment, Ranir forgot about the pain in his back.

The witch doctor stood up straight and looked up and down his body. "Magic will have to take care of the back, I'm afraid. I'll send for a water mage."

"I sent for Taryn already," blurted Ranir. She squinted her eyes. He realized she hadn't noticed Ramshi's quick appearance. "Ramshi came in for a moment so I sent him along."

She seemed flustered. "Fine," she said dryly

and began cleaning her tools and the cloth up. Nearly 10 minutes passed as Ranir lay in pain before Taryn teleported into the room with Ramshi.

"Ugh. I hate that," grumbled Ramshi, shuttering.

Taryn smiled as he walked over to his friend. "Ranir, what happened?" asked Taryn.

"I'll tell you later! Can you heal my back? I think it's broke," groaned Ranir. Taryn got flushed with a face of worry.

"Of course! I'll need some mana for that big of a spell." He looked down as Ramshi tapped him with a mana stone. "Thank you," he whispered.

Taryn siphoned the mana from the stone, pulling out red swirling energy into his palms. He set the stone down on the bed and began riddling off fire healing spells. Ranir's body shifted as his spinal cord snapped loudly back in place. He screamed as it was more excruciating than the first break. After several seconds, Taryn bogged down to his knees and Ranir was healed. The entirety of the pain had vanished.

Ranir rose from the bed and stretched left and then right. His back felt looser and yet stronger than ever before. "Thank you!" he yelled to Taryn in excitement. He turned to the witch doctor and nodded, "and thank you." He was more genuine with her. She gave a short nod and proceeded out of the room. As the door closed, Ranir held up his arm and casted," *Ertini Oltak.*"

Small arcs of lightning buzzed from his right palm as he he ran it over the wound. The familiar fatigue of magic healing was always more potent than simple spells. He unwrapped his arm and wiped the blood away, revealing a light pink scar. He looked up to Taryn and Ramshi. They were waiting patiently for an explanation. This amused Ranir. Without a word he walked to the door and opened it. He poked his head into the shaded corridors, expecting someone to be about. It was empty. He withdrew back into the room and shut the door, leaning his head against it. "I traveled through Lightning," he said casually.

"I'm sorry, you what?" spoke Ramshi.

Ranir turned around to see their confused faces glaring at him. "I summoned a storm, and then rode the lightning. About 5 acres away and crash landed into The Emphyrius." There was not a single sound from either of them. "Basically I teleported!" he yelled impatiently.

"Why didn't you just say that?" asked Taryn.

"Because I didn't teleport through magic. I did it through the elemental power of lightning...literally through a storm."

"Wh- How?" Ramshi seemed much more shocked than Taryn.

"I don't know I sort of pictured it and then, well, it just happened. I've been practicing controlling the element."

"That's great, Ranir!" bellowed Ramshi.

"If I can figure out how to do it the right way and control it, it could be useful."

"Absolutely," said Taryn. "So, Ramshi tells me you plan to use Balor as bait for another traitor, yes?"

"Yes! I looked for you all day. Where were you?" asked Ranir smartly.

"If you must know, I went to see Sora." Ranir smiled at him. "Not like that. We're going to be needing a lot more help to stop The Necromancer."

"Yes we are. That's why we want to shut down whoever his helping him. Do you think it's a good idea?" asked Ranir.

"Yes I do. It's not up to me, though."

"Right," started Ranir, "did you speak to The Emphyre?"

Ramshi seemed gleeful. "Yes I did and he said it's a great idea. He is expecting to see us all before we execute the plan before he heads out."

"Heads out?" asked Ranir.

"Well, he is the leader of Sythestine, Ranir. He has to show his face to those suffering in the world and hold meetings around the Kingdom with the City Leaders," boasted Ramshi.

"Oh yes, I forget that I'm now in ties with politics. I don't care much for them. When does he leave?" asked Ranir.

"Tomorrow night."

"Great, well we can execute the plan and find the other traitor or traitors tomorrow then," said Taryn. "For now, I'm going to bed before that blistering sun rises again."

Ranir decided it best to get some sleep. He was going to need energy If was going to be successful in providing help with the trap. The trio exited the infirmary with caution. Ramshi went left and Taryn followed Ranir right.

He was exited when he got back to his quarters. Immediately he stripped his robe and tunic off and walked to his mirror to see his back. For the first time, Ranir really looked at himself. His stubble had grown thicker on his face, giving him the look of someone older. His muscles were much more prudent than before he left Heramor. With each twist of his body, Ranir noticed his ab muscles clinching. For several seconds he stood still and admired his body for what it was. After a long day like this, he decided to skip a wash, and he found himself a comfortable spot across his bed. He fell asleep with his trousers and boots still on. He had no idea how long his nights and days were about to become.

Chapter 20: The Traveler

A swift change in the weather was born as fall began to finally set into Thrast. Ranir was awakening from his deep slumber. The events over the past day and a half had left him far wearier than he had expected. It was nearly midday when he rose from his bed. His body ached from a cockeyed sleep. His stomach growled angrily from his lack of appetite as of late.

Ranir sprung to his feet and slipped on his tunic and robe. He grabbed the cloak that was limp and stale on the floor. As he held it up and gazed at it, he realized that the robe and cloak were gifts from Eros. Besides Traveling, it had become clear now that Eros was deceitful. Ranir didn't want the robe any more. He decided that he would find a tailor and get new garbs.

For now he needed to speak to The Emphyre and make sure that the plan for the trap was set and everyone was in agreement on the specific details. He had slight uncertainty that the deception they had planned would be foolproof. Often he worried if he was making the right decisions. He didn't know long it would take, but he had one goal: stop The Necromancer Seldos.

As he set out to find Sythestine's leader, he noticed a drop in temperature in contrast to the burning summer sun. A cool breeze floated through the air, carrying the familiar aroma of evergreen forests. Ranir paused with his eyes closed and welcomed the scent. One thing that could always remind him of home was the woodlands surrounding Thrast. He reminisced his childhood running through the Heramor forest with Marnos and Selendt. He grew sad thinking of where Marnos might be now. He longed for the day when he could go home again. For now, he would only endanger the small village.

He opened his eyes, realizing the reality of his life as it was now. He had a purpose and a responsibility. He began trekking down the brick path around the east wing of the building. He had found, over the course of his time at The Emphyrius, various paths outside to get around faster. Inside the keep, many hallways bled into each other, giving the illusion of a shifting maze. There was so much of the building that he had not explored.

Making his way around the building, enjoying the fall finally setting in, he circled back inside and started his path up the spiral staircase that lead to various corridors. From there he knew the direct line to The Throne Room, where he assumes The Emphyre would be.

He entered the massive hall with an upbeat step. There was a slight excitement to having the trap planned and executing it without problems, though, Ranir feared that luck may against them and in the favor of darkness. Since he received his elemental power, it seemed like the world had only grown darker.

240

There was a heft group of men and women, garbed in royal cloths. Several of them had gold lacing in their robes, others will literal gold bracelets and neck pieces. Every one of them seemed to adorned with hair pieces and the finest cloaks Ranir had seem yet. Most of them shot discerning looks to him. Though it was recent he learned of most people's fear and disgust towards his residential stay at The Emphyrius, he still was aroused in disbelief. He had never had anyone, let alone most of the populates, jeer in his name. Ranir thought that maybe some day his efforts would garnish at least cordial, maybe even honorable. That would be, of course, if he succeeded and manged to live through the cursed actions of the dark sorcerer.

He paused before he proceeded. After an awkward silence, Ranir watched as The Emphyre approached him first. Ranir dipped into a low bow. If wanted to change his reputation for being The Lightning Rod, as well as hailing from a poor village across the continent, then he was going to have to start becoming more political. It may just become an advantage to trekking the world as well.

"Your Highness," said Ranir. "May I have a word with you, sir." The Emphyre rolled his eyes slightly, with a small smirk. Ranir knew that The Emphyre didn't like the title of Your Highness.

"Of course, Lightning Rod," he returned the tease. He outstretched an arm as he gestured over to a thin black door. Ranir led the way to the small entrance, unaware of where it would lead.

Pausing at the door, Ranir turned to The Emphyre who trailed him closely. Credin raised his eyebrows, granting permission for Ranir to enter first. As he entered the room, he was pelted with the musky stench of mouse urine and dust. He realized right away that the small door had led to a closet that, apparently, hadn't seen a cleansing in years. Why The Emphyre led here instead of a small, cozy office, Ranir did not know. However, he didn't plan to talk long.

The Emphyre followed him in, grabbing a torch on the wall of The Throne Room, and shut the door quietly. The air in the room was nearly difficult to breath in and The Emphyre instantly regretted choosing this location in which to speak.

"Had to be this closet, eh?" spoke Ranir in the dim light. Shadows danced around the empty storage closet from the cobwebs hanging from the ceiling.

"Sorry, it was close and I'm rather pressed for time. Do you know who those people are out there?" asked The Emphyre.

"Well, no. I don't hardly know anyone of your friends that bath themselves in gold. Maybe I should get to know them," Ranir joked.

"They are nobility of the highest classes within Sythestine." Ranir thought of as many aristocratic titles as he could.

"Where is Sora? Isn't she the leader of Killiad?" asked Ranir.

"Yes she is, but she is rather busy still with repairs from the first attack of Seldos," replied Credin.

"I see, well then. I won't keep you. Ramshi tells me that he spoke to you about our plan to draw out another traitor?" Ranir already knew that The Emphyre gave permission. He wondered what Credin wanted to say about it, to him personally.

"Yes he did. I think its well thought out and a great idea. My only concern, which is why I wanted to speak to you is this: Do not, I repeat, do not let Balor The Traitor escape from your site or you grasp, Ranir. Now that he is filled with Shadow Magic, he will be looking the resurrect someone in order to become a Necromancer." He wiped a bead of sweat from his brow. The narrow closet was humid and nearly suffocating. "I know that you know this, I just wanted to reiterate it one last time, as you know, I won't be here."

"I understand. I have no intentions of letting Balor go either. I've made the decision to do what I need to do to balance Gnariam, if that means execution of the damned, then so be it. You have my word," replied Ranir.

"Very good. You'll have Taryn there as well. He is highly trained in tactics. I have assembled a small group of archers to be on the rooftop of the crosswalk in case things go south rather quickly as well," he explained. "Just tell Ramshi when you are going to release Balor, he knows where to find the archers."

"Good. This is going to work. I know it," he lied. He was more-so terrified of failing and releasing more darkness into the world that halting The Necromancer at all.

"Good luck to you, Ranir. I have faith in you to do what's right. You are young, but you seem wise years beyond your age. For now, lets get out of this damn closet. I must prepare for our voyage, to too many cities," said The Emphyre.

"Thank you, sir. And good luck on your travels and diplomacy and what not," Ranir said. He hadn't the slightest indication of what exactly The Emphyre and his politically noble posse would be doing. He would rather paint rocks at the bottom of a river than to learn the dullness of governmental stratagems.

As they exited the tiny closet, it took a moment for Ranir's eyes to alter to the Throne Room's luminosity once more. The opposition of the dingy closet to the bright openness of the hall was immense, both in smell and sight. Ranir had never paid attention to how much the world smelled as much as he did at The Emphyrius. When he lived at home, growing up, everything was familiar and loosely discarded. The farm had the fresh stench of the cattle and fields. The forest, where he and his friends played and, as they got older, hunted, had a reciprocating aroma of fruit and evergreen trees all year long. Now in Thrast, he was smelling so many belongings of the world that he never paid attention to. Having magic had relinquished several tasks and much of his time, so much so that he had various instances to think, and to wander, more than ever.

Ranir bid his temporary farewell to The Emphyre Credin and made his way back through the stupendous maze of halls leading to the grounds below.

He needed to find Ramshi and Taryn both to pull off the arrangement. Several minutes passed as Ranir trekked, once more, across the deep green grass and brick steps directional to a sizable well-known door. Ranir had begun to set a pattern of these exercises to reach the respective surroundings of the bastion. He made it to Ramshi's office in a considerably fast time and bursted through the door without knocking, remembering Ramshi's conflict with him walloping on the threshold previously.

"Ramshi, I've spoken to The Emphyre," he said. "We are good to go. He mentioned about your ties with the archers for a safety net, not that it'll make much difference," he added slyly.

"Good and hey, you know never know!" replied Ramshi. "You gather Taryn, he should be waiting on you down at the foyer of the west wing. I'll gather the archers and send them to the cross walks. As soon as I get down to you, we will proceed. Gather your static stones, you may need them."

"Alright," Ranir said. "I'll see you in a few minutes. Be quick!" Ranir departed the room and set a course to his quarters first. He was nearly out of breath as he made it to his room. Rummaging through his satchel, he pulled on the two bracers that Ramshi had given to him inset with the static stones. He left the room, sprinting, to make his way to Taryn. His heart was racing. He couldn't tell if it was due to the excitement of the task at hand, or from his constant jogging around for the past half hour. He worried that he may need the to replenish his mana first.

As Ramshi had said, Taryn was waiting in a small vestibule in the west wing, which led out to the grounds, straight inline with the little shanty that Balor was stationed in. He was clad in the first black robe that Ranir had seen him wearing. Both of his massive swords were sheathed across his back. "What took you so long?" he asked Ranir. "Is Ramshi coming?"

"Yes. He is. I was getting these," Ranir said in between deep breaths. "He's getting the archers ready."

"Good, good. Well he should be here fairly soon." Taryn looked up and down at Ranir. "You need to start training more, you look winded already!" he teased.

"Yeah, yeah!" Ranir said in a breathy manner as he through his hands downward.

It was only a few seconds of waiting until the elder instructor came through the door. "Okay, let us head down there and see if we can draw out a snake, shall we?" he said as he swept past Taryn and Ranir without waiting.

Taryn followed closely behind Ramshi. Ranir paused with his eyes closed for a moment. "*Oh boy, please let this go right,*" he thought. He proceeded to trail the others down the dirt path to the shack. Per usual, several fire mages were placed around the prison. From outside, Ranir could hear screaming from inside the building. He looked at one of the fire mages who shrugged his shoulders and said, "He's been at this for awhile. Not long now, the darkness will take

246

him." Ranir wasn't going to let that happened before his snare was set.

"Open the door," he demanded to the red bearded fire mage. He paused for a second, staring at Ranir. "Open it," Ranir repeated in a stern tone. The man nodded to the others surrounding the door, gesturing for them to release the wards that were keeping Balor imprisoned and keeping others safe. As Ranir pushed the door open slowly, he felt a cool rush that sent shivers down his spine, reminding him how much darkness The Necromancer was spreading into Gnariam as each second passed.

From behind him, Taryn said, "Back up, all of you!" he commanded the entirety of the guards. Ranir took a step backwards as well, letting Balor have his freedom, if only for a brief moment.

Several minutes passed as they waiting for the Shadow Mage to exit. Everything around Ranir seemed silent with the exception of Balor scratching the floors and growling rabidly. He was fully prepared to unleash his elemental power should things go awry. "Let's back away, Taryn. Give him some distance, if it goes south, you can port to him quickly," said Ranir. Everyone was in agreement. The fire mages hesitated the least. They knew that they didn't possess the power to contain a Shadow Mage in the open.

As soon as they were about 30 paces away, the sounds that emanated from the room fell to silence. Suddenly, Balor exited the room with a rush and scattered about in circles like a wild cat, flailing his arms uncontrollably. White foam soaked his lips and it

247

seemed as if half of his hair had been pulled out, leaving deep red gouges in his head. His skin had smoothed over to a yellowish tone. Ranir steadied his hands and watched carefully. Suddenly, Balor scurried off. Taryn and Ranir looked at each other for a second, and went forward to follow Balor. Ranir realized quickly that his normal speed wasn't a match for the dark magic enhancing Balor's physical form.

For a moment, Ranir thought that they would lose him. As far as he could tell, nobody had stepped up to help Balor. The trap was failing. He reassured himself that Taryn could teleport ahead and stop him if he needed to. He wasn't ready to Travel again. The cool wind rushed past Ranir's ears. Suddenly in the wind, Ranir heard a well-known sound. "*Sssht!*"Ranir watched a black arrow zoom past his face and embedded into Balor's back. "*Idiots! That won't stop him!*" thought Ranir. In that moment, Ranir's heart skipped a beat as he noticed the arrow had splinters of glowing orange in the craft. It was the same ember-looking arrow that the assassin used against Detmés.

Balor thrashed in his sprint, reaching backwards to attempt to remove the arrow. He let out an earsplitting animalistic screech, and crumbled to the ground. He was moving so fast that his face was the first part of his body to smash into the grass, rolling forward and snapping his neck. His limp body rolled several times in a flimsy manner before halting on his stomach. Ranir and Taryn stopped. A deep brush of cold swept over Ranir as he watched Balor's arms reach out and brace himself. His head reeled upwards with several cracking sounds as he let out another scream. The arrow that pierced his back began to slowly smoke and glow bright orange. Balor arched his back for a second before the arrow exploded, destroying Balor in the process. Parts of his body scattered around with glowing purple energy. Ranir and Taryn threw their arms up to block falling pieces. He had never seen a body explode like that before.

"Who the Hel gave that order?" bellowed Taryn. He seemed more upset than usual. He looked back at The Emphyrius which was almost an acre away now. He began swirling magic into his palms and muttering under his breath. Within seconds an orange circle appeared beneath him and he disappeared into a portal. Ranir let out a deep sigh.

In less than a second, Taryn reappeared with the four archers that The Emphyre commanded. He let out a blast of fire, knocking all of the archers to the ground. One of them drew an arrow as he landed on his back as a warning for Taryn. "Do it. I dare you!" he screamed. "You aren't that fast, mage!"

Taryn dropped his hands. "Who shot him?" asked Taryn. Not one of them answered at first. Taryn blazed his hands with red fire, his eyes glowing bright crimson colored. "Who shot him!?" he screamed louder.

"Not us, that's who," said the archer still holding his lead on Taryn. Ranir wasn't sure if the archer was going to fire. He spat out a blue arc of lightning faster than the archer could react. The bolt smashed his bow in half, recoiling it back and smashing him in the face. The arrow fell at his feet.

"Then who did? They had an ember looking arrow! Just like the one that killed my brother."

One of the smaller archers spoke up with a squeaky voice. "Sir, the arrow came from the northwest tower. I saw it fly from there, I swear." He seemed to feel more threatened than the first archer. Taryn let his fire elemental withdraw. Looking down, his forehead creased as he deepened his thoughts.

"Do you remember what he said about my revenge not being taken right, or something?" he asked Ranir. "Do you think-"

"No," Ranir interrupted. That can not be the same assassin if that's what you're thinking. It just can't. You put a whole in her, remember?"

"But what if she isn't the one that killed my brother, Ranir? What if I killed a different assassin?"

"No. You tracked her, remember?" Ranir began to doubt his memory as he thought of how the Druid tricked his mind into tracking a beast through the forest of Heramor.

"Something about it doesn't feel right. Not now that I'm thinking of it." Taryn began pacing. The archers stood in silence and confusion. "Think about it, Ranir. We practically went straight to her and she came to us, baited us to attack. It was far too easy. Something's not right, I'm telling you."

The validity of Taryn's opinions struck Ranir in an ominous way. "I don't know, maybe there was magic involved, more than we think," he said.

Taryn and Ranir decided that they would investigate his brother's murder and this execution simultaneously. Taryn teleported the archers back to The Emphyrius, warning them to keep quiet about the arrow and assassin. He even threatened them with a Mentalist who could removed their memories. Upon returning to Ranir, Taryn said, "You know, I would like to see this 'Traveling' thing you talked about!"

Ranir laughed as he thought of crash landing into the keep again. "Maybe another time after I figure out how to land!"

"Oh come on, what better time than now, you are far enough away from The Emphyrius. If you break, I'll fix you again!" said Taryn.

Ranir thought for a few seconds. Taryn was right. He needed to practice Traveling while he was far away from people and buildings. More importantly, he wanted to aim for something softer this time. "Alright, I need somewhere easier to land. What's close?" asked Ranir.

"Too easy, you see that break in the forest there?" he said as he pointed to a distant void.

Ranir squinted his eyes, "Yes. I think so. What's there?"

"A small body of water. That should be soft enough for you to make sure you land feet first."

"Alright. Yeah. That could work," said Ranir nervously. His heart began working double time. He closed his eyes and slowed his breathing down to focus. In one smooth flow, Ranir threw his hand into the air and summoned a vast thunder storm. With the first strike of Lightning he pulled himself into the clouds. This time he seemed to have better control on his body and slowed time down for a brief moment to see his target. From the atmosphere, he could see the pond much more clearly. He imagined zooming his body in a hurl of lightning towards the water. Thrusting his arms in the direction of the pool of dark water, he pushed the power with a powerful driving force. In a blaze of blue and white flashing light, Ranir landed in the water. It wasn't nearly as painful as the brick and wood that he crashed through the first time he Traveled.

. "Yeah!" he bellowed as he slapped the water with both hands as he surfaced. The storm dissolved into a blue sky once more. He did it! He Traveled exactly where he wanted to go. As he looked around, he noticed the surrounding forest was singed and smoking. Several of the trees were split and splinters littered the top of the water.

"I guess water and lightning don't mix well!" Ranir heard from behind him. He turned around to find Taryn standing on the bank.

"What happened?" he asked.

"It seems that water amplified the lightning. You basically exploded in power from what it looks like," he said with his arms outstretched, referring to the charred woods. "Very interesting."

Ranir decided that he would walk back to The Emphyrius since Taryn wasn't strong enough to

252

teleport him back. Also, Taryn refused to try to teleport Ranir anymore after his first failed attempt.

It was nearing sundown as the pair made it into the keep. Taryn stopped Ranir at the foot of a staircase. "Ranir, we need more help."

"What do you mean?" asked Ranir.

"We need to recruit stronger mages and people that we can trust. There is still a traitor among us here. The issue with the assassin. The Necromancer. The truth of my brother's death. All of it. We need more help."

"You're right. I thought I was strong enough to handle the balancing responsibility. I am not," exclaimed Ranir. "Who can we trust? You know people, right?"

"Yes, I know some. I think we need to start thinking about getting a faction of loyal warriors together. I don't know how many we need, but we need to push the fight to The Necromancer," said Taryn.

"Alright, well who do you have in mind?" asked Ranir.

"I think you know the first person I have in mind. I've been trying to recruit her for awhile in our cause."

Ranir smiled. "Sora."

"Yes," said Taryn with a smirk. "She is powerful, as you have seen. She is a strategist, and she is loyal. We *need* to get her in our fight."

"I agree," said Ranir. He tried to think of anyone else he would know that could help. A few of the mages that helped trained him came to mind. He knew that Ramshi couldn't fight because he was old, but he would be a valuable asset as well. "So when do we go to Killiad? I might as well Travel over the desert. Feels good to know I can skip a saddle ride now!" The last thing he wanted to do was ride full speed across the hot desert again.

"Lets make a plan to go tomorrow. We'll gather what we need. We can take Ramshi with us. He is brilliant and knows more about many things than anyone I know," said Taryn.

"Okay. Tomorrow morning, be ready!" Ranir boasted. He ran up the stairwell and to his room. He was excited to know that they were going to be going on the offense now. Ranir hoped that they would surprise The Necromancer. Seldos had been a step ahead every single time until now.

As he got to his room, a large leather satchel was lain on his bed. He looked out in the hallway to see if anyone was waiting. As he returned to his bed and opened it, he was gifted with a new attire. He almost forgot that he stopped and asked a tailor for an upgrade. As he pulled the flaps open, he was nervous pulling out each piece of garments. His old robe was no longer going to be his statement. He separated each piece and looked over them. The tailor seemed to have gotten Ranir's order perfect, down to the color.

Included in the package was a pair of flat black leather pants, a black tunic with matching pocketed vest and a dark blue short robe. The robe only stretched down to his knees instead of to the floor per usual. Fitted on the back was an even deeper saturated blue hooded cloak. He fitted himself with each section to make sure they fit. They were snugger than his previous robes. He ordered them that way to subtract some of the drag and friction of the cloth robes. On the floor at the side of his bed was a small wooden box. Inside was a new pair of black leather boots and blue finger-less gloves.

As he dressed himself in all new garb, he gazed at his reflection in the mirror. The colors drew out the golden brown in his eyes. Now, he was ready to set out into Gnariam and fulfill his destiny. His next step was building a massive and powerful Allegiance.

Chapter 21: Allegiance

The next day, Ranir was up before the sun reached its bright yellow color. The humid clouds hung before the red sunrise giving his room a pinkish hue. Grabbing his large leather satchel, he swept across the room, picking out various possessions that he might need. If his and Taryn's plan succeeded, he didn't know how long it would be until their return to Thrast. This bit was more joyous than he thought it would be. There were many advantages and amenities that The Emphyrius held that he didn't know where else life would be as easy. However, Ranir truly misses the outdoors and traveling through dense evergreen forest. He missed the open countryside of Sythestine, albeit, not the desert, of course.

Ranir slipped into his new attire, admiring the crispness of the craft. The last part, the cloak, pulled all of the colors and textures together. Quickly, he rushed out of his room, with everything he needed. He made sure some items were certainly packed, including his bracers, daggers, The Thunder King's book, the pair of mana stones that he acquired and a white oak staff that he made through a series of boredom in the days passed. He thought about grabbing his bow and quiver, but decided it would be far too awkward in shape to add to his already impressive luggage.

Ranir aimed for Ramshi's office first. He hadn't conveyed the news of their departure to his teacher yet. Ramshi was certainly intelligent enough to offset his age and physical handicaps. Ranir had high hopes that Ramshi would share their quest to rally more recruits.

Upon entering Ramshi's office, Ranir found the old man in his chair as usual. "Ramshi, I need to speak with you."

"Ah! What is it, Ranir?" said Ramshi, seemingly startled by Ranir's sudden entrance.

"Taryn and I are leaving. We're going to take the fight to The Necromancer. The front of his attack's seem to halted for now. We've received no word of him attacking anymore," said Ranir.

"And where are you going I might ask?" His tone suggested a hint of disappointment or sadness.

"Killiad. We're going to try to convince Sora to join us. She is a great leader and one of the strongest water mages, according to Taryn." Ranir hopes that Taryn's uncertain infatuation with Killiad's leader wasn't clouding his judgment.

"I see," said Ramshi as he rubbed his beard.

Ranir paused teasingly, waiting to see Ramshi's reaction. "We want you to join us, Ramshi."

"I see," he repeated. "Well I won't be any good in a fight. No I think I'll stay here and-"

"We don't want you to fight!" Ranir interrupted. "You're the smartest person I know, and we could really use your expertise."

Ramshi chuckled. "Well thank you, Ranir. I'll think about it. When are you planning to leave."

"Today," blurted Ranir. "In less than an hour, actually."

"Oh what about my duties and training here?" asked the elder.

"I'm sure someone will cover your duties. This is more important."

"Alright," he said as he sprung from his chair.

"Alright!" boasted Ranir. "I'll get Taryn caught up, get your bag packed, but don't take more than you need. We're traveling light."

"Why, of course!" said Ramshi.

Ranir departed the room and sped to Taryn's quarters. He found the room completely empty. Strangely, it had the appearance of abandonment. The bed had fresh wraps, the shelves were cleared, and even the floor was swept. Taryn must have spent the night clearing out his room. Ranir wondered if he should have done the same. It was too late for that now. He strode out to the courtyards and worked around the building searching for the fire mage. He finally discovered his whereabouts.

Ranir's last place to look was the stable house. Taryn was inside one of the large wooden stalls with a massive black horse, and the stable master.

"He likes carrots at night time. Please just take care of him," Taryn told the large man.

"You got it, Taryn. He's in good hands. Good luck on your quest, and should you return, he'll be waiting for you!" said the man with a deep voice.

Taryn puts his hand on the horses head for one last farewell. Ranir had no idea that Taryn kept a horse in the stables, let alone the fact that he was this attached to the steed. He turned to Ranir, "Alright let's get to it, shall we?"

"Ramshi agreed to join us," said Ranir as he nodded. "I assume you'll be teleporting him. Until I really succeed in landing, I'll not be Traveling this time, especially moving forward into the unknown." Ranir thought of crash landing into a building again whilst they were on a dire quest such as this.

"That's understandable. We can get some of the mages together with stones and get you there. We may want to look at getting some goldeons for horses and lodging," said Taryn.

"Where we going to get those?" asked Ranir. "I haven't even seen money since I got here, not that I'm complaining." He suddenly felt guilty for having everything paid for at The Emphyrius.

"I have some saved up from hunting bounties." Ranir shot him a confused look. "I do get paid for my services here, you know."

"Well, maybe I should start looking for a trade!" Ranir teased.

"Ha! We don't need your unique talents going to waste on a farm, Ranir."

Ranir and Taryn ascended the hills of the courtyards and headed toward Ramshi's office. Before they reached the small room, Ramshi met them around a corner of a corridor. He was panting heavily like a dog and sweat was beaded on his brow.

"Come, quick!" he said as he raced off toward his office. Ranir and Taryn trailed behind him closely. When they entered the room, a sour smell lingered about. Sitting in a corner was a man dressed in all black. He was slouched over causing his hood to conceal his face.

"Who is it?" asked Ranir.

Ramshi leaned close to Ranir's ear and whispered, "I think it's the archer that killed Balor. His robes aren't from around here."

"Look at me!" yelled Taryn. His tone was driven by instant anger. The man didn't stir an inch. His breathing was deep and gurgling. It produced the sound of someone deathly ill, with phlegm in their throat. Upon further examination from afar, Ranir noticed a small pool of blood on the floor, seeping from the stranger.

"He's injured. And I don't know why he is here," said Ramshi. He moved behind the two elementals.

"I said look at me!" Taryn repeated louder as he reached for the strangers jowls. The man looked up just before Taryn touched him, causing him to backpedal. The strangers face looked the exact same as the sunken eyed assassin that they encountered in the forests of Heramor. Taryn's eyes grew wide. Ranir's heart felt like it had jumped inside his chest.

"Obirsha, The Fallen Son," said the stranger and his head dropped limp.

For a moment, there was a pause of bewilderment, then Taryn ripped a mana stone from his pocket. "Oh no you don't! You aren't getting away that easy you damn coward!" He began healing the stranger before he siphoned the stone as he wasn't thinking clearly. The stranger's body sprung to life as he tried to stand.

Ranir wasn't taking any chance on this one getting away. Using Surging Speed he forced the elemental magic into his muscles and let his fist fly into the man's revolting face, knocking him out cold. "What?" he asked Taryn and Ramshi as they looked at him, flabbergasted.

"Well," stuttered Ramshi, "that was eventful." He chuckled nervously. This was the first time Ranir noticed Ramshi in the presence of a physical conflict. He seemed more agitated and unnerved than Ranir would have expected. It made him slightly waver in his decision to bring Ramshi along.

"Ramshi, are you certain you want to join us?" asked Ranir. "There's no shame in staying safe."

"No. No I want to come along. I'll be fine as long as I don't have to fight." He nodded rapidly. "I shall embrace the quest for the greater good!" he said as he threw his fist to the air sarcastically.

"Well alright, how do you want to get him and Ramshi to Killiad?" Ranir asked.

"I'll port Ramshi and get a room. Then I'll come back for him," he said as he jabbed a finger toward the archer. "Then the mages will get you to

Killiad." He placed a hand a Ramshi's shoulder and began casting the orange fire ring around their feet.

"Don't take too long visiting your lady friend!" teased Ranir, bouncing his eyebrows up and down. Taryn cracked a smile and shook his head as they disappeared. Ranir waited for nearly 20 minutes for the Archemage to return. He kept a close watch on the assassin, imaging what spell he could use should he awaken.

Ranir began to play by throwing hands about and making sounds of lightning. "Bzht! Pew! Wah wah huh!" he got slightly carried away pretending to fight the assassin. It had a long time since he was in a playful mood. Marnos used to spar him with sticks, imagining they were swords, when they were younger.

Suddenly his heart sank and he froze still upon hearing someone behind him. "What are you doing?" said a soft, woman's voice.

Ranir turned around slowly with his hands still in casting form. "Nothing. Just waiting." He shuttered nervously and felt like his stomach was tied in a knot. The girl was stunning. She seemed similar in age to Ranir. Long, jet black hair flowed down her back and around her shoulders.

"And who is that?" she asked, flicking her green, cat like eyes to the assassin.

"Um, he uh, is...an assassin." Ranir said. He wanted to lie and not scare you away but the truth blurred out instead.

"Really? And just you guarding him?" she

teased. Her tone was playful, almost.

"Well, I'm-"

"The Lightning Rod," she interrupted. "I know." She giggled. Ranir felt his face flush and looked away from her.

"What are you-?" he halted as Taryn appeared in the room between them.

"You ready to go?" he asked. He turned and saw the girl in the green silk-looking robe. "Oh, Sagin. What are you doing up here?"

"You know her?" asked Ranir impatiently as he jumped to his feet.

"Well of course, Ranir. I know almost all of the mages here. Especially," he turned toward the girl. "The only earth mage within The Emphyrius. " Ranir's eyes grew wide. He had met only 2 earth mages and they were all but friendly.

"You're an earth mage? I thought that-"

"Yes everyone thinks that geomancers are loyal to only Gnariam herself. I seek to help the people that inhabit the world," she said.

Ranir shot a hinted look to Taryn, thinking, "she could go with us. She could be useful in a fight. She could help turn the tides of these battles. She's so beautiful!" He slammed his eyes shut, trying to block the latter idea from his reasoning. Taryn gave a half smile. He understood Ranir's desire to have her join them and have a nod.

"Sagin, do you want to come with us?" asked Ranir. His heart felt fluttery.

"For what?" she questioned.

"We're going to try to stop The Necromancer that's been plaguing Gnariam with dark magic. It seems he wants to take control of Sythestine. "

"I see. Well I can't just up and leave. I take care of so much here at The Emphyrius." She began pacing in the doorway for a moment. Ranir felt discouraged and regretted asking her. "Alright. If my sister can lend a hand in the fields and some people can help harvest, I can go."

Ranir was full of joy once again. He had never felt this way about a girl. "You can help teleport me to Killiad with Taryn!" Sagin stared blankly at him. "Oh. Right um, I am not a mage, can't teleport."

"Well I can!" she boasted. "Please give me a few minutes to sort things out, and I will be back." Her tone changed from intrigued to excited. She casted a teleport, "*Etuk Alansi!*" a bold green circle formed around her feet and she was gone.

Ranir stared at the threshold for a moment. "Mm hmm!" Taryn cleared his throat with hefty exertion, startling Ranir.

Ranir looked over to discover a broad smile on his face.

"Don't even!" said Ranir.

"I wasn't going to say anything," Taryn said with a chuckle. They both sat for only a few minutes and Sagin returned with a small leather satchel. Ranir noticed her hips were fashioned with a thin belt holding a beautifully crafted dagger.

"Ready!" she exclaimed.

"Great!" Ranir said as he pulled out a mana stone. "Take this. Leach the mana 'cause you'll need it."

"For what?"

"My Power makes it difficult, let's just say that." She glanced at Taryn with a concerned glisten in her slanted eyes. Taryn nodded to her once with his eyebrows raised as if to ask, 'Are you sure you want to join us?'

"Alright," Sagin said, grasping the stone from Ranir's palm. For a second, her hand lingered on his, and she slipped away. Ranir felt a lump in his throat, making it hard to breath.

"Alright, well, um. Yeah, we're all ready, so...yeah lets go, then." Ranir was certain his words were slurred.

Within minutes the trio, along with their prisoner was teleported into Killiad. Ranir wasn't sure where he was though. Taryn guided the port directly into the room that he had booked. Ramshi was sitting on a small chair with a dagger in hand.

"Oh thank The Gods! What took so long!" shouted Ramshi as soon as they appeared. It was so sudden that Taryn instinctively drew one of his swords and ignited one hand. Sagin stared at his fire wide-

265

eyed. She paced in a circle around to the front of Taryn, admiring the flame.

"You are an Archemage?" she asked with an overbearing volume.

"Sssht, don't say that out loud," Taryn blurted, "and yes, long story, I can create fire from the elemental power."

"Boy, am I glad I came along!" she shouted again. Taryn extinguished the fire.

Ignoring the wondrous teenager in front of him, he asked, "Ramshi, this is Sagin, I'm certain you know that. She will be accompanying us on this quest as well.

"Ah, yes. Sagin, how are you?" asked Ramshi as he sheathed the dagger.

"I'm doing great. Having an interesting day now!" she exclaimed. Ranir was taken aback by her sudden change in tone and manner. Now, she seemed more akin to a child than he did.

"We need to get him to a Mentalist, quick," Taryn said. He looked down at the assassin, still unconscious. "Ranir, did you kill him?" He shook the archer.

"No, I just punched him! Besides you can't teleport the dead, remember?" Ranir defended.

Suddenly the assassin stirred slightly, calming Taryn's potential alarming situation. "I'll be right back, just watch him. If you need to, sock him again," said Taryn. He departed the room in a near sprint.

266

Ranir dragged the wilted body of the bowman to a corner. As he let go, the assassin slid downward against the wall and hit his head on the floor. Ranir couldn't help but let out a laughing spurt. He cupped his hand over his mouth to silence himself, and looked back at Sagin. Her expression seemed like she was struggling to contain laughter. Suddenly the room erupted in hoots and cries of laughter. Ramshi walked over to the bed, shaking his head with a smile.

"Kids. The things that entertain kids!" he said sarcastically. Reaching for a pillow, he grunted, showing his age physically. He took the cushion over and situated it under the assassin's head tardily, with his arm extended as far as it would reach. The sounds of footsteps could be heard for several seconds ascending the stairs to their lofted room.

Taryn stepped back into the room. Sora was with him as well as a pale, thin man dressed in an all-white robe. "Ranir, this is Nanoc Savilar," he said with a hand on the thin man's shoulder. "He is a Mentalist."

"Nice to meet you, Nanoc." Ranir said with an outstretched arm, extending a hand to shake. The man grasped Ranir's, sending a chill through his arm. Nanoc's hand was as frigid as ice.

"Please. The pleasure is mine, Lightning Rod." Nanoc said with a deep bow. Ranir returned the bow respectfully.

"I've been meaning to ask, what is a Mentalist?" asked Ranir.

"Well, I'm glad you asked, Ranir. I'm a

Mentalist! A Mentalist is a mage, or hedge witch, that specializes in entering, alternating or erasing the mind of humans." He must have seen a threatened look on Ranir's face. "Don't worry, only works on non-magical humans. You've nothing to fear." His voice seemed as cold as his palm was and yet, he sounded sophisticated and respectful.

"Is it magic?" asked Ranir.

"Oh very much so. I'm still a mage, in my eyes anyway," he turned to look at Sora, "I was just gifted with mind instead of element.

"I see. That would be very handy, indeed. So you think you can get answers from him?"

"I hope so. Most humans crack easily. Others have been trained to resist Mentalists," explained Nanoc.

"Nanoc has agreed to join us on our quest. Sora has as well," praised Taryn. Sora turned to Ranir and gave a quick smile.

"That is great, Sora! Finally, we get some powerful mages on our team!" teased Ranir.

"Please, Nanoc," started Sora, begin the interrogations."

"As you wish, My Lord." Nanoc bowed and rushed over to the assassin. "It will help if he were awake. Would you mind?" He was staring at Ranir.

"Mind what?"

"Give him a little shock, please. Jolt some

energy into him. See if we can get a rouse." Ranir felt weird about using his power in such a manner but Taryn's and Sora's silence seemed like an agreement with The Mentalist.

Ranir summon his Element to one of his palms diminutively. A few arcs jumped around his fingertips. Sagin leaned in extra close to Ranir's hand. She looked like someone studying a foreign animal. Ranir glided over to the archer and placed his hand on the back of the man's neck. It didn't take much effort for Ranir to send out a small arc. A flash of blue energy lit up the corner and the assassin sat upright rapidly. Ranir jumped backwards. Before he hit the floor, Nanoc swept over and had both hands around the assassin's head, entrancing the archer with a magical aura that reminded Ranir of low hanging fog. The magic swirled from Nanoc's hand and appeared to enter the temples of the Archer.

Suddenly the murderer was still, his eyes wide opened and rolled backwards, giving the visual aspect of overflowing-white eyeballs. Nanoc was speedily muttering voiceless words under his breath with his head arching down. He paused and looked up to the group of mages around him. "He's ready, ask him what you want to know."

Chapter 22: Rogue

"What is your name?" started Taryn. He seemed to be the likely choice to interrogate the prisoner. After all, Taryn was, now previously, a bounty hunter in charge of tracking down criminals. Questioning people was a large task in his duty to getting closer to finding people. Many of his bounties throughout the years were magically capable of eluding him for long periods of time.

"My name is Pardim Malaaki," said the assassin in an airy voice. It nearly resembled a forced whisper slipped from his dry, cracked lips.

"Who do you work for?" asked Taryn.

"I work for The Necromancer."

"Who hired you to kill Balor, the cursed mage?" Taryn wanted to make sure he took his time with his questions because even under hypnosis, some people were capable of lying.

"The Emphyre." His words resonated through the entire room, echoing in the silence. Ranir's heart felt as if it ceased. The assassin gave a response that nobody was ready for. Taryn glared at Pardim with a furious silence. Sora cupped her hand to her mouth with a gasp. Ramshi grew pale in the face as if he had fallen ill.

"Is it possible he's lying?" Taryn finally broke the quietness to The Mentalist.

"Not likely. Let me search his memories and see what we find. Be quiet. I need to focus to dig deeper." He started muttering once more, squeezing his eyes tighter. Suddenly the flames from the torches began twitching, like a breeze was adrift in the room. The room grew colder.

"What's happening?" asked Ranir, whispering to not break The Mentalist's spell.

"He's resisting the probe," answered Sora. "I've seen this before. Don't worry."

No matter what she said, Ranir's vexation was set in, and wasn't going away until this entire ordeal had passed. Nanoc continued to pry into the mind and memories of Pardim. From the outside watching The Mentalist's face, it was only a matter of patience and trying to understand what was happening. For Nanoc, it was diving deep into, not only the memories but, the emotions and experiences of Pardim's life. After several quiet minutes, Nanoc said, "I have it," with a grunt. He seemed to be struggling in his mental battle with the assassin. "He isn't lying. I see them."

Ranir stepped around Nanoc to watch his face more closely. Through the thin membranes of his eyelids, Ranir could see Nanoc's eyes racking back and forth. "See who?" Ranir whispered.

"I see The Emphyre. He's asking Pardim to be at the Southeast tower...he's tasked him with killing the prisoner. The Emphyre is telling him not to harm you or Taryn. He's...ah...he's strong. I can't hold it much longer." Nanoc's breathing became heavier.

271

"Can you see if you find a memory of his past? Where does he come from? Where did he get that arrow?" Taryn began firing questions rapidly.

"I- I can't hold him. I'm losing my hold. Get ready to take him. Ah!" Nanoc screamed and ripped his eyes open, falling on his back with a thud. Pardim's eyes popped open as well. He screamed a foreign word as he placed one hand on the floor to lift his entire body. Horizontally afloat, he planted both feet into Ranir's chest before he had time to cast a spell. Both of Pardim's feet landed on the floor. He was crouched like a cat ready to pounce.

"A*stuk alo bis!*" cried out Taryn. An orange flame slithered like a snake and pelted Pardim in the chest.

"*Runel áshtin!*" called Sora from behind Taryn. As Pardim slammed against the wall, a wave of white water crashed against his face and paused, suffocating the assassin. Sora held firm as she channeled her control over the liquid. Sliding across the floor backwards with his hands and feet, Nanoc moved behind the mages before springing to his feet. Pardim thrashed against the wall.

Ranir was on his feet within a moment's notice. "Alright, let him down!" he bellowed over the sounds of Pardim's feet pounding the floor mixed with the deafening oceanic waves drowning him. As he demanded, Sora released her hold on the spell. Pardim went limp for a moment too long as Ranir grabbed him by his throat, picking him up against the wall with his feet hanging a foot above the floor. "Now you listen to me!" he screamed as he let the elemental power fill his eyes with pure white-blue energy. Pardim kicked once again and Ranir squeezed harder, feeling the strains of muscles in the assassin's neck.

"Ranir, stop. You're going to kill him and we need answers," demanded Taryn. Ranir released his hold and Pardim fell to the floor, landing directly on his side once more, clutching his neck. He let out a noisy cough and a deep breath. Taryn, Sora and Sagin stepped closer to close the gap between them and the assassin.

Pardim sat upright. "Disgusting swine!" he cried out with a scratchy voice. He slowly gazed upon each of them as he thought of his next move. He was trapped.

"Tell us, where did you get that arrow? Who do you actually work for?" Taryn asked Pardim directly, "and why the Emphyre hired you to kill Balor?" Taryn's breathing was heavier than Pardim's. He almost seemed equally nervous as he was raging.

The assassin was silent for a moment. Suddenly he spoke, "Hail to The Necromancer. Long live the Knights of The Fallen Son!" With inhuman speed he reached forward and pulled Sagin's blade from her belt and slit his own throat directly across the artery. Before he fell, he stabbed himself on the inside of his right thigh, severing another artery. His slid down the wall and landed on the floor, gurgling blood through his raspy breaths. Within seconds his body was still, his eyes wide open. Dark red blood oozed from the corner of his mouth.

None of them seemed to have time to even react and they didn't move after he ended his life. "No!" Taryn cried out, falling to his knees. Tears began to well up in his eyes. Sora placed a hand on his shoulder. In that moment, Ranir realized how much Taryn was relying on the assassin for answers surrounding the mystery archer that murdered his brother in cold blood. He had never seen Taryn grieve for his brother, even after he killed the archer so long ago. Ranir felt empathetic for his friend and felt his stomach twist inside.

"Taryn, we will have our answers. You will get your answer," he said, realizing afterwards that his words didn't sound comforting at all. "I'm sorry," he added.

"You're damn right we will," Taryn exclaimed dryly as he sniffed back his emotions, returning to his normal seriousness. Ranir was impressed at how well Taryn was able to hide his emotions by burying a part of him inside. "And I know just who to get our answers from, too." He turned and looked straight into Ranir's eyes. "The Emphyre."

"We need to find him. Where do we start?" asked Ranir. His fury for the treachery and deceit that The Emphyre had gone well past the point of forgiveness. He wanted to hunt down the man who he thought was a friend, a leader, a mentor. Behind Ranir, Ramshi was muttering under his breath, pacing back and forth. He face was hard in thought. "What is it, Ramshi?" asked Ranir.

"Didn't you hear where Pardim's loyalty was?"

"With The Necromancer, yes I-"

"No. He said 'Long live the Knights of The Fallen Son'," said Ramshi. His face seemed more pale than usual.

"What is that, like a cult?" questioned Taryn. "I feel like I've heard that name before." He shot a glance back at Sora who seemed as befuddled as the rest.

"The Fallen Son is Carmos, Eros's son, that he banished to Hel. The Knights were legendary thousands of years ago for trying to raise the Dark Lord." Ramshi scanned across their faces. Nobody was realizing the detrimental danger. "Come in! They were responsible for mass raids across Gnariam for centuries. If he is a part of The Knights, truly, the world is in more danger than just The Necromancer. Everything they do is for their benefit to please Carmos The Cursed." He took deep, shaky breath, "and if he was working for The Necromancer, something big is at play here."

"Let's not get unhinged, Ramshi. We don't know anything evident, yet. For all we know those memories could've been altered, right Nanoc?" asked Taryn.

"I suppose they could have. Another Mentalist could have worked him over before, a very strong one but yes it's possible. There have been people," explained Nanoc, "emotionally driven by false memories. Done terrible things."

"So first thing we need to do is find The Emphyre and get the truth," replied Taryn.

"Sora, you have political power that could help," said Taryn as he stood up. "Can you get to The Throne Room and find something that belongs to him. We'll need it. With his leave, there will be guards blocking the entrance."

Sora chuckled. "I'm sure I can persuade them." More than the other 5 in their group, she was radiant with confidence.

"I know you can," Taryn said with a quick wink. "Ranir and Sora, you'll come with me. We need more supplies and horses. Ramshi and Nanoc, stay here and keep that door barred. If it's us," he turned to the group altogether, "knock three times, pause then two more."

"That's why you should've taken the Leadership spot, not me," said Sora.

"I didn't want to be stuck in politics," he told Sora. "Let alone in Killiad of all places." His tone shifted to a humorous manner. "Alright everyone knows the plan. We will all meet back here to begin tracking down The Emphyre. He is our main goal right now."

"Luckily, after Alagien, The Necromancer hasn't been spotted yet. It may just by us some time to get out answers," said Ranir.

Without a word, Sora disappeared into a portal. Ranir and Sagin followed Taryn into the heart of Killiad.

As the hours crept into night, Sora was the only one who hadn't returned. Taryn had paid for rations and some supplies and blankets. The horses were saddled up and awaiting in the stables. Taryn was pacing nervously, "Alright I'm going to get her," he exclaimed. He didn't wait for a single person's opinion or permission. He vanished into a portal.

"So now what? *We* wait?" asked Sagin. She was growing rather bored being forced to stay in one room for so long. Her attention was almost always turned towards nature and farming.

"It appears so. I don't think it was wise for him to leave us though," replied Ranir. "Just stay alert in case anything happens." He looked over at the bloody blanket that they had thrown over Pardim's body. "We need to do something with that before someone downstairs notices a stench."

"I can help with that!" exclaimed Sagin, jumping to her feet. "It'll give me something to do as well." She strode over to the cold corpse and kneeled down, closing her eyes.

"What are you going to do?" asked Ranir.

"I'm going to give him a burial."

"How? I don't want to try to move the body and risk getting caught."

"Ranir," called Ramshi, "just watch," he gestured with his hands toward Sagin. Nanoc moved closer to get a better view.

"*Ornlekh Gnariam, na shini embril atasi,*" Sagin said softy, a near whisper. A green glow erupted from her palms as she cracked her eyes open. Slowly, she separated her arms, one running toward the head of Pardim, the other hovering towards his feet. The luminous energy from her hands seemed to light up the room, with a warm fluorescent tone. Ranir felt overwhelmed in a calming sensation. It reminded him of the first time he met Eros. The dimension of white fog had the same affect on him.

After several slow pauses, and waving her hands over the body, fanning it with the brilliance of nature magic, Pardim's cadaver began to twitch. Ranir's eyes grew wide. "What's happening?" he shot a glint to Ramshi who seemed to be unnaturally unagitated.

Sagin stopped channeling her earth magic and rose to her feet. As the fatigue had an imposing affect on her, she stumbled for a moment until Ranir halted her fall in a double armed embrace. Time seemed to slow for just a moment as her cheek pressed against his chest. He could feel his heart pounding faster and faster. Then she pulled away. "Sorry, Ranir. And thank you," she said with an enticing smile."

"Oh its, its nothing." They awkwardly stared at each other without a word for a few seconds longer. Ranir shook his head to break the trance. "Um, so what was all of that?"

"That is a Gnariam Burial spell. Just watch," she said.

The corpse was still twitching. It stopped and Ranir watched the blanket begin to wriggle. Something was moving underneath of it but not the body. He looked at Sagin with anxiety. She chortled and walked over to Pardim, pulling the cover back to reveal a body-sized bed of flowers and vines where the body used to lay. "This way," she explained, "Pardim's afterlife can go back into Gnariam. A little something to give back to Mother Nature, you see."

"It's beautiful," blurted Ranir.

"Thank you," she replied as she looked down. "I think I need to sit. That spell takes a lot of focus and mana to do right. Its a transmogrification of the human into plants. Not easy." She sat on the small, creaky bed.

The instant she sat, the room sounded like it had cracked open as Taryn and Sora reappeared in the room. "Help!" cried Taryn. He was holding Sora like an infant. Her once blue robe was stained in blood and she was unconscious. Ranir rushed over and helped lower her to the floor.

"What happened?" asked Nanoc. He immediately placed his hands to her head.

"What are you doing?" screamed Taryn.

"I'm calming her. Mood persuasion is the only magic I can do against a mage, relax. It will help her stay still."

Taryn let Nanoc calm her mind. "She was ambushed. The Emphyre is the enemy and he knows we're on to him. He has a mage with him, and I don't know who it is. She got the best of Sora until I got there. She was nearly dead. I need the mana stones!" he explained.

Without hesitation, Ranir rushed the stones over to Taryn. He siphoned the mana from them and ignited his hands in blood red colored flames. "*Atulashut!*" Taryn commanded and began rubbing the fire over Sora. Ranir watched in astonishment as the blood seeping from her wounds reversed its flow, sealing up the cuts. It appeared that she had been stabbed multiple times and cut as well. Within 10 seconds her wounds were cured fully. Nanoc cut his enchantment off and pulled his hands back.

That all sat around her for a moment. Suddenly she sat upright with a large gasp of air, her eyes opened broad. Taryn steadied her and clenched her in an embrace. "Oh I thought I might lose you Sora," he said in a shaky voice.

"Taryn, I'm fine. Thanks to you, I am alive." Taryn let go of her, allowing her to sit up straight. He looked over to Ranir who was smirking. Jokingly, Ranir raised his eyebrows in a flirtatious manner. Taryn squinted his eyes and shook his head.

"What happened, Sora?" asked Ranir. She rose to her feet in a demeanor that nobody could guess she was just dying.

"Well, I went to The Throne Room and there were guards. Even my rank didn't let them drop their force. So I waited until there was a shift change. It wasn't long," she explained. "Then, I went back and knocked them both out. Once I got in the room, I only found this," she had a small mirror in her hand.

"No, no, no!" shouted Ramshi. He grasped the

mirror from her hand and threw it at the wall. "That is his Black Sortár Mirror. He has a matching pair. When you look through one, you don't see your reflection, you see through the face of the other mirror. It's like a window. That's how he knew you were there, snooping around." Ramshi seemed more unnerved than he had ever been. Ranir was trying to discover if it was fear or anger, maybe a mix of both. "Now he knows who is all here." He plumped down on the bed.

"How could he use something like that? He's not a magician at all, Ramshi," said Taryn.

"The mirror is enchanted, not the user."

"Who can do enchantments like that?" asked Ranir.

"Mentalists," Nanoc spoke up. "Mentalists are more than capable of enchanting mundane objects to do certain things."

"Well, that is just fantastic. Let's just hope he doesn't know *where* we are exactly," said Sora. "Anyway, as I left the room an air mage blasted a hole through the door and knocked me down. She was powerful, too. She might have even been an Archemage. The guards came in to try to stop me, or....kill me...I don't really know. I fought them off but that mage was relentless. That's when Taryn showed up and I passed out."

"Can you still track him from the pieces of the mirror?" asked Ranir. Once again, he was cognizant of the vast amount of knowledge that he was still lacking in the world of magic.

"Maybe, I'll most likely need Sora and Sagin to help," replied Taryn. Both the water mage and the earth mage kneeled down next to Taryn. They all placed a hand on the small shard of mirror. "Okay, I will guide the rift, just focus on The Emphyre." He began muttering words that Ranir didn't know. He kneeled down on one knee, watching in amazement at how the three mages had came together to track down The Emphyre. He thought that it might take them awhile to find him. He was wrong.

Within seconds, Taryn locked on to Credin's location. "He's in Drâgok. Its a small village north of the desert. The house looks to be abandoned," said Taryn. They all pulled away from the spell.

"How are we going to get there? Can you teleport us all?" asked Ranir.

"Yes, if I have the location in mind, I can guide us all. Sora, can we leave the horses?" asked Taryn.

"Well, of course. I don't think you'll get your goldeons back though!" she blurted.

"I wouldn't dream of trying," he teased. He turned to speak to everyone. "Alright, everyone grab your supplies and satchels. Ranir and Sagin only had a leather satchel each. Nanoc had only a small pouch that hung to his hip and a back strap that held some rations. Ramshi had the most luggage, with him carrying his books with them. They all gathered in a circle. Taryn led the teleport, guiding them to Drâgok. Sagin and Sora lended their power to Taryn to get them all there safely. Ranir always enjoyed watching the colors blending together from different elements. Taryn's was always orange, Sora's blue, and now adding Sagin's greenish teleportation created a near gray color. Combining all four colors of the elements would cast a silver ring.

Suddenly, Ranir was thrust into the fray with the rest. In a flash of bright light, he was standing in a new room. His first instinct was to make sure that the entire group managed to stay together. He looked around, noticing something moving from the corner of his eye.

Sitting in a tall, red chair, nonchalantly, was The Emphyre. He sat with one leg crossed over the others, his snake like robe glistening in the candlelight.

He placed a black mirror on a small table beside him. He poke without a hint of panic. "Well, that didn't take long." His demeanor confirmed the group's suspicions. Ranir instantly became enraged. Without hesitating, he grabbed Credin by the lapels of his robe and jerked him from the chair. With a hard thrust he flipped The Emphyre over, smashing his back on the floor, cracking the hardwood floor.

"You traitor! How could you?" he roared. Credin's air was knocked from his lungs. Nobody in the group moved. Ranir was merciless as he lifted him again and threw The Emphyre into the chair. He had aimed to sit him down. Credit smashed through chair with a crash.

"Wait!" cried The Emphyre with a hand out to halt Ranir's wrath. "Let me explain. Ranir was silent.

Credin sat up with his knees bent. "Where to begin?" he asked the room.

"How about start from the beginning of your snaking around," said Sora.

"The beginning," The Emphyre snorted. "Alright, the beginning. When I was 14, my brother saved my life from a bear. But he was killed in the process as well. I was devastated."

"We don't need your entire life story, or why you chose to do what you've done. Just answer the question," barked Taryn.

"Just listen," replied Credin. "It's the whole story as you wanted. A little while later, my brother was breathed back to life by The Lord of The Winds. He became an air mage, you see. My father sent him away, disgusted by the magic. I went with my brother to Thrast, where he could get trained to control his magic. I learned a vast amount about magic as well. After years spent following my brother I decided, for my own life, that I would get into politics. I was jealous of his power, so I wanted power of my own. I slowly worked my ways through the ranks and became Lord of Thrast. My brother didn't care for government. Even through all of that, I was still in his shadow." He paused for a moment, as if choosing his words before he spoke them. "So I corrupted him. I pushed him to get a taste for more magic. I gave him mana stones that I helped steal. Eventually the lust set in, and he grew powerful...and dark. Shadow magic began to fill his heart. I created The Necromancer you see."

284

"The Necromancer? Like Seldos?" asked Ranir.

"Not like, my brother is Seldos," replied Credin. Ranir's stomach contorted. His enemy even having a brother seemed unfathomable. "For a long time, he would listen to me, but he grew uncontrollable. So during his wrath I had the idea of imprisonment. I couldn't kill him. So I exiled him into the mountain. I tricked him, and had some earth mages entomb him." The Emphyre's face looked full of guilt and regret. "I became the hero that rid the world of The Necromancer. I rose to a new rank, The Emphyre of Sythestine."

"You're not just a traitor, you're a liar to the entire kingdom and always have been. You are as vile as Seldos," said Ranir.

"So what, he got out?" asked Taryn.

"Yes, actually. And he forgave me, with a warning. He told me to stay out of his way or he'd burn down Thrast and all of its people. Then, your brother was onto Seldos's minions. An assassin and a Druid."

"I thought the Druid was a bounty," said Ranir.

"No, he was investigating on his own accord. After Taryn found you, things feel into place and then you became The Lightning Rod. I thought Gnariam had a chance to rid the world of my brother once and for all. I sent the mages to bring you back. They failed, obviously. Then Taryn brought you to me, finally. I pushed you to train for your exams, knowing that you needed a purpose. I gave you a purpose, Ranir."

"So you want forgiven?" asked Ranir.

"No, I just wanted you to know that I changed my ways and tried to fix my mistakes."

Taryn kneel down close to The Emphyre. Staring into his eyes, Taryn felt disbelief. "Nanoc, let's find out how much truth he is telling shall we? Dig deep, if you will."

"What? No! I'm telling the truth you ungrateful bastard!" Nanoc crept over cautiously. Ranir and Taryn nodded to each other's intentions and grabbed The Emphyre's feet, sliding him onto his back. They reached up and pinned him to the floor. Nanoc reaches his palms over Credin's temples and casted a spell. He Emphyre clawed the floor and squirmed for a moment, then he was still. His eyes roll back. Nanoc began to search through Credin's memories.

"Seldos is his brother...he forced him to turn dark. They worked together...Seldos wants to be the most powerful sorcerer. Credin wants the most political power. They plan to rule Gnariam, together." There was a long pause as Nanoc sifted through decades of memories. Taryn! He's lying! Your brother...he send the Druid to bait Detmés. Seldos sent the assassin from the Knights!" Nanoc's voice grew shaky as he revealed the treachery. "Detmés was getting close to uncovering their truth. They murdered him! Credin sent a second assassin to finish the job of killing you. Ranir wasn't expected." The group couldn't share the sight with Nanoc, but they could see the horror on his face.

"What happened to the one who murdered my brother?" asked Taryn.

"He's alive! He doesn't know where he went. Ranir! I see Verna. She knows his secret. He sent them to kill you all. He needed strong mages. Ranir your existence threatens their plan. They want to harness your power!" Ranir grew more furious and nervous as Nanoc rattled off various visions.

"Wait that's not-" he was interrupted as an arrow busted through the window and landed in the top of Nanoc's neck. Ranir and Taryn released Credin. A flurry of arrows ripped through the windows as everyone dove to the floor. The arrows flew into the room from several directions in relentless volleys.

Ranir crawled to the door. Suddenly the patting of footsteps could be heard on the roof. They were surrounded. Between pauses of the archers outside Taryn was throwing jets of bright orange fire aimlessly, yet they still couldn't see anyone in the dark. Sora and Sagin did their part to assist the offense.

"Don't you see? They think I've gone rogue!" shouted The Emphyre as he scrambled across the floor seeking cover.

"You are rogue! *Shunet*!" screamed Sora, blasting in the face with an orb of water, knocking him on his back.

"Ranir! Give me a stone, I have an idea!" shouted Sagin through the wallowing sounds of arrows pelting against and inside the house. Without hesitation, Ranir slid a mana stone to her. The rigidness of it caused it to bounce sideways. Sagin dove and caught it. She siphoned the stone completely dry. Ranir watched as she rose to her feet, her eyes glowed bright like a firefly in the night. She dropped the stone and opened her arms wide. "*Estak kawin afum ashal!*" she cried through the window, into the night. As her words left her lips, she dropped and smacked the floor with both palms, send a shock wave that loosed the floorboards and shattered the walls. Chunks of dry wood fell from the ceiling, sending an assassin falling into the room. The wind outside echoed with the sound of cracking trees and rocks. Screams from the assailants crawled through the gaps in the wall. The explosive energy exhausted Sagin and she collapsed on the floor. Ranir grabbed her hand and slid her effortlessly to the other side of the room, planting his boot in the face of the assassin.

Ranir knew that Sagin made the choice to cast the spell but it drove Ranir over the edge of controlling his emotions. As he let her hand fall, he turned around and drew the elemental power inside in a flash. There was itchy build up this time. He began to float above the broken floor and summoned a storm above them. Immediately bright flashes of blue lightning crashed down in the thousands around the house. The entirety of darkness was swept away in a blazing light, revealing hundreds of men outside, all dressed in black.

Without a thought, Ranir threw a lightning bolt through wall and leeched himself onto it, Traveling through the wall, into the open to unleash the elements on those trying to kill them. He flew feet first into one assassin, feeling his sternum crack under the force, sending him tumbling across the yard for a hundred feet. Reaching to the sky he siphoned the storm's raw energy, he casted out pure white chain lightning and held them in each hand. Like a steel chain, he began swinging the hot lightning through the air, lashing through several of the assassins. One man attempting to flee the carnage was severed in half. Ranir spun his body like a child playing, drawing the chains over his head. Suddenly, he felt fatigue creeping over him.

In that moment as he paused to catch his breath, a bright orange beam of fire shot passed him, instantly killing 5 more. As Ranir turned around he could hear Sora casting spells. He remembered the body of water that he landed in outside of Thrast. "Sora! Give them a wave!" he called out. He remembered her sister casting an ocean-style wave of water.

"*Shinis atu ef sim!*" she bellowed. Water instantly formed in from of her, a swell the size of a house. She thrusted it forward soaking a mass in front.

Ranir charged his hands and leashed out chain lightning. This time he let it flow. The blue and white arcs latched onto two assassins and raced into each person that was sipping wet. A brilliantly display of color and power sent a group of 26 stunned, shivering where they stood or lay. In that moment the rest of the men began called out retreat orders and they fled into the dark.

Ranir decided that he'd let them leave. His heart jumped in his chest upon hearing a scream from behind him. It came from Sagin. Ranir rushed into the house, knocking the door from the hinges. Standing in the corner where Ranir left her, The Emphyre was standing behind Sagin, with her dagger to her throat. "Credin! What are you doing?" Ranir bellowed.

"Taking her with me. I know if you let me go, you'll track me down again. So I'll use her for a little insurance. If you even th-"

A thin, red flame snapped sharply, like a dagger, through The Emphyre's eye and exploded through the back of his head. Ranir instantly charged Surging Speed and sped to Sagin, grasping the knife before it slit her throat in Credin's fall of death.

In contrast to the deafening tones of the battle, the cool night air fluttering through the battered house was near soundless. Sora mourned for her friend, Nanoc. He had been her adviser and ally for years. The Emphyre had been untrustworthy and manipulative his entire life. The fact that he was Seldos's brother was almost inconceivable. Ranir was certain that The Necromancer would certainly retaliate now.

The assassin that had crashed through the ceiling was now their prisoner. Sora had tied him to a chair. For now, they still had so many questions. More than anyone, Taryn wanted revenge on The Knights of The Fallen Son. He wanted revenge on The Necromancer. Moving forward, their premise laid on the fact that The Knights were once thought of as a myth, much like Ranir had once thought that magic was a children's bedtime story.

"Where do we go from here?" asked Ranir. Whatever their next move was, he could only hope to hinder Seldos even farther. They had confidence that they had just removed one of his most valuable assets and allies. The loss of The Mentalist was difficult and painful for Sora, but to Ranir, he was another casualty of this war. These were only battles that were leading up to the end.

"For now, we find this group. We find out who killed my brother," explained Taryn. "And we find out what they want. And if what they want is war, and to side with the dark sorcerer Seldos, then so be it."

"Taryn, we are not enough," stated Sora. "If he has the numbers and the power, we will lose."

"We need to get Thrast under control. The Emphyre is dead. Someone will need to step up and take control. No more Emphyres. Every city should have their own King," said Ramshi, "or queen." He nodded to Sora and Sagin.

"Sounds like it should be someone with wisdom and knowledge of both politics and the inner workings of the magical world," said Taryn. Ramshi nodded and looked at the floor.

"Ramshi," called Sora.

"Yes, my Lady?"

"You. You should lead Thrast. You know more of the magical world than nearly every mage that exists. You know more politics and strategies than most generals."

"Oh," he chuckled, "I appreciate that but I, I don't know if I could lead a city, especially the largest city in the Kingdom."

"King Ramshi," piped up Ranir. "I like it, has a smooth sound to it."

"Certainly," agreed Sagin.

Ramshi's face flushed red. As Killiad was the 2nd largest city in Sythestine, Sora was in control in the event that The Emphyre would die. There was nobody who could challenge her rank or rule. Walking over to Ramshi, she placed a hand on his shoulder. "Ramshi, you would make a fine King. You don't have to decide now. Maybe once we get back to Thrast, you can say what you feel."

"Alright," replied Ramshi, "I shall take it under advisement and process that. I will let you know soon."

Using the last mana stone they had, the group teleported back to The Emphyrius. Sora had informed the council of The Emphyre the events that had taken place. She temporarily took control as acting Emphyre. She did not announce the deterioration of The Emphyre rank just yet. She wanted Ramshi's decision first. Ranir and Sagin thought it would be wise to repack their bags and obtain more mana stones. They didn't expect to be at The Emphyrius for long. Taryn and Ramshi went to The Great Library to begin searching old texts on the whereabouts and locations of The Knights of The Fallen Son. Taryn was more driven than anyone and all the more suited to lead this expedition. Ranir decided that he would get a good night's sleep and begin his fresh minded searching in the morning. They were all going to venture into unknown territory, and they needed all of the information that they could get.

Chapter 23: The Knights of The Fallen Son

The next day Ranir was awake, it seemed, before all of Thrast. The sun was still buried in darkness. His dreams were filled with wondrous and terrifying imagery. He couldn't halt the rush of fear of The Necromancer's vengeful destruction. He worried for his friends. He had finally reached a point in his journey to call people friends.

As the sun creeped over the forest, Ranir decided he would put The Necromancer out of his mind and focus his efforts in helping Taryn and Ramshi search for The Knights. After breakfast, he set off toward The Great Library. He wanted to get ahead on his readings. The sooner they could find The Knights, the sooner they could close one more chapter of The Necromancer's plans.

He scanned the spines of thousands of books ranging from 'A History of Thrast' to 'Alchemy And Beyond'. As he continued to read the names, he realized that there was a vast amount of knowledge that he had never obtained. Out of curiosity, Ranir slid his hand across a section of books and randomly stopped to jerk the book from the shelf.

"'*Familiarity of The Divine*'. Such weird names," he said gazing at the black book. The text on the cover was shining silver. He opened the cover and began to read in silence.

'The true origin of magic started with divinity. The beginning has been lost in history. What is known, is the lineage of Prölin, The All Divine Father Who was the first God born with magic of Light. From that Light, came his son Gïran, the first born with magic of Darkness. There was balance in Fönthis. In that time, Gnariam was filled greed, lust and envy. Mankind was on the brink of destruction. Both the bearers of Light and Darkness sent their spirits to Gnariam as balance. In the great fall of Yldrinal, The Golden City in the East, Eros was created from the energy produced by Light and Darkness. Eros produced an explosion of energy when he came to form. The energy that destroyed the city scattered Light and Darkness into Gnariam. Eros returned to Fönthis, and created 6 Gods. Four of his children carried the power of the elements. One was made with Light, one with Darkness, to preserve balance. To rid Gnariam of Darkness, Eros banished his son to Hel. Lornil was the Daughter of Light, who spread her life force into Gnariam so that humans may always have a shade of light for all of time.'

Ranir slammed the book shut. He tried to wrap his mind around the history of The Gods. He never knew that many existed. Setting the book back to the shelf, he began to pick out several books in an effort to find anything else on The Knights, The Fallen Son, Hel or Eros. Most of the texts and manuscripts seemed mundane compared to the little black book.

The sound of the door opening startled him and he dropped a book, noticing a thin stick slide out of it. Without looking at whoever entered, he picked up the object. He observed it and saw that it wasn't a stick, it was a broken piece of ember looking wood, glowing with no heat. Ranir's eyes grew wide. He had only ever seen this type of one wood in the arrows from the assassins. What was it doing in a book?

"Ranir, what on Gnariam are you doing?" asked Taryn. He must have been the one to startle Ranir. Without a word, Ranir held the splinter up to his face. Taryn squinted his eyes with his eyebrows forced downward. "What is...?" he stopped and swiped the piece of familiar wood from Ranir's hand. "Where did you get this?"

"It was in one of these books. It popped out when I dropped the stack," replied Ranir.

"Which book?"

"I don't remember. I didn't see it fall out."

"Why would it even be in a book?" asked Taryn as both he and Ranir began flipping through the pages of the four books that crashed to the floor.

"Here!" said Ranir. He found a map of Sythestine. The book had a small opening punched through the right side pages, but not the outer cover. He handed the book to Taryn, not knowing what it meant. Taryn studied the hole and the spot on the map where the hole bled through. The map cover both pages, left and right. The hole stopped on the right side of the map.

Taryn took the book and set it on the table and put the sliver of wood up to it, discovering that it matched perfectly. "See this?" he showed Ranir the perfect mate. "I think this is a marker, Ranir."

"For what, though, is the question," replied Ranir. "Do you think its the Knights?" he asked.

"I'm not sure. I can't say why this particular book would have a map marked that easily. And if it is," he scratched his head, "then why did it just now get discovered? Maybe it was placed here recently."

"Where does the hole mark?" asked Ranir casually.

"The middle of Drâgok Desert, unfortunately. There isn't anything there but sand and Skorn."

Ranir stared at the book pages. Twisting his head to the left and to the right trying to piece together the very vague puzzle. He picked up the splinter and pushed it through from the backside of the right page and closed the map. Slowly he turned the ember-wood shaft with a little bit of pressure. The old page felt like it was being ground down to dust. He slowly opened the book again and pulled the stick free. Clearly marked on the left page was a small dot from the wood. "Taryn, what is there?" he asked.

Taryn spun the book around so that it faced him. He leaned closer to the map and then looked up as if searching the air for answers. "I don't know. I believe there used to be an abandoned village on the edge of that forest." He began pacing back and forth, making clicking noises with his tongue. "And if it is an abandoned village, what better place than that to hide a cult of assassins Hel bent on bringing The Fallen Son back, eh?" His tone shifted to excited. Ranir suddenly remembered the story of Eros's son that he banished. He wondered if Eros had made the right choice. With the God of Light spreading her power into Gnariam, he wondered how there could be balance if all darkness was concealed and forced to be in Hel.

"Taryn, if Carmos The Fallen is really locked away in Hel, and he is the God of Darkness, how can there be shadow magic and darkness on Gnariam?" asked Ranir.

"I don't know, Ranir. I'm not much into the history of things. Ramshi would be a better one to ask than me. I just want to punish those who are evil incarnate and those that had a hand in my brother's murder."

"I see, well. Maybe I will ask him then. He seems to know quite a bit about all of this," said Ranir.

"That he does, another reason Sora wants him to lead Thrast," replied Taryn as he continued to stare at the page. "I'm going to take this book and find a detailed map of Sythestine, I'll be back." He exited the room in a rush.

Ranir made his departure from the library and jetted off to Ramshi's office. He had other questions about the little black book he had found earlier as well.

Several minutes later as he entered the office of the elder teacher, Ranir made sure to bring the divinity book with him. "Ah, Ranir! I was just going to come looking for you. I think I know how to find The Knights," exclaimed Ramshi.

"Oh, yeah. I think we may have already found a location." Ranir explained to Ramshi about the ember looking wood and the map.

"I see. That is interesting. I've been through those books thousands of times and I've never seen a book like you describe, much less a book with a hole in it!"

"Taryn took the book to compare the map with a more detailed map. The marker on the map wasn't titled, but Taryn thinks there was an abandoned village there."

"Yes, there is an old village. Its one of the oldest temple structures in Sythestine. Some of the architects have written books and we have collected them in our library. The village was abandoned due to a plague about 1700 years ago. It was called Rafstal Village."

"Rafstal Village. I'll try to remember that." He paused as if to think of his questions before asking them.

"Very well. Let me know if you need my help again, Ranir. If you are planning to go there, please let me know that as well. I have a massive decision to make and need to really process my options and ponder a while."

"Yes, totally. I get that. I...I will leave you to it." He decided that maybe another time, he would ask Ramshi his philosophical inquiry. Ranir had many questions and he wasn't sure if Ramshi would be the one to answer all of them.

Ranir went back to the library to find Taryn with a monumental sized map sprawled out on one of the tables. "See this?" he said as he pointed to a spot on the larger map that matched to the map from the book.

"Rafstal Village?" Ranir blurted without looking first.

"What? No, there is nothing. Wait, did you speak to Ramshi?"

"I did. He said there is an abandoned village and a temple at that location. It was called Rafstal Village, 1700 years ago."

"Whoa, that is a long time!. I'd be surprised if the village still stands at all. The temple though, could very well be in decent shape to inhabit."

Ranir knew what the next step was without asking. "So when do we leave?"

"As soon as possible. Ramshi and Sora are going to stay here. Do you want to bring Sagin along?" he asked with a smirk. Ranir couldn't stop his cheeks from pulling back into a smile.

"No, not this time. It should be just us. If they range into the hundreds, we wouldn't be enough with all of us anyway. If its much less, maybe we can come to an agreement of sorts and they will seek justice, or something," said Ranir.

"I don't plan on doing much talking, Ranir."

Taryn's voice grew bitter and stern. "I plan on going to their home and destroying it. I want them to suffer as they have wrought suffering unto this world."

"Taryn, I know you are still mourning his passing, and I know that your revenge has not been fulfilled, but we cannot go into a horde of assassins simply blasting our way through them," replied Ranir.

Taryn sat down at the table and put his head down for a long pause. Then he looked up at Ranir and said, "You're right. I just hate them all and The Necromancer and they are doing as they please without a care who gets hurt."

"That is what Credin did for years. And now look, we got him, did we not. He got what he deserved," exclaimed Ranir.

"Yes I know. I've just grown...impatient."

"I will go get a bag packed and tell Ramshi that we will be off. You tell Sora," Ranir said without wasting another breath on stating the obvious in argument.

Taryn stood up and said, "Don't forget to tell your mate as well." He winked.

"Sagin is not my mate, Taryn. We are just friends. Grow up, would you?" Ranir could feel his face flushing into a deep red tone.

"I never said anyone's name!" Taryn said with a chuckle.

Without another word Ranir turned and went toward his room to get his bag packed for their next quest. He wanted to take even less this time, albeit he wanted to make sure that they had enough rations, etc for more than a one night stay.

After packing his small satchel and throwing it over his shoulder, he made his way to Ramshi's office and knocked on the door. He knew that Ramshi had no problem with Ranir barging in, but certain times, like now when Ramshi was trying to focus, he felt like being more respectful. "Come in!" came a voice from in side the room.

Ranir cracked the door open hesitantly. He wasn't sure why he felt nervous this time. "Ramshi," He said as he pushed the door open all the way. He didn't enter the room, merely stood shoulder against threshold. "I'm going to be venturing to the old village we spoke about."

"Oh? By yourself?" said Ramshi as he stood slowly.

"No. Taryn will be accompanying me this time." Something was flushing guilt into Ranir's mind. He knew that he was making the right choice, though.

"Well, alright." Ramshi's face was hardened. "Ranir..." He paused. Ramshi walked over to Ranir and embraced him in a hug. "Be careful, Ranir."

"I'm always careful," teased Ranir. He departed the doorway and made his way to Taryn. After several minutes he found Taryn in the library. Ranir assumed it might be where he returned to after they split up.

"You ready to ride again?" asked Taryn.

Confused, Ranir asked, "Ride?"

"Well seeing as I don't know exactly where this village is, I can't teleport there. The closest place I can reach is Drâgok. Then we would have to walk."

"So it's better to ride all the way and keep the horses with us?" asked Ranir.

Taryn laughed at Ranir's uncertainty. "It will be fine, Ranir. We won't need to ride as hard as we did across the desert." This seemed to calm Ranir's worries.

They made their way to the stables. Taryn was happy to see his large black stallion. Taryn's horse from Killiad was still among the hundreds of horses in the stable house. As if someone knew they were coming, the smaller tan and black horse was already saddled up with side satchels filled with rations. He turned to Taryn who winked and nodded. As they mounted up, Ranir turned toward the keep. He felt guilty about not telling Sagin about their departure. He would rather her stay safe at The Emphyrius instead of thrusting her into to trouble out of selfishness. They set off to the west for their unknown journey.

The cold, late fall winds swept over Ranir as the weeks passed by. Searching into the depths of several patched forests, the hunt for The Knights had proved fruitless thus far. "Taryn, I'm done," said Ranir through his dry, cracked lips. His voice was harsh from the steady inhalation of the bitter breeze. His face was nearly numb from dehydration and the gelid air.

"We will find them," said Taryn. His luck was better yet than that of the now 17 year old. For his elemental power flowed from fire, he constantly had warmth. Although, to Ranir, the cold wasn't his biggest concern. The fact that had been traveling by horse, or leading the horses by foot, for months without fail was disheartening.

"You've been saying that for weeks, Taryn!" bellowed Ranir. His temper had grown short over time, his bitterness deepened. Lately, Ranir and Taryn had more unfriendly conversations than anything else, when they did talk. The few days at the beginning of their journey were filled with excitement of a new, unmapped countryside. Now, Ranir detested the journey and no longer cared to find The Knights.

The dense evergreen forest that paralleled the desert stretched for over 200 miles. Strangely, even the desert was snapped cold. As they winds began to increase through the late fall, Ranir and Taryn had slowly gotten closer to the desert for warmth. Now the year was nearing its end and all of Sythestine was becoming a colorfully cold. Now and then, Ranir would get a little excited when they ran low on their rations because that meant he could go hunting, which also meant he got to run by his self for a day.

It was still early in the day as Ranir and Taryn scaled the lengthy, wooded hills. They had already been contemplating on the choice of abandoning the mission, when suddenly Ranir spotted the top of a smooth-looking white rooftop in the evergreen canopy down a hill. "Taryn!" he shouted as he pointed. The white was almost stained with a hint of green, making it nearly camouflaged with the needles of pine.

"What is it?" he said as he sprinted over the edge of the hill. Upon seeing the roof, Taryn pulled his map out and began calculating silently. "I don't think we're at the spot on the map, Ranir."

"The spot that someone stuck an arrow through? I'm sure it won't be that accurate, Taryn. Hell, that circle on the map alone could stretch 5 miles or so," he explained. "Who's to say that we didn't pass it days ago...or," he gestured with his open palm, "it could be right in front of us."

"You are right, let's check it out. I hope that its the temple...or at least the top of a house in Rafstal Village." The horses whined as they descended the steep hill. Taryn and Ranir held onto small yearling trees to steady their feet. It was a slow process as the leaves under their feet made their home on top of a muddy hillside. Ranir's horse was most hesitate to go down the slippery slope and started bucking its front end up, causing it to slip and drive down the hill much faster than Ranir wanted.

Ranir grabbed the reins, "Whoa, boy! Easy," he pulled hard on the leather straps. His stallion wasn't disobedient. It simply could not gain any traction once its hooves were filled with viscous soil. Taryn slowly crept down the hill with his large black horse behind him. It was evident that his black beast was much more disciplined and experienced in these conditions that Ranir's horse was. "Taryn, I can't stop it!" cried Ranir.

Taryn remained calm. "Hold the reigns, and get in front of him, Ranir. You have to lead him down the hill or he's going to slam at the bottom."

Following the elder mage's advise, Ranir sprinted down the hill, dodging small trees and overhead branches. The horse was still backpedaling so he managed to heave himself in front of the horse and pulled the reigns as apposed to trying to stop the stallion from inevitability. The horse bucked at first, nearly reeling Ranir backwards, but then gave in and tromped the rest of the way. As soon as Ranir's feet landed on the rocky bottom, he sprung his feet into the ground, leaping with ease and landing in the saddle, twisting the horse so he would evade a rather large, oncoming dead tree. To his surprise, it was a smooth transition and both he and the horse were safe. Steam belted from the horses face and body. The whites of the horse's eyes still showing his fear. "Easy, boy. Easy," Ranir whispered as he leaned down and rubbed behind its ears.

As Ranir waited for Taryn to reach the base of the hill, he proceeded around the building that they had discovered. At first glance, it looked like an old grain storage building that the ground had swallowed. As he crept around the old building he noticed an old rotten door. Upon further investigating, he saw swipe marks in the dirt. "*Someone has been opening this door,*" he thought. Slowly he approached door and heard a crack behind him. His heart skipped a beat and he froze, trying to listen harder. He swallowed in his dry throat and slowly began to turn around when he was cracked in the head with a blunt object, knocking him cold.

As he peeled his eyes open, Ranir slowly raised his head and saw that his hands were tied to the table as well as his ankles. His back was pressed flat against a wide stone plank. He quickly began to scan around him and saw Taryn laying a few paces away, similarly bound. "Pst." He looked around for signs of his attacker. "Taryn!" he called out louder. The Archemage slowly began to stir and groan. He appeared in pain, as if he was struck in the head as well. There was no sign of his horse or his dagger. With extra force he tugged on the ropes. Nothing.

"*Estashashek!*" he whispered. The ropes between his hands ripped apart with a snapping sound. He sat up quickly and arced lightning into the footholds. As he jumped off of the table he heard clacking of rock to his left and immediately casted a lightning shield around himself. As he stood still, the attacker appeared in a shallow opening. He realized that he was standing in a sunken church house, or more likely underneath, as he couldn't see any daylight, only torches lit the large room. Suddenly another appeared to his right, and one to his left. One by one, mysterious strangers appeared around the small hall.

"Who are you?" he called out. The room echoed strangely. "What do you want?"

"Thunder King!" they all yelled in synchronization.

"I'm not the Thunder King," he replied. "I am The Lightning Rod, Ranir."

"We are the brotherhood of The Knights!" they yelled together again.

"Alright, that's getting creepy. The Knights, eh?" He kept his head swiveling around to keep watch on all directions. "The Knights of The Fallen Son?"

This time there was no reply. In the same fashion, so to did the exit, one by one. One man stood still and waited until the room was clear. Ranir expected that the rest didn't go too far away. "What do you want?" Ranir repeated the question.

"We want you to do what you are meant to do!" the man called out.

"And what is that? Balance the world? Yeah I know my responsibilities."

"Balance? Yes. You are meant to replace Eros, The Lightning God. You are meant to become the new God, and release Carmos."

"Erm, I don't think so," Ranir said slowly.

"You will fulfill the prophecy. Release the Shadow King, The Fallen Son Carmos. Let darkness back into the world. Balance." The man stood his ground on his faith in The Fallen Son and was bold in his tone. He wore the same as the others, the same as the assassins.

"You would love that wouldn't you? You're all a bunch of assassins yes?" Ranir fired back with his own intimidating tone, or at least that was his intention.

"Assassins? No. Skilled yes," he said. There was a short pause as he looked down, then back to Ranir. "Why did you come here, Lightning Rod?"

"We came to find answers to who killed his brother...and then kill him," Ranir said bluntly, with attitude.

"We do not kill people," said the robed stranger.

"Don't give me that!" Ranir pointed to Taryn and let an arc fly out of his finger, snapping his rope. The fire mage jumped up on his feet.

"My brother was killed with an embered arrow!" yelled Taryn.

"*Talyrna!*" shouted the man. Ranir didn't know what the word meant, but it sounded like a curse. "There was a group of Knights that abandoned our mission, and fled to The Necromancer."

"The Necromancer is who we are trying to stop!" shouted Ranir. "Why would they go to him, if they wanted darkness here?"

"Some of our followers began to believe that The Necromancer is the reincarnation of Carmos The Fallen," replied the man. Ranir didn't know if he should trust him, but he felt truthful in his words.

"So where are the defilers?" asked Taryn.

"I don't know, we've sent scouts to track them down, and hope to stop The Necromancer all in one. So far, we've only failed."

"You are trying to stop *his* darkness, but you want Carmos to spread darkness?" asked Ranir.

"Yes, because true Shadow Magic is the key to helping truly balancing Gnariam. You must be the one to bring about the Balancing."

Ranir paused in his thoughts for a moment. He shot a glance to Taryn who shrugged his shoulders uncharacteristically. "Why don't we help each other?"

"You want us to help you, stop The Necromancer?" the man asked shyly.

"Yes, we need all the help we can get. We stop him, you help us find the murderer who took Taryn's brother's life. I will be in your debt."

"Ranir, a word," said Taryn, gesturing with his head.

"No. That is my final word, Taryn. Its a deal." He gave Taryn a stern look, as to say that is was final. The fire mage didn't say anything. A grim look came over his face as he rolled his eyes.

"Fine," agreed the stranger. "Where do we begin?"

"When we go after him, and we *are* going to go after him, I will call upon your help," replied Ranir.

"You have my word, so long as you keep yours."

With the new deal sealed with a potential enemy, Ranir and Taryn were led back outside. Ranir mounted his horse, and sat still for a moment. Taryn pulled his map out and gazed at the spot he best assumed they were. He assumed two days would suffice for a ride back to The Emphyrius. The had circled too far and cut back and forth, wasting time and steps in searching for The Knights. Taryn was well unsatisfied with the wasted trip. Ranir knew that it wasn't wasted. They set off back to Thrast. Ranir knew that one day would come, and they could use the numbers in a battle, especially as skilled as The Knights were in combat. He hoped that they would break the stranger's word of no killing policies if it meant helping stop The Necromancer. The days passed by rather quickly. Ranir was exhausted by the time they had reached Thrast and Taryn hadn't said much. Ranir simply left him with his thoughts, and went straight to his welcoming bed. As soon as his face touched his pillow, dreams swept over his mind with a fury.

Chapter 24: Perpetual Burdens

Ranir awoke in the darkness from the sounds of screams and explosions. He jumped out of his bed, still wearing the clothes from the night before, or rather hours ago. He slipped his feet into his leather boots and ran out of the room. From the corridor outside he could hear constant shrieking, both man and woman, and noises that measured to be the Emphyrius breaking apart. Ranir began sprinting down the hallway. His instinct urged him to find the source of the screams and worry about his own well being later. As he flew passed several people and opening doorways, sometimes slamming into people or objects in the hallway through the chaos.

"Hello?" Ranir screamed through the darkness. He made his way to the first stair case and paused to listen for directions of the screams. They appeared to come from below. He jumped over the railing and planted both feet firm on the top step of the turn around, then sprung over top of a man rushing up the staircase. "What's going on?" he asked the man as he spun around. The stranger didn't answer and continued his escape. What could be happening? Suddenly, Ranir came to a halt. His heart clenching in his chest. "*The Necromancer!*" he realized. "*How could he have found out so quickly?*" He thought of the several men that escaped Drâgok. "*Of course.*"

Ranir took a deep breath and focused. He bent

down and tied his boots finally. In a flash of Surging Speed, Ranir sped down the staircase leaping back and forth through the midst of people running. He made his way to the bottom floor and was instantly met with smoke. His elemental speed dissipated. A stream of white smoke shifted towards him with great speed, and slammed him against a wall. As he hit the floor, Ranir realized where the destructive sounds were coming from. It wasn't The Necromancer or his horde. This was the vocalization of mages that were loyal to the dark sorcerer. Kneeling on his knee, Ranir grew infuriated. As he stood, his eyes were glowing bright bluish-white and arcs of blue lightning littered across his hands and wrapped around his forearms. The color was overly saturated against the gray smoke, lighting up the entire corridor.

"*Ashu-*" he heard someone casting nearly right in front of him. Without hesitating, he interrupted the spell with his own Chain Lightning, wrapping the man up and jerking him off of his feet. Ranir caught him by his robe and looked to see if he recognized the mage. The man's face was as foreign as the ocean was to him. Ranir thrusted his forehead into the man's face, smashing his nose and knocking him unconscious. He tossed the mage aside like a stick. Suddenly the eruption of fire and water sped towards him with precision. The fire caught him in the chest sending him backwards off the ground. A second later, the water bolt crashed into his thighs, shifting his body midair. He tilted forward from the force of the water, and landed square on his chest. This reminded Ranir of the training that he had led with the mages, but different.

Ranir placed his palms flat on the floor and braced his body stiffly. He realized in that moment, that through the fog, he couldn't see the mages. That most likely led to the fact that they couldn't see him, only his lightning. He closed his eyes and drew the power into his muscles, feeling the power surging through his body. Using all of the friction he could muster, Ranir shoved his body forward horizontally, head first towards the plume. As he soared through the air he caught a glimpse on either side of him of magic. This was his moment. He exploded his power outward and spun his body, as if rolling down a hill rapidly. His lightning managed to attach to 7 mages in the darkness, stunning them and throwing them into the walls and ceiling. They soared in a counter-clockwise motion as did Ranir's twisting. He landed in a bear-like stance, hands and feet on the floor, then shoved his body upright.

The mages around him stirred and groaned. He thought about hitting them again, but he knew that there were more people in danger. Through the smoke and darkness, Ranir was able to make it clear through the keep and out to the front courtyard where he realized the full extent of the attack. Warriors were fighting warriors, mages against mages, he saw Taryn handling a large group by himself. As he heard the rush of water above him he turned around to find Sora on top of the crosswalk where he once aimed to land his Travel. For a moment, everything and everyone around him seemed to be moving and fighting in slow motion and silence. Magic was constantly flowing around The Emphyrius. Casualties were caught in the middle and sides. He knew that he needed to do something massive, and quick. He summoned the force of lightning to the surface of his skin once more. Suddenly a hand pushed into his, startling him. As he jerked his hand away and turned his was face to face with Sagin. "Sagin! Are you alright?" he bellowed.

"I'm fine, I can't find my sister, though. Can you stop them, Ranir?" He thought about that question as he gazed upon the twilight battlefield.

"I don't know. Maybe not by myself." He looked back to Sagin and she was staring hard at her palm. As he looked down, he noticed a small blue arc of lightning stretching from his finger tip to hers. "Can you feel that?" he asked.

Nodding she said, "Is that what it feels like all the time inside your body? Ranir, its pure energy. Can you leech your power onto others?"

He had never thought about the possibility of being a walking mana stone before. The thought almost haunted him for a second, thinking about people wanting to draw on his power. "I don't know. Let me try something." He closed his eyes and pushed the power forward as he did the lightning orb in the fireplace.

"It's working!" she cried. She pulled away from him, severing the connection. "Stand back, Ranir." He slowly backed away, casting a lightning bolt towards a swordsman sprinting toward him. "*Gnariam et sal eem athuna!*" she screamed into the night sky. Sagin thrusted her fist into the sky, then dropped to her knee, punching the soil like she did in Drâgok. Ranir braced himself for an earthquake again. It was a different spell this time though. Suddenly large roots began thrusting from the dirt and flying through the air like snakes striking their prey. One by one, thousands of fist-sized roots sprung from the ground, some reaching a hundred feet long, and drove through the torsos of many men and woman and mages. In amazement, Ranir glanced at Sagin. Her eyes were bright green once more, as if she was controlling every root simultaneously. He was as impressed as he was confused. Slowly, but surely, the noise of the battle began to dissolve.

Ranir wondered why the attack happened here and more so why such a small amount of combatants. Surely The Necromancer hadn't sent his full force. There wasn't a single dark magic user or Forsaken. For now the battle had ceased. Sagin slowly reeled the roots back into the soil and rose to her feet. Ranir slid over to her, expecting her to faint again. She looked up to him with a grin. "I am alright, Ranir." For some reason, he felt embarrassed and his cheeks flushed once again. It was an involuntary response when it involves Sagin.

"Good," he blurted. "I'm going to check on some people, make sure they're alright too." He made his way to the place where he saw Taryn. As he got closer, he saw Taryn's absence, only the warriors and mages that were scorched. With quick thinking he turned around and spotted Taryn and Sora on the crosswalk between two towers. They were safe.

Immediately his heart sank as he thought of

Ramshi. His eyes grew wide as he thought of how defenseless the old man was. He spotted the teacher's office window and sprinted toward the entrance. Instinct took over as he ran and he threw a lightning bolt through the stained glass on the third floor. As it left his hand he latched onto it, Traveling through the glass and landed perfectly on feet in the office. For the first time, he Traveled by instinct. For the first time, he landed exactly where he wanted and smoothly. The room was destroyed with splinters if wood and papers littering the floor. The door was blown off of its hinges and lay in pieces across the flipped desk. Ranir's excitement quickly turned to fear as he heard groans underneath the rubble. Through Surging Speed, Ranir began slinging debris with both hands. Suddenly he unveiled Ramshi on his back. His sleeping robes were torn and stained with sporadic crimsoned markings. Ranir's stomach twisted inside.

Kneeling down Ranir scooped the old man up, as a parent would pick up a child, and sprinted out of the room. In that moment, his teacher felt as light as air and time seemed to slow down. People that he passed by seemed like a blur of color and confusion. "Help!" he screamed out so loud that his throat burned. As he turned the steps toward the second floor, he was halted by a witch doctor. This was not the same woman that cared for him.

"Lay him down," the pale woman cried. Her once spotless white attire was stained black with soot and spotted red from her patients. Ranir slowly lowered Ramshi to the floor and saw that his eyes were closed.

"Ramshi? Here's a doctor! Ramshi?" he called again. Ramshi was not responding. The witch doctor placed a hand on his chest and waited several seconds. Slowly she removed her hand from his limp body and looked up to Ranir.

"I'm sorry. He's gone." Ranir sat back on his feet, struggling to breathe. Tears welled up and streamed down his cheeks. The world seemed to fall silent as he hunched over Ramshi's body as he let out a beckoning scream. It appeared as if no sound was produced. After a short moment, Taryn and Sora was by his side. They saw the flash of Ranir Traveling. Everyone within sight saw the power.

As the darkness transitioned into morning, Ranir realized that Ramshi wasn't the only one who lost their life. It wasn't until the sun literally shined light on the keep did he fully discover how much damage was done. Hundreds of bodies scattered throughout The Emphyrius, and the courtyards. Thrast mourned for their loss, as only they could, for they were the only city with open knowledge of magic. The full day was spent cleaning and repairing, getting the keep and it's acreage back together. No words were received on further attacks throughout the city, nor had anyone spotted the dark sorcerer.

At the sun's highest point, Sora steppes to rally the moral of the city and its people, as the new Queen of Sythestine, having done away with The Emphyre title. "People of Thrast, visitors Killiad, Alagien and," she gestured to Ranir, "Heramor." There were thousands of people in the northern courtyard of The

316

Keep, as it was now officially named. "As your new Queen, on this day, I give you my word!" Her voice echoed throughout the people and the forest behind her, reverberating off of the brick walls. "My word that we will not fall without rising back up. We will not cower in the face of danger. And we will not die in vain!" The crowd erupted in applause. "There is a darkness that has returned to Sythestine, to plague our Kingdom with Shadow Magic, and I stand before you to say that we will fight, as we have before. We will come together as nations of people and eradicate this disease that is The Necromancer!"

Ranir stood next to Taryn at the front of the crowd in case another wave of destruction was to be brought down on them again. He was thoroughly impressed with how Sora seemed to weave her words through the air as easily as moving a hand through a pool of water. "She is really good at this, isn't she?" asked Ranir. "She's going to make a great Queen."

Taryn smiled and kept staring at Sora. "Yes. Yes she is." He was fixated on her as if in a daze. The sun rippled across the silky streaks of her new, blue dress robe. "She has been doing this for so long in Killiad, it's only right that she steps up and takes the Silver City under her wings." There was a near sadness underlying his tones. Ranir wondered if Taryn was truly happy for her, or felt as if she was now farther than ever from him. He had never told Ranir about the history they had shared, nor had he admitted his feelings for her, but they were as obvious as a shadow on a clear day.

"To those of you wondering about why I am standing here, I am here to tell you as a personal witness to the crimes of The Emphyre Credin. For years, he was one of the main malefactor in helping The Necromancer Seldos, who we discovered was his brother." The crowd buzzed with gasps and whispers. "Not to worry," she continued. "We have taken the necessary precautions to eliminate the threat that he posed." Ranir wondered how many of the whispers stirring were those of citizens that believed in the truth. Most of them turned a blind eye to anything but gossip. "I have been crowned the new Queen of Sythestine. I know, I know," she held her hands to halt the rise of volume in the crowd. "The title 'Emphyre' is no longer. For now, I am Queen of the Kingdom, relinquishing Credin's throne. The Kingdom, as it has a broad array of people and cultures, does not need one leader, forced under one reign. I am going to be relieving my crown and taking control of Thrast. Each city will have their own King...or Queen," she said with a short bow, "and their own people to govern, elected by the people of each city...after all of this darkness passes."

The crowd seemed to changed their rhythmic tone to a prosperous auditory sensation. They appeared to enjoy the thoughts of electing their own Kings and Queens and being each city for themselves. For now, they enjoyed her speech. Taryn walked up to the front and stood beside Sora. Ranir was wide jawed and confused. "People of Thrast!" he called out. The crowd fell silent. This bewildered Ranir even more. They seemed to like Sora. They seemed to respect Taryn, or fear him; he wasn't certain which. "I present to, Queen

Sora!" he held his arms wide open and turned toward the new queen. The assemblage flared up once more in commendation and approving applause. Sora gave him and smile and bowed before her people, accepting them as they accepted her. "Now," he continued. "Not to bring sadness back into our hearts, but we must be ceremonious tonight. We have our dead to bury and honor." The people of Thrast was silent again, most of them looking to the grass or to each other sympathetically. "And we have life to celebrate. Please, lets pay our respects and send off our loved ones to Förnthis." This was the second time Ranir heard of this place. It seemed to be the afterlife, among the stars with the Old Gods. All together, the audience, Taryn and Sora included, kneeled and bowed their head. Ranir hesitated as he watched every shrink to the ground, the dropped as he realized that he should probably follow along. "*Gnariam sáv fénil!*" they all chanted together. The thousands of voices together amplified the volume and thrusted the beautiful words into the forest as if to say it to Gnariam herself.

After the citizens retreated back to their homes, the mages back to The Keep, and the towers were manned once again, a ceremony officially began. The sounds of large vräel horns could be heard deep into the evergreens and outside of the massive oak walls of Thrast. Individually, the dead were carried in a line through the forest. Most were carried on a flowered plank, dressed loosely in white cloth, upon a bed carried by the citizens. Ranir chose to bear a corner of Ramshi's bed, as did Taryn. Slowly, they marched to the sounds of drums and the horns that called a sad tale

319

of woe. Ranir was mentally prepared to lock his emotions inside, to honor Ramshi and his life, mentorship, and friendship. He couldn't stop the quivering of his bottom lip and the slow fall of tears that dribbled down his cheeks. Periodically he sniffed.

He remained steadfast in his hold on the bed. The aroma of pink and white flowers fogged throughout the forest, wonderfully blending with the constant pine that drifted about. Altogether, the ceremony was beautiful. After nearly a half hour of steady trekking the path, the massive group arrived at an open circle, where the trees had been cut down, and graves had been dug cleanly. To the far side of the funeral site, Ranir spotted Sagin. He hadn't thought of her since he left her in the courtyard looking for her sister. In that moment, though, wearing a beautifully tailored, dark green dress, she was stunning. Ranir felt embarrassed about crying, and used his shoulders to wipe away the tears. As he gawked at her, he noticed that her feet were bare, and the soil had left stains upon her hands. *"Of course, she must've helped dig the graves. Earth mages are wonderful!"* he thought.

As each person was carried next to a hole, and slowly lowered to the ground, Ranir watched as 12 mages pushed through the crowd, all adorned in dark green robes. Each of them were wearing a necklace that was inlaid with a green stone. "Who are they?" Ranir asked Taryn. Slowly they drifted apart, splitting up and spreading around all of the deceased.

"They are the Mourning Council, earth mages." Taryn kept his eyes forward.

"What are they doing?" whispered Ranir.

"Ranir! Watch!" Taryn hissed forcefully.

At that moment, Ranir realized that a ceremony of Thrast or of mages, perhaps both, were far more formal than those in Heramor. Ranir watched in amazement as the earth mages kneeled, placing their palms on the ground. It seemed as if they all moved in one, fluid unity. All 12 stones around the mages' necks began to glow bright. Suddenly roots like Sagin had conjured rose from the black soil underneath the beds. Beautifully, the roots sprouted colorful mixed flowers and lifted each person into the air, drifting them over top of the holes. The roots lowered them all into the graves. Ranir wondered why Sagin sat alone, and wasn't a part of the group of earth mages.

As the bodies were all lowered, Sagin stepped forward and kneeled in the center of the grave site. The rest of the earth mages flocked to her, surrounding her methodically. They all placed their hands upon her shoulders as the stones went dark again. Suddenly, Sagin's eyes glowed bright green through her dark bangs. She placed her hands in front of her arms open wide. "*Waelsihn Gnariam. Bethuel alin farnum,*" she called out loud. The drums and horns stopped instantly. Their echoes followed for a moment and then the forest was silent as well. Ranir's heart began to race. Her words felt like an ancient, forgotten language. All of a sudden the holes began to rumble with magic and fill with soil. As the dirt grew flush with the ground level, it stopped and fresh green grass sprouted, followed by a single rose bush on each grave. After the spell was done, Ranir realized that she was a part of the group after all. She was perhaps the most vital member of the group of earth mages. Looking at the site, now beautifully filled with grave marking flowers and lush grass, he hadn't realized that the stumps of the evergreen had also been swallowed in the ground.

As the ceremony came to a close and the citizens retreated back to the Silver City, Ranir waited behind. He wanted to speak with Sagin. He sat down patiently by a large tree. Sagin was still surrounded by the other earth mages; she was in the center, addressing them all. Ranir tried to watch her lips and understand what it was that she was saying but he could not. After several moment, she finally approached, gliding flawlessly in the grass. "Hello, Ranir," she greeted him with a short bow. He returned with his own awkward bow. "I am sorry for your loss."

"Thank you," replied Ranir as he dropped his head. He didn't know what else to respond with. "I just wish-"

"There is nothing you could have done," she interrupted. "And it is not your fault, Ranir." She placed a palm on his cheek. He slowly raised his hand and grasped her hand.

"Well. It almost is. If I would have just given in to Seldos then-"

"Then he would have taken your power," she stopped him again. "And we would all surely perish. Stop blaming yourself, Ranir. You can't save everyone. Ramshi wouldn't want you taking the blame."

"No, he wouldn't," he mumbled.

"No." She paused and looked back to the group of mages who seemed to be waiting on her. "I have to go, Ranir. I need to get back to my sister and the council and help them repair things."

"Oh yes. Good. You found your sister! I'm just going to go sulk for a while," said Ranir. Sagin gave him a quick smile, and trailed off once more without a word, heading back to her group. Ranir turned back down the trail toward The Keep. As he saw the large building, he decided that he wasn't in any mood to relive certain memories at the moment. Instead, he opted to turn toward one of the taller western hills.

As the sun set, Ranir sat down on a tall, grassy slope. He watched as the autumn sky transitioned from blue to pink, pink to red and then red to black. Many thoughts raced through his mind; Ramshi was at the forefront of his emotions which drove other memories forward. As the sky turned to darkness, Ranir sank down on his back into the dewy grass and began to fall asleep, watching the stars sparkling in the sky.

Chapter 25: The Fallout

Ranir had no more than just covered his eyes when he heard the ambient scream coming from the western forest. "Not again," he muttered as he sprung to his feet. Quickly, he dashed down the hill, kicking the tall grass with each stride. Through the darkness Ranir vividly saw a purple pulsating light inside the woods. His heart pounded as he recalled the same light before he foolishly attacked The Necromancer in Killiad.

As he neared the line where grass gave way in needle-covered ground beneath the pine, he heard the shrill scream again. This time he recognized that it was a woman's voice.

"Hello?" Ranir called in the black. Suddenly the purple glows disappeared. There was a wave of biting cold that slammed into Ranir. He couldn't hear any sign of life or movement. The forest seemed to consistently grow more ominous for several minutes as he waited, and listened. Then the crack of a stick broke the dead silence, startling Ranir. He stepped forward and a plume of black magic smashed against his chest, knocking him on his back with a thud. The air escaped his lungs. Once again, his view was covered in a starry night as he lay still. He heard the footprints coming out of the woods but he did not move.

Slowly, he tapped into his elemental power

without shifting it to the surface. Without sitting up or looking, he pushed a bright wave of lightning towards the forest. He heard of grunt of a man. The force of the lightning power slid him across the grass several feet. With all of his strength, he simultaneously jumped to his feet and casted a shield around himself. He was ready for a fight. Instead of Seldos, or any warrior, there was nothing before him. The air around him seemed to drag into warmth, like stepping closer to a fireplace in the cold winter.

Confused, he rushed back to The Keep. He went straight to his room and began packing his large satchel. He wasn't sure if a trip was soon, but he felt it in his stomach and heart that doom was impending. He dove into his bed after he was satisfied with his gear and supplies. The night drifted into a gray morning, which didn't seem to lift Ranir's spirit at all. He ran to Taryn's room and woke him, explaining what he had saw the night before.

"Its hard to say what it was. Sometimes, people will go into the forest for...alone time," he lifted his eyebrows and smirked.

Ranir snickered. "I don't think those were screams of joy, Taryn."

"With that spell og cold and getting knocked on your arse? I doubt it." Taryn said with a laugh. "Listen, today we may need your help with repairing Ramshi's office." He looked down. Ranir grew sad again. He knew that over time he would be alright, but for now they emotional wound was heavy.

"I can help," said Ranir.

"Good. Anything in there that you may want, I've talked to Sora, you can keep."

"Thank you," replied Ranir. He wasn't sure that there would be anything that he would be interested in, nor if he would actually keep it.

"After you eat, meet us up there. The council will also be along to prepare the office for a new teacher and trainer."

Ranir clenched his jaw. It seemed so easily that they would just immediately replace Ramshi, or try to replace him because Ranir knew that they could not. They would fail to put someone in his shoes, in terms of characteristics and vast amounts of knowledge. Ranir simply nodded and headed to the dining hall.

As Ranir finished his breakfast, he threw his satchel across his shoulder and forced his emotions into a joyous tone, deciding that he would not sulk anymore. He had too many things to focus on, and his responsibilities were far too important. As he made his way around a corner, he was plowed into by Sagin. She was sprinting and out of breath.

"Ranir! Come quick!" she bellowed and trailed back through the corridors. He gave chase and stayed at her heels.

"What's going on, Sagin? Is someone hurt?" he asked over her shoulder.

"It's The Necromancer!" she said between breaths.

His stomach twisted internally. He knew that The Necromancer hadn't given up that easily. "Where is he?"

"I don't know...Sora sent me to get you!" she panted.

Ranir realized that he wasn't getting winded as he usually did. He didn't ask any more questions, simply followed the beautiful earth mage. After several hallways and a flight of steps, they arrived at The Throne Room. As they pushed into the room, they were met with guards blocking the way to a large group of mages, including Taryn and Sora.

"Let him through!" Queen Sora Yelled at the guards. They gave a short bow and split to the left and right. "Don't you know who that is?"

"Sorry," said Ranir as he passed by them. He rushed to the Queen and without thinking bowed deeply to her. She returned the gesture with a nod. "My Queen, you sent for me?" He wanted to be formal, more for the crowd than her, and show his respect to the leader.

"Yes. The Necromancer has been sighted...outside of Killiad. From our scouts' best guess, his army measures over 10,000." Ranir's eyes widened. He thought that the army in Alagien was massive. This dwarfs that battle.

"What is he doing?" he asked.

"Nothing, the army is surrounding him, Forsaken, Mages, Assassins and Warriors, including nearly 500 archers."

Taryn was still, standing next to The Queen. "He's waiting for you, Ranir. Thrast was a warning...and bait to draw you out. That's our best guess," he said. Taryn's tone was serious, hardened even.

Ranir flexed his jaw. "How can we defeat him?" He was truly asking for advice this time. Ranir had learned in his as The Lightning Rod so far, that he wasn't able to save everyone. He wasn't strong enough, or fast enough, to defeat the enemy every time.

"You," muttered The Queen. "And Taryn. And the mages." She looked up to address the entire hall. "We're going to throw everything we have at him and his army!"

"Sounds like a lot of people are going to die in confronting him," one of the councilors said.

"If we do nothing, more people will die. Innocent people, like woman and children. We have to face this head off and radiate the world of his darkness once and for all. I for one will fight til my end," replied Taryn.

"How about logistics?" said a small woman in a golden robe. "How are we going to move an army large enough to combat his?"

"The mages are not strong enough to teleport a group that size," another councilor spoke up in the back.

Ranir thought of Sagin and the spell she did in the courtyard. "I have an idea. I may be able to give mana." The room was silent. All eyes bored a hole into his. "I discovered this recently, and have not tested its limits, but if we can get there altogether, we would stand the highest chance."

Ranir looked to Taryn, who was as surprised as the rest of the councilors. "That may work." He paused for a minute. "We need numbers."

"As we stand now," said Sora, "we are about 5,000 strong with Thrast. I've sent word to Drâgok and Alagien, drawing our mages back to help."

"And our soldiers in the northern forests are joining the fight as well. I spoke with the captain this morning," added Taryn.

"At noon, we will stage a formation in the eastern courtyard. Gather your men, spread word throughout Thrast." Queen Sora looked to Taryn. "We could use every person."

"Send your scout back to Killiad and rally as many as they can. If The Necromancer is going to give us time, we have to use it as best as we can," said Taryn. "I will teleport back to The Knights and call upon that favor." He shot a stern look toward Ranir. Queen Sora also gave him a slight scold of disapproval. "Hey, don't look at me like that, he" Taryn pointed at Ranir, "is the one who made the deal with The Fallen One's minions."

As the group began to dissipate, The Queen called out, "Ranir, hold here." He stopped immediately and turn to see her striding to another slim door, similar to the door that the traitor Credin took him to.

Taryn remained in the same spot as well, looking at Ranir with a slight grin.

Queen Sora returned carrying something shiny and silver. "This," she thrusted it toward him, "was found among the wreckage of Ramshi's room, and I think he'd like you to have it, more now than ever."

Ranir took hold of the chain mail and set it on the floor, pulling up the top folded section. It was a dark silver coated mail tunic. The links were not like those of warriors, but more resembled scales of a sharp fish. Each link was smooth, shaped like a diamond and overlapped in sequences. As Ranir waves it about, the normal jingle of mail was absent as well, it was as silent as silk. He laid them down and picked up the leggings that matched. They seemed to be tailored to his size coincidentally. "Thank you, my Queen." He bowed and turned to exit the room and Taryn halted him again.

"Ranir," he called as he through a metal stick to him. Ranir was still mid spin when he caught it, thinking it was going to be heavy. Contrarily it was as light as dead wood. Instantly, Ranir felt a draw to it, like magnetism. He noticed a quick arc of blue lightning flashed up the staff. "That," he pointed at the Rod," was made...by Ramshi, for you." Taryn approaches him slowly. "And this is from him." He handed a folded piece of yellow paper to Ranir.

He felt as heart quicken it's pace as The grabbed the note. He hastily opened the letter and read:

Ranir Trysfal,

I made this staff for you in theory with your elemental power. I don't know if it will work, it's made from metals and that have been reforged 21 times and smelted together. I believe that you can channel your power through it.

As always your friend, Ramshi.'

Ranir felt his eyes glisten and quickly rubbed them. He looked up to Taryn, "Thank you." Taryn nodded and nudged his arm.

"I need to go now, gather the...other troops," he said with a sarcastic smile. Ranir turned without a word and departed the Throne Room.

Ranir recalled the training and tutelage he had received under Ramshi. During his weapon training, the staff was his best weapon. At one point he could handle 4 combatants wielding swords, with a wooden staff. He was excited to test Ramshi's theory.

Ranir got into his room and figured he had about an hour before he had to get to the formation. Ranir set the staff on the floor and channeled his lightning. He slowly let a small arc latch onto the staff like chain lightning. Oddly, the staff felt connected to him unlike anything he had felt before. He pulled the staff with his thoughts and instantly the metal rod flew upward and smashed him in the chest longways. As it bounced from him, he caught it and spun it once with his right hand, each end swooshing through the air with a hum. He sat the tail end of it on the floor and let it drop, instantly magnetizing it again. The staff floated at a strong angle, one end still in the floor. He found tremendous joy as he could picture the utility of this weapon in a fight.

To test Ramshi's theory, he placed his hand in the middle of the staff and forced his lightning into it, guiding it down the rail. The end pointed at a wall released a bolt of lightning and burned a hole clean through his cloak hanging on the wall. The Lightning bolt seemed to be amplified by the Rod. He practiced several times throwing more lightning into the fireplace, immediately taking akin to it, as it felt as natural as his hands.

As time was beginning to drag by, Ranir slipped the new armor set on over his clothes and blended down, crouched, kicked into the air and jumped, testing the flexibility of the armor or the limits. There were no limits to its movement. As he maneuvered about, it seemed as if he wore just leather. He knew that it was going to come in use as well.

As the coolness swept through the window, Ranir gathered his things and made his way to the courtyard. As he approached he saw a massive group of people before him, awaiting on him. He looked around for Sagin. She would not be present. Part of him was glad to keep her a distance away from the battle going forth. The other part of him wanted Sagin right by his side. The Queen would also be staying behind despite her great power.

"Alright, he is here!" yelled Taryn from atop a stump. He seemed to be in a leadership position now. "Ranir, come to the center please." As he walked through the crowd, he felt all eyes on him. He felt nervous. The path between citizens and warriors alike closed as he passed through.

"Now, Ranir. The rest is up to you," said Taryn as he stepped down and joined the horde.

"Alright, um," he hesitated to think of commands. "So, everyone touch someone else to link us together like teleporting." He waited a few seconds to make sure everyone was touching. There was a small buzz from whispers. "Now, I'm going to push my power out, all of the mages siphon it like a stone, I think."

"You think?" called a stranger. Ranir ignored him and began releasing the power into the mages around him, surrounding the army in a blanket of static lightning. After several moments he began to feel fatigue like using a magic spell. "Alright! Now!" he screamed as loud as he could. He released his hold on the Lightning and watched as a bright white ring began to form around the entire army. The crowd stirred as they watched the gargantuan teleportation take place. He felt the familiar sting of the portal and held his breath. It a flash of white light, he felt the temperature drop instantly. He opened his eyes. Thrast was no longer their location. He turned to the North and saw the small gates of Killiad. "It worked," he muttered.

Quickly he and Taryn pushed their way to the south end of the army spanning nearly 2 acres. As he reached the front lines he was stopped in his tracks, gazing upon an army twice the size of Thrast's militia. He summoned the elemental force inside him; eyes glowing bright white. He looked over to Taryn.

The archemage's eyes were burning red, his palms engulfed in orange flames. He gave the order, "Attaaack!"

Chapter 26: The Battle of Veörn

Ranir was the first to let his power blast into the massive army. Channeling the full might of his lightning, he threw a lightning flash with his left hand, searing a hole through 2 Forsaken. He swung his staff with his right, brandishing a bright wave of blue and white lightning in the shape of oceanic waves. Taryn immediately followed the act with his own source of power. He shot a red beam of fire from both palms, nearly blinding onlookers and burning through a group before him. Instantly within two attacks, over 30 combatants were disintegrated. Ranir was satisfied with this, but he knew that they wouldn't be able to sustain attacking so heavily. As the two armies descended on each other, Ranir glanced in the sky as fire and water came from Seldos's mages. They were coupled with blasts of wind, speeding up the projection of the magic and causing them to amplify the damage. A one-two attack blasted into Thrast's army, killing almost 50 warriors and mages mixed.

"We need to split up!" called Taryn through explosions of magic and clanging of sword and shield. "Push the mages to the front. We have to focus on The Forsaken."

Ranir glanced around. In the dark army before him, they must have had the same strategy. Their mages and sorcerers, including Druids, were all pushing the Forsaken behind. "Alright!" He turned around and cupped his hands around his lips, "Mages to the front! Spread the word!"

Taryn recalled the same message to his right. Soon the robes mages were pushing their way through the front. Ranir realized just how many magic users had joined the fight. The Knights were pushing forward as well as the archers. Majority of the militia was made up of soldiers, warriors and even farmers. Ranir began striding to his left, Taryn to the right. He tried to focus on calculating his attacks and widely choosing his magic spells to add to the elemental power. A trio of water mages casted a wave of water together, an interesting idea that he didn't know was possible, and Ranir focused his own arc directly into the center of the torrent. The water instantly flashed bright blue and amplified his bolt of lightning, arcing and destroying the hydromancers. As the water crashed to the ground and splashed onto the other crusaders standing by.

Immediately, one after another, spells of casters were sent raging toward him. His shield stopped some of them. A couple fire balls and jets of water he dodged. The trickiest mages were aeromancers. Ranir couldn't see the direction of the gusts and was knocked to the ground several times. As he pushed the mages back, Ranir noticed warriors beginning to circle him with swords. Thinking quickly he called out, "*Zhunik Alhin!*" He slammed his foot to the ground, casting Polarity Shift. As his boot planted, a ring of lightning, light blue, almost faded in opacity, blasted outward. The men's chain mail and metal armor magnetized, pulling them toward each other. Ranir swooped to his left as all 5 men crashed together. Ranir blasted a deep lightning bolt, stunning and knocking out the champions. Suddenly he was rocked again by an air mage. This time, as he buried his foot in the dirt, he spotted the caster about 50 paces away, eyes glowing white. Ranir had only ever seen a mages eyes glow when channel extraordinary magic, like a mana stone. "He's amplified!" Ranir thought. Truth was, despite the danger, Ranir was enjoying the challenge of repetitive attackers.

Ranir began to walk toward the mage, spinning his staff to the left, then to the right, letting it roll between his fingers with each rotation. To the mage, it seemed like Ranir was being arrogant and showing off. In reality Ranir was statically charging his metal staff. The air mage muttered something and Ranir felt a blast of sharp wind hit him in the chin. As he stumbled back he let his elemental power flow through the staff, pointing it at the mage. A bright arc of lightning flashed forward. Ranir landed on his back. Quickly he rose his head to see his attacker. The aeromancer stood still, clenching his stomach. Suddenly he dropped to his knees as his arms fell limp. Ranir saw a small hole through the mage. He collapsed on his chest with a thud. Ranir didn't have time to gloat in his small victory because another warrior's sword was about to slash across his stomach just before a blast of water wrapped around his head and stuck like tar, drowning the warrior.

"Thank you," said Ranir to a strange looking water mage. She simply nodded and proceeded deeper into the battle. As Ranir watched her push forward a wave of fire descended on her, executing her instantly.

337

Ranir was beginning to feel less victorious and hopeful as the battle drove on. He jumped back to his feet, using his staff to stead himself. As he tapped into Surging Speed, the spells soaring overhead and around him, as well as the arrows, slowed down. Ranir didn't hesitate. He drove his feet into the soil for a strong projection and began sprinting full speed into the fray of man and monster alike. He knew that his strength and speed would allow him to do what he needed to before the speed dissipated and left him in the midst of enemies.

As he ran, he swung his metal staff over his head and began clipping combatants left and right. The instant clang of metal to body was chilling. Ranir could see one man's jaw slowly dislocate as he smashed the blunt weapon against his cheek. Using the reverberation of the metal, he let the momentum take his staff in a different direction. He swung it low, holding onto the very tip of the stick to increase his range. The metal staff broke clean through an assailant's shin bone, severing it where he stood. The blood flowing in slow motion nearly made Ranir sick. That didn't stop him from being relentless.

Ranir realized that he was exactly where he didn't want to be. Suddenly as he began to retreat back to Thrast's army, he caught a black and purple cloud heading for him out of the corner of his eye. He stopped and shifted his body to see where it originated. Between a couple of fighters, Ranir spotted the familiar dark mask of The Necromancer. He was armored as much if not more than Ranir. In that moment, his Surging Speed let go of its hold on time. Ranir was overwhelmed with dozens of champions around him. They did not wait and attack one by one. They ascended on his body altogether, making it impossible to run away or dodge them. Suddenly he found himself underneath hundreds of pounds of flesh, both human and rotting Forsaken.

He held his breath as his back smashed against the ground. Closing his eyes, he channeled his elemental force and released what he intended to be a thunderstorm, straight into the group. A massive surge of pure white lightning instantly turned the group on top of him into ashes. Like the spring fall of rain, so to did bones fall to the ground. He looked over to spot The Necromancer again. He wasn't sitting on his horse like he was just seconds ago. Ranir looked to his right. As his head just reached its full turn, The Necromancer caught him by surprise.

Grabbing Ranir by the armored tunic, he picked The Lightning Rod up like a child. Ranir casted his shield but Seldos did not use magic. This fight was personal for them both it seemed. The Necromancer planted his feet directly into Ranir's chest, smashing his armored scales. Ranir was knocked on his back again, 30 feet away. Pieces of his armored tunic flaked off and became lost in the soiled stampede of dark followers.

Ranir used the force of The Necromancer's punch and rolled backwards just as he landed, popping right back to his feet. The staff lay to his right, nearly halfway between Ranir and his nemesis. The Necromancer looked at it, "I've been waiting a while for this...Lightning Rod." His voice muffled and scratchy, just as he remembered from Killiad.

He must have expected Ranir to lunge for the staff because he jumped to it. Instead of the expected Ranir thrusted a lightning bolt to it, magnetizing it. He forced the metal staff into The Necromancer's mask, knocking him on his back this time. In that one swift move, the mask was sent flying through the air and under the heavy fighting. The Necromancer pulled his hood over his face more as he turned his back to Ranir.

Ranir paused too long, expecting The Necromancer to halt his attacks. He was so wrong. The Necromancer spun around and blasted Ranir directly point blank with another shadow spell, sending him flying through the air. It wasn't until Ranir felt his back smash through black rock did he realize, he had traversed the entire army and was at the base of The Veörn Mountains. Ranir sprung to his feet, twisting his shoulder back into place. Ranir casted his staff at The Necromancer again. This time he knocked the staff away, which is what Ranir wanted. As the dark sorcerer opened his right arm up to swat the staff, Ranir blasted him with a heavy blue lightning bolt in the chest.

The Necromancer was sent flying backwards, landing on his back and flipping twice before landing on his stomach. As he stood up, Ranir noticed his hood was down. He was curious to see the man's face after all of these fights and this time. The dark sorcerer looked up and Ranir's heart dropped.

Inside the hood, with a face completely scarred over on one side, even through the hair, was Marnos.

His best friend of his childhood was the one causing this damage. His best friend was trying to kill him. Ranir had been trying to kill his best friend. Emotions welled up in Ranir to the point that he nearly couldn't breathe. "Marnos?" said Ranir, letting his guard down.

Instantly, Ranir became aware that doing so was a mistake. "Hello, brother!" Marnos casted a black colored and embellished shadow bolt. Ranir was still so bewildered that he didn't even try to dodge or block the dark spell. Once again, Ranir was knocked backward, taking the air from his chest. Marnos walked over to Ranir, grabbed him by the armor again. Ranir did nothing. He was simply stunned by the revelation. "You took everything away from me, Ranir!" he planted a fist in the same dent on Ranir's armor, rocking him into the mountain. The Lightning Rod busted several large black rocks beneath the force.

"Marnos, wait. What happened to you?" Ranir called out with a palm forward, gesturing a halt. Marnos ignored Ranir's begging questions. He grabbed Ranir's hand, twisted it excruciatingly, and pulled Ranir closer, slamming a fist into his jaw. Ranir thought about which one hurt more, the fist on his left cheek, or the rocks that his right side smashed into. He felt the familiar hot taste of blood oozing from both sides of the inside of his mouth.

Marnos grabbed him again and picked him up, like he did in the alley of Killiad. This time, he pulled a dagger out and thrusted it under the armor of Ranir's tunic. The blade felt hot as it pierced his skin and into his gut. Ranir let out a bellow and felt his power taking control to protect him. Marnos yanked the blood stained blade out and thrusted upward again. The second time Ranir caught him by the wrist and stopped him.

Without a break, Marnos cracked his forehead against Ranir's, knocking him down yet again. Ranir began to feel his body breaking on him. Fatigue began to set in as if he were a mundane human. "Marnos, wait," said Ranir. He spit out a mouthful of blood. "This isn't you! Its the shadow magic."

"No, Ranir its you!" he kicked Ranir in the rib, sending him flying sideways several paces. The Lightning Rod began to see through blurred vision. His left eye began to swell shut from the headbutt. With a small window of relief, an arrow landed perfectly in Marnos's hand as he began to cast a spell. He turned his rage on the innocent archer, instantly killing him with a curse of black smoke.

Luck was on his side this time as it bought enough time for a certain Archemage to aim his revenge on The Necromancer. A massive wave of orange fire blasted down on Marnos. As he brought his hands up and created a smoky looking shield above him to block the magic, he didn't realize that Taryn was the one he released from his torture not that long ago. The elemental power was far greater than magic, and burned through the shield, scorching the palms of Marnos. He screamed out and shot a jet blade from under his long jacket, stabbing Taryn in the stomach.

"No! Taryn!" cried Ranir, furiously. Taryn fell to his knees, and slowly pulled the 8 inch blade from his navel. Marnos held his hand outward, calling the blade the same way Ranir called his staff. The blade ripped from Taryn 's hands and landed perfectly in Marnos's hand. Ranir had found enough strength To blast him again. This time, Ranir focused more on saving Taryn instead of finding answers or trying to talk to Marnos. It clearly wasn't working. The blue lightning crashed into Taryn's stomach, sending his spinning through the air.

Ranir crawled over to Taryn. Without a word, Taryn pulled a mana stone from his pocket and siphoned it. Instead of healing himself, he healed Ranir's wounds. As Ranir's vision cleared up instantly, Taryn felt backwards with a thud. His eyes slowly closed and his head rolled to the side. "No! No, no, no! Taryn," Ranir cried. "I won't lose you too! *Athik asztun shinak babat!"* he bellowed out, charging his hand with static lightning. He waved it over top of the knife wound in Taryn's stomach. The dagger was laced with poison, Ranir discovered. It took a lot more magic to heal that level destructiveness away. He dug deep in his psyche, and forced the magic to seal the gash. As it closed, Taryn quickly opened his eyes and sat up with a sharp breath. "You're alive!" shouted Ranir as he hugged Taryn.

He felt the fatigue of the magic draining him as he sat on the ground. He looked over and saw Marnos getting to his feet. "Here!" someone called to Ranir's right. A mage holding a blue stone out to Ranir. "Take it, and end this!" he nodded his head toward Marnos. Ranir siphoned the magic stored inside the mana stone and became instantly rejuvenated.

343

Two mages swooped in beside Marnos and began to heal his hands. "No!" Ranir yelled as he blasted them both with a sharp bolt, killing them both.

Marnos drew his hands up, now healed. Black fog erupted from them and he blasted it toward The Lightning Rod. Ranir put a shield around himself and ran straight forward, through the dark magic. As his shield let go, Ranir ducked under the spell and slid perfectly to Marnos. He jumped up and grabbed Marnos around his arms and back, squeezing with his full might. In a flash of burning lighting, Ranir Traveled with Marnos into the air. Immediately they were cloud level. Ranir looked down and saw the plateau where Taryn had first began to train him earlier in the year. A perfect, isolated spot to end the battle once and for all. Then, he shot down, still grasping Marnos. His feet landed like those of a fox, smoothly on the black rock. Just as he let go of his hold, Marnos thrusted his palms into Ranir's chest, catching him with a cloud of black and purple. Ranir stopped himself by hovering this time, slowly lowering his feet back to the rock.

Now they were alone, they were away from possible casualties. This would become a place of death. His or Marnos's, he didn't know. Ranir stuck his palm to the sky, reaching with his power. After a short moment, the swirling hums flashed through the air as the metal staff landed directly in his hands. He slammed it into the black rock at his feet. "Marnos, last chance to surrender. I don't want to hurt you, but you are sick and need help. Let me help you!" cried Ranir.

"I am not sick, Ranir. I am numb. I am unendurable, since you took her from me!" swashed Marnos.

"Who? Took who from you?" replied Ranir.

"You really are lost in this world, aren't you?" He paused. Marnos's voice was as smooth and innocent as Ranir had remembered. Now it was scratchy, and bitter. "Selendt! That's who! You killed her, because you had to go on this trip, didn't you? You just had to discover magic." There was a true sadness to Marnos's tone.

"I did not kill Selendt!" Ranir shouted back. How could Marnos believe that Ranir would kill one of his best childhood friends? "Verna drowned her, Marnos."

"No, I thought maybe that was the case, too." Marnos began pacing back and forth. Ranir readied himself for a surprise attack. "They brought her body back to Heramor a few weeks after...after she died. They said her body was marks of a lightning victim. Now who does that sound like...Lightning Rod?"

"No! That can't be right. The mages did that to her and to you."

"Now, I know you are delusional, Ranir. I saw the flash of a bright blue lightning bolt hit me. I felt the burn on my face! And my side. I felt the real power of you, brother. Friend? What were we, anymore? You, Ranir, are the real monster!" Marnos's voice was cracking and dry. Ranir thought that he had seen a glistening to his eyes, making the situation even more emotionally difficult.

Ranir lowered his gaze down at the ground.
Was it really his fault? He couldn't bear the fact that he
caused Selendt's death and the scarring of his best
friend. Tears began to well up in his eyes. He glanced
up to Marnos, "I'm so sorry, Marnos. I...I didn't know.
I...I tried to control it...to protect you and..and Selendt,
Marnos!"

"Wipe away your tears Ranir. I don't want to
see them for what comes next," said The Necromancer
coldly.

Ranir knew that he deserved to be judged and
punished for his mistakes, accident or not. Regardless,
he didn't want to die. Contrarily, if he did die, what
would happen to the citizens and soldiers of Thrast?
What would happen to Sythestine, and more so,
Gnariam? "Take me then, Marnos..."

"Oh, I plan on it. I plan on taking everything
from you. Your new fire mage friend, your new lady
earth mage, your new queen. I've already taken your
mentor. That did the trick to draw you out didn't it?"
said Marnos tauntingly.

In the heat of emotion, Ranir had nearly
forgotten about Ramshi's death. Instantly, he grew
irritated with Marnos's game. He became furious all
over again. "You can kill me, Marnos. But I won't let
you hurt all of them just to punish me." Marnos stared
down the steep, jagged mountain. "You hear me?"
Ranir screamed as loud as he could.

"My old friend...I hear you." As his words left

346

his mouth, he blasted a cold and dark spell toward Ranir. Immediately, Ranir thrusted his lightning into the spell. Both the light blue, and the dark purple and black met between them, locking into a stale mate. In that moment Ranir realized that The Necromancer matched his level of power. Bestial power wasn't going to carry the victory on this day.

"Marnos!" Ranir called through the crashing magic and elements before him. "It doesn't have to end this way!"

"Yes! Yes it does, Ranir!" replied Marnos through gritted teeth. The Necromancer dug deep and pushed harder. The center of the entangled power slowly drifted toward Ranir. He pushed with his mind, backing the dark magic again. They were compatible perfectly. Ranir tapped into his Surging Speed, to think, not to act. The lightning flowing from him arced in slow motion, as did the cloud of black and purple. Suddenly the bright sunny sky transitioned into darkness, as in Alagien. Ranir looked down the mountain and his heart began racing. Thrast's army was well under numbered. They were losing the battle. A dangerously beautiful array of color and elements cascaded back and forth between the mixed group.

Ranir remembered that he could weaken The Necromancer by destroying his disciples. That would mean letting go of the one hand pushing lightning, acting fast enough to thrust his element onto simultaneous targets. In that moment, he knew what he had to do in order to defeat Marnos. He was going to have push past the limit of his power, letting it consume him as he had been warned to avoid. There was no avoiding the inevitable. If Ranir wanted to save those that he had grown to love, and those that he had learned to accept, in his role as The Balancer of Gnariam, then he was going to have to give his every last breath to fulfill the end goal. He let go of his right hand and blasted a bright white arc of lightning into the darkening sky. Eyes glowing white, he channeled his elemental power and casted Sundering Skies together, "*Telétak Ashiá.*" The spell was designed around his power to create a surge of static charge into the sky, amplifying his thunderstorm. For him, it allowed him to control each lightning strike.

The center of their conjoined spells drifted toward Ranir once again. He pushed with his mind as hard as he could, letting beautifully blue arcs and streaks of lightning soar from the sky, landing perfectly into The Forsaken below, one after another in rapid succession. Suddenly, he felt the Surging Speed give way to normality. The spells began to push back toward Marnos. "No!" he screamed and fought back, driving the death spell to his enemy.

Ranir let out a furious cry. The lightning between them began to brighten. Ranir felt the power within begin to take on a different form. He was no longer channeling it. It was simply flowing through him. As The Forsaken began to die back and forth, allowing Ranir to drive the arc closer to Marnos, he released the Sundering Skies, feeling overwhelmed with fatigue. His vision began to blur and he screamed so harshly that his throat burned, pushing with his mind with all that he had, channeling the power to burn further into the dark plume before him.

Suddenly, Ranir noticed his fingertips began to crack like glass. His skin began to peel of like ashes from an ember. He was being consumed by the power that he once sought after. He was once a boy, excited for the truth to be heard about the actuality of magic. Now, he was a man, destined it seemed, to sacrifice his life for others in Gnariam. Marnos fell to one knee. Ranir knew this was his last chance to end it all, here and now. He found one last sliver of energy to push harder. Everything seemed to go silent as the lightning before him flashed brighter, covering the mountain top and the dark sky in a blanket of pure white energy, lighting up the forests and grounds around the black mountain. The massive surge of energy sent the lightning bolt burning straight through Marnos's chest.

All was dark. The Necromancer slowly fell backward in quietness. Ranir dropped to his knees, feeling completely numb. Time seemed to slow down on its own accord. As he looked to his right, Taryn teleported to his side, a moment too late. He could see that the Archemage calling his name, but he couldn't hear anything. He looked down as his entire hand flaked apart, revealing a light blue energy underneath the skin. Slowly, it worked up his arm and into his rib and chest. Then, he heard Taryn, "Ranir! Ranir! You did it. You saved us! We won! Ranir? No, no, no!" Ranir fell to his chest, collapsing in a pile of ashes. The Lightning Rod disintegrated into nothingness.

Chapter 26: A Debt Unpaid

Ranir opened his golden brown eyes. The wood on the ceiling mirrored the musky plank he was lying on. His entire body was throbbing with a dull pain. Sitting up, he could smell daub and straw, mixed with the mountain rain. Shadows from the candles danced about the room.

"Where am I?" said Ranir, the dark haired boy. He was near adult aged, a short scruffy beard covered his face.

"You are home. Well, my home, of course," replied a voice from a dark corner. Ranir couldn't make out who the deep voiced man was, in the shadows. He wasn't even sure that it was really a person at all.

"And just where would that be?" asked Ranir, sitting up and turning towards the shadowy corner of the room. Leaning forward from the creaking chair, the man shoved his face into the candlelight.

"That would be very near to your birthplace. Or rebirth is what I should say. We are in the Veörn Mountains," said the man.

Ranir could see shadows on the mans face, textured with scars and age. The golden light, from the candle flame, casted a foggy tone to his skin.

"What happened to me? And why am I back?" questioned Ranir.

The man stood up and moved closer to Ranir. Something familiar about him struck Ranir. He knew that he had seen this man before. He simply couldn't be certain, though.

"You have been given yet another chance. The Old Gods aren't satisfied with the balance yet," he said, speaking with a voice that resonated from deep in his chest. He spoke through a long black beard, which seemingly muffled his voice ever so slightly.

Disbelief perplexed Ranir. He couldn't belief that his actions had drew a response from the four old gods. He had thought that maybe his work was done. What more could they want?

"Even if that is true, that doesn't explain why I am back here, of all places," Ranir said.

The man seemed annoyed with the repetitive question. He pursed his lips together as he took in a hearty breath. Pausing for moment before exhaling, he grasped his beard in his hand, letting the thick hair pass though his fingers.

"Just know that you are meant to do more in Gnariam. Your responsibilities are not fulfilled so easily and all your questions will be answered in time," answered the man. He was stern with his answers. Ranir thought it all seemed like riddles to him.

The Stranger was clad in a dark and dusty cloak. His boots were worn down, and a couple patches dotted his pants. Besides the way his character was so steadfast and the manner in which he carried himself and his conversations, Ranir would have thought he was a beggar.

"So for now, go home. Or what remains of your home. You will be called upon when the moment is right. There is much to discuss," said the man.

Ranir looked out the window as lightning

dashed colorfully across the sky. A beautiful blue and yellow bolts dodged each other through the air. The thunder shook the entire shack. The arc of energy, spreading various hues of light, enveloped the room to a near blinding sense. Ranir could see all the details of grain in the old wood and the hole in the side of the far wall.

"Now, that is something I know," said Ranir, feeling the lightning in his core. It was as if that spark of energy was a part of him. He could feel the static raise his hair on his neck.

"How did this happen? Why did this happen?" he pondered to himself. Turning around to further question the man, Ranir was only left with silence, and an empty room. The man had gone. He began to recollect the events that transpired over this past year. He remembered that fateful night when he became The Lightning Rod.

As he stepped out of the small shack, into the storm, he felt the connection to the skies. He looked up, raised his palm to the black and connected with the lightning. Nothing happend for a moment. Ranir was confused. Suddenly a bright white arc descended and touched his finger, igniting a fire inside him that he thought was gone. He thought that he was gone. Who was the stranger? What did he mean The Old Gods were not satisfied. So much had happened and yet, once again, he was left with more burning questions than he could write down.

As he siphoned the storm into a clear sky, he heard a rock crack behind him. Without thinking, he turned with inhuman speed and channeled a rope of chain lightning, wrapping around a man dressed in a black robe. Whipping the man toward him, he realized it was a Knight. "Why are you here? Where is everyone?" Ranir asked.

"Oh Thunder King, we thought you were dead," the man replied.

"I was dead. I still don't know how or why I am alive again. Answer my question...now!" He squeezed the lightning harder around the stranger.

"I'm here to deliver a message!" said the man. Suddenly, in a cloud of white smoke, the man dissappeard from inside the circle of lightning. Ranir stood still for a moment, confused. He could hear breathing behind him. He spun around quickly and blasted a static hand outward.

The stranger caught his hand and thrusted both palms toward Ranir, releasing a plume of dust and wind, knocking The Lightning Rod backward. Ranir caught himself by hovering staticly. "Who are you?"

The man smiled, "I am The Master of The Winds, Ranir Trysfal." It was *The* Wind God."

Ranir's eyes grew wide. "Why are you here? Why am *I* here?" he asked.

"I am here to show you something, to tell you something, not the answer you seek, but the answer I give." Ranir disliked riddles.

"Show me what?" asked Ranir, beginning to get annoyed already.

"This," The God Of Air said as he thrusted a finger forward, casted a waterlike spell. Suddenly, Ranir was in a different place. It felt like a different realm. As he looked around, he saw the battle ground at the base of the mountain. He saw a man, dressed exactly like The Necromancer walking toward a victorious Thrast army. Time was frozen still. "That, is the real Necromancer. The real danger. *That*, is why my brothers and sister and I have brought you back, Ranir.

353

Our father didn't have a choice this time, though I suspect he wouldv'e done the same for his own gains."

"Who is it?" asked Ranir.

"Another answer you must discover for yourself. That, however, is now. You need to stop him, and he is not going to go down without a fight, Ranir."

"How do I-" he was interrupted by the snap of reality. Suddenly, he was alone again. He was frustrated at The Gods' riddles and the way they came in and out of his life without warning. He ran to the edge of the mountain and looked down. As he had seen in the vision, a Necromancer was approaching the survivors.

Ranir thrusted a bolt of lightning into the air, Traveling directly in front of The Necromancer. As his feet planted into the ground, Ranir punched his fist into The Necromancer's chest, sending him soaring backwards 20 feet away, landing with a crash into the rocky basin of the mountain. A flash of water smashed Ranir in the back, knocking him forward on his stomach. Suddenly, the sound of feet rushed by him. As he looked up, a robed hydromancer casted another spell, smashing Ranir in the face with cold white water.

He jumped to his feet and saw the mask of The Necromancer laying on the ground. He expected to see Marnos again, hoping that he lived through a bad dream, and that he could fix it this time. Instead, as the mage began to teleport, the sorcerer turned and glanced at Ranir. His face was so familiar and yet lost in memories as his heart jumped in his chest. He pushed up from the ground to clear his sight, confirming what he had witnessed. He was certain the identity.

"Father?"